## Praise for Gina Robinson's
### *THE SPY WHO LEFT ME*

"This first Agent Ex novel is good, old-fashioned fun. Full of laughter, intrigue, and, of course, steamy spies, it's a great weekend escape. Robinson knows how to balance a book with lighthearted romps and serious romance."
—*RT Book Reviews*

"At times laugh-out-loud funny, Robinson's foray into the world of James Bond has its poignant side, assuring that readers will be back for more." —*Booklist*

"Punctuated with Bond-worthy downhill car and bike chases and near-death surfing parties, Robinson's clever concoction of lust and longing is a refreshing tropical cocktail." —*Publishers Weekly*

"Mystery, mayhem, sexy spies, and lots of laughter. Gina Robinson writes a damn good book!"
—Christie Craig, award-winning author

"The action is fast and furious and the plot twists turn on a dime. Ms. Robinson seamlessly adds humor to her story that will keep the reader laughing as things keep going wrong." —SingleTitles.com

"A hilariously brilliant romp into the world of espionage and intrigue. Ty and Treflee are amazingly sympathetic characters and the world that Ms. Robinson has built for them to play in is dazzling and colorful. It isn't much of a stretch for the reader to hear the native birds sing and smell the coconut oil as they read this delightful novel!"
—*Reader to Reader Reviews*

## ALSO BY GINA ROBINSON

*The Spy Who Left Me*
*Diamonds Are Truly Forever*

# Live
## and let
# Love

## GINA ROBINSON

St. Martin's Paperbacks

This is a work of fiction. All of the characters, organizations, and events portrayed in this novel are either products of the author's imagination or are used fictitiously.

LIVE AND LET LOVE

Copyright © 2013 by Gina Robinson.

All rights reserved.

For information address St. Martin's Press, 175 Fifth Avenue, New York, NY 10010.

ISBN: 978-0-312-54241-2

Printed in the United States of America

St. Martin's Paperbacks edition / January 2013

St. Martin's Paperbacks are published by St. Martin's Press, 175 Fifth Avenue, New York, NY 10010.

10 9 8 7 6 5 4 3 2 1

*For all my Js*

Until death do us part. . . .

# CHAPTER ONE

LATE SEPTEMBER
COPACABANA BEACH
RIO DE JANEIRO, BRAZIL

*If a guy has to play dead,*
*Rio's the place to do it.*

Jack Pierce sat beneath a bright red sun umbrella at an equally bright red bistro table outside a kiosk along the promenade at Copa. Listening to the waves of the Atlantic Ocean and the buzz of Brazilian music, he sipped his third caipirinha. Spring in Rio—string bikinis, bare-bottomed girls, sunshine, heat, and Cachaca. Another mission accomplished. Beto Bevilacqua, hated drug lord, dead. Yes, this was heaven on earth.

Jack appeared to be aimlessly dreaming as he stared out over the beach, girls, and ocean, but he was on alert, as always, as he waited for his contact to give him his next mission. He listened to the sound of approaching footsteps on the wave-patterned black-and-sand-colored tiles of the promenade. Even though he wasn't wearing a watch, he knew the time. And his contact was right on it. Jack looked up at the newcomer when the footsteps stopped next to his table and fought to control his surprise. "Chief?" *What the hell?*

Jack regained his composure less than a second after it

slipped, and smiled, putting on his spy mask of inscruta-
bility. He wouldn't let the chief see him sweat, even
though it was damn hot outside. "This *is* a surprise. To
what do I owe the honor? Things get boring at Langley?
Or have you come down to check out the girls?"

Jack had been expecting his handler, code-named Talent, to show up. Only a handful of people on the entire
planet knew Jack was still alive. All of them in the Agency,
including the chief. But Jack still didn't expect the big
boss to pay him a personal visit.

National Clandestine Service chief Emmett Nelson,
head of the spying arm of the Central Intelligence Agency,
smiled down at him and pulled up a chair. "Jack. You still
have the accent? It blends in nicely down here."

Jack nodded. "Can't seem to lose it. The doctor says
my brain rewired it in as it healed."

Jack had been in a coma for several weeks after a horribly failed mission two years ago. They'd drilled into his
skull to relieve the swelling and pressure and save his life.
It was a miracle he survived.

Since he had recovered from the explosion, his speech
had been affected. He involuntarily spoke with a vaguely
Latin accent.

"You're looking good, too." Emmett studied him, in a
penetrating way only the chief and a master spy could. He
wasn't making idle chitchat. He referred to Jack's new
face and the fine job the Agency's plastic surgeon did re-
storing it after Jack had been blown up in Ciudad del Este
two years ago. The explosion crushed Jack's face and nearly
killed him. He'd had the final bit of reconstructive surgery
just eight weeks ago. He hadn't seen the chief since.

Jack turned his profile to Emmett and lifted his chin,
giving the chief a good look at what the U.S. government
had paid for. "I feel good—healthy and strong. What do
you think of my new nose?"

"It's a damn improvement over the original." Emmett winked. "The whole face is. You were an ugly mutt. Now you've gone Hollywood on us." The chief shook his head. "I should have told the surgeon not to make you so pretty."

Jack laughed. His doctors told him his face had been mush—shattered jaw, dislocated and broken nose, crushed cheekbones and eye sockets. The plastic surgeons reconstructed his whole face, straightened and thinned his wide, crooked nose, took off his identifying moles, gave him high cheekbones and slightly less deep-set eyes. He looked like the old Jack's handsome cousin—similar, yet different enough to fool his own mother. Like the man he'd have been if he'd had two better-looking parents and gotten the best possible combination of their features.

"Too late now," Jack said with a tease in his voice. "I'm not getting myself blown up again just so you can have another shot at getting my look right."

"Let's hope not," the chief said. "I had to bury your medical bills deep in my budget. You know how much I hate subterfuge." He laughed when Jack shot him a skeptical look. "When it comes to accounting."

The chief held a caipirinha of his own. He took a sip of it and grinned at Jack. "Word in the favelas is the remaining drug lords are running scared. Nice work."

Jack shrugged again. It had been a professional pleasure to kill Bevilacqua after he'd escaped from prison. "It's easy to do a good job when you love your work."

The chief set his glass on the table. "It's always rewarding to hear my employees have a high job satisfaction rate. I'll be sure to mention it to the director during my next job performance review."

It was well known in espionage circles the chief and the director didn't see eye-to-eye. Emmett was always baiting him.

"Just keep my name out of it," Jack said.

Emmett nodded and abruptly changed the course of the conversation to immediate business. "I have some disturbing news, Jack. The Rooster has been trying to track you down. Subtly, of course. He can't alert his bosses at RIOT that he failed to kill you.

"We don't know why he thinks you're still alive, only that he's trying to verify it and find you before RIOT realizes his mistake. If he finds you, he'll kill you. If he doesn't, but somehow makes a mistake and RIOT discovers he's looking for you, well shit, we can't have your cover of death blown. You've been too effective since Sariel 'died.'"

Sariel had been Jack's code name, after the angel of death. RIOT—the Revolutionary International Organization of Terrorists—was the Agency's nemesis.

"No," Jack said, silently cursing. "Thanks for the warning."

"This is more than a warning," Emmett said. "We know where he is." He paused. "I want you to kill him."

Jack couldn't believe his ears. *Finally.* He grinned and resisted punching the air in victory. He'd been begging for the chance to strike the Rooster since the RIOT bastard murdered Jack's buddy Kyle. Emmett had been promising him his chance—when the right opportunity presented itself. In Agency speak that meant when Emmett thought the mission had decent odds of success. This day kept getting better and better.

Jack lifted his glass. "To a successful mission and retribution." *Revenge.*

Emmett lifted his glass toward Jack's and knocked one back. "Ah, the Brazilians know how to make a drink."

At that moment, Jack didn't give a damn about Brazilian cocktails. He was ready to take the next flight out for destination Rooster. "I'll start greasing my sniper rifle immediately. How soon can I leave?"

"Hold on there, cowboy." Emmett studied him. "I haven't given you the details. This mission is more complicated than taking the Rooster out at one hundred yards with a rifle."

"A challenging kill—that's even better." Jack's beef with the Rooster was personal. He wouldn't mind killing him with his bare hands if he had to, not at all.

Jack could barely contain his excitement. He fought to stay calm, worried Emmett would pull the mission from him if he appeared too eager, too much like a loose cannon. He waited for Emmett to continue.

"Our sources say RIOT and the Rooster are planning to blow up an auxiliary meeting of the G Eight summit scheduled in Los Angeles for late October," Emmett said as calmly as if he were discussing the weather. "Without the Rooster and his expertise and strategic-planning skills, RIOT will be hard-pressed to proceed on short notice. Before you kill him, we want as much intel as we can get about RIOT's plans and the terrorist sleeper cells they're hiding."

Emmett looked out over the sparkling water and grimaced. "These damn G Eight summits are enough of a pain in the ass without the added threat of RIOT attacking. Too many ordinary protestors, anarchists, and rioters around during a regular meeting. Lots of security, but still a terrorist's dream."

Jack nodded, but his mind was elsewhere plotting and scheming. Besides being a personal dream come true for him, killing the Rooster was a career-making assignment. Not that a dead guy had much of a career. But Jack could make a killing, so to speak, if he got this one right.

The Rooster was RIOT's top assassin. He'd been dubbed the Rooster because he crowed about his kills. He was Jack's equal on the bad-guy side—his archenemy and nemesis. And the assassin who'd killed Kyle Harris, one of Jack's two best friends, in Afghanistan and blown Jack up in Ciudad del Este, ending Jack's life as Jack and making his wife, Willow, a widow.

Jack clenched his jaw, trying to hide his tic of excitement. "There's something you're not telling me. What's the catch?"

"He's in the States. We've tried, but we can't draw him out of the country," Emmett said, keeping his voice level and friendly so he wouldn't draw attention.

Jack was seasoned enough to hear the anger and frustration in it.

"The son of a bitch is wily," Emmett said. "He feels safe, thinks we won't hit him at home. Too bad the bastard has to be an American citizen, a homegrown traitor. We'd love to pull him in and interrogate him, but the Feds would insist on due process and the Rooster is smart enough to leak intel that would scare the American public and derail our intelligence efforts.

"No, we can't arrest him. We have to take him out with a targeted kill. Which means if you accept, you're off the grid. We want you to learn what you can about the operation, kill him, and get out.

"You can contact me, or Magic, or Talent, or the members of the Agency you've worked with since the explosion, but that's it.

"And if you fail or get caught, I'll deny any involvement and claim you went rogue looking for revenge."

Jack nodded. It sounded logical to him. "I expected no less."

Emmett took a deep breath and sighed. "Kill him in a way that looks like an accident to the authorities and general public, but sends a clear message to RIOT and the Rooster's handlers that we took him out. That we can, and will, take out their agents at our pleasure."

Jack nodded. "What's my cover?"

"How's your Italian?" Emmett asked in Italian.

"Decent," Jack answered, also in Italian.

"Very good." Emmett nodded. "Malene's worked out your cover. Your Italian accent will come in handy.

"You'll be undercover as Con Russo. Russo has an Italian first cousin once removed, Aldo Salemo, who lives in the small town where the Rooster is hiding.

"You'll be staying with him. The Salemos take in family with open arms without question whenever one of their own needs a place to crash for a while. They're just one big, lovable Italian *famiglia* with hundreds of cousins. Too many to accurately keep track of.

"Your cover as Con is as one of them. A city boy, workaholic public relations exec for a private firm who has been under too much stress lately." Emmett grinned in a way that let Jack know he understood Jack wouldn't love this cover.

"A public relations guy under stress, that's the best Malene could come up with?" Malene knew Jack hated office jobs and all that crap. What did public relations execs have to worry about? Why couldn't she get him something physical and outdoors?

"It's one of the most stressful jobs in the country. No control over circumstances or schedule. Always at the beck and call of the client. Always putting out firestorms when the client screws up or someone decides to sue. People with no control feel stress. At least that's what I've read in the news."

"You mean like assassins?" Jack smiled and shook his head. "I should ask for a raise."

"Complete this mission successfully and I'll put you in for one." Emmett paused as a group of tourists walked by. "Back to the business at hand," he said when they were past. "His *nonna* thinks he's overstressed. She's convinced he needs a break from the city, a few weeks in the country to unplug and unwind. So she called Aldo's *nonna,* who called Aldo, and now you have a place to stay in Aldo's detached guesthouse for a few weeks."

"And if I finish up earlier?"

"A public relations emergency can always call you home. You're going to love this place, Jack. Aldo runs a little winery and catering business on the premises. Malene says he makes a mean meatball. They melt in your mouth. And the men in the area like to hunt."

Emmett casually slid a small flash drive across the table toward Jack. "It's all here. Sound good?"

"Didn't know I had an Italian side of the family." Jack reached for the drive, but Emmett kept it covered with his hand and under his control.

Jack cocked his head. What game was Emmett playing? "It sounds homey. When do I leave?" He was itching to get going.

Emmett smiled and shook his head. "Not so fast. You still haven't heard the whole story." Emmett paused, turning a serious look on Jack. "What's the best way to get to a male spy?"

"What is this, a certification quiz?" Jack pulled back his hand and finished his drink.

Emmett stared at him, his expression completely serious. "Through a woman, Jack. Who did you die to protect and give a better life to? Who's always been your Achilles' heel?"

Jack swallowed hard and waited for Emmett to continue, using every technique he had for managing his anger and keeping his pulse rate from racing into the panicked, dog-mode thinking range. If your pulse speeds up too fast, you lose your ability to reason and process; you go dog mode.

"The Rooster's in Orchard Bluff. Pursuing your wife, Jack. Befriending Willow to find out what she knows and draw you out. You told me you never wanted to see her again, that you have to be dead so she can live the life she deserves." Emmett paused and lifted his hand, revealing the flash drive with Jack's mission details and cover story. "Are you still in?"

# CHAPTER TWO

ORCHARD BLUFF, WASHINGTON

There's nothing like the smell of freshly made caramel in the morning. Mix it in a latte. Stir it into a mug of warm cider. Or coat an apple with it. *Exquisite.* The day ahead was filled with heavenly, sweet salted-caramel possibilities.

Or would have been, if Willow Pierce didn't have a strong sense of foreboding, that feeling practically an assurance that someone she loved was in danger. She hadn't felt like this since Jack died two years ago to the day.

Willow looked at the rows of freshly jarred caramel sauce lining the counter of her candy kitchen and frowned. She picked up her cell phone to call her mother and check on her. It rang in her hand.

"Mom! I was just picking up the phone to call you."

"Willow, baby! You're all right? You're fine?" Her mother sounded as relieved to hear Willow's voice as she was to hear her mother's.

"Fine, Mom." Willow let out a breath she'd barely been aware of holding. "And you?"

"Oh, you know, I'm okay." She paused. "You feel it, too, then?"

"Yes," Willow said, nodding although her mom couldn't see her. "I thought you were in trouble. Who else could it be?"

Since Jack died, Willow only had her mom and Spookie.

"I don't know, baby."

"Do you think it's the day? An echo from two years ago?"

"The Sense doesn't echo."

Willow and her mother, all the generations of women in their family, were intuitive, sensitive. They shared what Willow's grandma called the Sense—a premonition of danger, the feeling your loved one was in trouble. And, on the positive side, a deep, glowing certainty when you met your soul mate. Willow had felt that glow once—with Jack. She'd also felt the opposite, the deepest horror of premonition, at the exact moment he'd been blown up.

"I know. It's crazy. But it hasn't always been right? Not one hundred percent?" She bit her lip, hoping her mother would reassure her. The Sense had to have been *proved* wrong at least once in the past.

"It's always right, baby. Perfect record."

"You're supposed to reassure me, Mom. Tell me no one is in danger, particularly you. Tell me everything will be all right. That you'll make sure of it. Lie if you have to."

Willow's mother laughed. "You aren't five anymore."

"What does that have to do with it?"

"You aren't as gullible as you used to be. I think you've realized by now that I don't have eyes in the back of my head and I don't have superpowers, either. Reassurances like you want are simply empty promises filled with good intention."

"Yeah, I know. But they're still nice to hear." Willow pictured her mom shaking her head in amusement. "Be careful today all the same, Mom. Take your meds. Postpone any skydiving lessons until further notice."

"As if that will be a problem!"

Willow teased her mom. She was afraid of heights. The last thing she'd ever do was skydive.

"And I'll do my part; I won't step on any cracks that will break your back." Willow would have winked at her mom if they'd been using Skype.

"My back and I appreciate that. You be cautious, too." Her mother sounded amused. "Drive safely. Don't run with scissors. No bungee jumping. Lock your doors. And be careful in that candy kitchen of yours."

Willow shook her head. "What could possibly go wrong in my state-of-the-art, highly efficient, beautiful candy kitchen?"

"Oh, I don't know, you could drop a vat of caramel on your foot. Slip with a knife. Or leave a batch of sugar syrup on the stove and forget about it like that time you were in the ninth grade and nearly burned the house to the ground."

"Who knew sugar was so highly flammable?" Willow teased her mom. "I'm never going to live that down, am I?"

"No, never. Sorry." Her mom paused and turned serious. "Treat yourself nicely today. I mean that, kiddo. Don't beat yourself up. Cry if you want to."

"I don't want to cry. Jack wouldn't want me to." She bit her lip again, puzzled. The Sense wasn't going away. The foreboding remained just as strong as ever. "At least we're both feeling it. Maybe we'll go together." Willow put a tease in her voice for her mom's benefit.

"Yeah, see you in heaven, baby. But not yet."

Willow smiled. "Not yet. I've got to go, Mom. Shiloh will be in any minute. We have a ton to do for the festival tomorrow—caramel apples to dip, chocolate salted caramels to coat, and white chocolate apple pie fudge to make."

"The candy show must go on." Her mom chuckled, still sounding relieved. "Be careful working over the flame. Handle the hot sugar with care. And throw some salt over your shoulder for luck."

Willow laughed. "I will. Love you, Mom."

"Love you, too." Her mom sounded reluctant to hang up. Willow heard her sigh and then the line went dead.

Willow disconnected and poured herself a cup of coffee, catching a glimpse of the apple country calendar on the wall. She took a deep breath, swallowing a lump along with a sip of hot coffee, trying not to burn her mouth. Death by scalding coffee. The Sense was making her jumpy. Maybe Mom was wrong; maybe it was just . . .

*Jack.*

Two Octobers ago, to the day, National Clandestine Service chief Emmett Nelson appeared at her former home in Seattle, all but carrying a folded flag and playing "Taps." He told her, in the gentlest terms she'd ever heard him use, that Jack was dead. *Dead.*

Given the sense of dread she'd had, she hadn't been terribly surprised. Two years later, though, it was still hard to even *think* the words.

Blown up by drug lords in Ciudad del Este. There was nothing left of him but a few bits and pieces. Barely enough to bury. Certainly not enough for an open-casket funeral.

The loss of his body didn't upset Willow the way people had feared it would. It was the loss of his essence, his spirit, his soul. His love and laughter. She missed him.

"Don't worry," Emmett had said. "We'll take care of you. Jack left you a nice widow's pension and a generous life-insurance policy." Emmett hugged her in the fatherly way he could put on like a second skin when the occasion deemed it necessary. "You'll always be a part of our clandestine family."

*Now that's reassuring. You can't divorce family, and evidently, you can't divorce the CIA, either. Or be widowed out of it. No matter how much you'd like to be.*

Emmett *had* made good on his promise to take care of her, though. She used Jack's life insurance and pension to

pursue her dreams. She trained under Seattle's premier
candy chef, the salted-caramel queen. Moved from Seattle across the state to apple country, to Orchard Bluff, a
comfortable piece of country living only fifteen miles
from Washington State's second-largest city, to escape the
memories of her life with Jack and try to move on. Paid
for the lovely piece of property and the gorgeous new
house with its daylight basement that housed her commercial candy kitchen and business. Provided her with
income as she worked to launch the business.

*Jack. If only I could see you again. You'd love this
place. But I'd give it all up to have you back.*

The anniversary of Jack's death was as good a day as any
for him to come back from the dead. *As Italian fashion
plate Con Russo.*

Why in the world was Malene, the Agency's cover life
artist, always trying to make him over? Just because he
had a new face didn't mean he wanted a new wardrobe,
too. He liked his camo and comfortably slouchy clothes.
He missed the shorts he wore in Brazil. She was always
trying to dress him up and make him into something from
*GQ.* Since the plastic surgeon had prettied him up, she'd
seemed even more determined.

At least this mission didn't demand he wear a tuxedo
like James Bond always seemed to. Small mercies. He flat
out refused to operate in formal wear.

As it was, the Loro Piana merino wool slacks he wore
were surprisingly comfortable. And the baby cashmere
sweater as soft as duck down. And warm. Used to Brazilian weather, Jack was freezing up here. But neither piece
of clothing was particularly stealth, especially in small-
town Orchard Bluff where denim reigned.

He just hoped he could pull this mission off. Despite
his months of acting lessons during spy training, Jack

wasn't Oscar-winning material. It was always better to be realistic about your shortcomings when embarking on a dangerous assignment. It kept you from getting cocky and complacent. From taking unnecessary risks.

The minute Emmett had told him the Rooster was pursuing Willow, Jack had only been more determined to do the job. Nothing could have kept him away. Now he only had to keep his rage at the Rooster for targeting his wife under control.

He'd made a vow never to hurt Willow again, to bow out of her life and let her find love with someone else. Someone who deserved her. Someone who wasn't a professional killer like he was. Someone whose sensibilities matched hers. Another vegetarian would be good. Someone who didn't eat anything that once had eyes. He'd eat anything, and had.

He had another good reason to let her go—Emmett was right. She *was* Jack's Achilles' heel, the one way to get to him. The precise tool the enemy needed to take him down and break him. He was a whole lot more effective when he didn't have to worry about her. And she was a damn sight safer without him.

The explosion, and the time when he was missing and presumed dead by the Agency and everyone else, gave him the distance, courage, and opportunity to give her a second chance at the life she should have.

But he'd also made another, higher vow, during his wedding ceremony. He'd vowed to honor and protect her. And he was a man of his word. But he wished for once his wife would develop better taste in men.

Things could be worse. If a guy *had* to be resurrected and fool his wife into believing he was still dead, October was the perfect month to do it. The haunted vibe of the season made for good theatrics as it thrummed through the crisp autumn air, highlighted by the rustling leaves in the apple trees overhead and the raucous cackle of a crow in flight.

It was the perfect atmosphere for a spook of any kind, even the clandestine variety.

Jack resisted the urge to punch the apple tree next to him in the orchard where he hid, watching Willow's house as he scoped out his next move before he introduced himself to his new "cousin" Aldo, who was Willow's nearest neighbor.

Malene sure knew how to pick his covers. Did she have to make things nearly impossible for him? How could he stay just down the street from Willow and keep the hell away from her?

Contrary to popular belief, his heart wasn't made of ice and buckshot.

It had taken NCS two years to find the Rooster. NCS and the U.S. government were nothing if not tenacious and patient. Like RIOT's deadly SMASH assassins, NCS didn't give up until they got their man. They may still not have found him if the Rooster hadn't taken an audacious risk and come after Willow to draw Jack out.

Courtesy of that little explosion in Ciudad del Este, and a skilled plastic surgeon, Jack didn't even need to dab on face paint or don a mask to be undercover. But were his new face and altered accent good enough to fool Willow, with her intuition and the Sense? Did she feel his presence already?

The doctors had dubbed his new accent part of Foreign Accent Syndrome. He was one of only a hundred people worldwide with this particular syndrome.

*Syndrome.* He shook his head.

*Okay, if that's what they want to call it.*

He thought of it more as a condition. Or maybe a pattern. At least the doctors hadn't labeled it a disorder. That would have gotten him kicked out of the Agency on disability. The CIA couldn't have assassins running around suffering from disorders, no matter how benign.

The nurses in Ciudad found it sexy as hell. He wondered what Willow would think of this new accent of his. If she'd find it sexy, too.

Hell, he wondered a lot of things, like whether she still loved him. And whether it was fair to even hope she did. It was better for his widow to move on.

He wasn't here to reconcile with his wife or disrupt her life and the peace she'd reportedly found. He might be hard, but he wasn't cruel. When he was finished here, he'd slip back into the shadowy world of espionage and Willow would still be a widow.

If the mission to kill the Rooster, who was going by the name Shane Kennett, went as Jack planned, Willow would never even realize he was alive and had been in town. And everyone would believe Kennett's death was accidental.

Jack was the one with the problem—jealousy. The irrational feeling she was cheating on him. Technically, a widow can't cheat on her dead husband. It was only when the dead husband was still alive that things got complicated.

Compartmentalize. That's how he dealt with his job. That's what he'd do now. Set his emotions aside. Focus on the goal. He *had* agreed to take this mission. He owed Willow for all the heartache he'd given her.

He simply had to make sure she didn't catch him in the act. He had no intention of upsetting her applecart. Jeez, that was awful humor.

No, no damn way Willow would find out. She believed he was dead. Why would she think otherwise now?

He felt like a piece of crap for hurting her. It hadn't been intentional. After the explosion, even NCS thought he was dead. The situation simply evolved from there. He was glad he hadn't been around to see Willow cry over him. He didn't deserve her tears.

Hidden in a commercial apple orchard across the street from Willow's rural home, Jack studied her large, custom-built ranch-style house. A daylight basement faced the road and contained her candy kitchen and retail shop. At least he had the satisfaction of having left her a hefty life-insurance policy. It looked as if she'd made good use of it, too. No regrets on his part there.

Damn his weak soul, he wanted to see her before he went to Aldo's. Get a good look at her so he could gauge her effect on him without an entire party full of people as witnesses. He had to know how he'd react to her in person. So he could steel himself and prepare for the evening ahead and the big apple growers' dinner he was expected to attend as Aldo's guest.

Just one quick look, one glimpse of her long, silky auburn hair as he imagined what it felt like in his fingers. One look into her laughing, peridot-green eyes. One more peek at the spray of freckles across her nose and the way her lips curved as she smiled. That's all he needed.

He'd have to use extra caution. Willow had always been intuitive, had the Sense, as her grandma called it. The years of living with him had honed it and trained Willow well in the art of realizing she was being watched, of the dangers of being loved by a spy.

And then there was their dog, Spookie, a shelter rescue. She'd be sure to recognize Jack and try to lick him to death. In general, Spookie was leery of strangers. So if she came charging out to him, wagging her tail, it'd be a dead giveaway. He missed that little mutt. Fortunately, he didn't see her around.

He mapped his covert path to a view of his girl. Willow's home sat on a rolling hill and a gravel drive wound up to it. He hated gravel. It crunched—a built-in alarm system. A nuisance.

An aggregate patio sat just outside the shop's door. Three small, round tables topped with pink-and-white-striped umbrellas and flanked by delicate wirework chairs for her guests dotted the patio. She'd placed a wrought-iron bench, surrounded by cornstalks and pumpkins, by the door in the shade of a maple tree. Flower beds skirted the patio and punctuated the rolling yard.

He swallowed hard and took a deep breath.

The orchard smelled like ripe apples and leaves moist with frosty dew. Anyone looking would have noticed the mist his breath made. Another giveaway he couldn't afford.

A gentle westerly breeze rattled the trees. Maybe it was only his imagination, but he swore he smelled the warm scent of caramel wafting out from Willow's kitchen. Caramel apples, now there was something to make him feel like home.

There were parking spots for three or four, maybe five, cars in front of Willow's basement, with a garage and spots for her own car on the level above, attached to the main level of the house.

A silhouette of a slim, curvy woman moved past the windows. His heart raced. He took another deep breath. The daylight basement faced east. With the morning sun bearing down on the windows, it was impossible to make her out for sure. But by the way his body was reacting he was certain the vague silhouette was Willow.

He stared, mesmerized. He'd always loved the way she moved—confidently, totally unaware of how sexy she was. He'd have to push in closer to get a real look at her. He'd give anything to hear her laugh and see her smile, to make her happy.

Jack pounded his fist against the Northern Spy apple tree he lurked behind, cursing beneath his misty breath and wishing he were a different kind of man.

On this second anniversary of his death, Willow remembered Jack in her own way. Sent flowers to the military cemetery three hundred miles away where his remains were buried. Had the cemetery staff place them. Jack wouldn't want her wrapped in grief. Stifled and stuck in the past. He'd always lived life in the minute. His job and personality demanded it.

She hated violence, didn't believe in killing, and preferred not to think about what Jack may, or may not, have done while living his moments in the name of national security.

Of course, some people would probably say going on a date to the growers' dinner on this particular day wasn't the most respectful way to remember Jack. And maybe they were right.

But they hadn't come up against Shane. He was persistence personified. He simply wouldn't take *no* for an answer when she tried to decline his offer to take her to the dinner. He claimed it would be good for her to be out among her friends on this difficult day, rather than feeling the pain alone. It was hard to argue with his logic. And his kindness and concern would have been flattering and endearing if she could just shake the feeling that taking her out was somehow self-serving.

She shivered, suddenly cold. That vague feeling of premonition that people say is like someone walking over your grave washed over her again. She shook her head to clear it. She was letting the day and the spooky time of year get to her.

Shane had never been anything but charming around her. Physically, he was a dream—well built and powerfully strong. But the Sense reacted as badly around him as if he were a serial killer. Crazy!

Just because he didn't make her heart trill didn't mean he'd committed multiple sins against humanity.

But it was puzzling. What did the hot, sexy organic apple farmer see in her? He could have had almost any of the single women on the bluff, and half the married ones made eyes at him. Why chase her?

She mentally shrugged. Probably the thrill of the chase. A man like Shane was a hunter at heart. Having been married to Jack, she recognized the type.

She scraped the bowl of caramel sauce in front of her with a spatula, drizzled the caramel into her coffee, and took a sip. She'd give the jars another few minutes to cool, label them, and load them up to take to Bluff Country Store. Ada would be waiting. Willow paused to admire the view out of her daylight basement windows.

Breathtaking. On this clear autumn day the mountain sparkled with a fresh crest of snow against a deep-blue sky in the distance past her neighbors' apple orchards. A gentle breeze stirred the dry leaves and bundles of cornstalks on her patio, which rattled against her window creepily. She loved fall and the childlike sense of imagination and fright, but she couldn't shake her very real sensation of foreboding.

Jack hid behind an overgrown arborvitae on the edge of Willow's property nearest her driveway, waiting for his chance to dart to her window for a quick peek or a long look, whichever he damn well had time for. He felt like a stinking Peeping Tom, and it didn't sit well with him. As Willow's husband he shouldn't have had to lurk and leer like a pervert.

*Willow.*

Her propensity for helping wounded animals got her

into trouble time after time. After living with Jack, she should have known better than to go after a stray. You can't cure a broken human being, even if you smother him with love and gentleness.

At least Jack would have the pleasure of taking out his wife's unsuitable date. For love of wife and country. How many men were officially sanctioned and paid to take out the competition? Sometimes a license to kill was a very good thing.

A car turned up Willow's driveway and parked off to the side. The crunching gravel gave it away. A young woman, no older than twenty-one or -two, jumped out. She wore black jeans, a white blouse, and carried what looked like a long pink apron. The help had arrived.

Jack trained his binoculars and watched as she opened the door. He heard the tinkle of the bell before it closed behind her.

A bold idea occurred to him. *What the hell? A guy has to live on the edge, especially if that's all he's got.*

The bell over the door tinkled. Willow felt the rush of cold, fresh air pour in all the way back in the kitchen, raising the hair on her arms from more than the cold.

"Hey, boss!" Shiloh called out to her from the front entrance.

"Shiloh? I'm back here." Willow let out a sigh of relief. Who had she been expecting? Jack's ghost?

Shiloh laughed. "Who else would it be?"

Willow glanced at the clock. Right on time, as usual. "We have a busy day ahead of us. Wash up and meet me back here."

Willow wiped down the counter, waiting in the kitchen for Shiloh to join her. The bell over the door tinkled again. A customer already? This was their lucky day.

"I'll get it!" Shiloh called back to her.

Eager to make a dent in the day's work, Willow didn't turn around to see who'd wandered in. She set up for dipping apples with her back to the counter as Shiloh asked if she could help the first customer of the day. The sexy, accented sound of a man's deep voice stopped Willow cold as she was stabbing a Popsicle stick into a prize-size Red Delicious apple.

"I can't believe I'm breaking the male code and stopping to ask for directions." He paused as if embarrassed. "But I'm hopelessly lost. And my GPS has betrayed me. Back down on the road, it said I'd arrived. But clearly, I hadn't. Not unless my cousin's vineyards have morphed into a shot-oiled road and apple orchards as far as the eye can see." He laughed. "I'm looking for Salemo Vineyards? Am I anywhere close?"

The hair on the back of Willow's neck stood up. Her heart raced. That laugh sounded so Familiar. *Like Jack's.*

Willow felt almost light-headed from the shock of hearing Jack's laughter after two silent years. She grabbed the counter in front of her for support and turned slowly over her shoulder to look at the man who had the temerity to impersonate Jack's laugh and give her almost frightening hope.

Their eyes met. He stared at her with a penetrating, searching, devilish look that was almost hunger. It momentarily took her breath away. Then he smiled, revealing killer dimples.

By any standard, he was gorgeous. Easily one of the most handsome men she'd ever seen—tall, athletic build, dark hair, immaculately dressed in perfectly tailored slacks and a sweater. Dressed the way women dream men should.

His face was perfection. High cheekbones. A strong chin. A straight nose. And those deep-brown eyes that danced with devilment. Arresting eyes. Eyes disturbingly like Jack's.

Looking at such masculine beauty, she'd never felt more disappointed. Or puzzled. His face was Jack's. And definitely not Jack's. The shape and structure so familiar. The eyes. Jack's eyes as surely as if he'd come back from the dead. The same twinkle. The same intelligent curiosity sparkling in them.

But his nose was perfect where Jack's had been crooked and slightly too large. Jack's face had had character. This man's skin was smooth and unscarred where Jack's had battle scars from serving his country and risking his life. Jack had been a man's man. This man was the metro opposite of her late husband. And yet she couldn't look away from him or help feeling as if she'd known him practically forever.

She had to force herself not to gape and stare. Although she supposed he was probably used to women watching him with their tongues hanging out.

She wiped her hands on her apron almost mechanically and floated to the counter, hardly aware of how she'd gotten there. "You're looking for Salemo's? You must be Aldo's cousin."

Who knew a Salemo relation could be God's gift to women? Short, stocky Aldo, with his cook's belly and love of fine food, had never thought to warn them. He'd certainly told them enough stories about others of his cousins, like hairy-backed Ilari, nicknamed Gorilla for obvious reasons. Those stories hadn't exactly inspired her to hope one of Aldo's male kin would render her, or anyone else, weak in the knees.

The man before her nodded, still smiling and holding her gaze. "Con Russo. Aldo's embarrassed, directionally challenged cousin."

She laughed to cover her sudden case of nerves around him. "Don't beat yourself up. People get lost on the orchard roads all the time." She extended her hand. "Aldo warned us to be on the lookout for you. I'm Willow Pierce. And this is my assistant, Shiloh."

When he shook Willow's hand, hers disappeared into his large, square, warm one. He held hers firmly, confidently, almost as if he wouldn't let her go—reminiscent of the way Jack used to.

Perversely, though she enjoyed the feeling of her hand in his way more than she should have, the hair on her neck refused to lie down and behave itself. What in the world was going on with her? She had Jack on the brain today. Hardly surprising, but . . .

This was crazy. Just the day and the season talking. And a single woman's reaction to a man with fantastic dark hair and Jack's laugh and eyes.

He broke the connection too soon, dropping her hand to shake Shiloh's with the same firm grip and flirtatious smile he'd given Willow. Shiloh smiled back at him like a girl dazed by a movie star. The man knew his effect on women and wasn't afraid to use it, that's for sure.

Willow cleared her throat and Con dropped Shiloh's hand. "You almost made it to Aldo's. He's our neighbor. For some reason, GPS can't seem to direct people all the way to his driveway. It likes to drop people in the middle of the road at the edge of his property and give up."

She pointed out the window. "Go back down our driveway. Take a right at the bottom. Drive about half a mile and take the first driveway on your left. You'll know you're in the right place when you see grapevines and tall metal roosters."

"Roosters?" He sounded almost disturbed by the word.

She nodded, not knowing what someone could have against roosters. "Aldo loves them."

"Ah." He still didn't look happy about the roosters.

"You don't like roosters?"

"Not generally." He winked at her. "They like to crow too much for my tastes."

She laughed. "Yeah, they do that."

There was an awkward silence while they stared at each other. Finally, he tapped the glass on the candy counter. "It smells fantastic in here. And these look delicious."

"I just made a batch of caramel sauce. It perfumes the air even better than baking bread." She couldn't look away from him.

Con studied the candy in the case between them.

"Would you like to try one?" She couldn't believe she sounded so eager. "We're generous with our samples."

He hesitated.

"Seriously," she said. "Have one. I insist. You should have some sustenance in you in case you get lost again."

He laughed again, Jack's laugh, and her heart stood still.

"In that case, I'll have one of those." He pointed to his choice. "One of the dark-chocolate ones with the salt on top."

When she saw which one he wanted, her knees nearly buckled. "The Lucky Jack?" It took her a second to find her voice and composure. This man who reminded of her of Jack also liked what he'd liked.

*This is just a simple coincidence. Lots of people like dark chocolate and salt. It's not a big deal.*

She took a deep breath and kept on smiling. "Good choice. Lucky Jacks are one of our most popular candies." Her eyes misted just a bit before she pushed thoughts of Jack aside.

"I named them for my late husband. They were his favorite." As she grabbed a tissue and plucked a caramel from the case she thought she could have bitten her tongue. It probably sounded as if she was making sure he knew she was single. Which hadn't been her intention at all. Or had it?

As she handed him the piece of candy their fingers brushed and she felt that shimmy of pleasure at his touch again. She could have sworn the brush was intentional. She suddenly wished she'd fixed up more and that her hair wasn't up in the tight ponytail she wore it in while working in the kitchen.

As he tasted her wares she watched, feeling like a child waiting for approval.

His eyes rolled upward and he sighed. "Delicious."

His accent was truly scrumptious.

"Flatterer," she said, just the way she'd have said it to Jack.

Con shook his head. "Would I lie?" He winked at Shiloh. "My cousin is having a big dinner at his place tonight, some kind of apple growers' party. Will you two be there?"

"We will," Willow answered before Shiloh could chime in. Almost instantly Willow regretted she'd be there with Shane.

"Good. I'll see you this evening then. Thanks for the directions." He nodded and turned to leave.

"Wait!" Willow reached into the candy case and put a half-dozen Lucky Jacks into a small white paper sack for him. "On me." She held them out to him. "A welcome gift."

He looked touched as he took them. "Thanks." And then he left.

She and Shiloh ogled him as he walked out of the shop. Willow had to remind herself to keep her tongue in her mouth. It wasn't because Con was handsome that he enthralled her. Or not *just* that, anyway.

He reminded her so much of Jack. It was almost eerie. And didn't make any sense. He even walked with a confident stride like Jack's.

The door closed behind him.

"I think that guy's my new old-man crush." Shiloh turned to Willow. "Did you notice the way he was dressed? Like he just stepped out of a fashion shoot." Shiloh sighed dramatically, teasingly. "His sweater looked so soft I wanted to reach out and touch it. And him. He looked hard and yummy beneath it."

"Yeah, I know the feeling," Willow said. "But believe me, he is *not* an old man."

He was most definitely in his prime.

Willow walked around the counter to the door and watched him get into his car and disappear down her long driveway. When he was out of sight she stepped onto the patio, listening to the dry cornstalks rustle in the breeze.

She hadn't felt a buzz of attraction like this for a man since Jack died. And she didn't understand it, felt almost treasonous for feeling it today of all days. Was she reacting to Con Russo only because he had something of Jack's spark?

As she turned to go back into the shop, Aldo's black cat crossed her path. Now there was an omen she didn't need.

# CHAPTER THREE

Willow walked back into the shop, only peripherally aware of Shiloh watching her with an expression of curiosity. She couldn't stop staring at the door. Jack was dead. No matter how much she wanted him back, he was gone. She didn't have the power to raise him from the dead. And she certainly never expected to meet someone like him again.

"Are you all right?" Shiloh sounded amused. "You look dazed. And dreamy. You aren't going to start doodling Con's name on napkins now, are you?"

Willow shook her head and managed a small smile. "He reminds me of Jack. Crazy, huh? It must just be the day."

"Wow, boss," Shiloh said. "Jack must have been hot."

Willow laughed. "Not like Con, but I thought he was sexy."

"I wouldn't know because you've never shown me a picture," Shiloh said pointedly, almost begging to see one now. "But if he looks like Con—"

"I haven't shown you a picture for a very good reason—I'm trying to move on. And he didn't look like Con. Except for the dark hair and eyes. And the height." That was another, more compelling reason Willow didn't flash Jack's picture around—the Agency had warned her not to. For her safety.

Shiloh put on a comical disappointed look and dropped

her quest to see a picture of Jack. "Is that all you noticed about him? His eyes? 'Cause his other parts were awfully nice."

Willow shook her head, ignoring the innuendo in Shiloh's voice. "We'd better get to work."

*That went well,* Jack thought as he got into his rented car in Willow's driveway.

This mission was going to kill him. He now knew his exact reaction to seeing Willow in the flesh—tight, clutching lust. Longing that made him ache to touch her. Dangerously tender feelings he thought he'd buried so deep they'd never resurface. He wanted to hold her in his arms and tell her he was sorry. For everything.

*Damn.*

Willow was the only woman who'd ever rattled him. She said it was because they were soul mates. He wasn't the romantic type. He'd never believed in things like starcrossed lovers. But he couldn't deny his connection with Willow still posed a clear and present danger to his mission and her life.

How was he going to face her at the party without giving himself away?

Jack was shaken and stirred—a bad, and potentially lethal, combination for an assassin/spy. He had a targeted killing to carry out. He needed to keep his head in the game.

Given what he did for a living, people accused him of having no conscience. Hell, he didn't issue the killing commands. He merely carried out orders.

But the way he saw it, he had plenty of conscience. If he failed this mission, the Rooster would attack the G8 emergency summit, killing diplomats and innocent civilians. Women. Children. Old people. Young people in their prime. People with nothing more than living their everyday lives on their minds. People who had no chance of fighting back or defending themselves.

Jack *was* their self-defense. They were on his conscience.

He pulled a caramel from the bag and took a bite as he buckled up. He'd rather be licking it off Willow's body, like he used to. Now *that* was heaven. He shouldn't have ordered his favorite. That was careless. And yet he was touched. She'd named the candy after him—the Lucky Jack. He wished he could have been sarcastic about it, but he *was* damn lucky. He'd survived that blast and lived to see Willow one more time.

He took another bite and stuck his key in the ignition. The engine turned over. He put the car in reverse and backed around until he was pointed down the driveway.

Willow had looked at him as if she recognized him. The Sense reacting to him? Or was he still, new looks and all, just a little too familiar?

None of it mattered. They couldn't be together again.

First he had to meet his "cousin." Then Jack planned to head over to Cooper Orchards and U-pick a box of apples as he scoped the place out and looked for his opportunity to strike. He was trained in a hundred different ways to kill. He just needed to know how to pick his poison. Literally.

Bluff Country Store was everything you'd expect of a country store—a story-and-a-half barnlike structure with varnished bare-wood interior walls and wall-to-wall country goods filling the shelves. It sold everything from locally made crafts and goods to touristy commercial dishes and pottery, basically anything with a farm or country motif. Roosters were a popular theme. And ruffles.

The back half of the first floor housed a deli with a candy counter where they sold Willow's chocolates and caramels. Off to the side they sold locally grown vegetables and fruit from bins.

The parking lot was gravel. Only the roads were paved around here, and many of them only shot-oiled. The winters were too hard on pavement.

The store had a large covered front porch filled with tables and chairs and stand-up signs advertising upcoming events and specials. In October, the porch was decorated with cornstalks, pumpkins, and gourds and the signs sang the praises of the Apple Festival.

Dodging the free-range chickens that roamed the lot pecking for pebbles, Willow parked as close as she could to the building. She shut off the ignition and jumped out. Someone had left a wagon in the lot. Bluff Country Store used little red wagons instead of shopping carts. She loaded it up with her caramel and headed to the store.

Ada looked down at her through the window as Willow hauled the wagon up the single step to the porch. She waved from behind the cash register.

"Here with our caramel, excellent! That's one thing going right," Ada said, coming out to greet her. "Let me get Matt to help you with that. Matt!" she called over her shoulder for her teenage son.

Ada put her hand on Willow's shoulder. "Leave it there. Matt will get it." She gave Willow a sympathetic look. "Things are already frantic around here getting ready for tomorrow. How are you holding up?"

Willow shrugged, ignoring the real reason her friend asked, pretending her day was just like everyone else's. "I'm harried and behind schedule. I still have apple pie fudge to make. What else is new?"

Ada raised a brow. "You sure you're okay?"

"I'm fine." And she was. Or would be if she could put Con Russo and his attractive similarity to Jack out of her mind.

"Are you as stressed about tomorrow as the rest of us are? All these last-minute details for the festival. You think you have things under control. . . ." Ada sighed. "I could use a little break. How about you? Do you have time for a cup of coffee? I have news." She winked at Willow.

"News? In Orchard Bluff? You mean gossip. Sure, I always have time for that."

Ada laughed. Willow followed her to the back of the store where the deli counter and café was located.

Ada grabbed a coffeepot from behind the counter and poured her a cup. "Cream? Sugar?"

"Black's fine. I've had my quota of sugar today. All of those tiny tastes add up. I've probably had my quota of coffee, too, but who's counting?"

Ada handed her the cup of coffee and pulled up a chair at a small, round table nearby. "Shane was in earlier."

Willow sat down across from her. "Making a delivery?"

"Yeah. He stopped by with a few crates of apples." Ada paused, looking as if she was debating with herself. "I probably shouldn't be telling you this. I'll ruin the surprise, but I think you should be forewarned. . . ."

Willow leaned forward like a conspirator. "Okay, that's way too ominous and intriguing. You can't leave me hanging after making a statement like that."

Ada laughed and immediately frowned, looking perplexed. "He bought you flowers, saying he wanted to perk you up today. Which seems natural enough and very sweet. It's just that he made such an odd choice."

Willow's heart thumped. "Not red roses? Please tell me he didn't. I'm definitely not ready for that."

"Relax," Ada reassured her. "I would have steered him away from something so inappropriate, especially given the day." She immediately looked as if she'd said something wrong.

Willow gave her a smile meant to reassure her.

"He bought you cockscomb. A large vase full of bright, beautiful magenta blooms. They're gorgeous, but, really, who gives them to a date?"

Willow sat back in her chair. "Cockscomb?"

"Yeah, odd, huh?"

"Well, it definitely doesn't send too strong a message or look like he's pushing too fast for a relationship. That's good. On the other hand, *You remind me of barnyard fowl*? Is that really a good message to send to your date?" She wrinkled her nose and noticed Ada wasn't laughing. "What's really bothering you?"

"He just seemed so pleased with himself for picking them out. Almost as if they were an inside joke. It was odd. They don't mean anything to you, do they?"

Willow shook her head and shrugged. "No."

"Well, okay, then. Just my imagination. I arranged them with a spray of greens. You'll like them. Try to act surprised when he gives them to you."

"You got it." She studied Ada. "Is something about Shane's flower-buying proclivities still bothering you?"

"It's probably nothing." Ada took a sip of her coffee. "I just think you should be careful around him."

Willow studied her suddenly serious friend. "You mean because of my delicate emotional state?"

Ada shook her head. "No, I know you're strong and can handle yourself. But there's just something about Shane that's a little off to me."

Willow sometimes had the same feeling about him, but she kept it to herself. "You must be the only one in town. He's charmed everyone else. What are you thinking?"

Ada waved her hand, making a dismissive gesture. "It's probably nothing."

"Oh, come on. Spill it."

Ada shrugged. "He doesn't seem like a genuine apple

man to me. I know he's just here for a few months to run Grant Cooper's orchard and bring the harvest in for Grant while he's in Phoenix taking care of his dying dad. But it seems as if Grant would have picked someone with more of a feel for the business."

Willow trusted Ada's intuition, but she didn't see the problem. "Why shouldn't Grant trust a college buddy from agriculture school? As suddenly as his dad got sick and Grant bolted out of here, he was lucky Shane's family could spare him from their orchards in the Northeast to come help out on a moment's notice."

"You're right." But Ada didn't look convinced.

"I just wish he'd pay more attention to his dogs. Buddy and Duke are such sweeties." Willow loved dogs. Shane treated his more like machines to serve him than companions. "They deserve some loving and kindness."

Ada laughed. "You're the only one who thinks so. Everyone else is scared to death of them. Those brutes are vicious."

"Not if you know how to handle them."

"You and your passion for dogs." Ada smiled and changed the topic of conversation. "Hey, have you heard? Aldo's cousin Con has finally arrived. Lettie saw him when she stopped by the Villa to drop off a punch bowl for tonight.

"She says Con is drop-dead, to-die-for gorgeous and if she were in her thirties, heck, if she were in her forties, she'd chase that man until he surrendered to his passion."

"I know. I met him." Willow blurted it out without thinking.

"You met him?" Ada's eyes lit up. "Then you have the scoop. Is Lettie exaggerating?"

"No. She may even be underexaggerating, if you can believe that." Willow winked at her.

Ada started laughing and clapped her hands. "Then

the ladies are *really* going to have fun tonight. No wonder Lettie was so delighted he'd be at the dinner."

Willow gave her a puzzled look. "Why?"

"You know we have a special charity fund-raiser every year at the dinner and it alternates between ladies' choice and gentlemen's? This year it's ladies' choice."

"Yeah?" Willow had only been once, last year. Her grief had still been too fresh for her to really enjoy herself. But everyone else had.

Last year the men designed the ladies' challenge—a competition to see how fast three lady contestants could assemble a precut wooden bench using only a hammer and screwdriver. No instructions.

The process for selecting the contestants was simple— people paid for votes and cast them for the attendees they wanted to see participate in the challenge. At the same time, possible participants could pay to have votes removed from their name. At the appointed hour, those with the most votes competed. It was all in good fun and for a good cause.

Everyone had had a good laugh at the bench-building process—the ladies really hammed it up. Of course the men had all voted for the women who were least handy with a set of tools. And the results were hilarious. Several of the benches were deemed un-sit-worthy. But they were all still auctioned off for charity. The winner, the one whose bench went for the most money, won a day at the spa and the privilege of presenting the check to the charity.

"As elected Town Grump, Lettie designed this year's challenge," Ada said. "I'm sworn to secrecy, but I'll give you a hint—Lettie loves dancing."

Orchard Bluff was basically two large loops of roads dotted with orchards. The "town" center, and *town* was a loose term, sat at the junction of the loops. Cooper

Orchards, the orchards the Rooster was purportedly babysitting, sat off the east loop on an offshoot dirt road.

*Of course it did,* Jack thought. All the better to stay out of sight and away from prying eyes.

What a perfect setup for an explosives-smuggling operation. Just a hundred miles from the Canadian border. People coming and going at the orchard all of the time. No questions asked if strangers stopped by and left with loads of boxes. Genius, really.

It would have been even better if the Rooster weren't pretending to be an organic farmer. But, as Jack knew full well, no cover was perfect. Especially those set on the fly.

Jack didn't believe the story about Kennett coming to town to help out an old friend in need. Kennett was here to pump Willow for information and draw Jack out while he planned his attack on the summit, pure and simple. Grant Cooper, organic apple farmer, was probably dead and buried somewhere on the property. RIOT assassins like the Rooster didn't leave loose ends and they didn't have friends.

Like all the farms of Orchard Bluff, Cooper Orchards sold fruit out of a metal, barnlike building next to the house. The Agency had heard rumors there was an old bomb shelter somewhere on the property. Jack was on the lookout for it. What an ironic and perfect place to build bombs. And hide out. If the bomb shelter existed, it was heavily shielded. The Agency hadn't picked up any transmissions from it.

Some of the homes on the bluff were large and fantastic. Others modest. Kennett had taken up residence in Cooper's, an old farmhouse on the modest side, with a steep, pitched roof.

As Jack pulled to a stop in the hard-pack dirt parking lot, he felt his adrenaline spike. *Showtime.*

He was here to rattle the Rooster's coop. Get him to

mess up and spill intel. Make him wonder—was Con Russo Sariel or not? Had he drawn out his prey? Or would he have to try harder?

Jack was prepared to play head games with him. And enjoy it.

Only one other car sat in the lot next to the barn.

*Good.* Jack didn't need any extraneous eyes watching him scope the place.

He'd already stopped by Aldo's, reunited with the "cousin" ten years his senior who—he hadn't "seen since he was a baby"—a piece of pure fiction—and settled in. Funny what people will "remember" and believe when you prompt them hard enough. Jack had never met Aldo before in his life. Aldo had no idea of Jack's true identity. And Jack intended to keep it that way.

Then he'd been ogled by the officially elected Town Grump as she delivered a punch bowl and tried to micro-manage Becky and Aldo as they set up for the growers' dinner, which raised money for a local charity. And finally escaped by volunteering to run to Cooper's to pick up the apples the Rooster was donating for the party this evening. Aldo, who was running around in a panic, was only too happy to take Jack up on his offer.

Jack jumped out of the car and went into the barn for a box. He was going to insist on picking as Aldo had requested. Aldo wanted the very crispest, freshest apples at his soiree. And it suited Jack's plan perfectly.

Jack would have preferred to roam the orchard at will, but U-pick apple farmers were peculiar about people free-ranging in their orchards and he didn't want to draw the wrong kind of attention. Farmers liked to point you to particular rows of trees they wanted picked first.

Jack stood in the doorway, observing the Rooster. It took every ounce of strength Jack had not to kill him on the spot. Jack flashed back to holding Kyle in his arms as he bled out after being hit by one of the Rooster's sniper shots.

A good sniper kills instantly. The Rooster had wanted Kyle to suffer and Jack to see it.

"Welcome to Cooper Orchards." The Rooster looked up from measuring apples into boxes in the back of the barn.

Jack was a master at reading body language. He watched the Rooster study him. He knew the instant Kennett sensed something familiar about him. Jack saw Kennett's confusion and kept his hand in his pocket on his weapon in case he needed to use it.

Jack strolled in, trying to keep his hatred from showing. "I'm looking for Shane Kennett. My cousin Aldo sent me over to pick apples for the big dinner tonight at his place. He said Kennett offered to donate as many as Aldo needs."

Kennett wiped his hand on a towel and came forward. "I'm Kennett." He extended his hand.

"Con Russo." Though his skin crawled, Jack accepted Kennett's hand and shook.

Kennett's handshake was crushing, a little too firm to be polite. More of a show of power and threat.

"So you finally arrived. Aldo's been talking about you." Kennett's gaze swept over Jack, leaving the impression the Rooster didn't approve of Jack and was assessing him.

No doubt the Rooster measured every new arrival in town against the possibility he was Sariel returned from the grave. That's why Kennett was here, wasn't it? To draw Sariel out.

"Good things, I hope." Jack kept his tone casual, though he guessed it would be evident to anyone watching that the two men disliked each other on sight.

Kennett laughed. "He forgot to mention what a sharp dresser you were." It wasn't a compliment.

Jack smiled back, making a note to scold Malene when he got back to Langley for making him wear these non–alpha male outfits. They put him in the weak position and he damn well didn't like it. He didn't care what James Bond did; real men on missions dressed to intimidate their opponents, not give them ammo to poke fun at.

Jack held Kennett's gaze. They were definitely two adversaries sizing each other up. He saw the indecision in Kennett's eyes—was Jack the one, Sariel or not?

*Good, let him sweat it.* Uncertainty was Jack's friend.

Kennett nodded. "Take your pick from any of the bins."

Jack shook his head. "Aldo says I should pick. He wants fruit right off the tree. Nothing else will do."

Kennett stared at him, shaking his head in the patronizing way bullies use. He was the kind of rugged, good-looking man women drooled over, before they realized he was a cold-blooded killer. And the type of guy other men had the natural inclination to punch out. Jack more than most men. Or so he imagined.

The Rooster laughed. "Sounds like Aldo. He's a perfectionist." He left off the word *prick,* but Jack heard it in the Rooster's voice. "Are you sure you want to go out in the orchards in those shoes? You're taking a chance with those fine leather loafers."

Jack looked down at his Italian leather shoes and back up at Kennett. "They're hardier than they look. I'll take my chances."

Kennett shrugged. "I grow a dozen varieties. Does Aldo have a preference? What do you want?"

*A quick way to kill you and get the hell out of here,* Jack thought. He could do it. No problem. It was the *making it look like an accident* part and the sudden appearance of an elderly couple also looking to pick that tripped him up.

"Aldo said Goldens," Jack said as the older couple strolled into the metal barn. He'd already studied a map of the orchard and knew rows of Golden Delicious apple trees provided him with the best area to scope out the place. Conveniently, his desires and Aldo's coincided.

Kennett handed him a box and gave him directions to the trees with ripe fruit. As Jack took the box, Kennett glanced at his watch. "A heads-up. I'm closing early today.

"I'm taking the hottest woman in town to the party." He watched Jack closely for his reaction. "Should be a good time." He winked at Jack.

Jack was a master at reading microexpressions, tiny, barely perceptible involuntary muscle movements that betrayed a person's true emotions. The Rooster was goading him to see if he was Sariel. It was written all over his face.

*Compartmentalize.*

The Rooster read microexpressions, too.

"I'm going stag," Jack said, letting his tone imply he didn't intend to finish the night alone. "I'll see you there."

There was no way in hell Jack was letting the Rooster go home with his wife.

# CHAPTER FOUR

The doorbell rang at precisely six. Willow's little dog, Spookie, barked and went crazy at the sound.

Willow hopped to the door with one white sandal in one hand and another in her other hand, trying to cram one onto her foot along the way. And doing an awkward dance in the process as she clattered across her wooden flooring with Spookie playing toy guard dog at her heels.

Why did Shane have to be on time, especially when she was running late? What was it with men? Didn't they understand the rules? *Give the girls a few extra minutes, boys.*

"Coming!" She slid the second sandal on, took a deep breath, and smoothed her blue chambray baby-doll shirt, contrasting red stitching, shirred bodice, empire waist, and all, as she came to a stop in front of the door. She'd loved this simple blouse with its stitched red and white country flowers on sight when she found it in town last week. Now she was wondering whether its innocent style was flashy enough to catch Con's sophisticated eye. Jack, however, would have loved it.

She ran her fingers through her hair. She'd spent an inordinate amount of time on it, trying to get it to look as if it always just cascaded in natural, loose waves about her shoulders with no effort at all. After all, she had to dispel that severe, prim image of her in a ponytail that was Con's first impression of her.

It was probably bad form to arrive on the arm of another man when all she could think about was Con Russo and how she was going to do everything in her power to get to know him better. She hadn't felt like this since the first time she'd seen Jack in that coffee shop in Seattle. And she'd do just about anything to hang on to that feeling, including being treasonous to her date.

Her heart felt as if it was waking again after a two-year sleep. And she blamed it all on Jack.

He'd set her expectations and standards for men high. She was always looking for him, for any sign of a hero, in any man she met. Right now she couldn't decide whether her attraction to Con was purely because he reminded her of Jack or not. But she intended to find out.

She put her finger to her lips and gave Spookie a stern look. "Hush. This is our guest arriving."

But Spookie ignored her and went crazy yipping and barking as Willow opened the door to Shane. Willow had never been much of a disciplinarian. Jack had trained Spookie. He had a way with dogs. Willow used to tease him that he could have been a dog whisperer.

Just as Ada had said Shane would, he arrived brandishing a lush bouquet of cockscomb. He handed them to Willow as Spookie hunkered down and growled at him in her attempt at a menacing stance. With his hair combed up in a faux hawk, Shane looked a bit like a rooster himself. *Maybe he's just going with a theme for the evening?* Willow thought to herself, half-amused.

"These are beautiful! Thanks." Was that surprised enough? "New haircut?"

"Yeah." He ran his hand quickly and lightly over the top of his hair. Then he grinned. "You look gorgeous."

Spookie chose that minute to attack his leg. A look calculated to kill crossed Shane's face as he glared at Spookie. It passed so quickly Willow wondered whether she'd imagined it.

She bent down and scooped Spookie up and stood aside to let Shane in. "Come on in. I'm running a little behind. Let me just put this killer dog of mine in the back and stick these in some water."

She carried Spookie back to the bedroom and, against her protests, gated her in with a child gate, dashed on a stroke of lip gloss, and returned to find Shane studying her living room.

He turned and smiled at her as she entered the room and went to the kitchen to fill a vase with water. "How are you holding up today?"

"I'm fine, thank you." Oh no, now he'd want to talk about Jack again. And her feelings. As if he were some kind of grief counselor because he'd lost his fiancée. Willow didn't want to talk. She wanted to be normal, feel normal, act normal, and be treated normally, not make people behave as if they had to tread delicately around her.

"You don't have to hold it all in, Willow. Not around me. I understand. I feel the loss every year on the anniversary of Crystal's death." Shane had told her about his late fiancée shortly after they'd met.

He liked to talk to her about Crystal and encouraged her to talk about Jack. But, frankly, she wanted to be dated because she was a desirable woman, not because she was a sympathetic ear.

NCS chief Emmett Nelson had warned her not to reveal anything about Jack to anyone, to always be on her guard. He shouldn't have worried. Her feelings, her memories, her thoughts about Jack were hers and hers alone. She wasn't about to share them with Shane.

Willow stuck the flowers in the vase and carried them

to the console table in her entryway. Shane came up behind her and put a hand on each of her shoulders, giving her a squeeze.

"I don't want to talk, really," she said.

"Come, Willow. It's okay to remember. Did he like to dance? Would he have liked the party we're going to tonight?"

"He hated dancing and loved social gatherings," she lied, thinking about Ada's hint that Lettie's contest would involve dancing. Jack loved to dance. But she'd only tell Shane that over her dead body. If he was going to persist with this, she was going to feed him as much misinformation as he deserved for not picking up on her less than subtle cues to back off. "But he would have loved Aldo's vegetarian lasagna." Another lie. Jack was a carnivore to his core, much to her dismay.

Shane lifted her hair off her shoulder and whispered in her ear, "I bet Jack was protective of you. I bet he'd have done anything for you. Saved you from any threat."

Though Shane's words must have been meant to be kind, must have been a compliment to Jack, they sent a shiver down her spine. She sidestepped out of his embrace. "Jack was a hero. He protected everyone. Let's go."

It was an unusually calm, warm October evening with the stars twinkling above to match the outdoor lamps, torches, and candles Aldo had burning outside his little establishment. It was a good thing, too, that the weather was cooperating. The Villa's two small buildings—the catering kitchen and the tasting room—could each be called cozy and quaint, but even together no one could truthfully call them spacious. Certainly not roomy enough for the number of people coming to the party. But the grange hall in town was decked out for the festivities that began the next day and unavailable to use.

The Villa was part winery, part catering company, and part "oh my gosh, I need something for dinner; a Villa lasagna is just the thing." Straight from Italy, Aldo had brought his cuisine and cooking skills with him. He cooked, catered, and sold frozen take-out lasagnas, polenta, meatballs, and pesto from his kitchen.

Pulling one of Aldo's frozen vegetarian pesto lasagnas from the freezer had saved Willow a time or two when she'd been too tired to cook.

He also made wine, reds and whites and, notably, apple wine for the harvest celebration. Tonight he was unveiling his latest apple creation—the Pink Lady blend. A perfect bottle as you cuddled around the fire with a special friend and thought romantic thoughts sipping Pink Lady bliss. Serve it up with some Brie and slices of fresh Pink Lady apples and romance was certain to follow. At least for weeks that's what he'd been telling anyone who'd listen.

"Remind me to buy a bottle of apple wine. For later." Shane smiled down at her.

Aldo's wife, Becky, greeted them as they stepped onto the patio. "Willow! Shane. Welcome." Becky grabbed Willow's arm and pulled them toward the bar where she'd been pouring apple wine.

"Come. Let's get you two each a glass of something. We're serving Aldo's new wine and my apple gold punch. And don't forget to sample the appetizer meatballs." She pointed to a warming tray filled with tiny bite-size meatballs. "Aldo spent all day on them. If everyone doesn't praise him to the hills, there'll be no living with him tomorrow."

While Becky talked, Willow scanned the party, looking for Con.

Becky handed Shane a glass of alcoholic punch. "Willow? What will you have?"

"Wine's fine, thanks."

Becky poured her a glass and held it out to her. "Aldo put out a vegetarian antipasto plate and made a pan of pesto lasagna just for you."

"That's sweet of him." Willow accepted the glass of wine. "Make sure you let him know how much I appreciate it."

Becky nodded and grabbed a roll of tickets from the counter. "Have you heard about this year's charity challenge? Five lucky men will be forced to square off in a country line dance competition. Last man standing wins a big-screen TV and a year of cable with any sports channels he wants.

"Tickets are a dollar apiece, or twelve for ten dollars. All proceeds will be split between the food bank and the animal shelter. How many can I sell you two?"

Willow pulled a twenty from her purse and handed it over.

Becky glanced at Shane as she counted out Willow's tickets. "Looks like you might be in trouble, Shane. She's buying a lot of votes. You'd better buy enough to counteract hers."

Shane reached for his wallet and handed over two twenties.

"Wise man!" Becky handed Willow her tickets and began counting out Shane's.

"I met Aldo's cousin earlier. Is he here?" Willow asked.

"He's here and he's already racked up a lot of votes." Becky handed Shane his tickets. "Many a woman here would love to see his moves."

Jack was a consummate loner and generally avoided social gatherings, except with his closest friends. Years of being beaten and bullied as a kid had trained a certain distrust of his fellow humans into him, and he was an introvert by nature. Tonight, however, he'd been enjoying himself—he liked a good cat-and-mouse game and pulling a fast prank—until he looked out across the parking lot and saw the Rooster arrive with his arm around Willow.

Sometimes surveillance really was the worst part of this job.

Willow looked beautiful with her hair cascading around her shoulders. She was wearing tight jeans and a blue top that showed off her delicate collarbone and creamy skin. Jack resisted the urge to ball his fists. He was supposed to look relaxed and like he was enjoying himself. If he'd had his way, he would have taken care of the Rooster right then and there. Then maybe he could enjoy the evening.

Jack's boss, Emmett Nelson, hated ex-spouses and lovers on the grounds they were security risks and WikiLeaks ready to happen. NCS had a policy about dating, marriage, and ex-lovers—they frowned on them all. RIOT had a stricter policy—no exes lived past the expiration date of the relationship. Period. Sometimes not even that long.

Jack worried the Rooster would eliminate Willow once he was done using her to draw him out. *Worry,* actually, was too mild a term. *Knew.* Jack knew the Rooster would kill her.

Worse, the RIOT boys liked to play with their food. Seriously, Jack would rather hand Willow over to a member of the old KGB, back in their glory days, than a RIOT assassin like the Rooster.

Fortunately, Jack had a plan to separate the asshole from his wife and get inside Kennett's lair for a look—a little vial of XTC in Jack's pocket should take care of the Rooster and make the party interesting.

Yeah, he knew. XTC was a date rape drug. Usually you used it to get some action, not prevent it. But, hey, what could he say? He was a creative guy.

Next to Jack, Aldo told a joke. Jack laughed to keep from erupting and running out to take a swing at Kennett.

This costume Malene had sent for Jack to wear to the party wasn't making his job any easier. He wasn't used to dressing like an Italian fop. High fashion—who needed it?

Malene had to instruct him how to wear the damn clothes. "Roll up the pant legs to just above your ankles, Jack, darling, and absolutely do not wear socks. It will ruin the look. Remember, you're supposed to be urbane."

"Urbane, hell. Who wears leather dress shoes without socks?" he'd said, mumbling something about blisters and a bad case of athlete's foot beneath his breath.

"You're not going jogging in them." Malene laughed.

But he had worn them to the orchard and had to pay for it later by having to polish them.

"I'll send along a pair of Odor-Eaters if you're worried about foot odor cramping your style." She had a wink in her voice.

Malene could be insufferable. But here he was, dressed as ordered. Why couldn't she dress him as an Italian jock? The woman had an evil, power-hungry side to her. She loved being in control.

But mainly, Jack worried about continuing the ruse and making sure Willow didn't suspect he was him, her husband. He was not Jack. He kept telling himself that. Jack had died two years ago. Maybe longer.

# CHAPTER FIVE

Jack had installed hidden cameras around the Villa so he could keep tabs on Kennett without having to constantly tail him. He'd been surreptitiously watching Kennett on the feed on his video watch since the bastard arrived at the party. He didn't like the way the guy had his hands all over Willow. Jack was sure that was to provoke him, a test to see if Con was really Jack and would out himself over Willow. Other than that, Kennett was a bore.

Jack had also been skillfully avoiding Willow, who was definitely seeking Con out. That woman could be persistent when she wanted to be. At this point, Jack didn't know who he should be more jealous of—Shane or himself as Con? He'd obviously made an impression on her earlier. Must be his new plastic surgery–provided good looks.

While it was flattering that Willow found Con so attractive, how could she just forget the real him, Jack, so easily?

This was a disaster of a mission and it was messing with his mind. He felt like he was developing split personality disorder. He didn't even know how to refer to himself.

He'd thought he was going to be the cat in this game, so why did he suddenly feel like the mouse? Kennett was openly suspicious of Con and rightly so. Any newcomer posed a threat, but one who bore a slight similarity to Jack? Any operative would use caution, and the Rooster was no dumb ass.

And then to make matters even worse, someone kept stuffing the ballot box with votes for Con. Jack did not want to compete in a country line dance-off, even if it would impress Willow.

Every time Jack passed by the voting, he had to buy more tickets so he could un-vote for himself. At this rate, he was going to go broke. He'd already run through most of his petty cash. Emmett would have his head for wasting Agency funds when he turned in his expense report for reimbursement.

Terrorists and torturers should take notes from charity fund-raiser organizers. Under the social pressure of supporting a worthy cause, there was absolutely no way even the cruelest of bad guys could resist buying tickets. It was either that or make a fool out of himself.

Lettie, the man-starved Town Grump Jack had met earlier, grabbed Kennett, peeling him off from Willow to bend his ear. Kennett was running neck and neck with Jack in the voting. Jack had the feeling Lettie was Kennett's biggest fan. There was some small justice in the world.

Willow seized her opportunity for freedom, wrenching herself free of Kennett's grip. Jack had to hold down a smile.

He excused himself from the group he was mingling with and circled out the back door, avoiding Willow, just in time to lurk in the shadows and spy on Kennett. Lurking in the shadows wasn't so bad. Jack was used to lurking and striking.

He made a bet with himself about how long it would take Kennett to extricate himself from Lettie, who droned on about some local drivel and made eyes at the Rooster, telling how much she was looking forward to seeing him dance.

Men in this town didn't like to dance. Which was why the women found this year's charity event so amusing. And the men were all trying to vote for someone else to face the humiliation.

It took Kennett a full five minutes to escape from Lettie. Jack timed it.

Not bad. He had to give his enemy a little credit.

Jack had a feeling Kennett would have loved to kill the official grump if ever given half a chance. Having escaped, he made his way to a six-foot-tall metal sculpture of a rooster Aldo had installed at the edge of the parking lot. Jack couldn't see the appeal, for the obvious reason that he hated roosters, but Aldo loved them and had half a dozen of the sculptures throughout the property.

Kennett stooped to pick up a rock. The lighting was romantic and dim, mostly candlelight, with some residual light streaming from the windows of the surrounding building. But Jack's eyes were sharp and adjusted quickly to the dark. He had a sniper's eyes. He saw Kennett drop a rock from his pocket onto the metal base of the rooster as he scooped up a new one and tossed it into the surrounding field, acting as if he were releasing pent-up frustration from having to talk with the grump.

*The old fake-rock drop trick.*

Jack grinned. That might be the oldest trick in the spy book, but it was still damn effective. There was no way to do electronic surveillance on a hard drop. An old-fashioned paper drop was the safest way to avoid detection.

He wondered whether Kennett had a contact at the party. More likely, one would be by after the party to pick up the drop. But not before Jack intercepted the data.

It appeared he had rattled someone's coop.

As soon as Kennett moved out of sight, Jack swooped in and retrieved the plastic stone. He pocketed the drop rock, walked casually to the men's room in the kitchen building, where he locked himself in a stall and used his lock-picking skills to open the rock. Inside it, he found a coded message. He snapped a picture of it with his cell phone camera and sent it to the tech gurus and decrypting staff at Langley. Within minutes he received a text instructing him how to alter the message to feed RIOT bad intel.

*Rooster, you are going to be in deep shit now,* Jack thought, trying not to grin as he made the alterations.

He replaced the message and pocketed the rock.

On his way out of the men's room, he got lucky. Kennett had his back to Jack and had set his drink down on the counter next to him as he made a point while talking to another grower near the punch bowl. Even better, Kennett was drinking apple gold punch, a warm, spiced cider laced with dark rum. Perfect.

Magic had always said sleight of hand was a highly convenient skill to have. And she was right. As the hour of the competition grew close, Lettie and her minions had been keeping an eye on all the possible contestants in case someone decided to bolt. Inconvenient, but it didn't slow Jack down. He always had something up his sleeve. In this case, it was his extra-strength homebrew XTC. He used the skills he'd learned at Magic's side during his rehab and slipped a dose big enough to sedate a horse into Kennett's drink. Why skimp?

Sometimes, you can't take the prankster out of the spy. Jack had to cover his tracks so when big, strong, *highly resistant to alcohol* Kennett went down after consuming only a glass or two of spiked punch no one would be suspicious. Aldo's cousin refilling the punch wouldn't give anyone reason for suspicion.

He grabbed a jug of cider that he'd filled with Ever-clear earlier and spiked the punch. Before the party he'd left empty Everclear bottles where they would eventually be found. He was hoping no one would ever catch the prankster and suspicion would be cast elsewhere. Like to a local. Hey, it was almost trick-or-treat time. Everclear in the punch was more fun than toilet-papering apple orchards.

Jack made his way back to the tasting building for the contest, dropping the rock where Kennett had originally placed it.

"Con!" Inside the building, Aldo flagged Jack down and waved him over. "Just minutes to go until they announce the unfortunate fellows who have to dance. You're trailing by just a few votes. But I have your back, *cugino*. I've been telling everyone who tries to vote for me to vote for you instead." Aldo let out a boom of a laugh and slapped Jack on the back. "Brilliant, eh?"

"My many un-heartfelt thanks. With family like you, who needs enemies?" Jack was only half-teasing. He had plenty of those already. If he completed his mission successfully, very soon he'd have one less. That made him smile.

"Eh! It's the least I can do. If you can't embarrass *la famiglia* for a good cause, life isn't worth living! Besides, you should show off. The ladies want to see it. We men don't care for dancing. But the ladies love a man who can dance." Aldo gave him another friendly, familial pat. "The family honor is in your hands now."

*Damn.* Now he'd have to buy more tickets so he could get himself out of having to dance.

Willow's pulse raced as Aldo pulled Con into the tasting room for the big reveal of which unlucky five men had won, or lost, depending upon perspective, the vote and would have to dance off against one another. Shane came into the building behind him, carrying a cup of warm apple gold punch. He slid in beside her.

"You're just in time," she said to him. "I was beginning to worry. You're in second place right now, just below Bob. I'm glad you didn't run out on us."

"I thought about it. But Lettie has people keeping tabs on me and guards posted at all the doors and escape routes. There's no way she's letting any of the victims bolt." He lifted his glass of punch and downed half. "For fortification and to cast away inhibitions."

Willow clutched twenty dollars' worth of tickets. One second before the stroke of eight, she was going to cast them for Con so he didn't have time to un-vote them.

She'd been unable to connect with him all evening. She had the feeling he'd been doing some evasive action and avoiding her. But that wasn't the main reason for her failure. No, the blame for that was 190 pounds of muscle named Shane who'd spent the majority of the evening either right at her side, eavesdropping on any conversation she had (he thought he was being sneaky, but she knew what he was up to), or, and this may have just been her imagination, watching her to see if she was watching Con. Yes, that was crazy. She really couldn't figure it out. Shane had only left her for a few minutes all evening. Once to go to the bathroom. And just now to get a cup of cider.

Of course, she *was* watching Con. With a very appreciative eye. But if she'd learned anything from living with Jack, it was how to conduct a covert operation. She'd been careful to be clandestine. She didn't think she'd given Shane any reason to be jealous. But she was probably about to blow all that when she spent her tickets on Con.

Shane's reactions and behavior around her puzzled Willow. He persisted in pursuing her, and yet there wasn't any sexual chemistry between them. None on her part and only halfhearted, feigned attraction on his. As odd as it sounded, it was almost as if he was acting a part.

Maybe Shane was trying to force himself to move on from Crystal's death by latching onto Willow. Maybe he thought their similar backgrounds of loss made them compatible. But it was a lost cause.

Willow was highly intuitive. And she knew chemistry when she saw it and, more important, when she felt it. There was no reason for Shane to be jealous and care whether she spoke with Con or not. And yet something about the way Shane acted, almost as if he was looking for her to make a move of some kind on Aldo's cousin, made her back off and go underground.

During her, she hoped, clandestine surveillance of Con she'd noticed a couple of interesting things. One, she'd seen him by one of Aldo's metal roosters pocketing a rock. For luck? Con didn't seem like the rock-hound type. And two, no matter how much the ladies wanted to watch him strut his stuff, he didn't want to dance. He kept trying to buy his way out of it. So, of course, she was going to make certain he danced until he dropped. And it wasn't the ladies' need for eye candy that motivated her.

You could tell a lot about a person by how good- or bad-naturedly they reacted under pressure or to a situation they found embarrassing. And how they took being ribbed. She'd know by how Con handled himself in the competition whether he was a man worth getting to know better. Or whether he'd never measure up to Jack.

Shane stood next to her, rocking on the balls of his feet nervously.

"You're right. Lettie's going to make you dance," she said to him, teasing. "I don't think she dreamed up this competition just to get back at Bob for last year. I think she just wants to see you shake your booty."

He shook his head, looking decidedly unappreciative of Lettie's desires. He pointed to Willow's tickets. "And you're planning to buy me out of this?"

She eyed him doubtfully. "Do you really think I can outspend Lettie? She's the wealthiest person here." Willow grinned. "Sorry, but I think you're in."

Con came into the building with Aldo. As they walked past her, an old, familiar feeling washed over her—the prickly glow and sense of danger that used to surround Jack. The hairs on her arms stood up, fueled by her earlier sense of foreboding. If she'd had a pinch of salt, she would have thrown it over her shoulder just then.

Instead, she studied Con. He was everything Willow liked in a man—broad shoulders, wavy dark hair, and a confident stance. She could see why he was Shiloh's old-man crush, though he was anything but old. Probably not a day over thirty-five. Jack's age, if he'd lived.

Dressed in a soft black V-neck sweater that practically screamed to be stroked as it strained across his shoulders, cashmere probably, casual mahogany-brown slacks rolled to the ankles, secured with a black-and-white-patterned belt, supple leather black shoes, sans socks, he looked very much in his prime. And way too sophisticated and city slick for Orchard Bluff. The opposite of the way Jack dressed. He wouldn't have been caught dead in such a totally metro outfit. But somehow, on Con, it worked.

A large digital timer was counting down the final minutes until eight. With two minutes to go, Lettie went to the podium at the head of the room, banged a gavel, grabbed a cordless mic, and called the room to order. "All right, citizens of Orchard Bluff, the hour of reckoning is almost upon us. Bob White, this is payback for that diabolical bench-building challenge last year." She pointed over her back.

Behind her stood a large whiteboard with a tally of

the votes. Bob White was in first place, Shane in second, two other local men in places three and four, and Con was in fifth by just five votes.

"Bob, I see the good ladies have made sure you're going to be dancing," Lettie said.

The crowd laughed.

Willow hoped her stash of vote tickets, and a perfectly timed casting of them, would ensure Con danced. He stood just a few feet away from her, rummaging through his pockets. She had a hard time not staring at him. He was so easy on the eyes.

Lettie led the crowd in a countdown. "Ten, nine—"

"Wait!" Con dashed to the podium, waving a bill around.

"A man who likes to flash his cash for charity." Lettie clapped. "Stop the timer. What can I do for you, Con?"

"Ten bucks says I'm out." Con held it out to Lettie with a big grin on his face.

Lettie leaned across the podium with a big grin. "More money for charity! Oh, but this is bad, very bad, for Clint. This puts him in fifth place. Clint, where are you? Start digging in your pockets for the animal shelter or you'll be dancing."

"Not so fast!" Willow's heart raced as she seized her opportunity and stepped forward. "Twenty dollars for the animal shelter and twenty-four votes for Con."

The stunned look on Con's face was worth every penny. As if she were a traitor. And yet he was amused at the same time. The curl of his good-natured grin almost stopped her heart—it was so strikingly like Jack's.

"Clint, you owe Willow one for this, you old codger. I expect to see you in her shop buying a pound of candy for your wife." Lettie banged the gavel. "Start the timer. Five, four, three, two, one!"

The buzzer sounded. The crowd cheered.

"Zero!" Lettie turned to Con. "We're good sports. And

we play fair, especially when we're trying to raise as much money as possible for a good cause. Before I pronounce your sentence, do you have any more money you'd like to donate to get out of dancing?"

Con pulled his pockets inside out and shook his head, hamming it up shamelessly. "Hey, Aldo, help me out? Lend me a few?"

"I'll throw in another twenty." Aldo grinned.

Con relaxed and did a victory punch in the air. "Yes! Family."

Aldo waved a bill around. "To make sure he dances."

Con stopped in his tracks and his face fell. The crowd roared.

"Anyone else have an opinion they'd like to throw some cash at?" Lettie looked around the group of growers.

"Ten for keeping him in!" someone else called out.

"I'll go five!"

"I have twenty tickets that say he's dancing," Sheryl the mail carrier said. "And I want to see a tush push!"

Con made a comical shocked face and slapped his hands on his butt as if he was tucking it in and keeping it firmly in place. "A what?"

Bob White came up, slapped Con on the back, and stuck his butt out. "It's a country line dance move, city boy."

"That is *not* what I'm talking about!" Sheryl called back. "Pull that big old butt in, Bob. Don't listen to him, Con. Nora will show you how it's done."

Lettie banged her gavel. "Con, it's official—you're dancing! The rest of you boys, get on up here."

Shane handed his drink to Willow. "Hang on to this for me. I'll be back for a victory drink."

Con, Shane, Bob, and the two others made their way to the front of the podium, looking sheepish and uncomfortable.

"There are only a few rules," Lettie said when they

were assembled. "No intentionally bad dancing. Some of you may not be light on your feet, but you're going to have to try. This is for charity and we expect you men to fight to win.

"If our judge taps you, you're out. The decision of the judge is final. No arguing. Got it?"

The men pretended to grumble but nodded their agreement.

"Good. Unlike the men last year"—Lettie gave Bob a stern look that got a good laugh—"who gave no instructions to the ladies, we women have risen above and brought in an expert to show you boys how it's done. Our very own Nora Renner has taught country line dancing for twenty years. Follow her and you shouldn't have any problems.

"Where's Roger, our disc jockey?" Lettie looked around. "There he is." Lettie smiled at him. "Nora? Ready?"

Nora stepped out to the front of the crowd and took a small bow.

"Take it away." Lettie clapped and stepped away from the podium.

Jack loved to dance. Yeah, it was a bit embarrassing to be a big, bad assassin who liked to trip the light fantastic. But what could he say? He considered dancing an athletic endeavor. He felt Willow watching him as Nora gave the men brief lessons on how to dance the tush push, Cotton Eyed Joe, and the Cowboy Boogie. Jack didn't need lessons, but Con probably did.

The men lined up, Jack and Bob in the front row and the three others in the back, with Nora at the front, back to them, calling out steps and leading.

Jack was debating whether he should throw the competition and get out when a blow to the back of his right knee with a steel-toed boot from behind took his breath

away and nearly felled him. His leg immediately went
numb.

*Damn,* Jack thought, fighting to stay on his feet. *A direct hit to gallbladder point 31.*

There are points on the body that if struck properly can
kill a person instantly. Striking others, like gallbladder
point 31, causes temporary paralysis. As a karate expert,
Jack knew them all. Unfortunately, so did his opponent.

It took a master to hit 31 with paralyzing precision.
And an expert to stay on his feet once struck. The Rooster
had caught Jack off guard. *This time.*

*Game on,* Jack thought, resisting the urge to fight back
and wishing he weren't under orders not to assassinate in
public. So the Rooster was trying to draw him out before
a crowd, was he?

Jack preferred a good, fair fight. Which was one reason he'd spiked the Rooster's drink. Any minute now that
XTC would start taking effect. Then it would be game
over for the Rooster.

While Jack waited for his drug to do its magic, there
was only one sure way to live through the evening—
swallow his pride and get out of this damned dance-off.
He pointed to his newly bum leg and limped toward the
sidelines, imploring the judge, a local woman, a friend of
Lettie's whose name he didn't know, "Hey, I'm about to
die in here."

The crowd booed and yelled at him to stay in.

"Con Russo!" Lettie's stern voice boomed like the
wrath of God over the loudspeakers. Or, more accurately,
like his angry mother's. "Stop hamming it up and trying
to worm your way out of dancing. That was just a light tap.
No more being a baby. The men in this town do not wimp
out." She shook her head condemningly. "Do I have to repeat the rules? No intentionally bad dancing. This is a
fight to the death."

She didn't know how accurate she was.

Lettie held the mic close. "Now man up! Get back in there, and stay in, until the judge tells you to get out."

Man up? That was a low blow. No one told Jack to man up or questioned his courage. If he weren't undercover, he'd show them what a real man could do with a well-placed karate chop.

A cheer rose from the crowd. The judge smiled and shrugged, looking like, *What can I do?*

*So that's the way it's going to be. The judge is just a figurehead to do Lettie's bidding.*

"Sorry about that, buddy," Shane said without the slightest hint of contrition in his voice. "My bad. I'm not much of a dancer." He flashed Jack a victorious look, as if he was relishing the thought of delivering a lethal deathblow in the next set.

Jack felt like a boat that was dead in the water. Dead on the dance floor—oh, the indignity. "One more move like that and I won't have a leg to stand on."

The crowd laughed.

"That's the spirit. Apology accepted," Lettie answered for Jack. "Can't fault a man for not being an expert dancer, can we, ladies?"

The ladies shrieked. Someone whistled.

Jack decided in that instant that Con was usually a good dancer, when he had two functioning legs, who picked up moves quickly. It fit with Con's metro image, so what the hell? Jack was running with it. Well, as well as he could with one limp leg. For now, he was going to have to heavily compensate with some splashy arm movements and butt-wiggling boogies. Until his leg woke up, his footwork was going to suck. He only hoped he was lithe enough to dodge the Rooster's blows.

Jack had to drive Kennett and get him to dance harder.

The more he exercised, the faster the drug would flow through his system, and he'd topple off his feet to his defeat.

Next to Jack, even with two good legs, Bob was struggling to keep up. The judge tapped Bob on the shoulder.

"Bob, you're out!" Lettie said into the microphone. "Get off the floor."

Bob looked stunned. "What? I didn't even hit anyone like Shane did. And the music hasn't even started. We're still learning the steps. Don't I get a second chance, too? I want that TV."

"The game began the minute you took the floor. You're simply not as pretty as Shane, Bob."

Bob pointed at Jack. "But Con's a hop-along casualty! He's dragging one leg. Let me stay in for him."

Jack shrugged like a good sport, rotated his hips, doing a sensual boogie move, and took a step toward the edge of the dance floor. "Good idea."

"Not so fast, Con." Lettie's mic squealed with feedback and everyone jumped. "We all know how eager you are to get out of this. But you can't fake your way out with the old bum-leg trick.

"It's time to take this to a vote. That was a pretty hot boogie, even one legged. What do you think, ladies? Is Con still in?"

The ladies whistled. "Con's in. Bob, you're still out. No arguing. The crowd's decision is final."

Bob left the floor with semi-good grace, grumbling only slightly. "That TV would have been awfully nice in my study."

Nora taught them a turn. Jack had to grab his right leg and swing it around manually. Which got a big laugh from the crowd. He was aiming for the Rooster's crotch. Everyone knows a blow to the jewels will take a man down. Sadly, Jack's aim was off and the bastard jumped out of the way. Next time, Jack would have to make an adjustment to his swing.

The two other men turned the wrong direction and were tapped out of the competition. But Kennett, that big ox, was still on his feet. Jack should have known someone with Russian ancestry, with their notorious tolerance for alcohol, would have developed a resistance to drugs as well.

"Looks like we just have two nice-looking young men left to compete." Lettie winked. "Wonder how that happened?"

More laughter.

"All right, you two," Lettie said. "Move in closer together. This looks like it's going to be a head-to-head competition. We're going to need to see you side-by-side to choose a winner. Remember—style points matter. I think it's time we put those moves to music. Nora?"

"We'll start with an easy one, gentlemen. Cotton Eyed Joe." Nora motioned for Roger to start the music and counted down the beat as the song began. "Five, six. Five, six, seven, eight!"

Kennett came out swinging, literally swinging, his arms at Jack's neck, aiming for the lethal pressure points there. Jack leaned back on his good leg just in time. Kennett missed jabbing him directly in bladder point 10, a knockout point, by that much.

"Someone's exuberant!" Lettie called out as Jack kept up with Nora only by doing a one-legged hop and moving his limp leg around by grabbing it with one hand and dragging it around. "Shane's winning points with his extreme arm movements."

"Quarter turn to the right!" Nora called.

Shane swung around, doing a karate kick. Jack ducked just in time to miss taking one to the head.

"A little less leg next time," Nora said.

"If I had any less leg," Con said, "I'd be on the floor."

The crowd laughed.

"I was talking to Shane, Con. Just follow my lead." Nora led them in a stomp, stomp, stomp move.

Jack's was more of a stomp, drag, stomp.

Kennett ignored her instructions. He swung around again, going freestyle, jabbing and parrying with Jack, going at his weak side, looking to hit the nearest lethal point as Jack limped around like a pirate dragging a wooden leg.

The crowd laughed at his antics, unaware Kennett was trying to kill him before their eyes. Jack couldn't fight back unless he wanted to kill the Rooster outright in front of everyone. Which was against orders. Besides, Jack didn't need an inquiry. And he most especially did not need Willow to see him kill someone.

Roger the DJ was quick to jump on Kennett's change-up of the dance routine. He switched up the music, and before Jack knew what was what he was dragging his leg through the Cowboy Boogie to "Footloose."

The good thing about the Cowboy Boogie—there was a lot of boogie, rotating hips, in it. Jack rolled his hips like a Chippendales dancer and seized full advantage, making the ladies scream and forget about his lack of footwork. Style points for him.

But the "Footloose" song lyrics drove him crazy, calling out his name, Jack, seemingly every other line. He had enough on his mind without having a song scream out who he really was. He should have heeded the song's warning and gotten back. But being him, he ignored it.

Now, not only was his leg numb and, of course, the Rooster was still trying to kill him, but his feet were killing him, too. Those damned Italian leather loafers had rubbed his heels raw. They weren't meant for dancing, especially sockless. Each move was torture, giving him another blister that stung. So when the song directed it, he kicked off his Sunday shoes in time to the music. Oh yeah, and one might have been intentionally flung at Kennett's head.

The Rooster dodged it and looked at Jack with murder in his eyes.

Jack felt a tingle in his leg and grinned back. A real tingle, as in his leg was waking up. Finally. Time to take this competition up a notch and strike when his opponent least expected it.

The Rooster launched a full attack, stomping across the floor in his steel-toed boots in time to the music, aiming directly for the vulnerable bare toes of Jack's gimpy leg. When was Jack's home-cooked XTC going to kick in? He knew he should have made it stronger. As in lethal.

As Kennett danced toward Jack, Jack looked around for help, like the judge. But she'd left the dance floor. This was now clearly a free-for-all.

So Jack broke out his secret weapon—a one-legged backflip. He caught the Rooster off guard and sent him stumbling backward out of the way, off the dance floor, and into a table against the wall.

*Take that. Next time, I'll show you what I know about hand-to-hand combat and lethal pressure points.*

"Footloose" ended. Jack was still on his feet and the Rooster was finally starting to sway. Barely. Jack had to do something to speed up the process.

"Give my worthy opponent a drink so he can keep up with me in the next round," Jack said. "He looks thirsty."

Willow stepped forward and handed Kennett his drink, but the bastard only took a sip and handed it back to her. Jack cursed to himself. There was part of the problem—Kennett had drunk barely half the cup.

"I paid for a tush push," Sheryl said from the sidelines. "I want to see it."

Nora gave Jack and Kennett a harsh look. "Do you two think you can follow directions and actually do the dance I'm teaching?"

Jack grabbed his leg. "I'm trying, teach."

People laughed.

"These two men are pretty evenly matched," Lettie said.

*That's a lie,* Jack thought. *I can dance this asshole under the table. And I would if I weren't dodging death-blows and hobbling on one leg.*

"Let's make this interesting," Lettie said. "Sheryl wants the tush push. But what song are they going to dance to? Willow? You got Con into this; you pick!"

Jack's gaze, and everyone else's, turned to Willow as she was taking a sip from Shane's cup.

*Nooooo!*

As she pulled it away from her lips to answer, Jack thanked small mercies and made a mental note to have Con knock that damn cup out of her hands if he had to dance into the middle of the mob to do it.

Her lips curved into a smile. "Lady Gaga's 'Poker Face.' Let's see them tush push to 'Poker Face.'"

Jack swallowed hard. Despite its lyrics that celebrated violence, Willow loved that song. He used to dance to it for her and with her. By requesting it, she'd just eliminated some of his favorite moves.

"That's just silly," someone said.

Lettie held up a hand to silence the protests. "The lady has chosen."

"People line dance to it all the time," Nora added. "We'll show you how it's done. Spin it, Roger."

Jack joined in with the music, doing his grooving as the crowd laughed. The tush push was meant to be done to certain songs and this definitely wasn't one of them. But he pushed his tush all the same.

"Stick it out there, boys!" a woman yelled, probably Sheryl.

Someone was getting her money's worth out of this show at least. The Rooster was tiring and backing off. Jack's leg was regaining motion and feeling. Finally able to really dance, he got caught up in the music and began pushing the Rooster to keep up with his moves. Forgetting himself for the moment, he hammed it up and swirled his hand around his face when Nora did, imitating Lady Gaga in the music video. Too late, he caught a glimpse of Willow's pale face and realized he'd gone too far. He'd sparked a memory in her of himself.

The crowd began to twitter.

Jack wasn't being all that funny. He glanced at his opponent and realized they weren't just laughing at his silly tush push moves or his theatrics. *Finally.* Shane was swaying on his feet as he tried to rotate his hips and keep up with Jack.

"Looks like your favorite's had a little too much, Lettie." Bob White sounded gleeful as he shouted over the music.

Willow stood on the edge of the dance floor next to the action. Con followed Nora's lead and circled his face with his hand in a movement mimicking Gaga in her music video. Willow gasped. Jack used to do that very move to make her laugh when they danced to the song. He was just doing what Nora did. Just as Shane was. A lot of people imitated that popular move. But that was Jack's *exact* flourish.

Willow felt suddenly short of breath and a little dizzy. And so tired. She needed something to drink. But as she lifted the glass to her mouth Con danced to the edge of the crowd a little too close to her. She started and stepped back just in time to miss being hit, spilling Shane's drink all over herself and the floor before she could touch it to her lips again.

Con mouthed, *Sorry,* and danced his way back to the center of the dance space. Shane started swaying. Willow blinked, trying to ward off the feeling she was about to pass out. Was Shane swaying or was she?

Shane stumbled, fell onto his knees, and collapsed onto the floor. Her gasp blended with the crowd's laughter. More than just Shane had had too much too drink.

Con shook his head. "Looks like my opponent has decided to sit this one out. He's just dead."

Willow's ears rang. *Ohmygosh. That's a variation of Jack's favorite line from* Thunderball.

She felt so dizzy. Her ears rang and the room closed in around her as she stared directly at Con.

"Jack?"

Jack heard Willow call his name, shoved past the crowd, and caught her before she crashed to the floor. Damn, he'd gotten too cocky. He never should have used that line, common as it was. Any Bond fan knew it, but Jack's using it was still reckless.

His heart raced. What had he done to Willow? One small sip shouldn't have sent her out like this.

"Water!" he called. "Someone get us a glass of water."

A crowd had gathered around Shane, too, mercifully keeping the full focus off of Jack holding Willow.

He wanted to cradle her and coo her back to consciousness. Beg her forgiveness for accidentally drugging her. If only Willow had been a germ-a-phobe, she'd never have drunk from Shane's cup.

And damn his weakness, even limp in his arms she felt good. He was worried about her, but with the small dose she'd gotten the drug should wear off quickly.

Becky appeared at his elbow with a pillow in each hand and began issuing orders. "Give them space. Make room for both Shane and Willow. Give them air!" She touched Jack's elbow. "Lay her down and get this under her head and this one under her feet."

As Jack did as he was told, he realized he'd made a serious mistake. *Willow suspects I'm me.* As schizophrenic as that sounded. It was damage control time. He reluctantly did as Becky commanded.

"Jack?" Jack frowned and, doing his best to appear confused, looked at Becky. "Who's Jack?"

It was a critical stage for the mission just now. Willow may have just blown his cover. He had to keep his head and use this situation to his advantage.

"Jack's her late husband. Died two years ago." Becky shook her head. "Poor thing. You'll have to excuse her. Today's the anniversary of his death."

"I'm sorry." He paused. He really was. It was his fault, after all. "And I look like him?"

Becky shook her head again. "I wouldn't know. I've never seen a picture. She doesn't talk about him much. She says she's still too emotional and can't without breaking up."

Damn, he had hurt Willow badly. It was for her own good, but hearing Becky say it aloud cut him to his hardened core.

Willow came to with Jack standing over her. Or, well, a man with Jack's eyes. *Con?* The two were blended together in her mind as she regained consciousness. She was confused. And still heavy lidded and sleepy. Con didn't look like Jack. But he acted like him and his eyes were the same as Jack's.

"Happens all the time," whoever he was said to Becky. "Ironically, I must look like a Jack. People call me that a lot." His grin was perfect and charming. "Must be my evil twin."

"Jack was not evil!" Willow couldn't believe she'd blurted that out. Too many years of defending Jack's sometimes violent job to her inner conscience.

"She's back!" Con smiled at her.

Her head buzzed. She wasn't thinking clearly and her social inhibitor had somehow been turned off.

The room buzzed with the hum of people trying to speak in hushed tones.

"No, no, of course he wasn't, hon," Becky crooned to her as she patted Willow's hand and looked relieved. "You gave us a scare. How are you feeling?"

Willow pushed up to a sit and stared at Con.

"Take it easy," Becky said. "Give yourself time to recover." She looked over her shoulder at the people around them and those who were attending to Shane. "She's fine. She'll be fine. She just got a little overexcited."

There was a collective sigh of relief and the buzz of conversation shifted to Shane, who was passed out cold.

Willow didn't want to recover. She wanted to stare at Con. Was he? Could he? Could he actually *be* Jack?

Willow shook her head to clear it. Someone appeared with a glass of water and handed it to Becky.

Becky put her hand on Willow's shoulder and held the glass out to her. "Drink. It will help."

Willow pressed the glass to her lips and took a sip. Drinking gave her a chance to study Con more closely.

NCS claimed they'd done a DNA analysis on the remains she'd buried and they were Jack's. Definitely Jack's. And the Sense, she couldn't discount that, either. She'd felt Jack being ripped from her at the very moment of the explosion that took his life. He'd been thousands of miles away at the time.

But Jack was Jack. She wouldn't put *anything* past him

and the Agency. If Jack had done anything else for a living, anything but living the covert life of a spy, she would have chalked those eyes, dance moves, smiles, and line from James Bond up to her own vivid imagination, especially given the day. She could have dismissed the Sense acting up now, claiming it was merely responding to her own emotions. She would have forced herself to admit the horrible irony of meeting Jack's twin by a different mother on the very anniversary of his death. How could fate be so cruel?

But Jack *had* been a secret agent. And secret agents were capable of any deceit. Even faking their own deaths.

She stared at Con, or Jack, or whoever he was, over the lip of her glass. If that was Jack standing there, pretending not to be her husband, acting like a casual stranger while her heart nearly failed, she was going to, going to . . .

Well, an ordinary person would say she was going to kill him. But Willow didn't believe in that.

She was going to teach him a lesson. Something civil and nonviolent so he'd learn the error of his ways. And she was going to get him back.

But what if he really was just Con, a man who reminded her of Jack? What would she do then? Something crazy like fall in love with him? And would it really be with him or would she only be falling in love with her memory of Jack?

Con squatted beside her and smiled kindly, looking her directly in the eye. "How are you feeling? It's very warm in here." He cleared his throat. "Becky told me this is an especially difficult day for you. I'm very sorry for your loss." He squeezed her shoulder sympathetically.

"I'm also sorry to tell you that your date has had too much to drink. He's passed out. A couple of the men are going to take him home and stay with him for a while to make sure he's okay. He'll be fine."

Feeling Con's hot hand on her and the warmth of his touch, she nearly sputtered her water in his face.

"Good." She paused, still trying to focus and clear her mind. Why did she feel so groggy? Almost as if she'd been drugged? "Did you win?"

He smiled at her, looking pleased. "Yeah, I did. I'm donating the TV. Lettie's going to auction it off and give the money to the animal shelter."

"That's so sweet." That's exactly what Jack would have done. Willow blinked back tears at the thought.

"I'm sorry. I'm upsetting you," he said. "Can I get you anything?"

There was no way she was letting this man who *might* be Jack disappear, walk right back into the twilight without her. Not until she knew for sure that he was Jack. Not even if he really was Con. Not if he was the man who could bring her back to life again after Jack. Until then, she'd have to keep him close at hand. If he really was Jack, he could disappear like a wisp of frosty breath, simply evaporate.

"Take me home." She forced a wobbly smile. "Please?"

She needed a plan. And she needed one *now*.

# CHAPTER SIX

Jack recognized that gleam in his wife's sleepy eyes. She was suspicious, wondering whether Con was really him, Jack. He didn't read microexpressions for nothing. He shouldn't have used his Bond line. *No more spy humor.*

Jack's mind was racing. He'd originally planned to knock Kennett out so he could break into his place later, after the party, and get what intel he could. So much for that plan now. He couldn't chance it if the men taking Kennett home were going to stay with him until he slept it off.

As Jack led Willow to his car, with his arm around her to steady her, he felt her studying him. "I'm sorry."

She tilted her head and looked up at him. "About what?"

"Everything—my zealous dancing. Spilling your drink. Somehow being an unpleasant reminder of your late husband. You looked at me and called his name just before you passed out. I feel somehow responsible." He didn't have to try too hard to look sheepish. He was completely responsible. He should have been more careful with his drink doping.

"Nothing about remembering Jack is unpleasant." Her voice trembled with emotion and her eyes shone as she looked at him.

*She misses me.*

Was she trying to kill him? It took all he had not to let any more emotion than the curiosity of a stranger show on his face as he beeped the car unlocked and opened the door for her. She was so slight, he could have carried her the half mile home. But he didn't think she'd go for that, and he didn't know how he'd keep his hands off her once he'd held her in his arms again. So he elected to burn the gas.

"Your late husband must have been some man." He tried to sound noncommittal, conversational. "Not Italian, was he?"

"Not that I know of." She slid in and looked up at him as he prepared to close her car door.

He caught himself acting as he used to, as himself. He liked to gently shut her in the car, protect her.

Willow stared up at him as if he was the second coming of Jack, a lover across time and death.

"Not that you know of?" He made himself slam the door just a little too hard. Or maybe he was more frustrated than he'd thought. He walked around the car and slid into the driver's seat.

She answered as he buckled up. "Jack was mysterious. He had a few close friends, but otherwise was pretty much a loner. He didn't like to talk about himself, his childhood, or his family. He said they were all unpleasant." She yawned and covered her mouth.

"His father is gone. I only met his mother and brother twice. At our wedding and his funeral. I didn't get much of a chance to get to know them on either occasion. Jack didn't keep in touch with them. His past is pretty much a mystery to me."

*His mother.* He was glad *he* hadn't had to deal with her at his funeral. Now there was a picture—the old lady putting on grief. Did she really have a heart? He was damned glad to be dead to her.

There are very few people who grow up to be killers. You had to either be a born psychopath or endure a hellacious childhood. Jack had had the latter and preferred to forget it, and the people who peopled it, as much as possible. There was one benefit in playing Con—he could make up a happy childhood and play off Aldo's great big loving family.

Jack stuck the key in the ignition. "A little mystery is good for a relationship." The irony of that statement was almost too much.

She seemed to catch it. "Is it?"

She stared at him with the moonlight reflected in her eyes and rolled down her window. Willow didn't like being confined. She loved the feel of cool night air blowing through her hair. And right now she was probably hoping it would wake her up. All she really needed were a few hours to sleep it off.

As if she willed it, a gentle breeze blew in, tinged with the crisp cold of autumn.

"That's what they tell me." He fired up the car and pulled out of the driveway.

The drive to her house took less than two minutes, even cruising along the gravel road at a whopping 25 miles per hour and resisting showing off with any extreme driving maneuvers. He'd have loved to take her for a long drive, show off his skills. But he had the feeling she'd sleep through it anyway. She kept nodding off.

He parked the car by the front door and turned off the ignition. "I'll walk you in."

"Afraid I'll pass out again?" Her tone was light, even as she studied him with intensity and suspicion.

*Ah, suspicious minds.*

"Just doing my duty. You look beat and I promised to see you safely home."

They got out of the car. He walked her to the front door,

resisting the urge to put his arm around her again. She looked steady enough on her feet to manage on her own, though she moved drowsily. There was a light on in the house and porch light on above the entry where they stood.

She unlocked and opened the door before pausing and studying him, lingering as if she was in no hurry to go inside and conversely looking at the same time as if she longed for her bed. She stood too close to him for comfort. His comfort. And looked up at him practically begging to be kissed. She looked so sexy with that sleepy, drowsy expression.

As he inhaled the sensual scent of her perfume, he wasn't in any hurry to leave, either. He looked deep into her eyes, mesmerized, when he knew he should take a step back and walk away. But he was held in place by the sense of peace he always felt in her presence. By the warmth of her personality and his desire for her and the way she used to love him.

Since he'd found her years ago, Willow had been the one good, truly good, person and thing in his life. In his world of violence and death, Willow would never harm anyone or anything. Especially him. She did nothing but love him. He didn't deserve it. He'd never deserve the love of such a gentle, caring woman. But it seemed so natural to kiss her good night, just as he had hundreds of nights before. Just one small kiss—

It was madness, but he bent his head toward hers. She angled her head and wrapped her arms around his neck, pressed her soft sweater into his until he could feel her warmth through the cashmere between them.

Every part of his body went hard and stood at attention as he gently brushed her lips. Willow kissed him back softly, tentatively, as if this were the first time, a first kiss.

He knew her theories about sexual chemistry and how a kiss would either reveal it or show it sadly lacking. He

should have restrained himself, but he could no more
stop himself than cease breathing. Longing thrummed
through his body and ran his blood hot with desire.

Her kiss, gentle and sweet as it was, almost broke him
the way hours of torture could not. She opened her mouth
to him. He had to restrain himself. He wanted to kiss her
as if he possessed her. Instead, he kissed her just deeply
enough to make her body tremble, until he knew she felt
the chemistry, too.

He could have lingered in that kiss, swept her in his
arms, and taken her to bed. But he came to his senses just
in time, pulled back, and broke the kiss, shaken. "Willow—"

"Yes?" She stared up at him. He read her expression
easily enough—she'd felt the desire, too. And then she
yawned again.

"I'm sorry. Again. I shouldn't have . . . I took advantage. You're overwrought. And tired." He took a deep
breath, reaching for that concerned stranger within him,
trying to fend off the husband who wanted her desperately.

She was breathing hard, if somewhat sleepily, and
staring at him, looking almost triumphant. Which fright-
ened the hell out of him.

Just then Spookie, the killer watchdog, barked and
came charging from the deep recesses of the house. Jack
heard her toenails clicking on Willow's hardwood floors
as she approached. Spookie appeared from around a
corner, growling. She took one look at him, and stopped
dead in her tracks.

It was a crucial moment. "Hey, girl," he said, kneeling
to get down on her level, where he could stare her in the
eye without Willow being able to see his expression. Many
people assume dogs, who have poor vision as a whole,
recognize their owners by smell and voice. But Jack knew

dogs inside and out. Dogs recognize their owner's faces and read emotion on them similar to the way humans do. He looked just different enough that Spookie would probably be confused. At least for an initial moment.

He loved that dog and hated what he was about to do to his poor pup. But it was for her own good. As he reached to pet her, he gave her a hard stare and a disapproving alpha-male back-off scowl. His little Spookie was a coward at heart. She whimpered and dashed off.

Why did Jack always have to scare off those he loved? Sometimes he hated this job.

He stood and looked at Willow, putting a heavy dose of apology and confusion in his expression and voice. "Sorry! I'm scaring everyone tonight. Dogs generally like me. Honest."

She stared at him without answering.

Just then he noticed a spray of cockscomb in a vase on her entryway table and his blood ran cold. From the Rooster, no doubt. A coded message for Jack, should he see it. No one else would recognize it as such.

*I'm close to your wife. I have access to her home. I'm after you.*

Jack composed himself and pointed. "What are those ugly flowers?"

"Cockscomb. From Shane."

"Interesting choice. They look a bit like brains." The flowers were probably bugged. Jack had to get them out of her house. "Wait. Is that a whitefly I see on them? Or aphids, maybe? You need to get those out of your house. They'll infect everything."

Willow looked alarmed. "I didn't notice."

He stepped past her into the house and grabbed the flowers. "May I?"

She nodded.

"I'll just take these away and dump them for you."

"Sure." Willow looked relieved to get rid of them.

Jack glanced down at the flowers and back up at Willow. "I'd better go. You look dead on your feet and need your rest. Good night." He turned to leave but somehow couldn't make himself go. He had to see her again, convince her he wasn't Jack. Even though of course he was.

He also had to distract her from Kennett. And he couldn't have her wondering all her life if he was still alive. He had to convince her otherwise. "Can I make things up to you? Take you out for coffee?" Coffee seemed safe. "Pay for your cleaning?"

"No need to pay for cleaning. I'll just toss these in the washer." She smiled. "But I'd love to go for coffee. Tomorrow morning? Before the madness hits?"

He nodded. "Name the place"

"Bluff Country Store. Ten?" She covered her mouth, trying to stifle a yawn.

*Good luck with that.* He made the best XTC around.

"I promise I'll be more awake and better company." She paused. "I don't know what's come over me."

But he did. "Sounds good. I look forward to coffee with a fully alert you." He smiled at her. "Don't beat yourself up. You've had a long, stressful, busy day. A few hours' sleep should fix you up."

She nodded. "Tomorrow then. Fully awake. And if I'm not, Ada's coffee will do the trick. That's probably what you were thinking, right?"

He laughed and nodded. As Jack walked away with the Rooster's coded flowers he couldn't believe he'd just made a date with his wife.

Willow shut the door and, holding back the curtains, watched through the side window by the door as Con drove off. When his taillights disappeared down the drive, she let her lacy curtains fall back into place and fell to a sit on the cold, hard floor. She was too unsteady to remain on her feet another minute. And too tired, too. At this rate, she was going to have to crawl to bed. That man, whoever he really was, had the power to take her breath away and render her unconscious with a look.

She'd never met a man with that kind of power over her before. Except Jack.

When Con had kissed her, she felt that jolt of attraction she'd known would be there.

She must be overwrought. Either that or Aldo had just created the world's first 190-proof wine and one glass had done her in. Something had gone to her head.

But the root cause of her unsteadiness was pretty simple—the uncertainty, was Con Jack or not? Was Jack very much alive? Or was fate playing a cruel trick on her by throwing his almost perfect twin in her face at the least opportune moment?

She couldn't believe she was even contemplating that Jack could be alive. That Con could be him. She must be crazy.

She ran her fingers through her hair. "Spookie! Here, girl! You can come out. He's gone."

Spookie came running from the back bedroom where she no doubt had been cowering. She paused at the edge of the living room. Sniffed. Tilted her head. Surveyed the area. Studied Willow. And, finally, scampered into Willow's lap for comfort.

As Willow mindlessly stroked Spookie behind her ears and crooned to her, she ran over the facts and circumstances as she knew them.

If Con was Jack, why hadn't Spookie recognized him? Shouldn't she have recognized his scent?

Willow frowned. Spookie wasn't a hound dog, a tracker. But still?

Willow looked up at the ceiling. Con sure tasted like

Jack. Looked just enough like Jack to make her doubt. His eyes were Jack's. And his dance moves. And his Bond lines and sense of humor.

If he was Jack, and still alive, and messing with her, pretending not to be himself, she'd, she'd . . .

She didn't know what she'd do. She wanted him back so badly.

And what about the opposite end of the spectrum—if Con wasn't Jack? Would a Jack look-alike be enough for her? Be better than no Jack at all?

Well, at least if Con's story was true and he was simply Con Russo, Aldo's distant cousin, then danger wasn't his middle name, right? In the win column for Con, her conscience wouldn't bother her over what he did for a living.

Marriage to Jack had taught her cunning and deception, how to get the intel she wanted, how to think like a spy. She drew on those rusty resources now, trying to think like Jack would have and see the situation from every angle.

She could contact Emmett using her emergency contact method. Tell him her suspicions. See if Emmett choked and spilled anything.

She pursed her lips. *Fat chance. Emmett never chokes. He'll probably just tell me I'm crazy.*

Then again, the possibility existed that Jack had somehow survived that blast without Emmett's knowledge. That Jack had contrived his own death and this was his way of coming back to her.

If that were the case, alerting Emmett would blow the whole thing. Still, if that were true, why hadn't Jack come clean with her and revealed himself immediately?

Could he have switched sides and was now a traitor or a double agent?

She shook her head. Her Jack would never become a traitor. But if that *were* the scenario she was dealing with, she should warn Emmett.

There was one more scenario—that Jack was under-cover and working for Emmett. In which case, Emmett wouldn't reveal a thing and would work to impede her from finding out the truth.

She took a deep breath and stifled a yawn.

Could Jack have amnesia? Not remember who he was? No, Con seemed too slick and with it to be suffering from amnesia. And if that were the case, why would Aldo believe Jack was his cousin Con?

She bit her lip. She wasn't living in the Dark Ages. Modern science gave her options like DNA testing. Home DNA collection kits for which one simply mailed the collected sample to a lab for testing. All she needed was his saliva, right? She didn't like cop shows at all, way too violent and too much death and gore. But Ada's husband, Paul, was a big fan of them and talked about them all the time. Willow remembered him telling her about an episode of *48 Hours* where the police tricked a suspect into giving his DNA by licking an envelope. And another where they tricked a suspect by inviting him out for coffee and stealing his paper cup after he tossed it away.

Garbage, evidently, was free for anyone to take. No legal issues involved.

Conveniently, she was having coffee with Con tomorrow. And Bluff Country used paper cups. Who knew she was so subconsciously genius? All she had to do was steal Con's cup and have it tested against the DNA report Emmett had sent her after Jack's death. If Con was really Con, he'd never even know what she'd done.

Now she just had to find a local place to buy a DNA collection kit, or get one online, and keep Con in town long enough to get the results back. How long would that take?

In the meantime, common old dirty trickery and PI work would have to suffice. She'd check up on Con's story. If she could stay awake long enough. She was as tired as if she'd been drugged. But she had to see if Con really was who he said he was.

She dragged herself to her study and powered up her laptop.

*I can Google with the best of them.*

If Jack was undercover as Con for the Agency, Emmett and his team would have set up a fake cover life for him online. But that didn't mean she couldn't use it to trip Jack up.

The laptop came up. She typed the name Con Russo in the search box.

*No Internet connection.*

"What!" She resisted the urge to thunk her head on the desk. "No! I'm having coffee with Con tomorrow morning. I need to know something about him. Now."

Why did everything happen at once? She was dying to get to the truth and now this. How was she supposed to check up on Con? Or order a DNA collection kit?

She grabbed her smartphone from her purse. There was more than one way to get what she wanted. Hooray for modern technology!

But her smartphone didn't work, either. Both the phone and the 3G were dead. No matter how many times she restarted it. *Great. Is there something wrong with the cell tower?*

Tomorrow she'd be so busy with the Apple Festival she'd be lucky if she had time to breathe, let alone sleuth. By the end of the day she'd be too brain-dead and tired to be effective. About like she was now. And that was assuming her Internet connection came back up.

She checked her Internet box. Sure enough the little lights next to DSL and Internet were ominously dark, not the bright green that meant they were working.

She stared at them. Sometimes they clicked back on after a few seconds or minutes. A watched pot never boils and a watched Internet box never comes back up, either. She powered down her modem and started it back up again. Still no connection.

She blew out a breath, grabbed the landline phone, and called her provider's twenty-four-hour help line.

"It's your modem, ma'am. It's dead," the help desk techie told her after running her through ten minutes of diagnostics through which she barely stayed awake.

"But it's done this before and always come back up."

"That was it in its death throes, then. Sorry. The easiest thing to do is replace it. I can send one tomorrow with a technician who can set it up for you. Or I can give you a list of local stores that carry it and you can pick one up and do the setup yourself."

The stores were already closed and she had no time to run to one tomorrow. "Send one out. I'm desperate to get my service back." Willow tried to keep the frustration out of her voice.

The techie chuckled. "That's what they all say. No one can live without Internet. I'll try to get our man out first thing."

As satisfied as she was going to get, Willow hung up and drummed her fingers on her desk as she powered off the laptop. She should call the cell phone company, too, on her landline, to find out what was wrong with her cell service, but she was just too tired. Too tired to grab her laptop and drive somewhere where she could get Wi-Fi. Driving in this sleepy state would be suicide. She'd have to tell Aldo his wine needed a warning label—"Do not drink this wine and operate heavy machinery."

She yawned again for what felt like the hundredth time, and her eyes felt heavy. She'd have to deal with everything in the morning. Maybe her cell service would be back up by then.

Her Internet service going out and her cell phone not

working simultaneously were freakily coincidental. It was as if she was being thwarted intentionally. But why? All signs pointed to Agency involvement. And Jack.

She'd have to be creative. And careful. Get to her tent early and talk to the other vendors as she set up. See what they knew or had heard about Aldo's cousin Con. Seek Becky and Aldo out and press for details. Look for inconsistencies in Con's stories. Hope she got 3G coverage somewhere outside the house.

Make a mental list of prying questions to ask him at coffee.

She'd find out who Con Russo really was.

She wanted him to be Jack. No matter what Jack had done, she needed Con, this stranger with Jack's eyes.

She'd put a bright face on things. Had been trying to move on, looking on the positive side of her life without Jack. But tonight had brought back all the memories—life was better with him in it.

She'd do anything to get him back—steal his DNA, sleep with him, tie him to the bed to keep him here.

*Anything.*

And if he didn't want her back? Or if Con was really just Con? She'd worry about that later.

# CHAPTER SEVEN

Willow's cell phone rang as she stepped out of the shower, belting out the distinctive ringtone she'd assigned to her mother. *Oh, good!* Her cell service was back up. She didn't need the ringtone to know who was calling. She could sense it. In fact, she'd been expecting it. Her sense of foreboding hadn't gone away and she'd bet her mother's hadn't, either. Diana Norris was in tune to the Sense much more than Willow was. The only question was—what had taken her mother so long to call?

Willow wrapped herself in her towel and grabbed the phone. "Mom! . . . Hey. I'm still among the living and doing fine. You?" She let her harried feelings out, hoping they masked her anxiety and crazy feelings that Jack was back and diverted her mom.

"I'm fine, too, kiddo, but confused."

"You still feel it, too? You aren't just calling to wish me luck at the Apple Festival today?"

"Luck and success," her mother said without missing a beat. "What happened last night? I was watching the Food Network when I felt something was wrong."

Willow had to proceed carefully. There was no reason to upset her mother further, not until Willow knew more. "The Sense must be overreacting. I got light-headed at the growers' party last night and passed out. Probably exhaustion from working so hard to get ready for the festival. Aldo's cousin took me home.

"Did I tell you about him? He just arrived yesterday. His name is Con and he reminds me of Jack." Which was the complete and honest truth. As far as she knew.

"Light-headed? Are you sure you're okay?"

"I'm fine, Mom. It was nothing. Just the day, you know."

Diana took a deep breath. "This Con reminds you of Jack? How?"

Willow hedged. "Oh, I don't know. Something about his eyes and his sense of humor."

Her mom was silent for a second. "I didn't want to bring this up, but I have a feeling about Jack. I can't explain it. I don't mean to upset you, but I feel almost as if Jack is still alive."

Which only confirmed Willow's suspicions about Con and made her more determined to get to the truth.

"Jack's gone, Mom. He really is." *Not.* At least, she hoped not.

Her mother didn't know Jack had been a spy. Jack had an advanced degree in chemistry. As his cover, he worked for the Drug Enforcement Agency, frequently being sent abroad by the State Department to help foreign governments determine the chemical composition of the drugs in their countries and trace their origins back to the illegal labs that manufactured them.

The story the CIA told about Jack's death was that he'd been on a State Department assignment in South America. While working with officials, he'd been an innocent victim of the drug cartel's dangerous wars.

The U.S. Embassy had sent his remains home. Because of Jack's military service in Iraq and Afghanistan, they were able to match the fragments of his remains to his military records. He was given a military funeral and buried as a hero in a military cemetery.

Willow's mother could never understand how her gentle, peace-loving daughter could marry a former military man. Willow had always argued back that his military service was in the past and Jack had the gentlest nature of any man she'd known.

"Jack never visited you before he left," her mom said. She meant this earth for spiritual realms.

And it was true—Jack hadn't visited Willow and said good-bye. She'd been angry at him about that at first. But Willow wasn't the kind to hold a grudge. She imagined he had his reasons. She thought the explosion might have had something to do with it, though she couldn't think what.

"Our men never leave without saying good-bye. Even that old cuss your dad's father, Grandpa Norris, woke me in the middle of the night, bounced the bed to get my attention, sat right on the edge at my feet, and glared at me as if I were the one holding him back." Willow's mother took a breath. When she got worked up she strung her words together. Every once in a while she had to pause to breathe.

"If that old man, who never had a good word to say about me in life, could take the time to stop by on his way out, why didn't Jack? I know he loved you."

Willow had no answer for her.

"The Sense isn't wrong," Diana said. "I can't knock this feeling that Jack is alive."

"I wish that were true, Mom. I really do." Her mother had no idea how much Willow would do and what lengths she would go to to prove Jack *was* alive.

Jack spied on Kennett's place from a hidden location just down the road. He'd barely slept all night, but the buzz from the thrill of the hunt kept him alert. He'd returned to the party and networked until two. Then watched the rooster sculpture until a RIOT courier showed up at three to pick up the drop. Jack had followed the courier to a house in the nearby city half an hour away and reported his location to the Agency.

Then Jack had headed to Kennett's, hoping to complete his mission. Unfortunately, the helpful neighbors spent the night. They must have subdued Kennett's dogs somehow. He had a pair of vicious, well-trained Filas. The two men had left together, without any noticeable chunks of flesh missing, a few minutes earlier.

Through his high-powered binoculars, Jack watched Kennett walk to his barn to open for business. Kennett moved like a man who'd been recently drugged.

If not for Kennett's helpful, conscientious neighbors, Jack could have taken Kennett out last night and scoured his place for intel. Followed him home and given him an IV drip of 190-proof alcohol, enough to give him alcohol poisoning resulting in death.

Jack was damn good with a needle. Barely left a mark.

Or he could have used a funnel and force-fed the bastard enough liquor to kill him. Jack had been tempted. It was an inventive way to kill. And a trick he might try later. Right now, he had another, cleaner plan.

Half of Aldo's guests had staggered home drunk last night. Buzz Foster had wrapped his Harley around a tree on his way home. And walked away. His bike hadn't fared as well, though. Probably totaled.

With all those drunks, the party had been the hit of the season. Aldo should thank Jack for his addition to the hot, spiced cider. It was a bigger hit than the pesto lasagna. For his part, Jack blessed Everclear for the loose lips it caused.

With very little prying, he'd collected good intel about his nemesis, Kennett. One very useful tidbit was Kennett's love of whiskey and his habit of tossing more than a few back at Beck's Tavern after a long day of work. Beck's was on the highway that ran north toward Canada.

No doubt he also met all kinds of unsavory contacts there. People had been smuggling explosives down from

British Columbia, Canada, since before the Millennium Bomber got caught in 1999. The border crossing at Cascade, B.C., was a whole lot less secure than the Peace Arch at Blaine, south of Vancouver. And conveniently located for Kennett just over two hours away.

Jack looked at the curving, shot-oiled road that ran in front of Kennett's house. It would be nothing, really, to hide in the orchards with a rifle and high-powered scope and wait for Kennett to come barreling home wasted one fine evening.

Jack grinned, picturing a rainy evening. That made for nice atmosphere. And slicker roads.

He could see it now. As Kennett came around a curve, Jack would fire a kill shot into Kennett's skull, causing an accident that would send Kennett into the orchard and the waiting arms of an apple tree.

Then Jack would swoop in, dig out the bullet if need be, torch the car, and be on his way. If the car exploded— bonus!

Jack liked explosions. Turnabout was fair play. The Rooster had blown up Jack, taken away his life and the lives of his friends. Sending the Rooster to kingdom come in a thousand tiny pieces would only be poetic justice. And the whole thing would look like a tragic accident.

Tonight? Jack wondered whether the Rooster would be foolish enough to go out drinking two nights in a row. Kennett was of Russian descent, hearty drinking stock— of course he would. As all drinkers know, one hangover cures another.

Jack glanced at his watch. Nine thirty. Time to head to his coffee date with Willow. This was where the operation got tricky: he had to keep Willow away from the Rooster until he killed him, flirt with her enough to keep her distracted, convince her he was not Jack, and not break under the pressure.

He hoped Bluff Country Store had stocked up on coffee. Call it a hunch, but he had a feeling there'd be a run on it this morning. And he needed his daily dose of caffeine more than ever.

Willow puttered around in her pink tent in the center of town amid the festivities, her mind on Jack, instead of where it should have been—on her business. Even her mother felt he was alive, and Mom was never wrong. As Willow filled tables with her candy and caramel sauce and thought about things, the more it seemed to her that both her high-speed Internet being down and her smartphone 3G being out at the same time was highly suspicious. Just the kind of trick the Agency would play to keep her from learning the truth about Con's real identity. They had phone jammers and all kinds of devices at their disposal. All she had were her wits.

If NCS was trying to stymie her by keeping her Internet and 3G out of service overnight, Jack's time in Orchard Bluff was short indeed. If Con was Jack, she was going to have to smoke him out immediately. If not sooner. Which meant at coffee, when she was going to steal his cup and get his DNA.

Her cell phone buzzed in her pocket. She pulled it out, looked at it, and frowned. Another apologetic text from Shane. And her 3G seemed to work just fine outside of the house, which made the case for a jammer. But she had no time to surf the Internet just now. She shoved the phone back into her pocket, ignoring it along with the other three texts Shane had already sent her this morning.

And if the man pretending to be Con really was Con?

She kept coming back to that. Her dad had taught her to think through situations with both the best- and worst-case scenarios in mind. If you could live with each extreme, then proceed. Otherwise, walk away. She had no idea if she could live with the middle, let alone the extremes. But she couldn't walk away; that much she was certain about. She'd always been a risk taker.

She wondered, in a completely irrational way, if she could stand seeing Con with another woman. He was so much like Jack it would feel like a betrayal.

And if Jack was back, what did that do to her widow's pension and the life insurance she'd received? Would NCS confiscate her tasty caramel business?

Finding out that Con was Jack created as many problems as it solved. More, really, when you got down to it.

But Willow had never been one to back off from challenges. Bring it on. She'd deal. She wanted Jack.

This was such a mess. Almost as much of a mess as her raging, twisting emotions.

And of course, there was the obvious question, if Con was Jack, what was he doing here? Who was he watching? What great, big, horrible disaster or nasty piece of espionage was about to go down? And why would anything like that happen in Orchard Bluff?

The thought sent a shiver up her back.

Yes, finding out Con was Jack brought up a whole host of problems and sticky situations. And not the lovely sweet and salty caramel kind of sticky, either.

If Con was Jack, what did she do then? Announce to her friends and family that his death had all been a misunderstanding? An unfortunate miscommuniqué? What story would she tell them?

That he'd been blown up while on a business trip? And had temporary amnesia and forgotten who he was? And thought he was Aldo's cousin?

That scenario sounded about as likely, and silly, as an old soap opera plot. In fact, she was pretty sure she'd seen it done a time or two too many. And he looked slightly different because he'd had reconstructive plastic surgery? Please!

Although, come to think of it, that's exactly what she thought. About the plastic surgery.

Had he really been blown up and the plastic surgery was necessary to repair him? Or had his whole death been faked in the first place and the plastic surgery a way to create a new identity, like people in the witness protection program?

So many questions. Too few answers.

All she really wanted to know was whether Con was Jack and, if so, whether Jack still loved her and would take her with him when he left.

She finished arranging a display of jars of caramel, surrounding them with fragrant sprays of dried lavender she'd grown herself.

She caught her reflection in a jar lid and frowned. Not just because of the fun-house optics that made her look like a round children's play figure. Or the dark circles under her eyes that her concealer and foundation barely disguised. She wore her pink Willow's Caramels cotton T-shirt with cap sleeves and printed with her logo. It hugged her curves and had a delightful V-neck. But it had not been designed to catch the male eye. Over it, she wore a frilly pink and black apron, also silk-screened with the Willow's Caramels logo. Very girlie. Too girlie, and not siren enough.

And jeans, her comfortable faded jeans, and Converse tennis shoes in what color? Pink. Altogether she looked like a birthday cupcake ready for a nine-year-old's party.

She cursed the impulse she'd had a year ago to design a brand identity so very homey and sweet that it lacked any sex appeal at all. Who would have thought she'd be trying to win Jack back after he was officially dead?

Back to Jack, after thinking about it all night, she'd come to a conclusion—if Con was Jack, he wasn't here to win her back. If that had been the case, all he had to do was reveal his true identity, sneak into her bed, and make passionate love to her.

She tried not to let her heart break over the thought. She had no time for pity parties. If Jack wasn't coming back to her, he had a good reason. Which didn't mean she couldn't break him down and win him back all the same. Her husband may have been a master at getting intel out of foreign terrorists and corrupt officials, but she had her ways of breaking a man, too. With love.

No, if Con was Jack, he was up to something. It could be as benign as making sure she was doing okay, surviving the new life he'd left her with. But Jack could have sent any of his old friends in to find out that intel. It would have been much safer to do so.

No, if Con was Jack, something was up. Something sinister.

Just then Shiloh slunk into the booth, wearing a matching costume to Willow's. With the addition of dark sunglasses. She moved as spryly as if she were eighty rather than twenty-one.

Willow frowned at her. "Morning, sunshine. What happened to you? Overimbibe last night?"

"Don't talk so loud," Shiloh whispered. "I haven't had a hangover this bad since my birthday. And this one isn't even my fault." She looked away from the sun glinting off one of the jars and scowled. "Damn the light."

She slumped into a folding chair behind the table. "Didn't you hear? Some asshole spiked the apple gold punch. Aldo found the evidence—empty bottles of Everclear. In the trash. The jerk didn't even cover his tracks."

Willow arched a brow. "Someone spiked the hot punch?" That sounded exactly like the kind of prank Jack would pull. After all, *loose lips sink ships.*

"Oh, that's right. You left before all the action." Shiloh

flashed a ghost of a smile and winced with the effort, looking as if her head were about to explode. "How are you feeling? How was Con?"

"I'm just great. Never better." Willow handed her a bottle of water, letting Shiloh think what she would. "Here. Hydrate yourself. Water cures the common hangover."

Shiloh took it. "Thanks. Wish I had coffee." She unscrewed the cap from the bottle of water. "Looking back, Shane was the first casualty. Someone mentioned he had a couple of steaming mugs of it. He's going to take some ribbing over it. A big guy should be able to hold even his Everclear better than that."

"Yes, poor baby," Willow murmured. "Any suspects?"

Shiloh shrugged. "No. Aldo thinks it's just a prank. Maybe high school kids. Though I told him high school kids wouldn't waste alcohol on getting adults smashed." She laughed and immediately grabbed her head. "Shouldn't have done that. Laughing hurts too much."

Jack arrived at Bluff Country Store uncharacteristically early, and surprisingly nervous, for his coffee date with Willow. Jack was born late, which meant Con had to be perpetually early. It was in the dossier. He looked around for Willow. Not here? Must be busy times at her candy booth. Either that or she was still making battle plans to out him as himself. He wouldn't put anything past her.

The air smelled of fresh coffee and apple cinnamon rolls. The pastry case was full and the candy case stocked with Willow's confections, including a hearty stash of Lucky Jacks that made his mouth water.

Con could buy Lucky Jacks. Nothing sinister in that. But Jack decided against it. Too many coincidences in character would only make Willow more suspicious. There was a saying in the spy business—*there's no such thing as coincidence.* Unfortunately, he'd told it to Willow more than a time or two.

He picked up a newspaper and paid for it, tucking the change into a tip jar on the counter. He found a table out in the middle of the seating area that would have to suffice. Unfortunately, there were no tables next to a wall, period. Back against the wall was the most secure position, but no one here in Bluff County Store seemed to care. Jack liked to keep all potential threats in front of him. He sat, holding the paper in front of him as he tuned in to the conversations around him out of habit, and studied the store.

A good spy always knows where the exits are. Jack did a quick scan of his surroundings. There was an exit in the front of the store and one at the side. The café area had a two-story ceiling. Stairs to the upper half story of the building were off to his right. The upper story had an open post-and-rail half wall, all the better to see the goods and entice shoppers up for a look.

Jack had no desire to wander deeper into this little piece of country kitsch than absolutely necessary. The view of ruffly aprons, pot holders, and dishes emblazoned with roosters and chickens was plenty enough for him. The upper story was definitely not an escape route. It was hell.

Around him, people discussed the first day of the Apple Festival. Simple stuff. People hoping to sell their crops, honey, handcrafted goods, and homemade goodies. As he sat listening to the clink of silverware and hiss of the coffee machine, he felt as if he'd stepped into a time warp. Happy Bluff, or something. A good place where people weren't afraid and were totally oblivious to the dangers around them.

If only they knew.

The door to the store opened and Jack's heart rate spiked. He resisted the urge to look up, but he felt Willow enter, caught a whiff of her perfume, and heard her call out a greeting to the girl behind the counter. He looked up from his paper just in time to catch Willow's eye. Willow waved to him, smiled, and walked over.

He loved to watch her walk. The way her hips swayed drove him crazy. She hadn't forgotten how to move. A quick memory of them in bed together popped into his mind unbidden. Okay, maybe bidden by the rhythm of her hips and the bounce of her breasts as she walked.

Jack, Con, neither of them could go to bed with Willow. Absolutely not. He had to banish the thought. Yes, Willow was intuitive. Yes, she knew his body as well as her own, had explored every inch as he had hers. But his had been slightly rearranged since the explosion, acquired a few new scars that might fool her. Lost a few distinguishing marks.

Jack could have fooled her. He believed as firmly in his powers of deception as she did in her intuitive sense. He could have fooled her, except for an old war wound. No, not the kind that made him impotent. The kind that gave him . . . an involuntary purr. Most men grunted. Thanks to a chest and throat injury that left a rattle when he became excited, Jack's grunt had a purr in it. Willow called him her big cat, her tiger, even after he pointed out that tigers can't purr.

"No, but they chuff, Jack," she'd told him. "The sound you make is really more of a big-cat chuff, much more powerful and sexy."

He swallowed a lump and pushed the memories away. Jack was here to make this kill and get out. No deep revelations. No reunions. He was a single spy once again. No strings, no attachments. That's the way it had to be, for all their sakes.

But he was walking a damn narrow tightrope just now as he balanced between keeping Willow on Con's string away from Kennett and at arm's length so Jack didn't take over and give himself away.

She stopped in front of him. "I see you found the place." Her voice was just sultry enough to let him know she was interested.

And send his heart pattering away into the danger zone.

Jack took a deep breath and looked up into her eyes the bright-green shade of August's birthstone, her birthstone. Willow stood over him, the sun from the window behind her lighting her auburn into a blaze of fire. She was summer's child. Always would be to him.

She wore a pink T-shirt, tight jeans, and pale-pink lipstick that emphasized her full lips and pale skin and made Jack ache to kiss her. As Con, he tried to appear neutral and only mildly charmed by her. But he had an insane desire to call her cupcake.

"Not too hard in this one-road town." He offered her a chair.

"You're chipper, too," she said as she sat. "You don't have the Orchard Bluff hangover this morning? Didn't party hard enough after you returned to the event? I suppose you know someone spiked the alcoholic hot punch? The news is all over town."

To the casual observer, her comments would appear offhand. But Jack knew her well enough to detect the undercurrent of accusation in her tone. She suspected he'd had something to do with the dastardly spiking. Which, of course, he did, and was proud of it. Pranking an entire town? That was epic. Who did she suspect, though—Con or Jack?

"Yes, it seems we have a fiend in our midst." Jack gave her a confidential smile and raised a brow as if he were about to spill some top-secret intel to her. "Publicly, Aldo's generally placing blame on some nebulous high school kid. In private, Aldo's accused his friend Beck of the mischief. Beck hasn't, to my knowledge, denied committing the crime. He reportedly thinks it's funny and tipped his hat to *whoever* thought the prank up.

"Fortunately for me," Jack said, lying easily, "I'm not a fan of hot punch. I stuck with the wine."

"Me, too. We were both lucky." She watched him closely. "Your accent, I can't place it. What part of Italy are you from?"

*Let the storytelling begin.* Fortunately, he'd memorized his cover story dossier. "Little Italy, Chicago." He grinned. "My father's from a small town just outside Naples. My mother is American, from Chicago. She says I mimic Dad. My accent is a mutt, a mutation of theirs."

Willow nodded and smiled at him from beneath her bangs with a come-hither twinkle in her eyes. "It's sexy, like the gravelly tone of your voice."

His heart skipped a beat as he picked up her clear signal. She was coming on to him. Whether she was pulling his chain or not about liking the accent, she probably thought she could trip him up and get him to drop it.

*Good luck with that, Wills.*

He hadn't been able to lose it in two years.

He smiled back at her as his mind worked like an opposing football coach's trying to determine his opponent's next play in this game of *Is he, or isn't he, her late husband?*

He had the feeling he was in for the Orchard Bluff inquisition. Willow could be persistent.

He tapped the table to distract her. "I asked you for coffee. What would you like?"

"A caramel latte. And tell Maddie, she's the girl behind the counter, to use my caramel in it."

"Only the best for you?"

"Why settle for anything less? Oh, and ask her to put our coffee in paper cups to go so I can take mine back to my booth with me."

He popped up and ordered the coffee. As himself, he would have ordered a dark-chocolate mint mocha. But as Con, he settled for cappuccino with a dash of cinnamon on top to maintain the Italian façade. Besides, it was in his dossier—favorite coffee beverage: cappuccino. Did HQ ignore his secondary personal preferences on purpose? He would have been happy with a vanilla latte. He could have disobeyed, but, hell, right now it was just easier to follow the plan.

He returned to the table to wait for their order, aware she had been studying him intently and continued to do so without embarrassment, looking for anything that would give him away.

"You're watching me like I'm still half apparition. I don't scare you today? And here I thought I had the power to make women swoon." He laughed, trying to be charming and not too intimate. "Even ghosts don't look as frightening in broad daylight, is that it?"

"Spooks don't scare me." She let the words hang in the air.

He got the distinct impression she was using a double entendre now, referring to his occupation.

"Really?" he said, in a tone that meant *you could have fooled me*.

"I was never afraid," she said. "Just startled by that line from *Thunderball*. For just a second, you sounded so much like my late husband." She looked him in the eye as if staring into his heart. "I loved my husband. If I could will him back to life, I would."

She sounded so sorrowful and sincere. And still hopeful. A lump formed in his throat. Damn, he hated this.

"Sorry to disappoint." He didn't have to fake his sympathy. She'd never know how sorry he was. He tried to change the mood. "In bright sunlight, there's only a passing resemblance, anyway, right?" He turned from side to side so she could see his face from every angle. Then he arched a brow, waiting for her affirmation.

She reached across the table and put a hand on his forearm as if she couldn't resist touching him. Either that or she feared he'd disappear, evaporate or something.

"Not many people here know this about me, but I have what my grandma called the Sense. It's hard to describe. Basically, it's a sixth sense that can tell when someone I love is in danger.

"I knew the minute that explosion blew Jack up." She looked him directly in the eyes. "But now I feel like he might still be alive."

Not cracking under that kind of emotional pressure was the hardest thing Jack had ever done, and he'd been in some tight situations. He'd been beaten nearly to death and he still wouldn't talk. But here he was, fighting not to crack now, because he loved Willow more than she'd ever know.

His heart raced. His mouth went dry. He wanted her. He could have her. Anytime. And that was the greatest temptation of all. He fought to keep his expression calm.

Fortunately, Maddie called out their order. "Tall caramel latte! Cappuccino!"

He jumped up to get them. When he returned to the table with the two paper cups and sleeves for each, Willow was still watching him with that unnerving look of hers as he handed her her coffee.

He sat down and raised his coffee to his lips.

She blew on hers and took a sip.

Was it his imagination, or did she stare at him just a little too hard as she watched him take a drink? And then the corners of her mouth curled up so slightly it took an expert like him to detect that small microexpression of smugness on her face.

She was happy he was drinking coffee? What the hell?

And then it hit him.

*Oh, damn! She thinks she can run a DNA test on me and find out whether I'm me or not. She's planning on using the old steal-the-coffee-cup trick. Like hell.*

He was going to take his coffee cup and DNA with him. In the meantime, though, playing a few head games could be fun. Someone needed to teach Willow how to use a poker face.

She studied him. "I love coffee shops. The first time I saw Jack, he was sitting at a table in one of the Starbucks in Seattle. It was a sunny day, like this one. Fall. September." Her voice was dreamy, faraway. "Kind of a coincidence, meeting you now, isn't it?"

He didn't answer, just smiled back politely and made a show of taking a nice big gulp of coffee. The kind of gulp that left lots of DNA on the coffee cup lid. Hell, he felt like spitting on it just to get her goat. But he restrained himself.

Willow couldn't let a silence go unfilled. Just as he figured she would, she stepped in and continued, "I was in pastry school at the time. Hurrying in before class for some caffeine so I could survive the morning. We had to be in class at five AM, like the professional bakers.

"Jack looked perfect, bright eyed, and fully awake. As if he never needed sleep. He looked up at me, caught my eye, gave me his devil-may-care grin, and I fell in love."

So she was going to torment him with memories. See if he'd go all gooey eyed and drop his guard. It was a decent strategy. It might work on a lesser man. But Jack would lie to his own mother to save the world or accomplish a mission. Not that that was saying much. He didn't like his mother. But he'd been confronted by tyrannical foreign dictators and all manner of terrorists and never, ever cracked.

She could sentimental him to death and it wouldn't do her any good. She should remember he never cried at the tearjerker movies she used to drag him to. He never cried, period.

"Fell in love? At first sight?" he teased her. "Before the guy even opened his mouth?" He shrugged. "That's better than fainting, I suppose." He winked.

She tilted her head and smiled. "That's the other thing about the Sense—it lets me know when I've found a soul mate. I knew right away with Jack." Her smile deepened.

*Damn that Sense.* The look she was giving him now meant either she knew he was himself or she'd found her next soul mate. Both of which were correct, but he wasn't falling prey to either.

A sane man would have run for the hills right then, terrified out of his mind by the smug, knowing look she was giving him, the one that meant he was already caught, snagged, snared, entrapped, bagged, and ready for the altar. But Jack couldn't run. He had a mission—convince Willow he wasn't himself and keep her away from the Rooster.

He took a deep breath and glanced heavenward for inspiration. As he did, a movement in the upper story caught his eye. A rack of ruffled aprons rustled and a large cast-iron statue of a rooster teetered on the open woodwork railing above him.

What the hell? Where did that come from? It shouldn't be there. If that thing fell—

Coffee still in hand, he bounded out of his chair, kicking it over behind him. He leaned forward to grab Willow and pull her out of the path of that rooster.

At the same time she jumped up with a look of fear on

her face. "Get out of the way!" She rammed into him with the force of her slight body so hard she sent him flying onto his back, knocking his coffee from his hand. She tumbled over with him, landing straddling him.

He looked up past her shapely, silhouetted form just in time to see the cast-iron rooster topple off the rail above them.

# CHAPTER EIGHT

One minute Willow was staring as dreamily as she could into Con's eyes, letting him know exactly where he stood—he was either Jack or her new soul mate—when the hair on the back of her neck stood up. Her mouth went dry and her pulse jumped into *fight or flee, run for your life* mode. An airplane from the local air force base rumbled by, shaking the walls. The next she looked up and saw a cast-iron rooster tumble from the story above, headed directly for Con.

She'd lost Jack once. She wasn't letting a rooster bean Con or Jack, or whoever he was, to death. Not on her watch.

She jumped out of her chair, threw herself at him with the full force of her 105 pounds, and knocked him on his back. He grabbed her, pulling her down with him. She landed breathing hard as she straddled him, her hair tumbling down around her face. The breathing hard wasn't just from the scare. She hadn't straddled a man like this since before Jack left for Ciudad del Este and was blown up.

Con rose to the occasion. She felt his arousal through his jeans. She thought about Jack, the passionate way he made love to her and purred. She'd give anything to hear him purr again.

The rooster crashed into the floor next to them, exactly where Con had been sitting, landing with an explosive bang that made everyone in the room jump but them. They were mesmerized by each other.

At least, she was mesmerized as Con stared up at her with Jack's eyes. A sense of complete calm washed over her.

She sat there, enjoying the view, until she heard the buzz of the room around them—the concerned murmurings, the sense of shock.

People began gathering around them.

Con cleared his throat and looked over at the rooster next to them. Willow followed his gaze. The rooster had hit the floor so hard that it left a dent.

Con held up his fingers to measure an inch. "Missed us by that much."

Willow recognized *Get Smart* humor when she heard it. So much like Jack, again. "Yes, it did, Max."

He grinned up at her. "You saved my life."

"Luck of the fall." She shrugged modestly. "You were trying to save mine."

"Did you see anything?" he asked.

*He suspects foul play. Just like Jack would.*

She shook her head as a shiver of fear washed over her. "No, nothing. Just a falling cock."

His words brought Willow back to reality. She became aware of their surroundings. Maddie hovered over them. A dozen other people crowded about them.

Ada pushed her way through the crowd toward them wearing a worried expression, a new dish towel, with the tag still dangling from it, in hand. Ironically, a dish towel in a rooster motif. "What happened? Are you okay? Should we call for help?" Ada fired the questions off too rapidly for Willow to answer.

"We're fine. The rooster fell." Willow pointed. It was probably time to get off Con. Lingering much longer would be highly inappropriate.

Ada scanned the damage and held the crowd back. "They're fine. They're not hurt. Give them room. There's nothing to see."

The cast-iron rooster sat in the middle of it all, looking, well, cocky. Remarkably, it had landed on its feet and seemed none the worse for wear.

Ada helped Willow up off Con. Willow would have loved to linger on his lap forever.

Con sat up, rubbing the back of his head and staring at the rooster. "Being coldcocked suddenly takes on a whole new meaning." He looked up at Willow. "You're sure you're okay."

"I'm great, fabulous." And on a certain level, she most certainly was.

Ada took a step closer to the rooster. "Where did this come from?"

Con pointed to the upstairs loft and stood. "Up there. It was sitting on the railing. I noticed it just before it fell."

"What? No! Old Cogburn here doesn't belong upstairs. On the rail? That's crazy. That's courting disaster." She frowned. "Who moved him? He has a corner downstairs in the rooster section where all the red and black country patterns are. He's been there since he came in six months ago. He's a hard old cock to sell."

Ada put an arm around her daughter Maddie.

"Maybe a customer moved him, Mom. Took him up there and saw something they liked better, then just left him there without thinking."

Maddie's theory explained the facts well enough for most of the crowd. But Willow felt as if a shadow had crossed her path. *Something wicked this way comes,* she thought.

More fodder for her theory that Con was Jack. Wherever Jack went, trouble was sure to be as well.

Ada's frown deepened. "No, but I would have noticed him from the cash register. I can see the railing from there. I keep an eye on it just because something like this could happen. He wasn't there earlier. I'm sure of it." She reached for the rooster.

Con stood and stepped in front of her. "Let me." He took the dish towel from her and, using it as an oven mitt, picked up old Cogburn. "I'd like to buy this from you. And the dish towel, too. It'll make a great souvenir, *the rooster that tried to kill me.*" He laughed. "Besides, Aldo will love it. I'm surprised he hasn't bought it already."

Con set the rooster on the floor and reached for his wallet in his pocket.

Ada put a hand on his arm and shook her head. "It's yours, my gift. I couldn't stand to have it around here anyway. Take it away with my compliments. Please. Just promise not to sue me." She shuddered.

"Sue you? For an accident? That's crazy." He gave her a warm smile. "You have a deal." He put his wallet back in his pocket and picked up Cogburn with the towel.

*Why with the towel?* Willow wondered as she inched toward Con's coffee cup. Victory was almost hers. All she needed was that cup.

Ada turned to her daughter. "Maddie, get a mop. Let's get this spilled coffee cleaned up before someone slips on it."

As Willow took another step toward Con's cup he blocked her. Ada made an end-round maneuver and reached for the cup on the floor just as Willow dashed around Con on the other side and bent to get it. As the two women nearly conked heads Con leaned down and scooped it up. "Allow me."

Still holding the toweled rooster, he carried the cup off to the trash can by the counter and Willow saw him toss it in.

*Curses, foiled again. How am I going to convince Ada to let me paw through her trash for that cup? And how will I know if I get the right one?*

* * *

Willow could dig through Bluff Country Store's trash to her heart's content, but she'd never find Jack's cup. He'd only pretended to throw it away. In reality, he'd hidden it under the towel with the rooster.

While he was recovering from the explosion Emmett had sent agent Lani Silkwater, code name Magic, to teach Jack sleight of hand to help him regain his small motor and shooting skills. He had gotten pretty skilled at it, exactly why no one saw him hide the cup.

Willow's attempt to gather intel amused him more than it should have.

He walked her back to her booth in the center of town with his new friend, old Cogburn, wrapped in a towel and bagged in a shopping bag from Bluff Country Store for added protection. He wanted to preserve any fingerprints on it. Not that he expected to find any of the Rooster's.

Jack lingered at the booth. He hated to leave Willow unprotected, but he had to get back to the guesthouse, dust Cogburn for prints, and contact Emmett. Old Cogburn was meant for him—a message from the Rooster: *If you're Sariel, I'm going to kill you.*

The Rooster had never been known for his subtlety. But then again, he'd never been known to miss before. That is, until he only *thought* he'd killed Jack in that explosion. Now the Rooster's perfect record was toast, and the hell of it was—he wasn't certain Jack was still alive.

The turn of Jack's thoughts was dark. He felt like grabbing his sniper's rifle and taking Kennett out right then and there. One well-placed shot between his eyes as he sold his apples should do it. A nice, clean kill shot.

That should send a clear message to RIOT. Jack could take out one of their assassins whenever he felt like it. Like now.

It sure seemed like a good message to him.

And hell, when weren't his shots always placed exactly where he wanted them? He made those guys on *Top Shot* look like amateurs.

But that wasn't the mission plan. Though he was sure as hell going to suggest it to Emmett as soon as he got back to Aldo's.

"Thanks for the coffee," Willow said as she apparently lingered, too.

Her assistant watched them as she helped a customer.

"Yeah, that didn't exactly go as planned, thanks to old Cogburn here."

Willow smiled and touched Jack's arm in the gentle way she had. "I think we need a do-over, something not quite so dramatic."

The store owner, her friend Ada, had made them each another cup to go. Willow set hers on the table.

Jack wasn't sure a nice, quiet meeting between them was possible. Not as far as his emotions were concerned.

"Let me make you dinner," Willow said.

The woman was not going to give up on trying to get his DNA. He read the sneakiness on her face as easily as he read coded intel.

"Monday evening? My place. I'll clear the house of all potential falling objects. Promise. Besides, it's just a single-story house with my shop in the basement. Around seven?"

Her tone was pleasant, flirty. Her eyes pleaded with him to accept. She was desperately hoping he was Jack. He could tell that much.

No doubt she was already devising another plan to out him as her husband.

Eating dinner alone with her at her house was dangerous business. And yet there didn't seem to be any way to decline without looking like a jerk and hurting her feelings.

He wanted to see her again, to spend a few more hours with her after he'd killed the Rooster and before he blew this town. Make sure she'd be okay. Say good-bye in his own way.

"Sure," he said. "Love to. Let me bring a bottle of Aldo's wine. White or red?"

"I'll get back to you on that." Her eyes sparkled. She looked too happy. And too devious.

Someone should really teach her how to hide her emotions better.

A crowd of customers wandered up. The festival was growing busier by the minute.

Willow glanced at her assistant. "I'd better go help Shiloh. She looks overwhelmed already. See you Monday?"

He nodded. "If not sooner."

She leaned forward, rising slightly on her toes, looking as if she was about to kiss him good-bye. As she always had.

He took a polite step back. *Nice try, Wills.*

She cleared her throat and looked down, probably to cover her embarrassment. "Great." She turned toward the table in her booth.

He started walking away.

"Wait!"

He stopped and turned toward her.

She handed him a bag of caramels, brushing his hand with hers as she did, a gentle caress. The kind of touch she knew he liked. "My compliments. Thanks for the exciting morning."

He took the caramels, trying not to let his reaction to her touch show—he'd felt it in a shiver of pleasure all the way up his back. "Thanks."

As he walked away, he looked at the bag she'd given him—her largest package of Lucky Jacks.

Yeah, she was sending a message. Damn, he had to work harder at fooling her.

He took old Cogburn back to Aldo's guesthouse, which

in reality was a small apartment built over the tasting room. He carefully unwrapped the old rooster and set it on newspaper on the table.

If Jack was right, and no doubt he was, he was always right about matters of assassination, the Rooster had worn gloves when handling Cogburn. The statue would not have any of the Rooster's prints. But Jack had to check anyway.

It's what Jack, or any good killer, would have done— leave no evidence behind, only prints that would implicate someone else: whoever had last handled the Rooster.

He got out his dusting kit and tested the rooster. Sure enough, no prints large enough to be the Rooster's. Just a few much smaller prints, likely Ada's or Maddie's. Which didn't dissuade Jack from the belief Cogburn had been pushed with intention. Had the attempt been successful, it would have been first-degree murder by rooster statue. Now wouldn't that have made a lovely headline?

It's a good thing it hadn't succeeded or Jack would have had to die of embarrassment. Can you imagine the jokes that would have gone around the Agency once they found out that Sariel had actually been alive and then been offed by the Rooster with a rooster? Jack's reputation would have never lived it down. So to speak.

Even though he was officially dead, Jack had a legacy to maintain and he'd be damned if he'd let Kennett sully it by killing him. Again. Especially so ignobly.

Jack needed to report in. He scanned the apartment for bugs and set up the shielding device he affectionately called the Cone of Silence.

Then he called Emmett. "Chief, the Rooster's trying to kill me. And my cover may have been blown."

# CHAPTER NINE

D on't be so dramatic, Jack. Of course the Rooster's trying to kill you." The chief laughed. "That's his MO. He doesn't care whether Con is really Con or not. He doesn't give a damn about killing innocent people. If there's a chance Con's you, he has to strike. Relax. Your cover's safe."

Jack took a deep breath. He didn't want to have to tell the chief about his screwup, but he had no choice. "Yeah, I know, Chief. I'm not worried about the Rooster. I can handle him.

"It's Willow. She's getting suspicious. Permission to kill the Rooster with a bullet and get the hell out of here?"

"What did you do, Jack?" The chief's amusement evaporated.

"I may have accidentally used one of my favorite Bond lines around her. But it's so common—"

"Jack! Did you learn nothing in the Agency acting classes? You can't act like you. You have to find your motivation and act in character as Con."

"Yeah, I know. But I'm an assassin, Chief. I don't usually have to do this undercover shit. And Willow has the Sense. Just because I may have danced like me—"

"Danced? No. Jack!"

"At the growers' dinner. I couldn't help it. I *was* in character. Mostly. The Rooster was trying to kill me during a dancing competition. If I'd been me, I would have simply killed him back. But instead I had to do something showy to distract the crowd from what was really going on."

Even though he wasn't Skyping, Jack could almost see Emmett scowling and shaking his head. "So even knowing that Willow knows your dance moves, you went twinkle toes on me. Is that what you're saying?"

"Well, when you put it that way, it sounds worse than it was." Jack cursed the Rooster beneath his breath. This whole scenario was making him sound like a wimp before his boss. "So? Permission to use any force, any means, necessary?"

"Permission denied. Stick with the mission, Jack," Emmett said. "The intel you retrieved from the drop is invaluable. We're still deciphering the details, but it looks like the Rooster was contacting other terrorist sleeper cells.

"But we need more. We want his plans for the G Eight Summit and we can't leave a mess behind and have local law enforcement breathing down our necks. Make it look like an accident.

"And for pity's sake, make Willow believe you're Con, not you. Stay the hell away from her if you have to."

By eleven, the town of Orchard Bluff was packed, not a free parking spot in sight. Willow worked on autopilot as her thoughts kept returning to Con and Jack.

Despite the accident, she couldn't keep the smile off her face. Con had acted so like Jack. Jack would have thrown himself in front of a bus to save a stranger's life. That's the kind of heroic man he'd been.

And Jack was *always* totally attuned to his surroundings. Sometimes annoyingly so. She'd be talking to him as they took a walk around the park by their house and he'd mention something out of the blue about a plane flying over. Or, "Look there. A beaver has been gnawing at a tree." Or, "There's new graffiti on the fence." Or some other detail she hadn't paid any attention to. Sometimes she wondered if he was listening to what she said at all.

Which was a long way of saying that Jack would have noticed that rooster as it began to topple. And he would have been looking for the cause, just like Con had done.

Brick by brick, fact by fact, she was building the case that Con was Jack, even without that blasted coffee cup. Either Con was incredibly helpful or he was Jack and savvy enough to know she wanted that cup and destroy the evidence. *Well, Mr. You're-So-Smart, I'm going to get your DNA and out you one way or another.* Even if she had to sleep with him and see if he purred like Jack.

Not that sleeping with him would be a chore, not if the tingles she'd felt while straddling him were any indication of the chemistry between them. It would be a great pleasure.

A commotion in the crowd caught her attention. Willow looked up from where she was making change for a customer to see Shane pushing his way through to the front toward her.

He came to a stop in front of her table. "Willow! I was making a delivery to the growers' booth in town when I heard about your mishap with a rooster. How are you? Are you okay?"

The breeze ruffled his thick light-brown hair, which brushed the collar of his open denim work shirt. Beneath the shirt he wore a red T-shirt with the apple growers' logo. He'd rolled up his sleeves to just below his elbows, showing off powerful forearms and giving a hint of his well-defined biceps. His thighs bulged in the legs of his jeans. The man was powerfully built and stocky.

Even now, Willow noticed women in the crowd noticing him. She noticed him, too. But not in a good way. She recognized his cocky stance as a threatening, dominant pose. It was the way dogs stood when they meant to in-

timidate intruders on their territory. And his concern
wasn't sincere—the words were right, but the tone was
faked.

He removed his sunglasses. "You're sure you're not
hurt?"

There was no concern in his eyes, either.

She quickly looked away from him, hoping he didn't
see the growing uneasiness in hers. "I'm fine."

"You haven't answered my texts." He was trying to
sound contrite, but that seemed false, too. There was a
tight edge to his voice that didn't jibe with an apologetic
spirit.

She stole a glance at him. His jaw was set, his eyes
hard. His fist clenched.

"I've been busy—"

"Look at me, Willow. Please. I'm sorry. What do you
want me to say? It wasn't my fault. Someone spiked the
punch."

"I know." She tried to sound neither angry nor encour-
aging. Just neutral, hoping he'd get the message she was
no longer interested in him. That she'd never really been
in the first place.

"The guys have been ribbing me all morning." He may
have been trying to sound light, but all she heard was
anger beneath a veneer.

Shane prided himself on holding his alcohol. Russian
ancestry, he claimed. Prize drinkers.

"I suppose Con was hungover, too? That's why he was
having coffee with you?"

Why should it matter to Shane what she did or whether
Con was hungover or not? Something kept her from telling the truth. Even though she knew very well he did not
have a headache and he had a perfectly good explanation
why. She held that bit of information back from Shane.
"Yeah, he was miserable. The same as everyone." She

wasn't going to apologize or explain herself. She could do what she wanted. She didn't need Shane's approval.

"Let me make things up to you. Come out with me tonight after you close up. Meet me at Beck's. I'll buy you a drink." He made his voice low and sexy. "We can loosen up together."

"No thanks, Shane. Now if you'll excuse me, I have customers waiting."

Shane's eyes darkened with anger, but he kept his tone friendly. "Sure. Another night." He tapped her table with his fist and walked off.

Willow tried hard not to shiver as she watched him go. Shane wasn't asking. He was commanding.

# CHAPTER TEN

Jack broke into Willow's house. He had a dog treat in his pocket for Spookie. But he wasn't overly worried about his killer attack dog. If the little ball of fluff failed to recognize him, he still knew how to make the scary face.

Jack, of course, was an expert lockpick. And he knew a thing or two about security systems. Which was absolutely useless information on this excursion—Willow didn't have one.

He frowned. *Wills, didn't I teach you that evil lurks everywhere?*

Emmett should have insisted she have one. Jack would remedy that now by installing his own, one that would alert him if she was in trouble. He'd have to be her security. Him and his bugs and GPS devices.

He had a bug-planting plan. He'd start upstairs and work his way into the candy shop in the basement below. He just hoped Willow didn't come home early and catch him in the act.

He stood in her living room and surveyed the area, listening for Spookie and doing a bug and camera sweep of his own, just to make sure the house was clear. He hadn't been in Willow's home before, no farther than the entryway, anyway.

Where was that little mutt?

He moved quietly, with the stealth of a trained assassin

and spook, as he cleared two bugs and a covert camera from the living room. His blood boiled as he thought about the Rooster watching Willow in her private moments. Using her to get at him. He swept the kitchen. Assured that the main living space was bug-free, he stomped around on purpose to alert the dog to an intruder.

"Hey, girl! Hey, Spookie, where are you, girl?"

He heard a yelp, followed by the click of dog toenails on the floor. Spookie barreled around the corner.

He kneeled and got down on her level so she could look him in the face. This time he let his joy at seeing her shine through as he smiled at her and coaxed her closer.

She ran up to him, tail wagging, pausing a few feet away to stare him in the eyes. She gave a happy bark, jumped forward, and licked his face.

He scooped her up and hugged her, scratching her beneath her ears as he slid a bug into her dog collar. "That's my girl! Good girl. Boy, have I missed you."

Then he rolled around on the floor, playing with her until they were both out of breath.

He set her on the floor, where she flopped onto her back, begging to have her belly scratched.

"You are a brazen hussy, you know that, right?" He scratched her tummy and stood up. "Time to get to work, kid."

He studied the living room. He recognized some of the furniture. But Willow had bought a bunch of new stuff, too. A new sofa. A large, bright area rug that covered the bare wood floor nearly from wall to wall.

Pillows. Damn, she had a whole lot of pillows. Floral affairs. Pillows with buttons. Some embroidered with ferns and leaves. She'd collected a regular pillow forest.

And she'd painted the walls a warm yellow he'd never have chosen. There was a bookcase full of cookbooks. A flat-screen TV. A feminine upholstered chair that no guy would be caught dead, or living, sitting in. The chair looked uncomfortable as hell.

There were a few picture frames, including a digital one, on the mantel of the fireplace, filled with photos of her mom and friends. A set of silver candlesticks she and Jack had received as a wedding gift, filled with beeswax candles in white. A crystal candy dish on an end table along with a fall floral arrangement in a vase he recognized.

But no pictures of him. Anywhere.

Agency policy. Emmett had told her to get rid of any or to keep them hidden. Never put them on display. For her own protection.

Jack was just surprised she'd obeyed. Grateful—no one in Orchard Bluff would recognize the slight likeness between him and himself—but surprised. And glad. He wanted her to be safe. Always. That's why he'd come back.

He walked around the room with Spookie on his heels, planting bugs in the kitchen. The guestroom. The bedroom Willow used as her study. Clearing the Rooster's monitoring devices and bugs as he went, seething as he found each new device. Thinking through the consequences of removing the bugs as he went.

Once the Rooster discovered his monitoring devices had all gone down, he'd be on even higher alert. Taking them down threw even more evidence on the fire that Con was Jack. But the thing about monitoring devices—to be effective, they had to be monitored. Today the Rooster would have to be out and about playing the part of the good apple grower at the festival. He wouldn't have much monitoring time. By the time he did, he'd be dead.

Jack found Willow's laptop on her desk. Earlier, on his way past to meet Willow for coffee, he'd seen a guy from a cell company delivering a new modem. She must have had modem problems.

Jack picked up her laptop, tried it out. The new modem was working. He swept it for keystroke-monitoring software and got rid of the Rooster's. He installed his own monitoring software and moved on to her bedroom. Spookie had a frilly bed in the corner. Willow had a new armoire, nightstand, and bed frame. But not a single reminder of him.

None of his clothes in the closet. No pictures.

He swept the room, barely containing himself from crushing the hidden camera he found to a pulp beneath his heels. Ground glass wasn't good for carpeting. Or Willow's bare feet. He restrained himself.

The Rooster was a dead man for violating Willow's privacy. For peeping at Jack's wife.

He ran his hands through his hair and plunked onto her bed. He scooped up the little dog. "It's like she's erased all traces of me." He sure as hell didn't like being erased even though it was necessary.

Spookie wiggled out of his arms, jumped down from the bed, and barked at the bed skirt.

Jack frowned.

Spookie growled again and barked. Thinking she smelled a mouse, he got onto his hands and knees on the floor and pulled back the skirt to see what had Spookie so riled up. He leaned down to take a look and found himself staring at several large, plastic storage boxes.

Spookie gave her happy bark. And it could have just been him, but he thought she looked triumphant.

He pulled the first plastic box out and opened the lid.

His breath caught. A lump formed in his throat. He set the box on the bed and scooped Spookie up to sit next to him.

Here was his life, his and Willow's life together.

A folded flag sat on top, a memento from his funeral. Beneath the flag, he found the DNA report Emmett had sent Willow, confirming that Jack's remains were those at the explosion site. It was a dummy, bogus report, of course. He had no idea whose DNA report this really was.

He removed the flag and the report and set them on the bed, revealing the treasure trove beneath. Had the woman saved every souvenir from their time together?

This was the Willow he knew.

He smiled as he lifted a small pink crystal-studded puppy collar and leash from the box. He held them up for Spookie to see. "Remember these, girl? Your first collar and leash."

Spookie barked and panted. She was probably just leading him on that she remembered. But he grinned at her anyway.

"Guess you've forgiven me for dressing you up like a fairy, then?"

He'd given Spookie to Willow for Halloween the second year they were married. To keep her company while he was gone. They both loved All Hallows Eve.

Willow used to say, "How can I not like it? I'm in love with a spook!" Then she'd laugh and kiss him.

Halloween was an excuse for her to make her candies and treats for the kids.

Jack frowned. He'd left Willow alone so often. So he'd gone to the pound and rescued the mildest-mannered, cutest, girliest puppy he could find. He knew a rescued dog would make his wife happy. She had such a tender heart and was always trying to save people and animals. Hell, she'd tried to save him.

He supposed he should have gotten her a killer watchdog. But Willow would never have been happy with a violent, aggressive dog. She wanted companionship, not protection.

Then he'd bought the collar and leash and a really stupid Sugar Plum Fairy dog costume. And dressed the dog

up, to both their embarrassment. And attached a card to
the collar.

He looked in the box next to him on the bed. Yep,
there was the card.

*To my sugarplum queen—a treat because you're so
sweet.*
    *Love, Jack*

Corny. Oh, well, she'd loved it when he knocked on
their door on Halloween night. She answered with a bowl
of candy—homemade suckers—in her hand.

He'd never forget the look on her face, the way her
mouth fell open all round and sweet and kissable when
she saw the dog in his arms. The way Willow had squealed
and nearly dropped the bowl.

The way he couldn't stop grinning. "I'm doing a reverse trick or treat." He took the bowl from her, set it on
the porch, and handed her the puppy with the really tiny,
stupid-looking tiara, tutu, and pink wings he'd put on her.

Spookie was hardly bigger than his hand.

Willow cuddled her against her cheek and crooned
loving noises to her. "Mine?"

"All yours."

He put his arm around them. Willow went up on her
toes and kissed him with the dog cuddled between them.

He'd grinned and cupped Willow's tight little ass. "I'll
expect my trick later."

And she'd given him a good one.

*Damn, I shouldn't think about that. That way leads to
frustration.*

Later, they cuddled in bed with the dog and ignored
the late trick-or-treaters who knocked on their door.

"She looks white and ghostly in this light," Willow
had said, studying the silky little puppy that slept on her

pillow. "I'm going to name her Spook. So I can be in love with two ghosts."

She liked to call him a spook. She liked it better than *spy*.

"The dog's a she. You'd better call her Spookie so you can tell us apart."

Willow punched him in the shoulder. And then they made love again. On the floor. So they wouldn't disturb the puppy.

Jack forced his thoughts back to the present. He looked in the box again. He found their wedding picture. And a picture they'd had taken in one of those cheap photo booths at the local amusement park on their first Halloween together. They were making funny faces.

Damn, they looked young. And happy.

He pushed the picture away and found a pressed rose. Probably the first one he'd given her. And a fifty-cent adjustable ring with a green plastic stone that he'd gotten from a machine at the grocery store. He'd wanted one with a heart-shaped pink stone. But you got what you got, as his mom used to tell him.

He'd mock proposed to Willow with it, testing out the waters to see if this beautiful girl he'd fallen for would ever consider tying the knot with a loner like him. She kept it now in the little black velvet box her engagement ring came in.

He swallowed hard and, leaning forward, rested his head in his hands, taking deep breaths.

He shouldn't be doing this. He had work to do. Why was he lingering here, tormenting himself with this walk through the past?

Call it morbid curiosity, but he pawed through the rest of the photos and other things in the box, resisting the urge to steal a picture of him and Willow together.

Now that would be suicide.

At the bottom of the box he found his old hairbrush, a few strands of his hair still in it, neatly tucked inside a plastic bag. Why had Willow kept this?

He shook his head. She was so sentimental. She probably just wanted to keep a small piece of him. Whatever her reasons, he couldn't leave the brush behind. It had his DNA in the form of hair follicles on it.

He took it. He'd have to clean it up, lace it with hairs from someone else, break back in later, before he left, and replace it. And hope Willow didn't notice it was missing in the meantime.

On the very bottom of the box, he found a flattened cardboard coffee cup sleeve from Starbucks. For a minute, he frowned.

*What the hell is this doing here?*

He set it down, shrugged, and hurriedly put everything back the way it was. As he kneeled to shove the box beneath the bed, he noticed the coffee sleeve on the floor.

Shit, he'd missed one item. He hurriedly opened the box and shoved the sleeve in beneath the flag and the report and the dog collar.

Finally, he shoved the box beneath the bed.

Willow hadn't forgotten or erased him. She'd just shoved him beneath the bed.

He ran his fingers through his hair once more. Enough soul-searching and reminiscing. He still had the basement to bug. "Come on, girl." He stood.

Spookie followed him to the kitchen. If Willow wanted his DNA, he'd give it to her. Well, he'd give her someone's DNA.

He grinned to himself as he walked to a cupboard next to the sink and found where she kept the drinking glasses. The top shelf was filled with her best ones. He removed one from the back, where she wouldn't notice.

He knew his wife. She'd use the special occasion

glasses when he came to dinner. Then, if the way she was eyeing his coffee cup was any indication, she'd pack his water glass away to send off to a DNA testing lab. He was going to make good and sure someone else's DNA was on that glass.

Not that it really mattered. The Agency would make sure Willow got a false report anyway. But Jack believed in dual redundancy and leaving nothing to chance.

He pocketed the glass and walked to the door to that led to the candy shop in the daylight basement.

"Sorry, my little spook dog. This is where we part company." He reached down, scratched her ears, and gave her the dog treat.

As she devoured it, he let himself into the basement, closing the door behind him, shutting Spookie out, just like he'd been doing for two years.

As he began his scan of Willow's shop, he picked up a low-level signal from something electronic. It wasn't a bug. He followed it to its source.

*What the hell?*

His blood ran cold. A remote-control phone jammer positioned to cover both the house and the shop. In Jack's opinion, there were only two reasons to jam service—to shut up inconsiderate jerks who talked too loudly in public places and to prevent someone from calling for help. Since Willow's home wasn't a public place . . .

# CHAPTER ELEVEN

Willow came home from her day at the festival physically exhausted but emotionally jazzed. They'd sold every piece of candy, every caramel apple, and every last jar of caramel sauce. Thank goodness.

She'd given Shiloh Sunday off. Even if Willow stayed up all night, she'd never be able to produce enough candy and caramel to stock her booth for Sunday's crowd. Anyway, she had more important work to do—snooping on Con.

Spookie looked up at Willow from her place on her favorite doggie pillow in front of the fireplace.

"Hey, Spook! Hey, come here, girl!"

Spookie lifted her head, looked at Willow, and put her head back down, curling up.

Willow frowned. Why was Spookie tired and listless? She didn't seem sick, just worn out, as if she'd played too hard. By herself? Not likely. Willow hoped she didn't have to make a late night run to the vet with her.

She went to the kitchen and got Spookie's dinner. But even when Willow rattled the bowl, Spookie didn't come. Willow picked up the bowl and took it to the living room.

"Okay, princess. Here you go."

To Willow's relief, Spookie stood up and ate. But she still looked plain old pooped out.

"What have you been up to while I was gone?"

Spookie cocked her head and barked.

"Yeah, now if only I were Dr. Dolittle I might understand that."

And yet Willow knew how Spookie felt. Willow was almost too excited and tired to eat, too.

She popped a microwavable meal in. When it was done, she grabbed a fork and carried her dinner toward her office. It was probably her imagination, but she could swear she smelled the faint remnants of high-quality cologne in the air. Things seemed just slightly off. Nothing she could put a finger on. Just . . .

Hadn't that pillow been in a different place? Why was the rug slightly skewed? Tiny, lightweight Spookie had never moved it before.

Someone had been here; Willow was almost certain of it. Someone like Jack. Or the Agency? Or someone the Agency had warned her about?

She was probably just being paranoid. Or overly optimistic, hoping Con was Jack and he'd been in to check up on her. She turned on every light to ward off the sense of creepiness.

When she inhaled deeply, she could still smell that ghost of cologne. Con's cologne? She'd shaken a lot of hands today. Met a lot of people. Hugged too many friends and acquaintances to count. It was possible someone's cologne had rubbed off on her and that's what she smelled now. Still . . .

She couldn't get the hair on the back of her neck to lie down properly. Again. Was there a product on the market she could buy to tame it?

In her office, the light on her Internet box was lit. Her new modem was working. Just for kicks, she tried her cell phone. It worked now, too.

If Con was Jack and he'd been here, what had he been looking for? Would he be watching every move she made?

If so, he'd know exactly what she was up to. And if someone else had been here?

She had to get out of the house and think.

She grabbed her laptop, her purse, and her keys. She'd been too tired last night, but tonight she'd go find an all-night café with Wi-Fi. Or even park in one of the orchards and use her smartphone or see if she could piggyback on one of her neighbors' Wi-Fi connections. She'd find out what she could about Con and see what she could find out about getting an exterminator out to the house—the kind who killed electronic bugs and surveillance.

*Get too cocky, Jack, and you're going to tip your hand.*

At least she hoped this was Jack's handiwork. That would be joyous news. And the alternative was just too frightening.

Jack hid in the woods, surveying the parking lot of Beck's Tavern. Word on the street hadn't let him down. Small-town small talk had told him everything he needed to know about Kennett's habits. The Rooster liked to drink, always had, which played into Jack's hands nicely.

Kennett had been in Beck's about half an hour. He'd parked his truck at the middle of the lot near the building where light streamed out from the bar windows onto it. No doubt Kennett wanted it where he could keep an eye on it, suspicious bastard.

Jack grinned. With his night-vision binoculars trained on the window, he had a clear view of Kennett as he downed beer after beer.

Jack's trigger finger itched. He ignored it as he waited for Kennett to leave his perch by the window. Sooner or later the son of a bitch would have to take a piss.

And then Jack would spring into action. In the meantime, he was cold, even dressed in his warm camouflage jacket. And a raccoon was making eyes at him. Not exactly the date he envisioned for a Saturday night.

As if Jack had willed it, Kennett got up. Jack became immediately alert as he watched Kennett walk away from the window toward the interior of the building. Jack grabbed his duct tape and moved to the edge of the parking lot.

When the lot was clear of onlookers, he slunk through the shadows and crouched in the dark in front of Kennett's truck. Jack ripped off a half-inch piece of reflective silver duct tape and placed it on the front bumper directly below the center of the steering wheel. He did the same in line with it above the windshield.

*Two pieces of duct tape mark the spot.*

It was a daring plan but ingenious.

Just as a drunk stumbled out of the bar door, Jack slid back into the shadows of the forest. He ran through the woods to a back road off the highway where he'd left his car. He tossed the duct tape in and poured himself a cup of coffee from the thermos he'd brought.

There was really no hurry. If Kennett followed his regular pattern, he'd be in Beck's for another hour at least, maybe more. Didn't the seasoned assassin know that routine killed?

It made Jack's job way too easy. Maybe Kennett thought no one noticed or cared what a local apple grower did. Maybe he was just trying to fit in. Jack didn't waste too much mental energy trying to figure Kennett out. He didn't really give a damn.

He fired up his engine and put the car in drive. Time to get into position. Better an hour early than a minute late. His dad had drilled that into him with plenty of punishment for incentive.

Jack hated to admit it, but the old man had been right on this point.

Jack refused to take any chances and blow this kill. He had to get out of Orchard Bluff before things became more complicated than they already were. He didn't know how much longer he could fool Willow. Or keep her at bay.

Fifteen minutes later, he parked out of sight in an orchard, facing the road Kennett would be coming down as he headed home. Jack had found a perfect place to attack Kennett—a bend in the road lined with trees on either side. A tough little curve to negotiate sober, when there was no frost on the road and the puddles weren't frozen.

Jack turned his car to face it, aiming his headlights in the direction Kennett would be coming from. He'd blind the bastard and be able to see his reflective tape so he could take aim.

A five-gallon gas can stood on the passenger floor beside him. All the better to burn Kennett to a crisp with. A sniper's rifle equipped with a night-vision scope rested on the passenger seat. Jack wasn't heartless. He'd kill Kennett before he torched him. Not that he deserved mercy.

After sweeping Willow's house of the Rooster's bugs and jamming the phone jammer the Rooster had installed at her place, Jack was still seething. He tried not to think about the Rooster watching Willow's every move since he'd come to town, listening in on her conversations and calls, tracking her movements, installing a jammer.

This was Jack's fault. Even though he was dead, he'd put her in danger. And he'd be damned it he'd let the Rooster near her again. He was going to end this.

At just past midnight, Jack turned on his headlights, grabbed his rifle, and got out of the car. His unwitting informants in town said Kennett always left the bar at midnight. Superstitious bastard. Didn't like to be out past the witching hour?

Jack lay on the ground in front of the car and trained his scope on the bend in the road.

*Any minute now, Rooster. I'm waiting for you.*

Willow left the Bluff Country Store parking lot a few minutes after midnight. Their empty lot had been a good place to camp out and borrow their Wi-Fi.

What had she found out about Con? Too little and too much.

Con Russo was a man with many friends, many talents, a boatload of relatives, and a thorough social network presence. From all appearances, he was an outgoing connector personality. Willow didn't personally recognize a single one of his Facebook friends, Twitter followers, or LinkedIn connections. But he shared quite a few with Aldo. Those must be relatives. Very legit seeming.

She still didn't buy it. But maybe that was just her blind optimism talking. Or maybe her blatant cynicism.

Con was a man with a past—a well-detailed one. College pals. Old girlfriends. Girls who could be new girlfriends.

Willow frowned. *Ugh! Girlfriends.* She felt her temperature rise.

If Con was Jack and pretending to be dead and taking advantage of his single status as Con to go out fooling around, he was in some deep doo-doo. Deep, deep poo.

In his defense, Con's online status was *Single, not in a relationship.* But since when did anyone tell the absolute truth online?

The thought of Jack, or Con, with someone else made her horribly, wickedly, intensely jealous.

*Inhale. Breathe deeply. Purge all violent thoughts.*

Being antiviolent was becoming harder and harder since Con showed up. Con, who from all online appearances was the complete and total opposite of Jack, who liked to keep a low profile.

Willow frowned. She'd spent half the night Googling the man, only to come up with a big fat regular life? What a waste of time.

The Agency was good. And no doubt Jack, if Con was Jack, had committed this fiction to memory. He'd always had a top-notch memory. Though it was still possible she could trip him up.

She wished she were as gregarious online as Con. Her caramel shop could use someone with his online sensibilities. Maybe she could get him to tweet an endorsement?

She decided to follow Con's online presence to keep tabs on him. She sent Con a friend request on Facebook. He could deny her, but if he was Jack that would be a giveaway, wouldn't it? A slap in the face of a friend. If Aldo found out about that, he'd go Italian ballistic on Con.

That might be worth seeing.

What was she thinking? There was that awful violent streak showing up again.

She got on Twitter and followed Con. Good thing he didn't have to approve that. *Let's just see if he keeps up his regular tweeting, shall we?*

If Con was Jack, the Agency was probably doing it for him. Willow had her doubts whether Jack would be able to keep up with so much social interaction.

One thing did stand out as suspicious—he didn't post good, clear, full-on pictures of himself. Which was an indictment in itself. The Agency wouldn't want pictures of an altered Jack all over the Internet. But it was still inconclusive and not definite proof of anything.

The moon was out, drifting eerily in and out of a light cloud cover as she headed toward home. Ground fog hugged the dips and hollows. It was a perfect Halloween atmosphere. The perfect night for a haunting.

Not what Willow needed to think. Not with all the creepy things that had been happening since Con arrived. She had to go home to an empty house that someone might be monitoring. Spookie wouldn't be much help. Despite her name, if she saw a ghost she'd turn tail and run. Willow forced herself to look on the positive side and how beautifully silvery the night looked as the frost settled in.

She'd have to be particularly careful on Loop Road Two at that bend near Shane's place. Deer loved to hang out in the orchard there and eat culls. With a nearly full moon, more than likely there would be a mob of them.

That curve was sharp. And the fog hung low in it. If it was going to freeze and be slick anywhere, that bend was it.

Willow gave herself a pep talk. "Mobs of deer, sharp corners, frost, and freezing fog—bring it on."

None of that scared Willow as much as the thought of losing Con before she found out whether he was actually Jack. Or if he wasn't, whether she could let herself fall in love with Con and love him for himself.

# CHAPTER TWELVE

The fog hung close to the lowlands around Jack. Damn, he hoped it didn't obscure his vision when Kennett came. Jack hated weather complications.

Near him in the orchard, a ten-point buck nibbled low-hanging fruit. He had five or six does with him who ate culls and windfall. And two more does in the orchard across the road. The nearly full moon must have brought them out. The grower who owned this orchard wouldn't be pleased. And neither was Jack. Deer were too damned unpredictable.

Just then a pair of headlights swung into view. Jack's two pieces of duct tape lit up. He aimed six inches beneath the top one, took a deep breath, and held it as he rested his finger on the trigger.

Just as he began applying pressure to the trigger, one of the damned does ran into the road. She stared into Jack's headlights and froze. Jack eased up and swore.

Impaired by alcohol and blinded by Jack's headlights, Kennett swerved too late to miss the doe.

Jack heard the sickening sound of four thousand pounds of metal hitting flesh. Watched the deer fly and crash to the ground just off the road. Shane's crunched truck veered off the road and slammed head-on into a big old granddaddy apple tree with an impact that shook the orchard.

*Looks like Lady Luck is on my side tonight.*

Jack hadn't even needed to take a shot. The doe had

done his work for him. He jumped to his feet, slid into his car, and turned off his headlights. If anyone came by, Jack didn't want them to spot him.

He grabbed his gas can, slung the rifle over his shoulder, and watched Shane's truck. Shane didn't move.

*Excellent.*

The doe's mournful, whining bleat carried through the silent night, ghostly and eerie. After he took care of Shane, Jack would put the deer out of her misery.

He took off at a run toward the accident site. He was nearly halfway there when the lights of another car coming around the bend lit up the ground fog. Jack swore to himself and fell to his belly on the ground again, hoping a Good Samaritan hadn't just arrived on the scene to disrupt his mission.

To his dismay, the car slowed and pulled over to the narrow shoulder of the road. The driver put the emergency flashers on.

Jack put his scope to his eyes to get a better look just as a woman stepped out of the car.

His heart pounded. *Damn it all! What's Willow doing out now?*

As Willow ran to Shane's truck Jack lowered his rifle and listened to the deer bleating over the sound of Willow calling Shane's name.

"Shane! Shane! Can you hear me? Are you all right?" Willow stood on her tiptoes and banged on the driver's window of Shane's truck.

*No response.*

The front of his truck was crumpled into the tree and smoking and hissing. Had Shane even braked?

The dark shape of a wounded deer lay on the ground about twenty feet away. The deer bleated mournfully, raising the hair on Willow's arms and neck.

*Poor, poor thing.*

Willow leaned in to peer into the driver's side window. Her breath fogged the glass. She wiped it away with her sleeve.

Shane was slumped over the wheel. A trickle of blood, black in the moonlight, ran down the side of his head.

He wasn't moving. She tried the door, but it was either jammed, locked, or both. She tried the passenger door. Same thing.

She looked around desperately for help as she pulled her cell phone from her pocket and dialed 911. "There's been an accident on Loop Road Two. Shane Kennett hit a deer and wrapped his truck around a tree. . . .

"No, he's not moving. I can't get to him. His doors are locked or jammed shut. And the deer's hurt and crying. Send an ambulance. Please, please hurry!"

She barely registered what the operator told her, except that help was on the way. Her fingers shook as she slid her phone shut and the deer continued to cry.

She should have asked them to send a vet. She'd been too upset to ask. Somehow she made it to her car and found her emergency kit and blanket.

She grabbed the blanket and went to the deer.

"You'll be all right," she crooned to the doe as she put the blanket over her. But she lied. She had no idea whether the deer would live through the night or whether the coyotes would come for her.

Willow wrapped her arms around herself and shuddered. Then she went to Shane's pickup and leaned against it as she waited for help to arrive.

Jack watched Willow and the accident from a distance. Was she covering the deer with a blanket? His Pendleton wool Yellowstone National Park blanket? That thing cost several hundred bucks.

He shook his head at her tender heart as he settled in. No way he was leaving Willow alone with the Rooster, even on the hope he was dead.

The fog covered Jack's misty breath as he waited. About five minutes later, an ambulance, a paramedic crew, and the police arrived.

It didn't take them long to get Kennett out of the car and load him onto a stretcher while the police interviewed Willow. Unfortunately, Kennett was moving.

Finally, they loaded Kennett into the ambulance and it sped off. A tow truck arrived. Willow got into her car and pulled away. Jack seized his opportunity to head to Kennett's to gather some intel.

Willow dropped her keys on the kitchen table and collapsed onto her sofa, still shaken from coming upon the accident. Shane drank too much. He wasn't careful—

*Duke and Buddy!* Shane's killer Brazilian Filas. They were really just softies when you knew how to handle them. Who was going to feed them now? To Willow's dismay, Shane kept them on the edge of hunger. He fed them once a day right before he went to bed. But he hadn't made it home today.

*Oh, the poor things!* She couldn't stand to think of his dogs hungry and thirsty and on their own. He treated them badly enough as it was. Behind his back, she frequently stopped by, brought them treats, and showed them some gentle loving. She had those vicious dogs eating out of her hand. She was almost as good with dogs as Jack had been.

She got to her feet. She really didn't want to go past the accident scene again. What about that poor deer? But she couldn't sleep, knowing Duke and Buddy would be scrounging for food. They'd be locked in the house. Fortunately, Grant Cooper had shown her where he kept a key hidden outside. Shane was just staying in Grant's place while he was here. She doubted he'd moved the key.

The thought of going into the old farmhouse creeped her out. Built in the 1920s, it had all the eccentricities, creaks, and moans one would expect of something its age. Local legend held that the previous owner was a crazy old loon who haunted the place.

But instead of sensing a haunting, all Willow felt at his place was a vague sense of evil. And totally perplexed that any sane person would have picked the hideous wallpaper in the kitchen.

Locals knew that Old Man Terrence had died in his bed in the house a few years into the twenty-first century. He'd wanted to pass away in his 1960s bomb shelter, just in case the end of the world came while he was dying. He wasn't convinced the Soviets no longer existed, claiming the breakup of the USSR in 1991 was all a clever hoax. He didn't want them dropping the bomb on him during his final minutes.

His son, who hated his old man, refused his last request. Terrence hadn't changed a thing in the house after his wife died some years before he did. He died in his fussy bed upstairs, surrounded by dusty pink frills, cursing until his last breath. Rumor had it that he haunted the bomb shelter, waiting for final annihilation so he could be vindicated for all the flack he took about the shelter all those years.

His son sold the house to Grant Cooper. He'd only made one improvement—he'd locked the bomb shelter.

Ghost of Old Man Terrence or not, Willow didn't want to go there alone.

She grabbed her cell phone and called Con.

Having tranquilized Kennett's dogs and locked them in the bathroom, Jack was making a thorough examination of Grant Cooper's home, if you could call it that. House, maybe. The place was about as homey as the mausoleum of an old lady. The peeling floral wallpaper alone was enough to set Jack's teeth on edge. The Rooster had picked a hell of a place to roost while he was here.

Jack's cell phone buzzed. *Damn, what now?* He looked at the number. *Willow.*

*Shit.* He couldn't ignore Willow. He glanced at his watch. One AM. Con would be asleep at the guesthouse. Jack answered, trying to sound groggy, as if he'd just been pulled out of sleep in Aldo's comfy queen-size guest bed.

"Con!" Willow sounded relieved, frustrated, fragile.

Jack suppressed his instinctive protective urges. "Willow?"

"Did I wake you?" Willow asked.

Jack would have told her, *No, I had to get up to get the phone anyway.* Since that's what Jack would do, Con couldn't.

"No problem. What's wrong? What's happened? Are you all right?" He knew very well what had happened. She'd inadvertently foiled his mission and rescued the enemy.

Wives on missions—a damned nuisance! Every spy he knew said so.

He could hope Kennett had died due to his injuries. Death by deer seemed like a good, ironic end to an assassin like the Rooster. Jack certainly wouldn't be shedding any tears over him.

Sadly, Jack wasn't optimistic. The crash didn't look lethal. And Jack was a pretty good judge of lethal.

"I'm fine. It's Shane. He hit a deer on his way home." She launched into a brief explanation that pretty much matched the facts as Jack had observed them.

At appropriate intervals, he made sympathetic noises.

"Now I'm worried about Shane's dogs," Willow said. "He feeds them right before bed. I know he'd appreciate it if someone stopped by tonight and fed them. I'm the only one who can handle them."

*Damn. The best-laid plans.*

"I don't want to go to his place alone this late at night. It's, well, it's creepy out there in the best of times. I know it's a lot to ask, but would you go with me?"

Jack didn't want her out there alone, ever. Besides the dogs, which were a bit loopy right now, any number of terrorists or assassins could be hanging out at Kennett's. Just as Jack currently was.

Jack jumped in to head her off. "You stay where you are. I'll go."

"Oh, that's sweet. But you'll need the key. I know where one's hidden. It's kind of tricky to find in the dark."

*Like hell he did.*

"And Shane's Filas will tear you apart if they don't know you."

He glanced toward the bathroom door. *Not if you come armed with sedatives.*

"They're bred to be aggressive and obey only their master, but they're really just sweeties at heart once you get to know them and learn how to handle them," Willow said.

Jack doubted that. Filas were so aggressive they couldn't be trusted around anyone other than their owners.

"I'm the only one who can handle them. They like me. They'd attack anyone else. I still don't know how Sam and Gus got past them the other night when they took Shane home. He must have been coherent enough to handle them."

Willow had disarmed Kennett's guard dogs. Why did that not surprise Jack? She had him cornered. He couldn't figure out how to wiggle out of this one and stop her from coming to Kennett's.

"I'll pick you up," he said. "Give me fifteen minutes to wake up and throw some clothes on."

Damn, now how was he going to explain the drugged dogs?

As promised, fifteen minutes later, bundled in a designer jacket only a dandy like Con would wear, Jack pulled into Willow's driveway. He'd only had to drive back to Aldo's, making a quick stop to put that deer out of her misery on the way, and retrieve his blanket, change, and head back out. A hell of a feat for fifteen minutes. He didn't even have to get out of the car to get Willow. As he expected, she'd been waiting and watching for him. She dashed out of the house, breath frosty in the night air, the moment he pulled up.

Seeing her made him want to wrap his arms around her and protect her. If he had half a brain and an ounce of courage, he'd grab her and run somewhere neither RIOT nor the Agency would find them. Unfortunately, such a place didn't exist, not to his knowledge. Too many before him had tried to run and failed. Whether it took five minutes or ten years, RIOT and the Agency would find him. He rubbed his hands together and smiled at the woman he loved enough to die for and stay dead for as she got into the car.

"Con!" Her eyes lit up when she smiled at him. "Thanks for coming."

They made the four-minute drive in silence.

The Cooper house stood dark and foreboding in the fog and eerie blue light emanating from a mercury vapor light on the pole above. It didn't take much imagination to picture it on the front of a Halloween greeting card. They got out. He followed Willow to a plastic rock with a key hidden inside and then to the front door.

"I can see why you don't want to go in there alone," Jack quipped. "Freddy Krueger won't be waiting inside with an ax, will he?"

Willow laughed and shook her head as he followed her to the door. "Yeah, it's a bit of a fixer-upper, isn't it? Grant isn't really into home repair. But the fog is adding to the atmosphere. Don't believe all the ghost stories you hear around town about it, either."

"There are ghost stories?"

She ignored Jack's question, slid the key in, and unlocked the door.

He angled to get past her. "I'll check it out first."

Willow blocked him with her arm. "You'd better let me. Duke and Buddy will tear you apart."

"I think you just crushed my machismo," Jack said.

She gave him a smile that made him want to kiss her as she reached into her pocket and pulled out two dog treats. "Sorry, but you don't have the proper ammo."

"Dog treats? That's all it takes?"

She shook her head. "And a lot of love and attention." She lowered her voice to a whisper, even though there was no one else around to hear and Willow didn't know about the Rooster's secret, and deadly, occupation.

Good thing Jack had disabled all of Kennett's bugs and security devices earlier. Jack was pretty sure that feeding Kennett's dogs and invading his private territory was tantamount to signing your death warrant.

"I'll let you in on a little secret—Buddy and Duke think I'm their owner. But don't tell Shane. It will hurt his feelings."

Hurt his feelings? Who the hell cared if Kennett got his tiny feelings hurt? Jack frowned his puzzlement at

Willow. Why would the dogs think she was their master and did he really want to know?

Willow nodded as if he'd asked a question aloud. "Yes, really."

Willow seemed to know what she was talking about, so he followed her in. Plus, old Duke and Buddy were going to be lethargic and wobbly on their feet for another four or five hours at least. He'd given them a gentle dose of PromAce. There was really no danger.

"Brace yourself. The boys can be exuberant."

*Not tonight,* Jack thought.

Willow flipped a light on. "Duke and Bud! Where are you boys?"

Nothing but the complete lack of pitter-patter of big bad dog feet, and the wheezing of the old house as the furnace kicked on. The kitchen was empty.

Willow let out an ear-piercing whistle.

Jack jumped.

She waved the dog treats in the air, made that sucking noise people use to call dogs, and patted her thighs. "Here, boys! Here, boys!"

"I thought Filas were vicious guard dogs," Jack said. "Shouldn't they be attacking us by now?"

Willow frowned. She turned to Jack, a look of fear and apprehension on her face. "Duke! Bud!"

"Are you sure going looking for them is a good idea?" Jack said.

She grabbed Jack's arm. "Something must be wrong. Usually, they'd be beating down the door before I even got out of the car. What if they've gotten out and are gone?" Her voice cracked.

She really cared about them. That was Willow—always falling for the dangerous types.

"We'll find them," he said. He knew exactly where

they were. "Do they have a kennel or dog beds some-where?"

"Shane's mentioned their beds are in the living room." She hesitated. "But I've never been in there. Shane doesn't like having people over." She looked around the place. "And who can blame him? This place is a dump. He re-ally should talk to Grant and convince him to fix it up when he gets back."

Jack had the feeling Grant was never coming back and just hoped he and Willow didn't stumble upon his dead body while they were feeding the dogs. If the Rooster had any common sense he'd buried Grant in the orchards somewhere. In a deep grave.

Jack looked around and sniffed. "Is that beer I smell?" Yeah, he'd staged an explanation for the dogs' drugged behavior.

"Yeah, I smell it, too, but that's nothing. The house al-ways smells like beer."

"Ah yeah, but look at that." He pointed to the counter where a six-pack lay tipped over. And then to the floor where two broken bottles lay, surrounded by traces of their contents.

Willow's hand flew to her mouth. "Oh no!"

"Yeah," Jack said, really playing for Willow's sympa-thies. "Look at their water bowls—empty."

Her eyes went wide. "The poor desperate things! Dogs will drink anything when they're thirsty. Alcohol can kill them. We have to find them!" She took off for the living room.

"Wait a minute! Hold on. What if they attack?"

He followed her deep into the house.

She turned on lights and waved the dog treats around like talismans. "They won't."

He nearly ran over her as she came to a sudden stop in front of him. "There you are!"

The dogs lolled in their beds where Jack had left them, looking three sheets to the wind and smelling of beer. He'd doused their muzzles with it for authenticity.

"Oh, poor babies!" Willow squatted and called to them.

One of the massive dogs lumbered to his feet and swayed as he took a step toward her. The other just raised his head, looked at Willow as she waved a dog treat, and put his head back down.

"They look as drunk as you said their owner was," Jack said.

Willow ignored him and ran to them. She fell to her knees to pet them before Jack could stop her. As she stroked them and tried to coax them into eating the treats, she looked up at Jack. "What's wrong with all the dogs around here lately?"

"What do you mean?"

"When I came home this evening, Spookie scared me, too. She was so tired, she didn't come running to see me when I came home, like she usually does. And she was too pooped to play."

"But she's okay now?" Jack's alarm just popped out.

Willow looked at him, studying him. A triumphant look shone on her face, as if she'd pulled a fast one over on him and gotten him to reveal a damning fact. "She's fine. Thanks for your concern."

*Damn.*

The cause of Spookie's tiredness hit him a second too late—he'd been playing with her while Willow was gone. He'd probably worn poor Spookie out. The little mutt was no doubt out of shape from too little exercise and too much pampering.

He would have laughed aloud if Willow hadn't been there, studying him as if something was up as she rubbed one of the Filas behind the ear.

Jack put on an innocent expression. "How is it that those two let you get so close?"

"I told you, they think I'm their mistress. If Shane lets them outside, they'll go to the end of the driveway and howl and whine for me. I've spoiled them, really."

Jack gave her a quizzical look, hoping to prod her into telling the story without him having to ask outright.

"Do you think we should call the vet?" she asked Jack.

"They're pretty big dogs. They probably weigh more than you do," he said, slowly, knowing they'd be just fine but wanting to appear concerned. "I only saw two broken bottles. That doesn't seem like enough to do them any real harm. I think they'll be okay. Get some water in them so they don't dehydrate and let them sleep it off."

"Yeah, you're probably right. Watch them a minute while I clean up the mess, will you? I don't want them stepping in the glass."

"Are you sure I'll be safe with them?" Jack put on a worried expression and nodded toward the animals.

"They're sloshed. I think you'll be fine."

"What if they're mean drunks?"

Willow laughed. "You'll be fine. They look like sleepy drunks to me."

"All right then." He tried to sound uncertain, though he was completely confident he was safe.

"If they make a move, yell, and I'll come running." Willow winked at him and walked off toward the kitchen. He heard her banging around in there and then the tinkle of glass as she swept it up and dumped it in the garbage.

Finally, she came back into the living room. "Come on, boys! Come on, Duke."

The rusty-brown Fila stumbled after her. Buddy just looked at them and put his head down as if he wanted to go back to sleep.

Jack followed Willow and the dog into the kitchen. She led the dog to his water bowl and made him drink.

"Watch this guy while I give his brother a drink."

"And she leaves me with a dangerous animal a second time."

She rolled her eyes and ignored Jack as she went to give Bud a drink. She was back quickly with the bowl and set it by the other water dish. "I wonder where Shane keeps their food?"

"The pantry?" Jack suggested.

He watched as she went to the pantry with the dogs' food bowls. She rustled around and opened a fifty-pound bag of dog food, grabbed a scoop, and filled the bowls to heaping. "The dogs are how I met Shane."

Probably accidentally on purpose. The Rooster would have studied Willow and known exactly how to get to her, what she liked, what would attract her. He'd know she loved dogs and would have used them to meet Willow. How long had the Rooster suspected Jack was still alive?

"He's a private man, kept to himself except for going to Beck's several times a week and Bluff Country to have coffee in the morning.

"Then he bought Duke and Buddy from a breeder across the state. He brought them into town in the back of his truck. They were practically pups and so cute. They'd howl for him while he was in having his coffee. I couldn't stand it. The poor things were so lonely. They needed a mama.

"So I started making larger batches of treats when I baked for Spookie and bringing them along when I went to Bluff Country. Duke and Buddy fell in love with me. Didn't you, Duke?" She rubbed the dog's head.

*Who wouldn't fall in love with you?* Jack thought.

The furnace shut off. The house popped. Something

banged overhead on the second story. The house shook and the sound of irregular footsteps echoed on the stairs.

Duke gave a pathetic, weak growl that any self-respecting Fila should be ashamed of. The dog took three steps as if he was going after an intruder, then stumbled, and fell over.

*Great, just great. Thanks to me, even the guard dog can't walk a straight line.*

At the same time, Willow screamed. The next thing Jack knew, she was wrapped in his arms. And she felt damn good there.

He curled himself protectively around her. Jack cursed beneath his breath, ready to go for his gun, hoping Willow didn't feel either gun bulging in his pants.

# CHAPTER THIRTEEN

This operation was going to kill Jack in more ways than one. Or blow his cover. All kinds of dire thoughts crossed his mind, like a SMASH assassin hiding in Kennett's house, waiting to take him out for double-crossing RIOT. And Willow and Jack being in the wrong place at the wrong time and ending up as collateral damage. Although Jack *was* responsible for the double-crossing. He might have appreciated the irony if he hadn't been worried about Willow's safety. SMASH was RIOT'S death squad. They were ruthless.

Jack hadn't gone to all this trouble for the cover of death to be killed as a by-product of someone else trying to take out Kennett. And yet if he acted to protect himself and Willow, he'd blow his cover. *Hobson's choice.*

For the moment, he chose protecting his cover. Only because the house had gone stonily silent.

And so had they. Neither of them spoke.

After a safe, but tense, interval, Jack whispered, "What was that?"

Willow looked up into his eyes. He had to hold himself back from kissing her. She smelled of something that gave him ideas of a tumble in bed, and if there were a SMASH assassin on the premises this might be Jack's last chance to kiss her before his death became real.

She looked up at him, inching her lips closer to his,

totally unaware of the real potential for danger. "Old Man Terrence haunting the bomb shelter?"

*Oh, shit! She thinks we're playing scary movie or haunted house here.*

"Bomb shelter?" Jack stared at her intently. "I've heard rumors about one and a ghost. Is it beneath the house?"

"Beneath the apple barn. The entrance is a trapdoor just behind the cash register. Shane keeps it locked with a padlock."

Jack arched a brow, trying not to inch closer to Willow's lips now that the threat of danger seemed to be waning. A SMASH assassin would have shot them by now if he intended to. Still, losing his head in a kiss wasn't the smartest idea. "A padlock will keep a ghost out? Never heard that before. Maybe someone should tell those guys on *TAPS*."

"I love your accent," Willow said, out of the blue. "It's sexy." She pressed into him.

Good thing he still had the designer jacket on. It kept him from feeling the soft, delicious warmth of her body and losing control.

"I think the lock's more to keep curious kids out."

"Do you believe in ghosts?" he asked.

Willow let out a heavy sigh. "I believe in life after death." She paused. "I have to."

She didn't know how on target she was. After all, he was still alive after his official death. He wished he could reassure her; instead he kept his face neutral.

Beside them, good old Duke staggered back to his feet and lumbered toward the door into the living room, doing his best to growl and bark. His bark still didn't score high on the menace scale. But Jack gave him credit for trying. If that drugged guard dog was game for checking out the house, so was he. No one could say a dog outdid him in the courage department.

Jack forced himself back away from the siren look in Willow's eyes that was calling him to renounce his cover, took a step out of kissing range, grabbed a can of soup sitting on the counter next to him, and handed it to Willow. "Duke and I are going to check out the house. Stay here and defend yourself."

"With soup?"

"Sure; paired with a strong throwing arm, soup is good ammo. If someone threatens you, let him have it."

"My fastball won't make the majors. And this will float right through a ghost."

"If you see a ghost, run like hell for the car." Jack shrugged and pointed after Duke. "My partner's leaving without me."

"No way." Willow shook her head. "I'm not staying here alone. This reminds me too much of a scene from *Halloween*."

"Which one?"

"All of them."

"You aren't babysitting."

"I'm watching the dogs."

She had him there. "Okay, I guess that counts. Just stay back." He followed Duke through the living room toward the stairs.

Duke howled, made as if he was going to dash to the stairs, and fell over with the effort. Jack took pity on him and moved toward him, hoping to help the poor dog to his feet. It was the least he could do. But Duke growled at him and bared his teeth as Jack approached and reached for him.

"Jeez," Jack said, pulling his fingers back out of nipping range just in time. "Dogs usually like me."

"I've heard that before," Willow said, sounding completely unconvinced. "Duke, leave Con alone."

Jack gave up on the dog. A tennis ball lay at the bottom

of the stairs. Jack was certain it hadn't been there before. He picked it up and held it for Willow to see. "Looks like this may be our culprit." He looked up the stairs.

"Poltergeists?"

"Settling houses. There's a bin of balls for the dogs at the top of the stairs. When the furnace shut off, the house shuddered and this ball rolled out and thumped its way down the stairs. That's what I'm guessing. It was only footsteps in our imaginations. Stay here while I check the second floor out."

She rolled her eyes. "What about the bang we heard before the footsteps? That was right over our heads."

"That's what I'm going to check out."

"I'm going with you."

"No way." Jack used his firm *don't argue with me* tone. "You stay here and run for help if I don't come back in a reasonable amount of time."

She looked at him, shrugged, and went to comfort Duke as Bud snored in his bed. "Call if you need help and we'll come running."

Jack laughed. "Maybe *you* will, but I'm not counting on the dogs."

At the top of the stairs, out of sight from Willow, Jack drew his gun. A floorboard creaked as he entered the master bedroom. He scanned the room, gun in front of him, ready to take out any intruder.

Kennett's dead friend Grant really needed to fire his interior decorator *and* his cleaning lady. The place was a mismatched hodgepodge of ugly and uglier. A lot of the old-lady décor up here, too. And the musty smell of a house that needed airing and dusting.

Jack hadn't had much time in this room before Willow called, but everything looked pretty much as he remembered. Except for a work boot, which had toppled off a shoe rack onto the floor. That explained the thump they'd heard.

He relaxed. Simple explanation—an old, settling house, and sloppily stored shoes falling off shelves. Nothing sinister there.

He surveyed the room all the same. His gaze fell on the nightstand and the hair stood up on the back of his neck. Someone *had* been here. In the last fifteen minutes while he was doubling back for Willow.

Kennett's alarm clock was in a different spot. Jack could tell by the dust pattern on the nightstand. There was now a clean spot on the wood where the clock should still be. The settling hadn't caused that.

He checked the closet and underneath the bed. Then he moved to the bathroom and two remaining bedrooms.

"Everything okay up there?" Willow called to him from the bottom of the stairs.

*Yeah, just peachy. But empty. Whoever was here is long gone now.*

"Yeah. I think I found the culprit." He raced back to Kennett's room and grabbed the boot. He carried it to the top of the stairs to show Willow. "This fell out of the shoe rack."

Willow put a hand to her heart, let out a breath of relief, and laughed. "Scared spitless by an old shoe."

"Yeah, we're a pair." He grinned, trying to keep his anxiety from showing. "I think our job is done here. The haunting is debunked."

She shook her head. "This time. Next time we'll have to be more scientific. We'd better bring a deluxe EMF meter and an EVP spirit box."

The kind of spook that worried Jack wasn't the kind that showed up on EVPs. Still, he grinned. "Those sound cool. I like gadgets."

"Yeah, I can tell by the way your eyes lit up."

"Let's get out of here." He grabbed her arm. "It's creepy being here uninvited. What if Kennett comes back and finds us?"

She nodded.

"This stays between us. Neither of us can mention anything about being here, feeding the dogs, them being drunk. . . ." Jack tried to sound casual. But his sense of urgency must have slipped through.

Her eyes went wide. She nodded. "Sure. Mum's the word. This random act of kindness is just between us."

Con drove Willow home and walked her to her door.

"Thanks for coming with me." She paused, not wanting Con to leave, not wanting to go back into the house alone. These past few days had just been too much. And tonight—all the hurt and injury, she was overwhelmed. She needed comfort. She needed Jack.

Con took her in his arms. "Hey, it's all right. The dogs are fine, thanks to us. Shane will live. You're just tired and need some rest." He tipped her chin up and looked into her eyes.

Her breath caught.

His face bent to hers.

She leaned up into him. Their lips met and it was like coming home. To Jack.

She wrapped her arms around his neck and opened her mouth to him. The Sense screamed at her, *This is Jack. This is Jack!*

It was an ethereal knowledge deep in her soul. This man was Jack. She just knew it. He had to be. And if he wasn't, she wanted him anyway.

She opened her mouth to him and suppressed a groan of pleasure. He tasted like Jack. He kissed like Jack, with a gentle probing dance of his tongue. With pressure to keep her melded to him as if they really were one.

But this man kissed her hungrily, the way Jack did when he'd been away on a mission too long.

Jack *had* been gone too long. Far too long.

Con pulled away from the kiss suddenly. He ran his hand through his hair and stuffed both of his hands into his pockets as if he didn't trust himself to keep them to himself. As if he was on the edge of losing control completely.

She thought about pushing him, this man who could be Jack, to the edge, inviting him in. Begging him to come in. She wanted her tiger. She wanted to know for sure whether Con was Jack or simply a man she could love. She wanted to make love to him and hear Jack's sexy chuff. Or Con's grunt of pleasure. Either sound would tell her the truth.

The chuff would give him away as *her* Jack. She wanted Jack back, no matter what he'd done, or where he'd been, or where he was planning to go from here. But she hesitated just a second too long.

He cleared his throat and stared at the ground. He was under control again.

Sadly, she knew she'd missed her opportunity. Next time she wouldn't think; she'd simply act.

Con pulled his keys from his pocket. "Good night. I'll see you Monday."

On Monday, he wouldn't get away.

# CHAPTER FOURTEEN

On Sunday morning before seven, Jack lounged in a leather recliner in Aldo's guesthouse reading the Sunday paper and sipping a dark-chocolate mint mocha that he'd had to drive twenty minutes out of town to get. Yes, he'd gone rogue and gotten what he wanted, damn it all. He had to satisfy one of his cravings before he went crazy and went to Willow's to do what he really wanted—make love to his wife.

Which would blow everything to hell.

The sun still wasn't up. Jack liked the peace and quiet of the morning.

The guesthouse was a one-bedroom, one-main-room, one-bathroom affair. The kitchen occupied the wall opposite where Jack sat in direct line to the bedroom. Though the kitchen was small, Aldo had spared no expense on it. He'd lined the counters with fine Italian marble, installed Italian tile backsplashes, and put in top-quality stainless-steel appliances. A round, four-person table and chairs completed the ensemble.

The apartment was homey and upscale, decorated in a rooster motif and Italian design, with vases and wreaths of fall flowers. Except for the rooster motif, Jack liked it. He'd like it even more once Kennett was dead. Damn, that man had nine lives.

Jack opened the paper to the Sunday crossword and pulled a pen out of his pocket. Doing the crossword cleared his mind and opened him up to creativity, which he sure as hell needed right now—a creative way to kill. One Willow wouldn't inadvertently interrupt.

He'd thought about sneaking into the hospital where Kennett had had to stay overnight for observation and taking Kennett out. He'd even scoped it out. But it was too dangerous and had too little chance of success. Too many medical people around to revive Kennett. Not enough time to figure out their schedules. Too many questions would be asked. In a cost-benefit analysis, the risk of failure outweighed the chance of success. So Jack would have to chill, be patient.

He started the crossword. *A five-letter word for low point . . .*

He became so engrossed in the puzzle, he almost didn't hear the gentle click coming from the kitchen. Almost. He cocked an ear.

*Click. Click, click. Click.*

The little apartment was full of pops and hisses, the bump as the gas furnace ignited and kicked on, the whisper of the furnace fan. But this was something different.

Jack pushed the footrest down, set the paper and pen in the chair, and stood, listening. *Click. Click, click. Click.*

Not an explosive. Not a detonator noise he recognized. It sounded like . . . an oven turning on and warming up. At that moment, he glanced across the room at Aldo's beautiful glass-top stainless-steel oven. The electronic display glowed orange-yellow, happily lit to display the setting and rising temperature.

*Broil. Four fifty. What the hell?*

He hadn't turned the oven on.

Acting on instinct, Jack pushed the recliner aside, jumped out of the line of fire of the oven, and rushed toward it. Standing off to the side of it, he fumbled with the controls, found the OFF button, turned the thing off, and opened the oven door at the exact instant the oven fired a bullet at him.

It whizzed past him and where he'd been sitting in the chair and sliced through the wall between the bedroom and living room. If he'd slept in and been in bed or was still in the chair, he'd be dead.

Jack swore beneath his breath.

*Damn that Kennett! What the hell else has the Rooster booby-trapped?*

Jack took a look around the room with a trained eye. His range of motion around the apartment was limited until the oven cooled down and he could disable the gun. He couldn't risk stepping into the line of fire. Place a gun in an oven, heat it up, and it will discharge.

*Very creative, Kennett. Not particularly effective, but creative.*

Had it been successful, no one would have suspected Kennett, not when he'd been in the hospital having his vitals checked every half hour. Jack wondered whether the Rooster had slipped in and set the oven timer or he'd rigged it so he could arm it remotely. *Remotely* seemed like the most efficient and certain way to make a clean kill. And the Rooster was sneaky—the gun had been quiet. He'd even used a silencer.

Jack did routine sweeps of the guesthouse for bugs and monitoring cameras, which had most certainly thrown the Rooster off and made him take a gamble that Jack would be in bed at the time of the shooting.

Jack shook his head. He had to take that asshole out soon.

The bathroom wasn't in the direct line of oven fire and was the next most lethal room in the place. Jack had been out all night and was so groggy when he got home and again when he'd gotten up, he hadn't paid much attention when he'd used it.

He scoped it out now with a keen eye. An aerosol can of germ-killing cleaner sat on the heating vent.

Heat an aerosol can up and it will explode. Jack wasn't certain the vent would blow hot enough air to explode a regular can, but he had a feeling this can was specially modified to blow up when the Rooster wanted it to. He removed the can and stored it in the explosive containment container he'd brought.

He unscrewed the showerhead and found it filled with powder that would produce poisonous gas when water coursed through it. A careful search turned up nothing else.

Jack didn't scare easily.

He went back into the kitchen. The oven had cooled enough for him to take a look. He grabbed a pot holder from a drawer and, using caution, removed the pistol from the oven. He shook his head.

The serial number had been filed off and he was certain there'd be no prints. Jack set it on the counter and followed the line of fire into the bedroom, where he dug the slug out of the wall.

He didn't like the fact that the Rooster had gotten past his security measures. Time to step up things around here. He grabbed his laptop and listening gear and did a quick check on Willow's place to make sure she was safe, lingering a second to watch her as she sat sipping her morning coffee, braless in a sheer tank top, as she pounded away on her laptop. He knew what he'd rather be pounding. He also knew what she was doing when he looked at the keystroke-monitoring software. She was trying to get the dirt on him.

*Good luck, baby.*

When he was satisfied she was safe, he grumbled and forced himself to turn off the laptop and think about something other than Willow. He was going to have to fix

Aldo's walls. And jam the gun to make it look as if it hadn't fired. Just in case Kennett came back for it. Which Jack was sure he would try.

Well, good for him if he did. Jack was going to lace the damn thing with poison.

Jack took a look out the window. The sun was rising over the mountains to the east, lighting up the world with a breathtaking sunrise. A herd of deer walked across one of Aldo's fields.

*Damn deer.*

It was hunting season. Too bad he didn't have a license. He could go for a taste of venison.

Jack grinned. He might not have a license to hunt deer, but he sure as hell had a license to kill the Rooster. In fact, Jack had something even better—a direct order.

He returned to his newspaper, picked it up, and began to hum. As a kid, he'd made all kinds of things out of newspaper—hats, boats, papier-mâché masks, and volcanoes. As an adult spy, he knew exactly what he was going to make out of this one—a paper crossbow. Yes, few people, even those in law enforcement, realized that an arrow fired from a paper crossbow could be perfectly lethal.

And destroying the evidence, so easy! Burn the crossbow and presto, no weapon. It was archery hunting season. And accidents did happen. . . .

Willow sat at her kitchen table with her laptop open, going over Con's online presence again, frustrated in her search to out Con as Jack. At least she'd sold out her caramel yesterday and didn't have to be in town manning her booth.

She grabbed her smartphone and studied the picture she'd secretly snapped of Con yesterday.

She saw a straight nose instead of a crooked one. Perfectly white teeth instead of slightly imperfect ones. A

slightly different shape to his cheekbones, more promi-
nence. And Jack's eyes. *Jack's.*

Which all fit if he'd been blown up and had reconstructive surgery.

She needed help, big-time. Scientific help. She had to
find out the truth before Con left town and disappeared.
Because if he really was Jack, he'd disappear without a
trace.

Willow needed a DNA collection kit. She could ven-
ture half an hour out into the neighboring big city and get
one. No big deal. But it wouldn't do her a bit of good if
Con left town before she got the results. It would take
three to ten business days at least; that's what all the Web
sites said. And, of course, she needed that DNA report to
compare the sample she took from Con to.

None of the test kit sites mentioned anything about
comparing their results to a findings sheet. They all com-
pared samples to samples.

She also needed a good bug-sweeping company. But
none were open until Monday.

She closed her computer. It was almost eleven. The
stores should be open by the time she got there. She'd better grab the report and take it along so she could ask
about it when she bought the kit.

Now that she thought about it, she also had Jack's hairbrush with several strands of hair on it. That might work
better. Maybe they could test that. But she was loathe to
part with even a strand of it. She hoped the report would
suffice.

Of course, the CIA had Jack's DNA on file. But she
couldn't have their lab run the test. She'd never trust Emmett to tell her the truth. Especially since she suspected
him of concocting Jack's death.

She slid off her chair and rushed to the bedroom, got

on her knees, and pulled out the memory box she'd made
to remember Jack.

The box was slightly out of place, skewed. She didn't
remember leaving it like this. Oh, well, she probably accidentally hit it with the vacuum or something.

She pulled the box out from beneath the bed, removed
the lid, and carefully lifted the folded flag, feeling, as always, the deep sense of loss. Beneath it was the report,
and then the little crystal dog collar that always made her
tear up.

And then, her heart stopped. The coffee sleeve from
the first time she met Jack sat on top of everything else.
The hair on the back of her neck stood up. This was becoming its permanent position.

She always kept that sleeve at the bottom of the box.
*Always.*

Someone had been through her box.

*Jack.*

She swallowed hard and pawed through it, looking for
Jack's brush. Nothing. It was gone. She took every item
out one at a time. Jack's brush had vanished.

She would never, ever have misplaced it.

She swallowed hard as a horrible suspicion dawned
on her—the report she had was probably bogus. That's
why whoever had been in her room hadn't bothered to
take it. The hair on that brush, however, was Jack's, un-
doubtedly Jack's.

She pulled her own hair and resisted screaming. Jack's
beautiful dark hair was gone. Her precious memento and
her one true chance at Jack's DNA, gone.

She sat on the bed, freaked out of her mind. She truthfully didn't know whether to feel more scared or more
optimistic. Someone had taken that hair. Who even knew
about this box besides her and Spookie?

The only person with motive to take the hair was Con,

if he was Jack. But how could he know about it? She'd never mentioned it. But if he was a spy . . .

She had to think. Think, think, think!

She needed help, really needed help now. There was only one person she could trust to help her. Well, actually two—her good friend Staci Fields and her husband, Drew. Drew was a CIA agent and had been one of Jack's best friends. Drew was with Jack on that fateful mission when Jack was blown up. Drew had been injured, too. Just not fatally.

Willow couldn't believe Drew would have lied to her all this time. No, if Jack was alive, Drew must not know. His wife, Staci, had been with him on the mission to the city of smugglers and drug lords, Ciudad del Este, Paraguay.

Jack and Drew were assigned to bring down a dangerous drug cartel. At least, that's what Jack told her, all he could tell her. Willow had always been opposed to violence and, unlike other wives, had never gone on one of Jack's missions with him. Staci had begged Drew to finally take her on a mission, so he took her to Paraguay.

Willow sighed. That mission had proved to be fateful for her friendship with Staci, too.

Drew relented and finally agreed to take Staci with him, provided she stay in a separate apartment from his and that they both keep her identity and their relationship a secret. Somehow, Willow never did know how, the horrible drug lord Beto Bevilacqua discovered that Staci was Drew's wife, tracked her down, and tortured out of her information about where Drew and Jack were going to be that fateful night.

The Bevil, as the Agency referred to Beto, sent his men out after Jack and Drew. The drug lord's men blew them up. Drew was badly injured. Jack was blown up into pieces, many too small to recover. Staci blamed herself for what had happened, saying she'd told the Bevil where to find Jack and Drew.

Willow sighed and shook her head. She believed in forgiveness and had never blamed Staci. What was there to blame her for? For thugs torturing information out of her? Staci had spent a week in the hospital herself. And then she'd separated from Drew because of her guilt. They'd only recently reconciled.

Willow sighed again. Staci had apologized a dozen times, even though Willow asked her to stop. Finally, they'd drifted apart. Willow realized it was because of Staci's guilt.

Jack, Drew, and a third friend, Kyle Harris, met as trainees at the CIA training facility The Farm. All three men were from Seattle and became good friends. When they each married, their wives became good friends, too. Kyle was dead, gone before Jack. Murdered by terrorists in Afghanistan. Willow and Kyle's widow, Mandy, kept in touch. But Willow really missed Staci.

If Jack was alive and Drew could prove it, it would relieve Staci's burden of guilt. And Drew would want to know that his best friend lived; of course he would. Drew would help Willow find out for sure, wouldn't he? Maybe bend a few Agency rules? To get his best friend back?

Because bend them he'd have to. Willow didn't want NCS chief Emmett Nelson to get wind of what she was up to. Not until she knew the truth about Con. She needed Drew's help if she was going to find out the truth.

She closed up the box, stuffed it back under the bed, grabbed her cell phone, and auto dialed Staci.

"Staci, I think Jack's still alive. He's here in Orchard Bluff, pretending to be someone else. I need your help."

# CHAPTER FIFTEEN

"What?" Staci's shock reverberated through the phone. "Let me get Drew. Skype me back and the three of us will talk."

Willow did as Staci asked, though she felt nervous, as if she was being watched. She probably was, by whoever had been in her home and taken Jack's hair.

When she got through to Staci again on Skype, Drew was sitting next to Staci, holding her hand. In typical spy form, the camera was positioned so Willow couldn't identify where they were.

"I think I'm being watched."

Drew interrupted her. "You definitely are. Someone's installed CIA-grade keystroke-monitoring software on your laptop. It's probably nothing to worry about, just us making sure you're okay.

"I've disabled it remotely using an app I have. But I can't sweep your house from here. We'll have to speak guardedly. And, of course, I'll recommend a sweeping service. You should get the house cleaned as soon as possible."

Willow nodded. "I'm already planning on it."

"Good." He then gave her further instructions. "In the meantime, we'll all need to speak in low voices. Willow, pick up your laptop and walk around the house as we're speaking. Even in a thoroughly bugged house it's impossible to place bugs so that they cover every inch. When you're walking around, anyone listening in will be likely to lose bits of information from time to time. It's the best we can do on the fly."

"Got it." Nervous as she was, she was eager to move around. Pacing was a good thing. Willow picked up her laptop and began roaming. "We're clear. I'm wandering. How do you like the tour of the house? Do you like my new pillows?" Willow pointed her laptop toward her pillow-covered sofa.

"Very nice." Drew said, but he sounded less than enthused.

What was it with men? Why didn't they appreciate a beautiful decorative pillow? Must be something in their genetics.

"Willow," Drew said softly, gently, when Willow turned the laptop screen back to focus on her. "I know this anniversary is a hard time for you. It is for all of us. But I saw Jack. . . ." He took a deep breath, as if it was difficult for him to talk about it. "I saw Jack during the explosion. He couldn't have survived the blast."

Drew sounded genuine in his grief and belief. But Willow was not going to budge. She knew what she knew—Con was Jack. She had to convince Drew to at least consider the possibility.

"I know, Drew. I believe you saw what you saw. But you have to believe *me*. I know my husband. And this guy in Orchard Bluff who calls himself Con, he's very likely Jack." It was hard to keep from speaking loudly when she was so excited and emphatic about the possibility. She had to force herself to modulate her voice.

"This isn't about the Sense, is it?" Drew asked.

Her friends knew all about the Sense.

"Not just, but it's been niggling at me. It's more than that, though. It's his eyes—" She grabbed her cell phone from her pocket. "Let me show you." She brought up the picture of Con and turned it toward her computer camera so Staci and Drew could see.

Staci gasped. "He does remind me a bit of Jack, only—"

"—more perfect," Willow finished for her. "As if he's had reconstructive plastic surgery."

Drew was frowning.

Which didn't surprise Willow. She didn't expect to be believed. At first.

"Does he sound like Jack?" Drew asked.

"Yes, but with a gravelly voice and a European accent. He never loses that accent, no matter how hard I try to trip him up. I don't mind, though. It's sexy." She grinned at Drew, trying to get him to smile back at her.

"Jack's good with language and accents. Not as talented as Kyle was, but damn good still," Drew said slowly, raising Willow's hopes that he was at least considering the possibility Jack was alive. "Foreign Accent Syndrome would also explain the accent."

"Foreign what?" Willow asked.

Drew explained. "It's rare," he finished. "But it happens. And if Jack lived, and I'm not convinced he did, his brain has been rewired by the blast so he can't help but speak with that accent. It's involuntary. Tell me more about this Con guy."

Willow launched into her story as she made a circuit of her house.

When she finished, Drew's expression was unreadable, calm. She recognized that particular expression as one of Jack's spy faces. They must have learned it at The Farm. Anyway, that expression was better than blatant disbelief. It meant Drew was thinking about it.

Staci looked optimistic and excited. "You really think Jack's alive? And fooling you? But why? Could he have lost his memory?"

"Lost his memory? I've thought of that. But Con is way too with it and he has a complete social media presence with a full life. No, he hasn't lost his memory," Willow said.

"As to why he's trying to fool me? I really don't know why. But I need to find out. And for that, I need a DNA test."

Drew was slow responding. Staci clutched his arm and implored him, "If there's even the slightest chance this Con is Jack, Drew, we have to help Willow." She lowered her voice and whispered to Drew, but Willow had keen hearing and caught the gist.

Staci felt she owed this much to Willow.

"We can't leave Willow, and ourselves, in the agony of not knowing for sure," Staci said.

Drew glanced between his wife and Willow on the computer. "If he's Jack, there's a reason the Agency doesn't want anyone to know. And Jack. He'd have to have an awfully damn good reason to keep this from all of us."

"Yes, I've thought of that, and I agree. He has a reason; I just don't know what it is."

Drew stared directly at her through her computer screen. "I could lose my job for digging around in this." He set his jaw. "But, damn it, if he's Jack . . ."

He gave Willow a sympathetic look. "What will you do if Con does turn out to be Jack? Can you keep it secret? Can you live with the fact that Jack doesn't want you to know he's still alive?"

"If he's Jack, he'll have a good reason. And I promise, I'd never try to pry it out of him."

"If he's Jack, and we find out it's him, you can't confront him. You could be blowing a highly sensitive mission." Drew ran a hand through his hair. "You can really let him be Con for the rest of his life? Live your life without him?" He gave her a truth-serum stare.

No, she couldn't. But she needed Drew's help, so she lied. Fortunately, she didn't have Staci's problem with lying. Staci had never been any good at it. "If Jack's alive, I'll just be grateful and let fate take us where it may."

"You're trusting to fate now?" Drew sounded skeptical.

Willow nodded. Yes, she trusted fate to get things right, including bringing Jack back to her.

They sat in silence for a minute while Drew thought. "I know a guy who may be able to help. He owes me a favor."

Willow let out a breath she'd hardly been aware of holding and came to a complete stop. "Great! What do I need to do?"

"Keep pacing, for one," Drew said.

"Oh, sorry."

When she was back in motion, Drew gave her instructions on how to collect a DNA sample and contact his guy.

"Don't we need a sample of his DNA to compare it to?" Willow asked, explaining that she didn't trust the report she had.

"I can get a copy of the Agency's DNA report," Drew said.

"How long will it take to get the results?" Willow asked. "I'm afraid Jack will disappear. If I had my choice, I'd be with him every minute."

"With my guy and a good sample?" Drew answered. "Less than twenty-four hours."

Willow nodded. *Less than twenty-four hours!* "I'll get the sample tomorrow evening and overnight it."

They chatted for a few more minutes and then signed off.

Great, now all she had to do was preserve Con's drinking glass, mail it to Drew's guy, and she was golden.

Unless she could get Con to let her swab the inside of his mouth with the swabs the kit provided. But somehow that seemed less than subtle.

*Here, prove you aren't my dead husband* seemed a crazy thing to ask him, even for her. If he was Jack, there's no way he'd go for it. And if he weren't, she'd just scare him away. So she had to go for subtle and hope he didn't insist on helping her load the dishwasher.

Willow sighed. She was going to do her own test for Jack tomorrow night. Good scientists always used every means possible to verify their results; why shouldn't she?

She was going to feed him and bed him. That was the plan. Cook up an absolutely stunningly delicious dinner—chock-full of every food Jack despised—and see if he could choke it down without giving himself away. Then take him to bed and make him chuff. She tingled at the thought. The menu was already running through her mind.

A fresh pea salad, Italian-style. Jack hated peas. Eggplant Parmesan, because, of course, she didn't cook or eat meat. And Jack loathed eggplant. And for dessert, apple dumplings, with the flaky crust she'd learned in pastry school. Because this was apple country after all. And Jack didn't like cooked apples. And to add insult to injury, she was going to put cheese in the crust. Plenty of it. Many people loved cheese in their apple piecrust. Jack wasn't one of them.

It was just too bad Jack didn't have any food allergies she could exploit. A nice peanut allergy or gluten intolerance would have made her life a little easier, temporarily.

If Con could make it through the meal she dreamed up and not gag, she'd give Jack props for being a better actor than she thought.

His chuff, however, was involuntary. She grinned, grabbed a piece of paper, and began making a shopping list.

Despite Drew's counterintelligence tactics, Jack heard *most* every word Willow exchanged with Drew and Staci when he listened in on the voice-activated bugs he'd planted in Willow's house. Yeah, he was damned good with a bug.

Hearing Drew's voice again, and Staci's, Jack swallowed hard. Damn, he missed them, particularly Drew. Soon enough Jack was sure they'd cross paths on a mission again. Drew understood what it meant to be a secret agent, the constant need for lies. Hell, Drew lied with the best of them. He'd forgive Jack. Jack hoped. At least Drew was making excuses for him already.

Staci he wasn't so sure about.

And Willow? Hearing her voice, the urgency, the desperation, the longing . . .

She was going to let fate do what it would? He only half-believed that.

Jack almost broke down, almost decided to trudge over there and tell her the truth.

He took a deep breath and drew upon his training on how to endure torture, how to avoid spilling sensitive information, how to resist, damn it, resist. This *was* torture, heinous punishment.

If he were an ordinary guy, not a trained killer, he'd charge right to her. Beg her forgiveness. Make everything up to her. Take her in his arms, make love to her, and show her just how much he missed her.

But he wasn't. And he couldn't. Because he loved her.

Willow didn't really know who he was or what he did and had done. And who he was and what he did were the antithesis of everything Willow believed in and loved.

He could blame who he was on his childhood. He'd been the scrawny kid of two backwoods parents who moved around way too often, always had too little money and dreams that were too big. He was quiet, the opposite of socially adept, and a huge disappointment to his stout, stocky bully of a father.

Jack's father berated him emotionally and disciplined him to the point of physical abuse while his mother looked the other way. He still had the scars to prove it. Mostly emotional ones now. The explosion had covered many of the physical ones.

Jack reacted by becoming a prankster and acting out in school, trying to use humor to diffuse things. Which led to more beatings—from both his dad and the other boys who didn't appreciate Jack's pranks. Or his intelligence. He had always been a whiz at math and science, which only seemed to irk those with lesser gifts.

When he was thirteen a group of boys beat the shit out of him after school. When he finally got home, his dad beat Jack again for scaring his mother, losing the fight, and not coming right home after school. Something in him snapped.

He knew it was only a matter of time before he was picked on and beat up again. Hell, no fight was going to be a fair fight any way Jack looked at it. Bullies always traveled in groups. Jack didn't have any friends, period, let alone anyone who'd play backup for him. He decided to go down fighting next time, dirty, and teach the next guys who took him on a lesson so no one messed with him again.

He studied how to fight. Put on boots with steel in the toes. Bought a switchblade. And then next time he was jumped after school he fought like a scrawny alley cat. No finesse, just anger lashing out.

He slashed the main bully, got him on the ground, and

started kicking him, unable to stop. It took all the other boys to pull Jack off before he killed him.

Jack sent the main bully to the hospital. He wasn't sorry. He had absolutely no remorse. His dad beat him after that, too. But the other boys didn't mess with him again.

Too bad he moved shortly after and had to start all over again in town after town. That wasn't Jack's last fight. Not by a long shot. After taking his share of beatings, he finally wised up, bought a gun from a thug off the street, and learned to shoot. He had an aptitude, a real talent, and practiced until he was skilled. After a while, word of his proficiency got around. No one bothered him anymore.

If he hadn't been such a loner, he would have been an asset to just about any gang. But no one had enough courage to approach him and he liked his solitude and reputation.

Jack got an ROTC scholarship and went to college. Emmett recruited him into the Agency in college, where Jack was studying math and chemistry and had pulled a good many pranks. Emmett had Jack's juvenile and academic records. He told Jack the Agency had been watching him for years, since high school and before. His intelligence, interests, and ability to lash out and strike at others without conscience made him a perfect candidate to be a CIA assassin. It was either that or end up in prison. Because Jack was going to end up killing someone one way or another. The CIA could train him to do it with finesse for a cause. But first he had to pay his debt to his country. But the Agency would see he got all the right assignments, get him assigned as a sniper.

It sounded like the perfect opportunity to Jack. He agreed with Emmett's assessment. Jack sure as hell didn't want to spend his life in prison. Little did he know that besides being a thrill and giving him the opportunity to use his talents to do the right thing, the CIA was its own kind of prison.

Willow, gentle, gentle, loving Willow who took in every stray, didn't know any of this about him, except for the bare essentials of his abuse at the hands of his dad and a few bullies. Nothing about the way Jack fought back. Nothing about what he was trained to do and did for the Agency. She thought he was just your garden-variety intelligence-gathering spy.

He met her after he'd trained at The Farm and made his first few kills as a spy. At a time in his life when he felt as if there were nothing but violence and hate in the world. And he was simply fighting back the tide. At the time when he wondered whether the violence he saw, the violence he lived with, would completely overtake him and he'd be no better than those he fought. If he'd simply become a killing machine.

And then there she was, a woman so peaceful and serene, so full of good, that she calmed his soul and gave him hope—for himself and humanity. And miracle of all miracles, she fell in love with him. Someone actually loved him, for the first time in his life.

From then on, he fought for her and all the people like her who must exist in the world somewhere, even if he never saw them. But mostly for Willow, so she'd never see the violence. So she'd never change.

If she ever found out the truth, she wouldn't love him. And he'd lose everything, including his drive to do what he did, his faith, his peace. He was convinced of that. The explosion in Ciudad del Este gave him the opportunity to set her free without burdening her with guilt over who he really was.

So he cooled his heels, forced himself to remain calm.

He wouldn't let Drew get in any trouble over him. But he did have to alert Emmett that Willow was trying to get a fast read on Jack's DNA. Knowing the chief, Jack believed Emmett was probably anticipating it.

Not that Willow would succeed. As Jack had already noted, that report she was counting on was bogus.

He made another note to himself—he had to replace the hair on that brush he stole with someone else's. Jack never took chances.

He was thinking a few strands of his "cousin" Aldo's would do nicely. Aldo's was a close visual match. Or hell, any nice dark-brown hair from a brush at the barbershop.

Jack looked in the mirror. Yeah, he was getting a bit shaggy. He could use a trim. Besides, he wanted to look his best for this date he was supposed to have at Willow's tomorrow.

Jack grabbed his smartphone. He had a Facebook friend request from Willow. And a LinkedIn request. And she was following him on Twitter now, too. He grinned. *Nice try, Wills.*

He accepted all her requests. *Good luck tripping me up and spying on me this way, babe.*

He wouldn't slip up and she wouldn't learn anything. The Agency kept up his online persona. He didn't envy the guy who had that desk job back at Langley.

Jack was only responsible for tweeting a few personal things about his stay in Orchard Bluff. He rolled his eyes. Social media was a pain in the ass.

Which reminded him . . .

He sent out a tweet. *Need a haircut.*

*Yeah, scintillating.*

Then he dialed the big house, as Aldo called the main house. Aldo picked up.

"I'm a shaggy dog," Jack said. "Can you recommend a good barber?"

# CHAPTER SIXTEEN

W illow pulled to a stop at Shane's house as close to the back door as possible. He'd called her and asked her to pick him up from the hospital, apologizing that with the festival going no one else was available. It had cut into her plans for the day, but what could she do?

He opened the door and got out of the car slowly, stiff from the accident and his injuries. The old-man movements were directly at odds with his athletic build. Almost as soon as he stood he staggered and leaned against the car, gripping the roof for support.

"Easy. Take it easy. Are you still dizzy?" Willow rushed around to the passenger side to help him. "Don't pass out on me. Don't you dare. I'll never be able to move you." She was only half-joking. He was over six feet tall and stocky.

"Nothing to worry about. Stood up too fast." He gave her a half grin that should have made her heart race but somehow fell short of its intended effect when it didn't reach his eyes.

Still, she smiled back. "Take a deep breath." She stared up at him into his hazel eyes and rubbed his back with one hand to comfort him. "Here, put your arm around me." She took his hand and guided his arm around her shoulder. "I'll help you in."

"There's an offer I can't refuse." He slung an arm around her, leaned in, and spoke softly, as if the admission was hard to make, "Sorry about this, Willow. The doctor says the dizziness should go away in a day or two."

Shane's breath warmed her neck but not her heart. His arm was solid on her shoulder. He smelled clean, like hospital soap, but Willow felt uncomfortable around him. The vulnerable look he gave her should have made her melt into emotional mush. Only . . .

She couldn't explain it, but it seemed put on, as if he was acting a part, overacting maybe, trying to play on her sympathy. It was crazy, but since Con came to town Shane had been acting differently. A little too possessive. A little too much in competition with Con in all aspects. It was almost as if Shane was trying to make Con jealous. Which made no sense. But then, what men did often didn't seem sensible.

Jack had always teased her that she was a sucker for a wounded animal. Somehow, Shane had picked up on this, too. She couldn't help feeling he wasn't quite as helpless as he seemed.

She adjusted his weight on her shoulders and helped him down the sidewalk to the house. "We'll take it slow."

"With my arm around you, slow's just fine."

Half the women in Orchard Bluff would have gone weak in the knees just then from his nearness and the tone of his voice. But Willow's land legs were just fine.

Inside the house, the dogs went wild, barking and growling as she and Shane approached the kitchen door. Thank goodness the dogs were back to normal.

Shane called out to them jovially, "It's me, you big fools. Calm down in there!"

"They sound happy to see you. You think it's safe to go in? Or will they plow us over with enthusiasm?" Willow hoped her relief at their complete recovery didn't show. "Your boys are a little too exuberant sometimes." She unlocked the door. "Brace yourself." She pushed it open.

Duke and Bud barked happily, charged Shane, and jumped up on him, nearly toppling them both.

Shane stood his ground, pulled Willow to him, and stared into her eyes, trailing his gaze to her lips. "Told you I'd protect you." He cocked his head and lowered his lips toward hers.

Willow stepped back. "Better give Duke and Bud a little affection. I think they're jealous, and that's the last thing I need."

A look of anger flashed across Shane's face. He covered it, but not quickly enough. He laughed, but it felt forced, and released Willow to play with the dogs. He seemed just a little too steady on his feet all of a sudden.

Shane roughhoused with them a minute, then looked up at her, a frown on his face. "Do Duke and Bud seem different to you?"

"No, why?" Willow tried not to panic, hoping she hadn't made a mistake by not taking the dogs to the vet. "What do you mean?"

"They seem . . . subdued."

She laughed. "You call this subdued? They nearly knocked us over."

"Yeah. That's what I'm saying. They *should* have bowled us onto our butts."

"They look fine to me."

"They must be hungry. I didn't get a chance to feed them yesterday." He scratched Duke's ears.

Shane looked over at their dog dishes. She followed his gaze. Both of them were licked clean, just as they'd been when she'd arrived with Con last night. They dogs had eaten every last crumb she'd given them, thank goodness!

She breathed an inward sigh of relief. There was no reason to tell Shane she'd fed them and they'd been drunk and sluggish. Because he hadn't left them enough water and they'd gotten desperate.

She grabbed Shane's elbow. "Let's get you settled in and then I'll come back and feed them." The dogs were really going to love her once she gave them an actual morning meal. "Where would you rather be—upstairs in your bed—"

"I'd love you to put me to bed."

She ignored his innuendo. "Or down here on the sofa? I say sofa—it'll be more convenient once your admirers start arriving. You're going to have a stream of visitors once the festival closes up for the day. I hope you have plenty of room in your freezer for all the casseroles coming your way.

"Ada told me she sold out of your favorite apple fritters nearly the minute she opened. Be prepared to put on a few pounds." She paused. "So what will it be?"

"You've convinced me; the sofa it is."

"Good." She helped him into the living room.

He stopped suddenly just inside the door and frowned. "Someone's been in here." He turned to look at her. A subtle shade of anger and fear colored his tone.

She froze and her heart raced. She'd been in here with Con, but they hadn't touched a thing. Shane was beginning to look like a paranoid nutcase.

"What? What's wrong? How can you tell? Is something missing?" She pointedly looked around the room, which was, frankly, a mess, the same as it was the night before. "It looks to me like Old Man Terrence's ghost escaped from the bomb shelter and played poltergeist." She laughed.

"Yeah, I need to pick up. Never mind," Shane said, shaking his head. "You're right. Must be the drugs and the concussion messing with my head."

She relaxed.

He studied her. "On second thought, I think I'd like to lie down in my bed and sleep awhile. Help me up to my room?" Anxiety had crept into his voice.

He did look suddenly pale. Something was off with Shane.

"Sure," she said. "Do you think you can make it?"

"With your help."

She helped him up the stairs. He paused at the entrance to his bedroom and studied it.

"Are you okay?" she asked him again. Because it looked to her as if he suspected someone had been in his room, too.

"I'm fine."

"Sure? You look as if you expect to see Old Man Terrence's ghost in here now."

He laughed. "Spooks don't scare me."

He sounded almost as if he was trying to convince himself. Spooks scared her, but not the kind he was thinking of.

"Well then, let me just fluff your pillow and pull back the covers." She led him to the bed.

He wasn't paying attention to her. Instead, he scanned the room as she opened the bed for him. He walked to the window, which was closed and latched. A small wad of paper lay on the floor beneath it, a smashed wad of paper.

Shane picked it up, smoothed it out, and glanced at it while she pretended to be busy.

She caught only a glimpse of it. It was a geometrical design of overlapping circles. She'd seen the pattern before in an art book—the pattern was called the Flower of Life.

Shane crumpled it and, in a flash of anger, hurled it against the wall.

She looked at him, startled. "Something wrong?"

He turned and looked at her. "No, just a note to myself that I misplaced and ended up on the floor. Something I was supposed to do and forgot. Too late now." He smiled, but it looked forced. "No big deal."

She patted the bed. "Come. Lie down."

He sat on the bed and pulled off his boots. He winced as she helped him into a reclining position.

He took her arms in his hands before she could straighten and pull away. "Come back later? Stay with me awhile and keep this invalid company?"

She smiled back at him. "That's a tempting offer. I'd like to, but I have too much to do. I've got so much caramel to make, I can't even tell you. I completely sold out yesterday. But don't worry. I've got you covered. Your neighbors, the Buckleys, will be stopping by later to see if you need anything.

"I'll make you a tray with your medicine and some snacks before I go."

She did have too much to do, but it wasn't making candy. She had to find out whether Con was her husband or not. Much too much to do.

Jack's newspaper crossbow was a thing of beauty. And had proved absolutely worthless to him since he'd constructed it. In fact, he'd almost crumpled it up in a fit of anger as he watched that bastard the Rooster act an invalid and lean on Willow for help into the house. Watching a terrorist make a pass at his wife was really more torture than a dead man should have to endure.

He flashed to a memory of the Rooster in Ciudad, and the elated look on his face as he detonated the charge that blew Jack through the second-story window of the building. Of landing on his face, smashing it to hell, and passing out in the street below. Of his last conscious thought for nearly a month—*I'm a dead man. Willow, forgive me for leaving you.*

As Jack watched the house, Kennett finally appeared in his bedroom window, holding a piece of paper and looking scared and angry. Jack got out his high-powered

military-grade spy binoculars and took a look. He wanted
to know what was on that paper. No good. The light
shone through it and he couldn't get a read. He whipped
out his superzoom spy camera and snapped a shot, hoping for better luck reading it later.

Willow left ten minutes later. Jack stayed and watched
Kennett's house for several more hours, but the bastard
refused to step outside for even a split second all day. Jack
couldn't get a shot off at him. Worse, a fellow farmer
came over to help sell apples for Kennett and people were
trooping through without end.

Jack went back to the guesthouse disgusted and tried to
read that note that had upset Kennett. No luck. He would
have to question Willow about it, subtly of course. Jack
hadn't seen her. And happily, she didn't return to Kennett's.

Yeah, he checked the tracking on her car. After leaving Kennett's, she'd gone directly into the city while Jack
had gotten a sample of hair and replaced it for his in Willow's memory box. If the address recorded on the GPS
tracking device was any indication, she was no doubt
buying that DNA collection kit Drew recommended.

Monday was even worse. Every woman from Orchard
Bluff over the age of twelve showed up bearing a casse-
role, a pie, or a thermos of soup for the poor, unfortunate
accident victim.

It was hard to stage an archery accident with so many
women fluttering around.

Jack retired to the guesthouse, frustrated. He checked
it for guns in the oven, aerosol cans on the heater, and any
other hazards he could think of, even though Kennett
wasn't likely to have been out of sight of one woman or
another longer enough to do any damage. Jack even unscrewed the showerhead and checked it for poisonous
powder before he jumped in and cleaned up for his dinner
with Willow.

He'd meant to have killed Kennett and been gone by now. But since that hadn't gone according to plan, he may as well have dinner with his wife. Though he was walking on dangerous ground and he knew it.

He showered with a different soap than he'd used when he was with Willow, used a different shampoo, shaved with a different brand of shaving cream, and splashed on a brand of cologne he knew she detested to throw her off and act as a kind of Willow repellent.

As he combed his hair on the opposite side, he caught a glimpse of the temporary tattoo, *eamus catuli, Go Cubs,* painted on his left arm to throw Willow off. He'd always loved baseball. But being from Seattle, he preferred the Mariners. He donned the slacks from another of the stupid sissy outfits Malene had sent for him to wear—a sweater, slacks, leather jacket, and, mercifully this time, Italian leather boots.

One of the hazards of going on a date undercover was risking having his gun discovered. As Con, he wouldn't be carrying. As Jack, he never left the house without protection.

Conversely, conceal his gun too well and there'd be no way to reach it in an emergency. He could wear one under a sports coat. Maybe. But he'd look damn odd never taking the coat off once during the evening. Especially if things got hot at Willow's. Which he had to make sure they didn't.

He had a tiny microrevolver that fit into a belt buckle. But that only worked if he was dressing like a cowboy.

*Good job, Malene.* He strapped on an ankle holster with his NAA Black Widow mini-revolver in it and put on black dress socks and the metro boots. The boots covered his little piece nicely.

He studied his shirtless self in the mirror.

*Not bad.*

Even his scars looked better. He used to have a hairy chest. But the explosion did a number on him and left him with too much scarring. Now he was the hairless wonder. It had also done a good job of obscuring any scars Willow would recognize with the ravages of burns and skin grafts. The plastic surgeons had done a fantastic job on his face, which had been smashed to bits but remarkably unburned.

He'd regained his muscle tone and fitness. He'd worked like a demon to rebuild his frame and strength, but his chest would never be real pretty to look at again.

He flexed his biceps and grinned at his own folly.

Good thing he'd never gotten a real tattoo. *Willow Forever* tattooed in a heart on his biceps would have been hard to explain. Which was exactly why tattoos were against Agency policy.

He didn't expect Willow to ever see him shirtless. But again, Jack prepared for every contingency. She'd be suspicious about the burn scars, but he had a story for that.

He put on his shirt and sweater. The sweater would hide a holster and a bigger gun than the one strapped on his ankle. But unless he missed his guess, Willow would hug him and feel him up for weapons.

Instead, he packed the drinking glass he'd stolen earlier and gotten Aldo to drink from and a bigger gun, a compact service pistol, in the man bag Malene had sent. He just had to make sure Willow never dug through it.

He ran through the sleight-of-hand procedures and tricks agent Lani Silkwater had taught him during the past year. In case he needed them to switch the glasses after dinner.

Lani had worked undercover as an assistant to the famous magician Rock Powers for several months. Much to the chief's chagrin, Lani had married the great illusionist against orders, run off on him, and begged Emmett to keep her deep undercover and out of Powers' sight. Marital regret is such an ugly thing.

Being the gracious, sympathetic guy the chief was, not, he assigned Lani the onerous and, some would say, boring duty of building Jack's spy skills back up, including teaching him a little magic. A few parlor tricks.

Emmett rightly believed working magic tricks would help Jack rebuild his muscle dexterity so he could regain his shooting skills. It had done more than help him regain muscle movement. It had helped build his confidence. And it was fun as hell.

Lani was a great teacher. Very patient and the one person who sympathized with Jack's desire to allow Willow to think he was dead. At times, Lani said she wished she could accomplish the same, because rumor had it that Rock wouldn't rest until he'd reappeared her. That's what she got for skipping out in the middle of the act. Rock wasn't going to rest until he got his rightful prestige—Lani reappearing in the box he'd put her in—and wiped the egg off his face. If she could fake her death . . .

Jack had reassured her, death had its own set of problems.

Jack took a deep breath. Spookie could be a problem this evening, but he'd worked out a plan. He was bringing her a special dog treat to woo her. He'd play nice to her and wave it in front of his little dog when he first got there. Then he'd claim the treat had won her over. Problem solved.

Jack grabbed the wine he'd bought from Aldo, his wallet, the man bag, the Halloween wrapped doggie delectable, and his keys. Jack would have brought Willow flowers. It was too soon and too dangerous for Con to show that kind of romantic interest. Con had to be aloof, a slightly flirtatious but generally *let's just be friends* type of guy.

* * *

Willow glanced at the clock. Con would be arriving any minute. The house was clean, of electronic bugs and hidden cameras as well as of dust and dirt. She'd set the table with her best glasses, dishes, and flatware and the silver candlesticks she and Jack had received as a wedding present from his friend Kyle. She'd made a centerpiece of gourds, Indian corn, and leaves around the candles, creating a homey, romantic fall look.

She'd turned down the lights and judiciously lit candles around the room to create an intimate atmosphere. Candles that smelled of vanilla and pumpkin spice to offset the smells of eggplant Parmesan wafting out of the kitchen. She wanted to spring the meal on Con so she could gauge his initial, surprised reaction.

Dinner simmered in the oven. Apple dumplings ready to be covered with hard sauce sat on the counter. A fire of seasoned fir crackled in the living room fireplace, perfuming the room. And Spookie was corralled back in the bedroom by a child safety gate.

Willow had debated and debated what to wear to this DNA-snatching evening. She wanted to look hot, delectable, and totally casual. As if the evening were no big deal. Even though she meant to seduce Con.

She knew a thing or two about what men found sexy, Jack in particular. She put on the outfit of universal appeal—tight jeans that showed off her butt, tall black pumps, and a formfitting, scoop-neck white T-shirt. So easy, but so effective.

The doorbell rang. *Let the games begin.*

# CHAPTER SEVENTEEN

Willow met Jack at the door wearing the sexiest outfit he could imagine—a white T-shirt with no bra. It took every ounce of determination he had to look her in the eyes, not her beautiful, bouncing cleavage. Not to stare at the dark buds of her nipples poking through sheer white fabric, not to imagine that T-shirt wet and clinging to her skin—

*Stop it, Jack. Control, man. Control.*

"Con, you're right on time." She took the bottle of Zinfandel he held from him and hugged him. He got a deep breath of the perfume she wore—there it was again, his favorite. The one she wore to let him know she was in the mood.

Damn, why did he have to be wearing a leather jacket? He couldn't feel the brush of her breasts through it. He just wanted a tiny feel. Just one.

Willow stepped aside to let him in.

He looked around the room and tried to clear his head from thoughts of her. "Where's the little dog? I brought her something." Jack pulled a dog treat from his pocket. A preemptive strike was best. And he was looking forward to seeing the little mutt.

"Oh, I gated her in the back. No sense scaring her." Willow winked.

He raised a brow. "I'm that frightening?"

"You're not frightening at all," Willow practically purred, and gave him a salacious smile.

He swallowed hard.

She set the wine down on the entry table. "Let me take your coat." She paused and looked at the leather man bag slung over his shoulder. "And bag."

Damn that Malene for making him carry a man bag. At least it was a place to carry a weapon and was totally unlike anything he'd wear on his own. But it was not alpha-male behavior. He set the dog treat on the entry table and handed her the bag.

"I'll just set the bag here in the entry if you don't mind."

Fine with him. He wanted it within easy access. He shrugged out of his jacket and handed it to her.

At first whiff, the house smelled heavenly of burning wood and spice. On second breath, he detected the stink of eggplant Parmesan.

So that's the way she was going to play things, was it? She was going to try to smoke him out by going for the gag response. Feed him foods he hated and watch to see if he slipped up.

He hadn't thought Willow could be so cruel. He had a sudden vision of the dinner ahead and food after food he despised. Crafty little minx.

She could try, but he'd eaten worse. Far worse. He'd survived on grubs and bugs in the wilderness for an entire week, consumed parts of a cow, bull, pig, horse, chicken, kangaroo, octopus, squirrel, and rat no person should ever eat. Hell, no one should ever eat rat, period.

If he could manage all that, he could chow down eggplant without blanching. He wouldn't enjoy it, but he'd eat it.

"Something smells delicious," he said, partly to goad her and partly to throw her off track.

"Eggplant Parmesan. I thought since you're Italian, and I don't eat meat . . ." She hung up his coat in a closet nearby and picked up the wine and dog biscuit.

"Good thought." He followed her into the living room, walking past the dining room, where the table was set for two. The living room glowed with candlelight. And was suddenly filled with mementos from their life together that hadn't been there on his previous nefarious visits. "You have a beautiful place."

"Thank you. I like it." She carried the Zinfandel toward the kitchen. "What can I get you?"

"Wine's fine."

"Good." She set the dog treat on the counter, grabbed a corkscrew, opened the wine, and poured two glasses. She grabbed the glasses, handed one to him, and raised hers. "To new friends."

"To new friends, may they become old friends." He clinked.

She watched him drink over her glass as she took a sip. He could almost see the triumphant gleam. Yeah, she thought she was getting his DNA for sure this time. But the joke was on her.

"Aldo recommended this Zinfandel. He knows his stuff."

"Yes, doesn't he? This is heavenly."

He noticed a pink lipstick ring on her glass. Willow didn't wear lipstick often. A normal guy would assume she'd fixed up for him. Jack assumed she wore lipstick to mark her glass, so she knew which one to test for his DNA.

"Let me just get the appetizers." She disappeared into the kitchen, reappearing a minute later with a silver tray he recognized as one from their wedding. She held the tray out for him.

*Ah, shit, mushrooms stuffed with Gorgonzola.* In

general, you could call him a cheese man. He loved just about any kind of cheese. Except Gorgonzola. And he despised mushrooms with a passion. They tainted anything they touched. His distaste might have had something to do with a near-miss experience with a Destroying Angel in France. Never trust nefarious French cooks.

But he smiled, took one, and popped it in his mouth, making sure to wash it down with a big gulp of wine. If he kept this method of drowning out the bad flavors up, he'd pass out by the end of the evening or end up in Willow's bed. He couldn't afford to do either.

"Delicious," he said for her benefit, and took another. Yeah, he was a glutton for punishment. Anything to keep up a convincing cover.

"Dinner's in the oven. It will be ready shortly." She nodded toward the living room. "Come on in and have a seat."

He followed her into the living room. She sat on the sofa, leaving plenty of room for him to sit next to her, and gave him a flirtatious smile. He took the chair opposite her, preferring the view and distance from her and her tantalizing body. His hormones were raging, threatening to overcome his good sense and control.

Sitting too close to her, he wouldn't be responsible for his actions, like reaching out and touching her in all the right places. A spark of disappointment crossed her face, tinged with a determined look that said, *Play hard to get if you like; I'll play harder and win you over.*

Yeah, he'd seen that look before. And damn it all if she wasn't right. She could win him over, way too easily. Hell, one accidental breast brush would do him in, in the sex-starved condition he was in. Beautiful women had an unfair advantage when it came to prying intel out of male spies, especially former lovers.

"That falling rooster interrupted us the other day before I had a chance to find out anything about you," she said with a twinkle in her eyes. "Like what you do for a living, your favorite color, highest level of education, sports you played in high school, hobbies, you know, coffee-date essential intel."

Had she just used *intel* on purpose? She wouldn't get a rise out of him so easily.

He laughed. "Yeah, that rooster was a conversation stopper." Let the game of twenty questions and trip-Jack-up begin. As if he were going to come right out and tell her he was an assassin for the CIA. He hadn't told her the truth about that yet. Why would he now?

"Let me see, to answer your questions—I'm a public relations exec for a small firm. I travel a lot for the job. Favorite color—red. Bachelor's degree. Baseball. Hiking and playing guitar. Did I get everything?" He'd hit the cover life dossier essentials.

"I think you covered the icebreakers." She took a sip of wine. "How long will you be staying?"

He shrugged. "I have another week and a half of vacation." He'd be here long enough to kill Kennett and find out what kind of mischief he was planning for the G8 summit.

"Speaking of Aldo, he and I tried to pay the deer-hitting invalid a visit. You know Aldo, we went armed with a lasagna and two dozen breadsticks. Turns out we shouldn't have bothered. We could barely get near the place. Every woman in town was streaming in with some kind of food for him.

"Kennett better hope he recovers quickly, before the women of this town feed him to death." Which wasn't a bad idea. What if Kennett suddenly developed a fatal case of food poisoning? It was something to consider. Shouldn't be too hard to find a Destroying Angel or Death Cap mushroom to bump him off with. The woods around Orchard Bluff were great mushrooming territory. So Jack had heard Aldo mention.

She laughed. "Food is the way we show our love around here. Speaking of Shane, I have something to tell you. This will give you a laugh—when I brought him home from the hospital, he nearly gave me a heart attack. The moment we walked into the living room, he was convinced someone had been in there.

"I couldn't see how he could tell, unless he had hidden cameras installed. Everything looked the same to me."

Jack had to work hard to keep his concern from showing and laughed politely. "Did you fess up to feeding his dogs?"

She waved her hand. "Are you kidding? No way. It's much more fun to be clandestine." She watched Jack closely for a reaction.

She'd have to work harder than that to get Jack to admit to being the hardened spy that he was.

"No, I had to fall back on my excellent lying and acting skills."

"He believed your innocent act? You fooled him?" Jack liked the shared intimacy of their secret, but he was wondering what had set Kennett off and worrying that he suspected Willow of seeing something she shouldn't have.

"Oh yeah."

"We were so careful not to disturb anything," Jack said, acting confused, as Con would. He had been careful. Damn careful.

"I know! We even cleaned up the beer the dogs spilled."

Jack's turn not to give himself away. "What about the dogs? How were they? Had they sobered up by the time you got Kennett home?" The drugs should have worn off by then.

"They were fine, but Shane thought they looked sluggish. That man is too observant. Of course, I couldn't tell him they'd gotten drunk, thanks to him. Poor babies, they were only fending for themselves."

"Good. I'm glad the dogs are fine." Jack frowned. "But why did he think someone had been in the house? That's weird."

"That's what I thought." She became suddenly serious. "And his paranoia continued. He was dizzy. I had to help him upstairs to bed."

Jack didn't like the sound of that.

"Again in the bedroom, he looked as if he thought someone had been in there. He was scared, almost as if he'd seen a ghost."

"Really?" *What would have scared the Rooster?*

She nodded. "You know what was even more odd about Shane? I've been thinking and thinking about this and still can't make any sense of it.

"He picked up a wad of paper, a smashed wad of paper, that was on the floor beneath the window. I was opening the bed. He didn't think I saw. But when he unfolded it, he paled and looked angry.

"When I asked him about it, he claimed it was a note to himself, a reminder about something he'd forgotten to do."

She had Jack's full attention now.

"But I saw what was on that piece of paper and it wasn't a note."

"What was it?" Jack asked.

"A geometric pattern called the Flower of Life."

*SMASH!* Jack had to work hard not to give himself away. That note was a message from SMASH to Kennett, a warning—screw up again and we'll take you out. Jack had seen one of their threatening notes before.

RIOT must have realized the Rooster had passed them bad intel. They generally weren't the forgiving sort. Which meant that either the Rooster was too important to take out before the G8 auxiliary summit or they suspected someone else had tampered with the drop and were hoping to smoke them out. Either way, they'd view the bad intel as meaning the Rooster had been careless and would eventually have to be punished. Jack just hoped RIOT didn't suspect him as being the source of the Rooster's screwup. He was also disappointed that SMASH wouldn't be killing the Rooster for him. They were much crueler than he'd ever be.

And damn it all, too, Kennett would be even more on his guard now that he knew SMASH was watching him as well.

"That's odd," Jack said, remembering to be Con. "What do you think it meant?"

"No idea," Willow said. "But it is odd behavior."

Just then a timer dinged.

Willow popped up and headed to the kitchen. "Let me check on dinner."

Jack watched her walk away, salivating over the gentle sway of her hips, aching to touch her. She looked so fine, sleek, and sexy when she walked in heels. All lovely, long legs, and cute butt. He watched her curves as she grabbed a pair of oven mitts, bent over the oven, and pulled out a dish of eggplant Parmesan. Every part of him ached to touch her, just walk up behind her, grab that fantastic ass of hers, and take her in the kitchen.

He swallowed hard and tried not to think about it. Making love with her had too many dangerous consequences, most important giving himself away as still among the living. Although it would probably get him out of having to eat eggplant.

It was just too damn bad Willow had decided to play the game this way. She was a terrific cook and he'd been salivating all day over the thought of eating her home cooking again. Her talents in the kitchen were just one of the many things he missed about her, though by no means the thing he longed for most.

He'd have to make the best out of a tasteless situation. Savor the sauce, so to speak.

Willow set the dish on a ceramic trivet on the table.

"Can I help you with anything?" Jack asked, still admiring her form.

"Thanks, sweet of you to offer, but I have everything under control."

Oh, shit, did she! His sweet little Willow had taken torture to a new level. He watched as she went to the fridge and pulled out a cold pea salad in a clear cut-crystal bowl. He almost gagged just looking at it.

He hated peas, especially cold peas. The only thing worse was canned peas, and unless he missed his guess, she'd probably found a way to incorporate some into that grotesque salad. Maybe there'd be bread?

He was quickly rethinking his plan. Giving himself away in the height of passion was a lot more appealing than trying not to gag on peas. He sighed inwardly and called up his training. He'd eaten bugs and raw entrails, just not in a lovely romantic setting being served by his wife. Somehow, without the imminent threat of danger to his life hanging over his head, just the temptation of giving in to hot sex, the thought of eating peas seemed about as bad as eating grubs. Situational gastronomy.

"Dinner is served!" Willow said with a sly smile.

Willow watched Con closely as she put the food on the table. He was all smiles, charm, sparkling eyes, and wit. Not a touch of dread on his face. He'd handled the mushrooms well, too. But then, he'd only eaten two. A man of his size and appetite should have scarfed down a dozen.

She set the eggplant Parmesan on the table next to the pea salad, directly in front of him, and poured them each a glass of water and another glass of wine. Later, she'd just pack up one of those lovely glasses, stuff it in the collection bag for protection, wrap it up, and overnight it to Drew's guy. She already had the box ready to go. In less than twenty-four hours, Jack's game would be over. Maybe sooner if she could get him to bed. He'd never be able to hide that sexy chuff of his.

She smiled at him. He was so easy on the eyes. It was hard not to stare at him. She'd noticed, too, that he was having a hard time looking away from her.

She raised her glass. "Bon appétit!"

He nodded, raised his to hers, and clinked. They both drank.

She handed him a set of serving utensils. "I'm casual. I like to eat family-style. You don't mind serving yourself?"

Yes, she was taking pity on him, in a way. And this was also a test—would he take a big enough serving to throw her off?

"Casual is just the way I like things." He took the utensils and served himself a respectable portion of eggplant, took a nice spoonful of pea salad, and then loaded up on bread.

She passed him a small bowl of grated cheese, trying not to look too gleeful as she watched him closely. Jack loved a good Parmesan-Reggiano or a nice pecorino Romano. He hated exactly two types of cheese—Gorgonzola and Mizithra. Guess what was in that bowl?

Con was sharp enough to smell the Mizithra without being obvious. "No extra cheese, thanks. This food looks rich enough and delicious as it is."

*Very good, Jack. Totally diplomatic.*

She watched as he took a large bite of the main course. Now, while he was distracted by trying to pretend to like the eggplant, that is, if he was really Jack, was the time to grill him about the finer details she'd learned on his Facebook, Twitter, and LinkedIn accounts. She opened her mouth, but Con cut her off.

"This eggplant is heavenly. Absolutely the best I've tasted."

She closed her mouth. He sounded genuine. He wasn't obviously gagging. This was a disappointing test. She so wanted him to be Jack. Which meant—she wanted to see him gag.

"Hey, I've been meaning to thank you in person for the friend request on Facebook," Con said before she could speak again. "And the follow on Twitter."

*Oh, shoot and darn!* If Con was Jack, he'd taken the offensive and probably studied the heck out of those accounts. With hope springing eternal, she'd ignored the obvious evidence that Con would pay attention to the accounts and Jack wouldn't. Which would mean that the man across the table from her was Con. That had been her theory, anyway. Now she rejected it as a foolish test of identity.

"My pleasure." She felt her face go warm as she realized that Con/Jack must surely know that she knew a lot more about him than she'd let on earlier.

But the man in front of her didn't seem to notice her discomfort. At least he was kind enough not to comment on it.

"Did you see those pictures of my cousin Vinnie? That guy is a crack-up, a real prankster!" His eyes shone with admiration. "Has Aldo told you any of the family stories about him?"

"No, I'm afraid not."

"Oh, you have to hear this." Con/Jack grinned and launched into a story. "Vinnie and I were in Las Vegas last year. . . ."

Jack had always been a fantastic storyteller. Con was

equally talented. He soon had her laughing along with him, entertained and asking questions, enjoying herself in a way she hadn't in over two years.

If Con was Jack, he was trying to be cagey, taking the offensive to spill all the info on his social sites so she couldn't grill him and get him to slip up. Yes, her husband the spy was a tactical genius. Which had been one downside of being married to him. He generally outwitted and outplayed her. She warned friends and relatives never to play Risk with him, especially not Secret Mission Risk. He was killer at that.

Little did Jack know, though, that he was giving himself away the more he talked and tried to convince her he was Con, getting so caught up in the details that he forgot to mask his classic storytelling style. And even though he spoke in a gravelly voice that wasn't Jack's and he had that sexy European accent that he never accidentally dropped out of, Jack's wit shone through.

On the other hand, he answered the questions she peppered him with as easily as if he'd actually lived the life he talked about. Which was an argument for Con. And everything he said jibed with what she'd researched. She made a few mental notes of details to check later. But she doubted she'd catch him in a slipup.

Willow was enjoying herself so greatly, and they were talking so much, that time just slipped away and the dinner on their plates got cold without her realizing it until too late. They'd been so animated in conversation, she'd forgotten to eat more than a bite or two. Con's plate was suspiciously untouched, too, that sneaky man.

Everyone knows that cold eggplant Parmesan is simply no good, no good at all. She couldn't force him to eat it. He'd outplayed her again. Finally, she looked down at her plate with an exaggerated expression of regret. "Our dinner's gotten cold." She smiled weakly at him. "We were so busy talking, we forget to eat. It's no good now."

"No good now?" He smiled back, took a big forkful of eggplant Parmesan, and popped it in his mouth. "Delicious," he said after he'd swallowed. He reached for his wineglass to wash it down.

"You big liar. It is not! Not cold." She passed him the basket of bread. "Here. We'll just have to fill up on this and dessert."

*Curses, foiled again! Drat that lying, spying man.*

# CHAPTER EIGHTEEN

When having dinner with the enemy, or your super-sneaky, up-to-no-good-trying-to-out-you-as-her-husband wife, evasive action and diversionary strategies are absolutely essential tactics of battle. Both of which Jack used to his advantage. Hell, he always could tell a good story.

One small bite of pea salad and one large forkful of eggplant for the cover; one long, funny story to save his stomach. And now he'd won—the offending eggplant Parmesan would soon be going down the disposal.

However, dinner was waning. And he had yet to make the big drinking glass switch. Lani had coached him to create a diversion. Diversion was the soul of magic.

With that in mind, he *accidentally* bumped his dinner plate. Which then *accidentally* landed in his lap, eggplant side down.

"Oh, shit!" he said, and looked at Willow apologetically as he pulled the plate and his serving of eggplant from his lap and set them on the table.

Willow jumped up as he dabbed at the red sauce in his lap with his cloth napkin. "How bad is it?"

"It's red sauce." He made a face he thought the dandy Con would make, a face that regretted the damage to the pants. Jack, however, wouldn't be mourning their loss.

"Let me get you something." She ran to the kitchen, wet a clean dish towel, returned with it, and proceeded to dab at the sauce in his lap. Which proceeded to arouse him. He had the feeling she was "dabbing" that way on purpose.

Score one for Willow. He cursed silently to himself. He hadn't thought far enough ahead.

He cleared his throat and grabbed her hand before things got sticky. Her eyes glistened with triumph. She knew very well what she was doing.

"Water isn't going to be strong enough. Do you have a stain stick?"

He knew very well she did. And he'd also moved it slightly from its regular spot earlier, when he'd sneaked in and replaced "his" strands of hair. It would take her a while to find the stain remover and buy him time. As Jack, he would have died from embarrassment being so worried about his pants. Con, though, was a different matter.

"Oh, of course! Stay there! I'll go get it and be right back. Don't move."

Yeah, he could hardly wait for her to return and rub him with the stain stick. In retrospect, he should have leaned over and dragged his sleeve through the sauce. She dashed off toward the laundry room, which was out of sight of the living room.

Jack grabbed his water glass, rushed to his man bag by the door. Got the glass with Aldo's DNA out, poured the water from his glass into it, stashed the glass from dinner in the bag, and returned to his chair. He returned the glass to its spot on the table, pulled a packaged disinfecting wipe from his pocket, cleaned his wineglass of all DNA, and smiled. Sometimes the spy's life was just too much fun. Besides, Jack had always loved a good prank. And, oh yes, he was pranking Willow, big-time. And planned to take things a step further if he got the chance.

Willow had left the child gate open when she rushed

through to the laundry room. Spookie came bounding out, barking happily to see Jack.

Perfect timing! Jack jumped up, grabbed the dog treat from the counter, cuddled Spookie, and fed it to her. "There, girl, I'm glad to see you, too."

Willow returned to find them fast friends, Spookie sitting happily at his feet as Jack continued to wipe his pants with the damp towel.

"Spook, what are you doing here?" Willow's tone was total mom voice.

"She escaped your gate. Don't scold her, Willow. She and I have made friends. I gave her that treat I brought her and she warmed right up to me."

Willow's eyes narrowed. She looked just the slightest bit suspicious. "How's the stain coming out?"

"Stubbornly."

Jack had turned his chair to face sideways to the table. He sat with his legs apart, feet firmly planted on the floor.

"Let me see." Willow boldly came up and kneeled between his thighs, wielding the stain stick.

Oh, shit. He had an exceptional view down her shirt to her naked breasts. As she wielded that stick like a pro and rubbed him all the right ways, he rose to the occasion and her nipples budded up, adding to his agony.

He was certain she knew what she was doing as she massaged the stain remover into his crotch, lightly touching his family jewels as she lifted the fabric of his pants away from his skin to more vigorously attack the stain. Resting her hand against his inner thigh, temptingly close to his balls.

All innocent, and incredibly erotic to a man who'd been way too long without his wife.

She rubbed and dabbed. Clung to his thigh with fingers that innocently massaged. Leaned in so close she could have kissed his lap, until he thought he might start panting.

Okay, he'd screwed up with this maneuver and given her the tactical advantage.

However, if the way her pupils were dilated when she looked up into his eyes was any indication, she was feeling things, too. "There. That should do it."

No, that didn't do it. And no, he wasn't going to lose his resolve and do it.

"I think this is the best we can expect. Hopefully the cleaner will have more luck." Looking at him like that, she was so totally tempting and begging to be kissed.

Jack leaned down, feeling as if he could simply fall into her kiss when Spookie barked and pawed his leg, begging to be picked up and saving him from certain temptation.

Willow frowned at the dog. Yeah, she was trying to tempt Jack into a roll in the hay. Not today, damn it.

"You belong back in your room," she said to the dog.

"Oh, she's fine. I like dogs." He reached down and scratched Spookie behind the ears.

Willow rose slowly and set the stain stick on the tablecloth. "Let me just clear the dishes and make some coffee to go with dessert." She shot Spookie a warning look, grabbed the offending plate and her own, and headed for the kitchen.

Jack gave an inward grin, grabbed the two wineglasses and the pea salad bowl, and headed for the kitchen with Spookie on his heels. All the DNA was long gone from that wineglass, but he was going to give Willow a scare anyway. In the kitchen, he set the salad bowl on the counter and went to the sink.

"Just set those on the counter," Willow said.

Maybe it was only him, but he detected a note of worry in her tone.

"I'll hand wash them later," she added.

He set them on the counter, pushed up his sleeves,

and turned the water on. Before Willow could stop him, he rinsed his wineglass thoroughly, making a show of running the dishcloth around the rim. "You cooked; the least I can do is help clean up."

Willow spun around from where she was loading the dishwasher and grabbed the glass out of his hand. "No, absolutely not. You're my guest. No helping out."

She grabbed his shoulders, spun him around, and pointed him to the living room. "Please, go make yourself at home. I'll just be a minute in here. I want to get some of the pans soaking. The rest can wait."

He hesitated.

"I insist," she said.

Oh, what the hell? He would have liked the pleasure of running the pea salad down the garbage disposal, but he acquiesced.

He watched her from the living room as she grabbed the drinking glasses and set them aside. He imagined she was just itching to get his glass wrapped up and mailed off to Drew's DNA lab. Well, the joke was on them.

His phone buzzed. He pulled it out of his pocket. The screen lit up with a video security feed from the guesthouse. You had to love a smartphone. He'd programmed it to alert him to any intruders.

Oh, look, there was Kennett creeping around the place.

Jack remotely armed his defense mechanisms. If Kennett so much as pried open the door, he'd be a dead man. Which would make Jack's job that much easier.

The equivalent of an anvil would drop on Kennett's head—the horseshoe Aldo had hung above the door for luck. And not the actual horseshoe, a replica made of tungsten, which was twice as heavy as lead or steel. Jack had had Emmett overnight it to him and hung it himself for luck just this morning.

Kennett being killed by a symbol of luck seemed like poetic justice and great irony to Jack. It would look like a total accident. And Kennett would look like a jealous bastard. *Job well done, Jack.*

But the Rooster didn't try the door. He got out a jack-knife and used it to pin something to the guesthouse door. Jack got the feeling that whatever motivated Kennett to pin his missive to the door wasn't honorable.

Willow walked into the room, carrying two apple dumplings covered with sauce. Jack didn't like large mounds of cooked apple. Call it an idiosyncrasy of his. And he was willing to bet the piecrust that covered the dumplings was laced with cheese. The thought made his stomach turn. Jack began to reassess his long-held belief that he liked cheese. For a guy who professed to love cheese there were many applications of it that he outright detested. And Willow had just exploited every one.

He quickly cleared the screen of his phone before Willow reached the sofa.

"Something important?" she asked as she handed him a bowl with a beautifully done dumpling and a paper napkin.

The dumpling looked as if it had come right out of an issue of a cooking magazine. Willow's pastries were always things of beauty. This one even had a sprig of home-grown dried lavender artistically laid on top of it.

He'd love to photograph it. But he wasn't eating it. No way.

She stood over him with the other dumpling for herself in her hand, silhouetted and backlit so that he could see her curves through her shirt. Her dark nipples budded and bounced enticingly near his face, begging him to reach up and stroke them.

Her voice was a gentle purr. Her perfume wafted

toward him, heavily laced with pheromones, no doubt, because every pore in his body reacted to her.

He had to get the hell out of here. Now. Before he did something really stupid and reckless. Because he was losing his will to fight temptation. And he had to get rid of that note Kennett had left and do possible damage control before anyone else saw it.

"Those look delicious and tempting." He nodded toward the dumplings, but he was thinking of her breasts. "But I have to run. Emergency work situation. Big PR problem for a client. Damn the cell phone era. We're never out of touch."

She kept smiling, but disappointment clearly clouded her face. He wondered whether she was more disappointed that she wasn't able to seduce him or to get him to eat the cheese-infested dumplings?

She straightened. "I'll just wrap this up for you."

He watched her walk off toward the kitchen, his body aching and his heart constricting.

He was doing the right thing, wasn't he? Yes, absolutely. Absolutely.

Willow watched Con's taillights as they disappeared down her driveway. Part of her was achingly disappointed— she'd scared him off, failed to seduce him, and she'd been looking forward to a good tumble and release. She wouldn't hear her tiger chuff, but at least she had his glass.

That man was Jack, her Jack. He had to be.

How convenient that he'd spilled his dinner in his lap. She'd taken a few liberties with the cleanup. She would have loved to take about a dozen more seductive, indecent liberties. She almost had him when she stuck her breasts in his face as she delivered the dumplings.

But business called. Spy business?

She was still wondering what Jack was up to in Orchard Bluff. If Con was indeed Jack. Which she was convinced he was. Other than seeing her, what *could* he be up to? What could possibly happen in Orchard Bluff?

It really didn't matter now. As disappointed as she was by Con's sudden departure, she now had her proof.

She ran to her bedroom and grabbed the packing box she'd stuffed with popcorn for packing cushion earlier. She took it to the kitchen and carefully, lovingly, put the water glass Con had used in the collection bag, wrapped it in packing paper, nestled it among the popcorn so that no damage would come to it, taped it up, and put the mailing label on it.

Then she grabbed her coat and keys. Drew had given her instructions on where to take the package and who to see to guarantee it would go out immediately.

You had to love spies and their networks that never slept.

Back at the guesthouse, Jack deactivated the deadly horseshoe. He would have done it before he left Willow's, but it only took him a minute to get back. There wasn't time for anyone else to accidentally spring the trap.

Unlike Kennett and his SMASH ilk, Jack abhorred collateral damage. He didn't tolerate it. Which made his kills harder to orchestrate and carry out.

Jack got out of the car in front of the guesthouse and walked to the door. Sure enough, there was the knife with the note pinned beneath it to the door.

The Rooster had a touch of the dramatic in him.

Jack pulled the knife out of the obviously once crumpled and now smoothed out note. Kennett was recycling either paper, or threats, or both. Very eco friendly and organic farmer–like of him.

Jack whipped out his penlight and shone it on the note.

*Huh.* That geometric design Willow had talked about— the Flower of Life. SMASH's calling card. Obviously Kennett's copy.

Jack mulled over the various meanings of Kennett's message to him. It could be, *You're a dead man.*

It might mean, *I know you're Sariel.*

Or it could be, *I know you're the SMASH assassin who's after me and I have your number.*

Most likely it meant at least two out of the three. Kennett had good reasons to kill him: One, he thought Jack was out to kill him, guilty on that count; Two, killing a rival SMASH assassin, if that's what Jack turned out to be, would prove Kennett's worth and prowess to RIOT and maybe get him off the shit list; and finally, killing Sariel would cover up his initial mistake.

None of this boded well for Jack.

Jack shrugged. Fine with him. This was now out-and-out war.

He'd wanted to kill Kennett quietly, staging a small accident that would allow Kennett to keep his dignity here in the community. Nothing that aroused the citizens of Orchard Bluff to the danger that had been in their midst. Hell, he'd been willing to let them bury Kennett in the local graveyard.

Now, however, a bigger, better plan formed in Jack's mind. He was going to blow Kennett to kingdom come. In his bomb shelter. The irony appealed to Jack.

But first he had to get into that bomb shelter and scope it out. He had the feeling it was the Rooster's command center.

# CHAPTER NINETEEN

Shiloh burst into the shop on Tuesday morning with pink cheeks and her clean apron in hand just minutes before they were scheduled to open. Willow watched her push her way through the cluster of women that had begun forming at the door fifteen minutes earlier. Holding their steaming mugs of coffee and tea in the crisp October air, they looked like an innocent lynch mob ready to pounce on Willow. But why? That was the question Willow wasn't really sure she wanted to know the answer to. She had a bad feeling, a really bad feeling, about what was in store for her once she opened.

"We'll open in five." Shiloh's breath rose in a puff through the air, coming out in energetic bursts with her words. "Just give us five."

Shiloh slammed the store's door behind her, locking the crowd and her frosty breath out with a decided click. She leaned back against the door as if to brace it against a marauding mob of women. "Have you looked outside? What's going on out there? Why are the town's big six gossips out there, waiting to pounce?"

"Yeah, I've seen it. Lettie arrived a quarter of an hour ago. She came with Dottie Lundgren."

"Jeez," Shiloh said. "What did you do to upset the Town Grump?" Her tone indicated Willow was in big-time trouble.

"No idea."

Shiloh glanced over her shoulder out the small window in the door. "That group is out for blood. Individually, they're good at terrorizing. As a group"—she shuddered—"they're like watching a *Saw* movie. They're scary and they have psychological torture down to an art form."

"I've been up since dawn turning sugar, butter, sea salt, and cream into sweet salted caramel. We'll kill them with kindness and sugar if they cause any trouble." She looked past Shiloh out the window at the group of gossipy women at her door. "I have no idea why the Visigoths are attacking. They should be at Ada's having their morning coffee, not taking it to go. Isn't coffee supposed to calm the savage beasts?"

What in the world *was* going on out there with those six? They never varied their morning coffee routine. Willow had a bad feeling. Strange things had been happening since Con had come to town. She thought she was the only one who'd been affected. Now it looked as if someone had put something in the apple crop. The entire town must be going crazy.

Shiloh winked at Willow. "That rumor that the Food Network is featuring your candy on one of their shows hasn't been resurrected again, has it?"

Willow laughed and shook her head. "You're not still blaming Ada for that? She was just joking that we could use a visit from a Food Network star to perk things up around here and boost sales. I don't know who overheard, misheard, and started the brushfire by spreading the rumor. I wish I could find the culprit. I'd hire them to do my advertising. Never hurts to have a bigmouth on your side."

"Odds are it was one of those six." Shiloh frowned. "Something has them going."

"Yeah, I know. I'm as perplexed as you are." Willow peeked out the window again. "What do you think they want?"

"Besides sweets? No idea. I know what I wanted—a decent parking space. They took every one. I hate parking on the street. I almost parked in the Villa's lot. But you know how Aldo hates it when you park and don't buy a lasagna."

Willow peeked out the window again. "I hope this isn't some kind of prank." Which immediately made her think of Jack. Jack loved his pranks. "It's not even Halloween yet."

"What makes you think it's a prank? Let's flatter ourselves and think your caramels have finally caught on epically." Shiloh grinned at her.

Willow couldn't help but smile. There was a reason she kept Shiloh around.

"How was your dinner with the mysterious Con?" Shiloh switched topics abruptly as she tossed the apron over her head and tied the strings around her waist. She watched Willow as closely as a mother looking for a child's lie as she waited for her answer.

Something in her tone made Willow suspicious. It was less, *How was your evening with Con, hint, hint, wink, wink, did you do the deed?* and more, *Something is rotten in Orchard Bluff.*

Willow answered with a certain amount of hesitancy and evasive action. "Fi-i-i-ne," she singsonged, stringing the one-word answer out.

Shiloh pursed her lips and shook her head. "You're hedging, boss. I need details." Her tone still wasn't as light and youthful, eager, spill-the-details Shiloh-like as Willow expected out of her.

Living with Jack had made Willow something of an expert at detecting lies and cover-ups. Shiloh either knew something, suspected something, or was trying to cover something up. None were good scenarios.

The ladies outside grew louder. Willow put a tray of

freshly made sea-salted lavender caramels into the re-frigerated glass display case. "Why do I have the feeling I'm in for the Orchard Bluff inquisition?"

"What do you mean?"

*Way too innocent and nervous there, Shiloh girl.*

"That wasn't your usual salacious *How was your evening with a hot man?* tone." Willow began filling another display tray with caramels. She glanced up at the clock. Two minutes until the crowd rushed the door. She was running behind, too, feeling like a contestant on an episode of those crazy timed cooking shows as she arranged the tray.

"I can put more innuendo in if you'd like." Shiloh washed her hands, wiped them on a paper towel, lowered her voice, and wiggled her eyebrows. "How *was* your evening, boss?"

Willow shook her head. "You're right. I liked it better without the innuendo." She paused. "Why do I get the sense something's up that I don't know about?"

Willow hated the thought of peaceful Orchard Bluff going covert on her. She'd had enough of that life with Jack. "What's up with you?"

Shiloh sighed and finally looked Willow in the eye. "Nothing."

Willow gave her the piercing *tell me the truth or spend the afternoon scouring candy kettles* stare.

Shiloh caved, sort of. "It's just . . . well, what do you know about Con?"

"Con?" *Oh no, please don't let small-town politics and suspicion rear their ugly heads now, at the worst possible time.* If the citizens of Orchard Bluff turned on Con, they'd run him out within days. She needed Con around long enough to prove he was really Jack. And she needed Jack around forever. And if Con was simply Con, she was getting the feeling she needed him, too.

Another terrible thought occurred to Willow—was she the cause of this sudden suspicion? Had someone found out she'd been Googling Con and checking up on him? Seen her buying that DNA sample taking kit? Had she inadvertently aroused suspicions?

She'd been so incredibly careful. She'd practically worn a trench coat with the collar turned up and dark glasses as a disguise. And she'd gone deep into the city to Drew's contact specifically to avoid the prying eyes of the people of Orchard Bluff.

In the year and a half since she'd been here, she'd quickly realized she was a lot more anonymous in the city. Small towns, even peaceful, loving little small towns, loved nothing more than gossip and speculation. Willow remembered the gist of a quote from *Pride and Prejudice*: "What do we live for but to entertain our neighbors?" That was too true here.

What sort of horrible rumor had someone started? Did they think Willow was trying to prove Con really was Aldo's cousin and not an imposter? Or the daddy of her hidden child? She didn't have a hidden child, but in a town like this nothing was beyond the imagination.

She had to calm the savage mob.

And right now Willow simply needed to play it cool with Shiloh, who could be the town's inside informant. "I know all I need to about him."

*Except whether he's actually Jack, for sure and certain.*

"I'm just saying, it might be wise to find out a little *more* about him before you become too attached to him." Shiloh looked timid for the first time Willow could remember since hiring her.

"Too attached?" Willow laughed. "I'm not going to run off and marry him." She shook her head as if Shiloh had just said something very silly. If Willow was right, and she believed she was, she was *already* married to him. So clear conscience, no lie there. "Why the sudden concern?"

"We like you, Willow," Shiloh said, hedging again.

Willow got the distinct impression there was something she wasn't saying. "And?"

"Con's from Chicago." Shiloh cleared her throat and looked down at her colorful Converse tennis shoes. "We don't want him to sweep you away with him."

Willow shook her head, bemused and confused. "One dinner and the town's worried I'm going to run off with him?"

Well, they had part of it right. If Con was Jack she'd follow him anywhere, run with him to the moon.

She felt that deep sense of longing again so strongly she had to resist the urge to clamp her legs together. The desire to track Con down and make love with him nearly overwhelmed her good judgment and common sense.

She and Jack used to make love every day when he was home. When he went away on a mission it was torture without him. The moment he walked back in her door they ripped each other's clothes off. She felt an emotional and spiritual connection with Jack when they made love that she could only liken to the high of listening to a favorite piece of music and letting your spirit soar with it.

"Well, you know what they say," Shiloh said. "Lonely widows and all. They can fall too easily for any handsome man who comes along."

Willow rolled her eyes. "On the very off chance I did suddenly decide Con was the one, I wouldn't run. I'd stay right here among my friends."

The clock on the wall chimed ten. Willow took a deep breath and sighed, eager to be distracted from this conversation. "Time to let the marauding horde in." She grabbed her key, took a second deep, calming breath, prayed for peace, and unlocked the door.

The group of women pushed in.

Lettie was first in the door. She'd held the Town Grump position more times than anyone else and felt it gave her extra rights to speak her mind.

She cornered Willow by the windows before she could escape to safety behind the counter.

"Oh, honey," Lettie said without preamble. "We heard about your dinner with Aldo's *purported* cousin last night. What were you thinking having a strange man over to your house all alone?"

He wasn't a strange man. He was almost certainly her husband.

"I wasn't all alone. I had Spookie. And Con's not a stranger. Aldo knows him. What do you mean by *purported*?" This was bad, worse than Willow originally feared. She couldn't help sounding defensive.

Lettie clicked her tongue. "Just what I said, hon. Is he really Aldo's cousin? How would we know for sure? Aldo has thousands of cousins. You know how those big Italian Roman Catholic families are—no birth control, mixed with the temperament of Latin lovers. They multiply like rabbits. It's impossible to keep track of everyone. I bet even their mothers don't know who's who and where's where.

"I heard Con's not related to Aldo at all. He's just a drifter taking advantage of Aldo's hospitality and you. He's out for your money." Her eyes snapped as she nodded to make her point. "Has anyone checked up to make sure he is who he says he is?"

"I heard Con's already taken advantage of three other women," Dottie said from Lettie's elbow. "Love 'em and leave 'em Con is what they call him. Showers women with attention, gets them to buy him expensive presents, borrows their money, and absconds with it."

"I bet he's a bigamist," Brenda Hayes, a small, round

woman who owned an apple orchard just outside of town, said. "That's what I heard, anyway. Probably has half a dozen children, too."

"What about Shane?" Lettie nodded her head and shot Willow her accusing stare. Shane was obviously Lettie's favorite, even though he was a newcomer and a short-timer in Orchard Bluff, too. "Ever thought about his feelings?"

"I—" Willow couldn't keep up with the ambush.

"Con's wanted in three states," Sheryl Cramer, Willow's rural route mail carrier, interjected, cutting off Willow's response as she handed Willow her mail. "And I vote for Shane, too. He's a good man. Always closes his mailbox nice and tight so the spiders and rain don't get in. Very polite, that man."

She gave Willow a gentle, nudging elbow. "And handsome, too, in an all-American way. Has character to his features. Who likes such dark, perfect looks as Con's, anyway? He's much too slick for our tastes."

But not Willow's. She loved Con's perfect good looks that reminded her of Jack's imperfect ones.

Willow had to put a stop to this blatant rumor growth before either they made Con into an ax murderer or she exploded. She already felt herself growing hot, and it wasn't just due to the crowd of warm bodies and hot tempers around her.

She mouthed across the room at Shiloh to call Aldo and get him over here as soon as possible. Aldo, with his exotic Italian accent and expressive gestures, could surely calm the women down. Most of them would quiet just to hear him talk.

"Calm down," Willow stepped in to rush to Con's defense. "That's all rumor and hearsay. You've all met him. You liked him. He's a charming man, really sweet. He even brought a treat for Spookie when he came over last night."

"Of course we like him! That's part of his nefarious plan to throw us off the scent. It's always the charmers you have to watch out for," Lettie, who appeared to be the ringleader, said. She was taking her role as Town Grump way too seriously. Keep acting as she was and they'd have to rename her Town PI or maybe simply Town Snoop and Busybody.

"He acted like a perfect gentleman." In fact, he'd acted way *too* gentlemanly for Willow's tastes. She wanted to taste him. If he was Jack, he was showing a good deal of restraint. She felt the sexual attraction thrumming between them and knew he did, too. She'd read somewhere that men's testosterone levels dropped when they had sex less than once a week. They eventually got used to the drop. She hoped that explained Jack's sudden ability to resist certain temptation.

Willow had to calm the women down and reassure them. Where in the world had they gotten these ridiculous rumors in the first place?

"Perfect gentleman, now is that any way he should be acting around a beauty like you?" Linda Herman asked. "He should be making a move like a real man. The guys who hang out at Beck's would be all over you in a minute, probably less, if you gave them half a chance.

"That just proves our point. I knew the man was a fake. He's trying to throw her off guard so he can move in with his charming ways and elegant clothes, and steal her money now, too!"

"Steal my money!" Willow couldn't believe what she was hearing.

"Like we said, that's the way all con men operate, honey," Lettie said. "Move in on susceptible widows, marry them, and abscond with their insurance settlements. If they're pretty like you, it only sweetens the pot, if you know what I mean."

Willow bit back what she really thought. There was no way the Agency would let her be taken in by a con man.

"Yeah, he didn't even have the decency to pick a good cover name," Willa Bentley, who owned the best Golden Delicious orchard on the bluff with her husband, chimed in. "Con! He could have been more original."

"Probably trying to throw us off track," Lettie said. "You know, hide in plain sight."

A sea of heads nodded.

Willow waved her arms in a *cease and desist with this craziness* motion. "No, no, no."

"Yes." Lettie nodded.

"Where did you get these crazy ideas? Has anyone asked Aldo?" Willow looked around the crowd as the finger-pointing began. "Or confronted Con directly?"

"Con would only deny it, wouldn't he? Smile at us, charm us until we melted under that hot accent of his and warm, chocolate eyes, and then send us on our way still in the dark and under his spell."

"And you know Aldo. You don't insult his family without proof. He'd never sell us another lasagna again," Lettie said.

The part about Con charming them was probably true.

"You're not giving Aldo enough credit," Willow said. "If he believed for a second Con was an imposter, he'd protect me and Orchard Bluff and send Con away. I know he would. Where did you hear these things?" Willow glanced over at Shiloh, who'd just snapped her cell phone shut.

Shiloh nodded to Willow and mouthed, *Aldo's on his way.*

"I heard it from her." Lettie pointed to Willa.

Willa pointed to Dottie. She pointed to someone else. This was like a game of round-robin, nearly impossible to discover a ringleader or the source of the misinformation.

Willow shook her head. "I'm grateful to you all and appreciate how you want to protect me. Really, I am.

"But you don't have to worry about me. I'm not as gullible as you think." She snapped her fingers as she remembered how she'd snooped on Con herself. "I've already screened Con. I did a thorough Internet search on him before I invited him over. He's exactly who he says he is." *Not.* He was her husband, Jack. He had to be.

"I can show you. I'll just grab my phone. If you'll just let Shiloh take your orders while I go get it—"

"Hold on here." Aldo burst through the doors, waving and making Italian hand gestures that Willow didn't care to know the meaning of. "My cousin is who he says he is. I have my ninety-five-year-old *nonna* on the phone and she confirms.

"Nonna, let me put you on speakerphone. You tell these ladies and set them straight about Con." He punched a button on his phone and held the phone up so the crowd could hear.

Nonna's raspy voice filled the air. She let loose a string of rapid-fire Italian that scared the ladies in the room into pin-dropping silence.

Aldo grinned and nodded along. Willow was close enough to him to hear him whisper, "Give 'em hell, Nonna," beneath his breath.

"You see?" Aldo said when his grandmother finished.

"Yes, but what was she saying?" Lettie asked. "None of us speak Italian. We need a translator."

"Again in English, Nonna," Aldo said into the receiver.

His grandmother began speaking again. "Con Russo is my Aldo's second cousin once removed. He has the Salemo good looks, but that's only from his mother's side. He's my cousin Sal's . . ."

Willow wondered how the Agency had convinced Aldo's *nonna* that Jack was her relative.

* * *

Jack wandered into Bluff Country Store around ten, hoping to get away with ordering a coffee drink he really liked. The store was suspiciously quiet. None of the usual crowd lingered about. Which was good for his coffee ordering but roused his suspicious nature.

On top of that, the few locals who lounged at the tables, reading their newspapers and sipping coffee, gave him the evil eye. Yeah, he'd been a spy long enough to recognize the evil eye when he saw it. And he was definitely seeing it now.

Fortunately, he doubted any of them had assassin skills to match their looks. Who among knew how to make a crossbow out of their newspapers, for example? It was an acquired skill.

Making sure to steer clear of the second-story ledge above and, therefore, any *accidentally* toppling objects, Jack went to the counter where Willow's friend Ada refilled Stan Herman's coffee cup. So there still were a few people who drank a plain old Americano cup of coffee. Unfortunately, with Ada behind the counter, Jack would have to stick to his approved drink list.

Stan walked away. Ada turned her attention to Jack and glared at him. Yes, glared. What the hell? What had he done to upset her? Against his strong sexual impulses and drive, he'd behaved perfectly around Willow. No animal advances. No taking her on the living room rug like he wanted to. Nothing but gentlemanliness as far as the evening stretched. Hell, he'd even helped her with the dishes. The fact that he'd had an ulterior motive shouldn't count against him.

"What can I get you?" Ada's stare held all the warmth of the frost on a pumpkin, and her eyes snapped with anger.

"I'll take a *grande* pumpkin spice latte." Still, not his

favorite drink, but better than a cappuccino. And it was on the approved cover list.

"To go, I take it."

Now there was a subtle hint. So he wouldn't be lounging in the cold atmosphere of the store and picking up any helpful local gossip.

She rang it up and took his money. He watched her as she made his drink just to make sure she didn't spit in it. When she'd finished it, she plunked it on the counter so hard that coffee splashed up through the drink hole of the to-go cup lid.

Sometimes the best way to get intel was the direct approach.

He looked Ada straight in the eye, giving her no wiggle room, and put on his most sincerely apologetic tone. "Have I done something to offend you?"

Ada held a dishrag. She looked as if she wanted to swat him with it. Instead, she thwacked the counter. "Willow is my good friend and I will protect her to the end. Especially from gold-digging men who are after her widow's inheritance. Mess with her and you *will* mess with me, buster.

"The eyes of the entire town are on you, Con Russo, or whoever you really are. You are *not* going to break our Willow's heart and run off with her money. Nor will we allow you to trespass on Aldo's hospitality a moment longer, you, you fraud!"

If Jack hadn't been trained to be cool under pressure and had lots of experience facing down much badder guys than Ada, his heart might have stopped.

But the SMASH note pinned to his door and all the ladies of the town trooping through Kennett's house came suddenly to mind.

*Touché, Kennett. Good move.*

With a few well-placed lies, some hints, and a bit of innuendo, Kennett had just enlisted the entire town to be his eyes and ears and keep watch on Jack.

The Rooster, that bastard, was definitely scared, but Jack tipped a figurative hat to him. Kennett just proved he was good with a tactical move. And he knew small towns.

*I'm going to get you, you bastard. Soon. Try all you like to trip me up; that only strengthens my resolve.*

Fortunately, NCS had an app for everything. Jack laughed and pulled his smartphone from his pocket. "You don't believe I'm Aldo's cousin? Would you believe his dear old *nonna*?

"Phone, call Tia Salemo."

"Aldo Salemo, you should be ashamed of yourself for dragging your poor old confused dear granny into this." Lettie glared at Aldo after he ended the call with his grandmother.

The other women crowding the store nodded their agreement and murmured encouragement to Lettie.

Aldo glared back at them. "Nonna is not confused. Are you insulting my *nonna*? No one insults Nonna and gets away with it." He made an Italian hand gesture that Willow was pretty well convinced meant something rude.

Lettie ignored it. "Do you have any Mafia connections?"

"I have a distant cousin in the porn industry in LA."

Lettie's eyes narrowed. "But he doesn't off people who disagree with him?"

Aldo looked confused. "No."

"Then, yes, I'm disagreeing. I'm not calling your granny a liar. I'm just saying, at her age it's easy to be mistaken.

"You have to throw this imposter out, Aldo. Kick him right out of that guesthouse of yours and boot him out of town. You can't harbor a fugitive."

"Fugitive? Who are you calling a fugitive? Someone in

my family? You'd better take that back, Lettie, or no meatballs for you. Not ever again." Aldo crossed his arms and glared at the ladies.

"Slow down, everyone. Let's not get carried away. All we have to go on so far is malicious, unfounded gossip." Willow had to stop this lynch mob, but if they wouldn't listen to Aldo's grandma, whom would they listen to?

Although, privately, she had to admit she didn't believe Aldo's *nonna*, either. There was no way Con Russo was real, not if he was Jack. But Jack may have assumed Con's identity. Still, she wasn't going to let these women scare the fake Con, if that's what he was, away. At least not until she knew for sure whether he was Jack or not.

Lettie crossed her arms, too. "I will not take that back. It's the truth."

"And *I* will not stand for someone calling Nonna a liar. And I will not throw my cousin out based on idle gossip. Salemos stand by and protect the family," Aldo said.

"And I will not stand for the town interfering in my personal life. I'm a big girl. I can take care of myself. So far, Con's done nothing wrong and nothing more than accept my dinner invitation and prove himself to be a charming dinner companion.

"Now, let's eat caramel." Willow waved to Shiloh. "Bring out a tray of samples.

"The rest of you clear a path so I can get behind the counter. I expect you're all here to buy candy." She gave them her piercing, fierce stare, the one she hardly ever used.

Just then her cell rang. She pulled it out of her apron pocket. "Ada?"

"Thank goodness I caught you," Ada said. "Have you heard about Con Russo? He's a fake and a bigamist, a wanted felon who has wives in five states. I should call the cops, but I wanted to talk to you first.

"He was just in. Don't worry, I sent him packing. Any man who'd mess with you is not welcome here. Of course, I sold him a coffee first. Profit is profit.

"So, should I call the FBI?"

"Not you, too," Willow said, heart pounding. "No, you should not call the FBI. I thought you had better sense than to listen to these horrible rumors. Where did you send him?"

Willow crossed her fingers. *Please don't let him leave town.*

# CHAPTER TWENTY

I'm sorry, Willow. The DNA doesn't match. Despite his uncanny resemblance, your friend Con isn't Jack." Drew Fields stared at Willow through his computer screen as he Skyped with her. He'd disabled monitoring software before giving Willow the news. And, of course, Willow had had her house swept. They could all speak freely. Staci sat beside him, holding his hand and shooting Willow sympathetic looks.

Drew looked as broken up as Willow felt. "No! That can't be true. He is Jack. He is. He *has* to be. I had dinner with him last night. He tells stories like Jack. He . . . he's Jack."

It was a good thing Willow was already sitting down; otherwise she'd have collapsed with shock. This couldn't be true. All day long she'd been defending him, protecting him, sending him texts, direct messages on social media, and trying to get to Aldo's to warn him. But the town seemed to be conspiring to keep her from physically reaching Jack. "There has to be a mistake—"

"DNA doesn't lie." Drew's tone was soft and sympathetic. "My guy checked it twice."

"The sample—"

"The sample was fine, Willow," Drew said. "More than fine, excellent. There's no mistake. The DNA on that drinking glass doesn't belong to Jack."

Drew's phrasing sparked a thought. That sneaky rascal Jack. What if he'd somehow tampered with the sample?

Willow squinted and stared back at Drew and Staci. "Who *does* that sample belong to?"

"A male of Italian descent," Drew said. "Dark haired, healthy. Marker for marker it basically matches your description of Con."

Willow balled her fists. Oh, that man was good!

"Is there any way Jack or someone inside the Agency could have tampered with the sample? This sounds like a classic Emmett smoke-and-mirrors trick."

"Willow, I think you're in denial, hon." Staci looked genuinely sad for Willow. "Don't hang on to false hope. I wish Jack was still alive almost as much as you do. But let this go."

Drew squeezed Staci's hand. Willow was observant. She saw him tense. "My man is outside the Agency. Dependable, loyal. He owes me his life. I trust him. He can't be bought off.

"The Agency, however, is damn good. But we were all careful. The odds of them getting to this sample are slim to none, Willow."

"Jack could have done it. I don't know how, but if Jack has been faking his death for two years, I wouldn't put anything past him," Willow said.

"The package arrived undisturbed, the seal unbroken, our coded message inside, all of our precautions and verifications intact. My guy was on the alert for any tampering."

Willow took a deep breath to ward off tears. She couldn't believe it. She *wouldn't* believe it. She wouldn't let Jack go. Not again.

"Is there any way you can do some discreet inquiring within the Agency? Something low-key and beneath Emmett's notice."

Drew looked as if he was about to refuse.

Willow cut him off before he could speak. "I know it's a lot to ask. You know I wouldn't if it weren't so important."

"If I ask about Jack, flags will immediately go up," Drew said.

"So don't ask about Jack. Dig around and see if the Agency has any reason to be in Orchard Bluff. If Jack is in town, there's a reason."

Drew pursed his lips. "I'll do what I can. No promises, Willow."

"No promises, I understand completely." And she did. She understood how much Drew's career meant to him and knew the risk he was taking for her. But like her, Drew would do anything he could to bring Jack back. Drew had been Jack's best friend. It was the trump card she held over Drew and she half-hated herself for using it, but she didn't see any other option.

"You know that if I do find out anything sensitive, and all our stuff is sensitive and top secret, I won't be able to give you any details. The most I'll be able to do is say the Agency has an interest in the area."

"I know. Thank you, Drew."

He looked embarrassed by her heartfelt thanks. He shrugged.

"Just don't hold on to such a slim hope, Willow. I'm concerned about you, that you're still in total denial. Damn that Sense of yours." He gave her a crooked grin.

She grinned back in return. "It's never wrong."

He shook his head and became solemn. "Seriously, I'm concerned. If DNA evidence from Con himself won't convince you, nothing will. When will you give up?"

*Never.*

Which she didn't say aloud. She didn't have to. Drew caught her expression and sighed.

"Hope springs eternal," she said. "Staci, how's your mom doing?"

"If you're going to start gossiping and engaging in girl talk, I'm out of here." Drew shook his head and stood to leave.

"Bye, Drew. Thanks!" Willow watched him walk away.

"Mom's spending Sam's money and doing surprisingly well. She still doesn't suspect a thing. . . ."

Staci's mom had unknowingly been married to a traitor who was selling national security secrets to a dangerous terrorist group. Willow, of course, didn't know all the details. Just that it had been Drew's mission to capture Staci's stepfather, Sam.

Somehow Sam had been blown up while on a "fishing trip" at Victoria Harbor. Well, of course Drew was involved. Even more interestingly, that mission had saved Drew and Staci's marriage. They were just days away from signing the final divorce papers when Drew got the assignment.

The spying life was notoriously hard on marriages. Yet somehow the Agency had a low to nonexistent divorce rate. Odd, but love was fickle. And the chief, Emmett Nelson, was a master manipulator. Willow always thought he somehow had a hand in the high rate of marriage survival.

Rumors in the Agency had been circulating for as long as Willow had been married to Jack that Emmett's own marriage had failed years ago. Though it was hard to picture the kind of woman who would dare marry Emmett. It sparked the imagination, that's for sure. Emmett never talked about her or the marriage. And all the records had been sealed.

If Willow could uncover any intel on Emmett's defunct marriage, she'd have power over him. Immense power. Enough to get him to help her discover if Con was really Jack. Which, of course, he was. He had to be.

However, daydreaming about blackmailing Emmett into helping her was futile.

Willow chatted with Staci for another half hour and signed off feeling amazingly cheered, given the news she'd just received. She was determined, absolutely determined.

The Sense was not wrong and neither was she. Con was Jack. He had to be. And she was resolved to prove it.

Jack had left her no alternative. She mentally shrugged. She had to sleep with Con. *Tonight*.

Before Orchard Bluff ran him out on a rail or in an applecart, whichever was handier.

Jack couldn't lie to her with his lovemaking. Of that she was certain—he had that telltale chuff, that almost purr.

And sleeping with Jack, or even Con, would be no hardship. None at all. Not sleeping with Con, though, was simply hideous torture. Every part of her being ached for him and his touch. Some parts of her more than others.

She'd have to be sneaky to outwit and outplay the people of Orchard Bluff who'd been trying to keep her from Con all day. Somehow they'd organized and been taking shifts to make sure she didn't get near Con.

She'd barely had a spare minute since she opened the shop. The one time she'd tried to sneak out and over to Aldo's, Sheryl had intercepted her and scooped her right back into the store.

Even now, if she looked out her bedroom window she was sure she'd see a shadowy figure keeping watch. She was under surveillance.

But no one, absolutely no one, could keep her from Jack. She hadn't been married to a spy for nothing. She could operate covertly when the need arose.

She mentally mapped out a plan. She'd sneak out the back way, head to Aldo's guesthouse on foot, and take a

shortcut so none of the good people of Orchard Bluff
intercepted and deflected her the way they'd been doing
all day.

She'd dress in camo. No, not Jack's old camo. Night
camo. Black jeans, sexy black boots that came to her
knees. She had a pair Jack had given her before his last
mission—shiny, stiletto heels that laced up the front and
back, lined with downy fur that ran up the lacing. Jack
once told her no hetero man on the planet could resist a
woman wearing those boots.

She was going to make Jack put his money where his
mouth was.

She'd put on a black button-up blouse, black lace thong
panties, sexy bra to match. Black trench coat. Black
gloves. Jack loved her in sexy black.

Put on dark makeup—smoky eyes, pouty lips, and seductive perfume.

Yesterday, she'd tried to torment Jack into revealing
himself by feeding him everything he detested and wearing see-through white to tempt him into a tryst. Tonight,
black was her friend. Jack had a fantasy he'd always
wanted her to enact where she played an enemy agent out
to seduce him. It was time he got his wish.

As he finished his nightly weight-lifting routine in the
guesthouse, Jack cursed the Rooster for making his life
and job infinitely harder. And turning the town against
him. And preventing him from going to a real gym.

Jack made a muscle and frowned. Not bad, but he
feared he was getting soft.

The good people of Orchard Bluff wanted to run him
out. Aldo had defended him and insisted he stay as long
as he liked and finish out his vacation. But Jack's days in
Orchard Bluff, dead or alive, were definitely numbered.
And with the controversy surrounding Con it hardly

seemed like staying was going to help reduce Jack's stress level.

He had to kill Kennett and get the hell out of Orchard Bluff before he lost his mind and did something foolish with Willow, like chuffing his brains out and blowing his cover. Or someone, namely the Rooster, "accidentally" mistook him for a deer and took him out in much the same way he'd been planning to kill the Rooster with his newspaper crossbow. Still hadn't gotten a decent shot. The citizens of Orchard Bluff were watching him too closely.

Much as Jack loved Willow, he was no good for her. She'd never understand his lifestyle or condone it. She'd *really* never forgive him for killing Kennett, especially because Jack could never reveal the evil, villainous bastard Kennett was. Top-secret intel was a pain in the butt sometimes. And a definite impediment to love.

Jack had a plan, a big plan that would go boom in the night.

Tonight, Jack had a little prep work to do. A bit of surveillance, if he could escape the prying eyes of every apple grower from here to the Canadian border.

*Evil will appear good and good will appear evil,* he thought. And that was never truer than now. Kennett had the people of Orchard Bluff snowed good and well.

Shirtless, Jack slipped into a pair of black jeans. Put on his thick wool surveillance socks and black army boots. He rubbed eye black cream beneath his eyes and was scrounging around for a shirt when his doorbell rang.

*Who the hell can that be?*

He grabbed his smartphone and looked at the front door cam. A shapely woman in a black trench coat stood silhouetted in the front porch light, looking like every fantasy he'd ever had.

Damn, Willow was even wearing the sexy boots he'd

given her. The ones no straight man in his right mind could resist. Images of the mind-blowing sex they'd had while she was wearing those boots flashed through his mind. Suddenly a cold shower seemed like the best idea in the world. That and a tranquilizer shot intravenously. Nothing short of that was going to calm the desire coursing through him.

He took a deep breath and weighed his options as the doorbell rang again. Ignore her and hope to hell she went away and got home safely? Or answer the door, let her in, and risk blowing a cover two years in the making and ruining Willow's life again?

There didn't seem any middle ground. He couldn't rely on his self-control, which was why he had to blow this place. Soon.

He made a split-second decision. He couldn't leave her out there. What if someone saw her? What if Kennett saw her? Kennett would use any weapon he could against Jack, especially because he thought Jack was either Sariel or a SMASH assassin poaching on his territory and trying to get to him through Willow.

No way would Jack let Willow become collateral damage. Damn, if Kennett ever had Willow in a spot where he could harm her Jack would crack. She was his one weakness, the one thing that affected his ability to be the perfect assassin. His one vulnerability. He must never let the enemy know that. That's another reason he had to leave Willow behind. She interfered with his ability to get the job done. Though she was also the reason he did the job in the first place.

When cornered or captured, spies were trained to take a suicide pill rather than spill valuable intel to the enemy. Jack knew the drill. He was cornered, surrounded, and bound by his heart. Which left him no alternative.

He grabbed his bag of chemicals, rifled through it,

pulled a vial, extracted a pill, and stared at it for half a second. Damn, this was going to hurt him way more than Willow would get hurt. It was fast acting, too. But it couldn't be helped. He popped the pill without water. He had maybe ten minutes before it took effect.

He dashed down the stairs without thinking and threw open the door.

Willow looked up at him through smoky bedroom eyes, not even arching a brow in surprise at his attire, or lack of. Her gaze traveled leisurely down the length of his body, from his eyes with the eye black cream beneath them, down his bare chest, past his nipples that hardened along with the rest of him under her appraising eye. He had to resist the urge to flex his muscles like a peacock parading for his lady. Okay, he may have flexed, a little.

Two could play the seductive stare game. Damn she looked hot in that trench coat and tight jeans. And those tall-heeled boots to her knees. Her moist lip gloss sparkled in the lamplight, making her lips look full and ready to be kissed, possessed. And he wanted to possess her.

He knew what she was up to. He'd asked for this fantasy before. Why the hell hadn't she given it to him then, when he could have enjoyed it?

"Let me in before someone sees me." She glanced around furtively and then smiled up at him again in the way she used to when she had sex on the brain.

He stepped aside and let her in. But only because he knew in a few minutes there'd be no way he could perform.

She closed the door behind her and faced him, standing too close to his personal space in the small entryway at the bottom of the stairs leading to the guest house. "You didn't reply to any of my texts or direct messages. I hope you don't think I'm a nutcase or exaggerating. So I came to warn you in person and convince you I'm not. Someone's been spreading vicious rumors about you."

"Now why would someone do such a thing?" He enjoyed letting his gaze travel down her body. "Hot coat. Playing secret agent?" He may as well call her on her game.

Her eyes sparkled. "Maybe."

He let his gaze travel over her again, hoping, though knowing it was bad for him, that she wore nothing beneath that trench coat. "Halloween's still a ways away."

She laughed in that twinkly way that turned him on, and reached up and stroked his cheek just below the eye black.

Her touch singed, made him hot all the way through. He had to fight to stand still and act uninterested, hoping she didn't notice the way his body reacted to her. Being alone with her was dangerous business.

"Like my outfit?" She took a step back and twirled for him, pointing her foot so he could get a good look at one of those boots that only gave him ideas he shouldn't have.

Oh, damn, he liked it way too much.

"I had to sneak out," she whispered as if they were being bugged. "They're watching me."

"Are you into conspiracy theories now? Who's watching you?" he teased. He had to stall for time. Give his pill time to work, though he dreaded the result.

"Everyone, the entire town. I'm here on a serious mission, Con. You have to believe me. The town is up in arms. They want to throw you out. They haven't forgiven you for that dance performance, and that was just the beginning of your faults in their opinion."

"What? Charming, lovable me?" He was going to pull her chain until the end. He may as well flirt with her and have some fun. It wouldn't last long.

"You can't tell me Aldo hasn't told you about his encounter with Lettie and her gang at my shop this morning. She's still mad you beat her favorite at the growers' dinner and has been gunning for you since. Aldo had to call his *nonna* to defend your honor.

"People are saying you're a swindler, a con man, a heartbreaker who's out to ruin me and run off with my bank account."

"They're still saying that? Even after my great-aunt defended my honor with such vigor?" He shook his head and took a step into Willow. If he wanted her bank account, there were easier ways to get it. "You don't believe them?"

"No. Should I?"

He arched a brow. "I may be a bad boy, but I'd never pursue a woman for her money."

Her eyes lit up in response. She rubbed the greasepaint she had picked up stroking his face between her fingers. "Are you playing dress up, too?"

"Yeah, just practicing for Halloween. Trying out some looks, you know." He should have wiped off the eye black before answering the door. See? She messed with his head and his concentration.

"Shirtless is a little cold for a Halloween costume around here." She ran her hand over his bare shoulder and down his arm, hesitating at his tattoo. "Nice tat. *Eamus catulie*. What does that mean?"

"It's obvious you aren't from Chicago. Go Cubs." He grabbed her hand and squeezed it, then took her arm. "Come on in where it's warm."

Oh, this was too easy and utter torment.

"Love to." She let him lead her up the stairs.

"I'm flattered you came out on this dangerous mission just to save me. Did you walk over? I didn't hear a car."

She smiled and untied the belt of her coat. "Very perceptive. Yes, I did. I like the bracing night air."

His breath caught for just a second as he waited for that coat to fall away. But she was in no hurry to shed it or open it and let him see what was beneath. She was going to torture him, too.

Well, he couldn't act too eager. He had to be somewhat in Con's character. "Let me get my shirt. I'll drive you home." He turned toward the bedroom.

She grabbed his arm and caressed his biceps with a gentle stroke that sent a shudder of pleasure through his entire body. "No hurry. You wouldn't happen to have some tea around? Something to warm me up?" She stroked his arm again, her tone heavy with suggestion.

He removed her hand from his arm before he lost his will and took her in his arms and ravaged her right there. "Aldo has some green tea around here somewhere. I'll look for it." He turned toward the kitchen.

She stopped him. "Don't bother. I know my way around. I'll get it." She slid off her trench coat, one slow shoulder shimmy at a time.

Damn, one fantasy dashed. She wasn't topless. But she was the next best thing—wearing a sexy black bra beneath a sheer black button-up blouse that may as well not have been buttoned at all. It fell open to her navel.

She was really putting him through the wringer now. His mouth went dry, which was better than salivating all over her.

As she tossed her coat over the back of the sofa, the backlight lit every luscious curve of her body.

His gaze naturally rested on her chest, where he got a hot view of the round curves of her breasts. He had to resist the urge to reach out and touch one. He cleared his throat, trying not to sound hoarse with desire. "A button or two has come undone."

She smiled and trailed a light touch across his chest, then looked down at her own and shrugged. "Really? I hadn't noticed." She didn't button them.

Oh, she really was trying to kill him.

Unfortunately, his pill wasn't. He had to stall for a few more minutes until it kicked in.

She walked seductively to the kitchen, pulled out the electric teapot, filled it with water, and plugged it in. He watched her hips and her beautiful butt as she reached into the cupboard for cups and tea bags.

He felt like an adolescent boy who'd just gotten his first look at a copy of a porn magazine—about to lose it.

She was doing this on purpose, damn her. Tempting him to take her to bed and break his cover. He balled his fist. He was going to hang on and not crack under this exquisite torture no matter how hard and uncomfortable matters became. Until his meds kicked in and things got ugly.

"Would you like a cup?" she asked, her voice sweet and seductive.

He'd like so much more. "Sure."

He took a seat in the recliner where he had a nice view of her working and where she couldn't come over and sit too close to him. He left the big sofa for her.

"Does Aldo have any mint and honey?"

"I—"

"Oh, never mind." She kneeled down to look into a low cabinet where Aldo kept supplies. He watched the sweet curve of her butt and the light shine through the thin material of her blouse. She stood. "Mint and honey."

The teakettle whistled and boiled. Willow poured two cups, then walked to the bar. What the hell was she up to there?

She reached for a bottle of rum. "Here it is. Deep, dark rum. Aldo always has the good stuff." She walked back to the kitchen and poured a generous shot of rum into each mug of tea. She brought the two cups and set them on the coffee table, which sat perpendicular to the chair.

She stood over him, looking down at him with smoky bedroom eyes. "These should really cool for a minute. No use burning our tongues."

The next thing he knew, she straddled him in the chair, knees on either side of his hips. Her long hair tickling his chest as she lowered her crotch onto his and rubbed against him.

He couldn't hide it. She had to feel him bulging against her. Even through two pair of jeans, the sensation was killing him. This was like being a teenager again and desperately trying to get to the next base, fully clothed groping. Only he was trying not to get to the next base, fighting his baser nature. He grabbed the arms of the chair to keep from stroking the breasts that met him in the eye.

*Oh, damn.*

Just then, he felt the first tremor, the tiny rumbling in his gut that meant the pill was working. Just a few more minutes now. He hoped he could hang on long enough, because after two years away from her all he needed were two exquisite minutes. Just two, though he'd love more.

His mission was riding on a razor's edge; everything depended on his fast-acting pill to act faster, damn it. Because there was no way he was stopping himself. In another second or two, he'd lose it.

"Con," she said on a near moan, whispering a name that was, and was not, him as she ran her fingers through his hair and sighed. He wanted to hear her moan and call his real name. Call for Jack. But that was lunacy.

He swallowed hard.

She leaned down and sucked his nipple.

He sucked in a deep breath and lost his control, reaching out and stroking her breasts.

She unzipped his jeans.

He pulled her face up to meet his and brought his lips

to hers. He grabbed the handle for the recliner and pulled it, sending the chair into the reclining position, and Willow tumbling on top of him as he kissed her, one hand tangled in her hair. The other held her tight.

He wanted to feel her, all of her, every last inch.

He slid his hand up beneath her shirt and stroked her back as his lips possessed her mouth.

He needed to feel her bare breasts on his chest. He released her waist and fumbled with the few remaining fastened buttons on her blouse before trying to unfasten her bra.

He'd just freed her blouse when his stomach turned over and a wave of nausea hit him.

They both heard the rumble and gurgle—it was loud enough to wake the dead. Fortunately, it was going to keep this dead guy from being outed as still alive. Damn, he just had seconds now to make it to the bathroom.

He pulled away from her kiss. "Sorry. This is a bad time for this to come up," he quipped as he pushed her off him as gently as a man in dire need of a bathroom can. Actually, it was perfect timing. One second later and—

"Excuse me." He dashed for the toilet. Good thing he'd always been fast. And, despite his mother's fanatical training, left the lid up when he was on his own. He made it just in time.

It was a shame he'd had to resort to such extreme measures to keep himself under control. Aldo had cooked him a terrific dinner. Now it was going to be a while before he could look a manicotti in the face again.

"Con?" He heard Willow's trembling, worried voice as he bent over the porcelain throne and retched.

"I'm fine," he finally managed to say as he gasped for breath. "Must have been something I ate."

She appeared at the doorway to the bathroom. It was a humiliating position to be in, but she looked at him with nothing less than the loving compassion of a wife. Yeah, Willow had seen him like this a few times before.

"I hope it's not contagious." He wiped his mouth, took a deep breath, and tried to grin. "Sorry."

No, it definitely wasn't contagious.

"Don't worry about me. Bad timing," she said, sounding almost suspicious and looking so good he almost forgot his nausea.

He was almost desperate enough to ignore his condition and proceed with the ravishment. But after two years apart they deserved a better reunion than that.

"Yeah," he said.

"Can I get you something? Let me stay and take care of you—"

"No, no, I'd rather you didn't see me this way any more than you have to. Please."

"I guess I'll be going then. . . ." She sounded hesitant as she turned to walk away.

"Don't go alone." He didn't mean to sound so alarmed. She stopped and stared at him.

"Call Aldo and have him take you. I insist."

# CHAPTER TWENTY-ONE

A ldo walked Willow to her front door. "Thanks for believing in Con." He shook his head. "I don't know what's gotten into this town. Suddenly my cousin is this big, bad man who uses women and takes their money.

"Salemos are many things. Dishonorable, bah! That is something we are definitely not. We are *not* thieves. We don't care that much for the money, only the passion of life." As he sighed, his belly jiggled. "If I didn't have to make a living, I'd say, *No meatballs for any of them.*"

Willow smiled at him. Aldo and his meatballs. He'd been kind enough not to mention her sexed-up look. She'd dressed for Con's eyes only. "Don't take it too hard, Aldo. It'll blow over. Once they get to know Con better, they'll forget all about this nonsense."

"They won't get the chance. Con is already making noises about leaving early. He doesn't want to put me out or make things worse. If he leaves, it will put an end to all this rubbish. That's what he says."

"What?" Her worst fears were coming true. She couldn't let Con leave.

"Maybe *you* can convince him to stay longer?" Aldo said with a lifted brow. "A beautiful woman possesses powers of persuasion that I don't, eh?"

Willow laughed softly. *If only.* Aldo was her only ally. Then again, if Con was Jack he was here for a reason and he wouldn't leave until that reason was fulfilled. If only she knew what it was. Maybe it was time to find out.

"I'll try," she said, and meant it. She didn't want Jack to leave. Ever. She unlocked her front door.

"Good night," Aldo said.

She slid into her house and locked up behind her, pausing a minute by the narrow windows on either side of her front door to watch Aldo walk back to his car. Spookie came running in to greet her.

"Hey, girl." Willow scooped her up and cuddled her.

Willow had been so close, this close to everything she needed. She'd only missed it by a fraction of a second. Okay, maybe five minutes, tops. She felt a frustration—sexual, emotional, and overpowering—so strong and complex she almost didn't have words for it.

At that minute, Willow just needed to be near Jack. She carried Spookie into the bedroom, set her on the floor, and pulled her memory bin of Jack from beneath the bed.

*Oh, Jack. No matter what you've done, I love you. Even if you've faked your own death, come back to me. I'll forgive you anything.*

It was a mantra she'd repeated many times. She'd said it before and she would say it again—there was nothing Jack could have done that was so bad she wouldn't love him. Even deserting her for two years and letting her believe he was dead. She trusted that he had a good reason. She lifted the lid of her memory box and tenderly pulled out one memento after the next—the flag, the dog collar—

She gasped. *What?*

Jack's brush was back. She picked up the gallon-size plastic bag that contained it and stared hard at it, heart pounding in her ears.

*No, this can't be.*

She hadn't missed this before. She hadn't. It was one of her most prized possessions. Someone had replaced it. Only two people, or entities, had a reason to steal it in the first place—Jack and the Agency. Only two had any reason to replace it—the same two suspects.

Her heart surged with joy and hope. She smiled a happily evil smile.

*Jack, you prankster, you. You can't fool me with Cubs tattoos or by wearing cologne I hate.*

Jack would have known she'd tried to get his DNA and made sure she had none to compare a test sample to. NCS would have done the same.

She held the Baggie up to the light and stared at it closely. Something was off. She frowned and opened the Baggie, gently feeling a strand of hair.

*This isn't Jack's.*

She knew the touch and feel of Jack's hair. Con's hair felt like Jack's in her fingers. This was imposter hair, replaced to throw her off.

She thought about the convenient timing of Con's sudden nausea. Food poisoning? Stomach flu? No, she thought not. It would have been just like Jack to take something to make himself sick. He probably had syrup of ipecac on hand. Or something stronger. The man never could resist her. And after two years? He'd have to be made of ice. No, Jack needed a sexual suicide pill to stop him from having sex with her and blowing his cover. She knew he did.

*Oh, Jack, you're good. But I'll get you yet.*

When he'd been in the military, there was nothing Jack loved better than a good recon mission. Nothing like the excitement and adrenaline high of being out in enemy territory, spying.

As a spy, he didn't technically do recon, which was a

military function. Spies were supposedly noncombatants. The thought gave Jack a good laugh. Tell that to the bastards he'd killed in the name of freedom and protecting innocent lives.

Now, he would have loved this recon mission more if his stomach wasn't still sore from all the retching he'd done earlier. The things he did in the name of duty.

He pulled a bottle of bitch-in-heat urine from his pocket and sprinkled it along the primrose path Kennett had planted leading from his apple storage barn to the orchards. Old Duke and Buddy were soon going to be feeling some of the sexual frustration Jack had felt earlier this evening.

Jack looked at the dark flowers in the moonlight and shook his head. A floral pathway seemed kind of girlie, but what did he know? It was Cooper's anyway.

Jack wound through the orchards, sprinkling urine and creating a maze of sexual frenzy and disappointment for Kennett's dogs that should keep them occupied and out of Jack's hair for hours.

*Welcome to the club of sexual frustration, boys.*

Jack didn't need pheromones to keep him frustrated. He had Willow.

Jack emptied the bottle, screwed the lid back on, and returned it to his pocket. He wore his night-vision goggles, camouflage fatigues, and had reapplied the eye black in the area beneath his eyes. If anyone caught him, he'd have a hard time explaining himself. Then again, they weren't that far away from Aryan Nation territory. Not that that explanation would win him any friends.

Jack shook his head at the residents of Orchard Bluff. They were still keeping an eye on him. He'd seen four cars drive past Aldo's before he left for the orchards. Aldo lived at the end of civilization on a street that went nowhere and probably had three cars a year cruise farther

than his house. Good luck to the Orchard Bluffers trying to stop him. He'd sneaked past them without any
problem. They didn't know whom they were dealing
with.

If he wanted to, he could sneak over to Willow's and
whisk her away, too. But that would blow everything. Not
that he wasn't tempted, all the same.

Any second now, Duke and Buddy would get a good
whiff of Jack and come running to tear him apart. Until
they caught the scent of something infinitely more seductive and headed off in pursuit of fun that didn't exist. And
took their raucous barking with them.

Jack grinned as he heard the patter of approaching
paws. The hounds of hell would come pounding around
the corner, hit the bushes, and head off in hot pursuit of a
willing female. Or unwilling. Dogs didn't care.

Sure enough, the two dogs barked and bared their
teeth, heading directly to where Jack leaned against the
barn in the shadows, invisible to anyone in the house.

Kennett stepped out onto the porch in his boxers and a
T-shirt and called out after them, "What do you see,
boys? What's out there?"

When they caught the scent Jack had planted, they
took an abrupt right turn and, barking, ran down the floral path to total frustration.

*Boys and their hormones!*

Kennett shook his head. "Damn, dogs! Stop waking
me to run after squirrels and deer!" he yelled. Then he
stepped back inside.

Jack watched the lights go off in the house in a pattern
that led to the bedroom. The Rooster had gone back to bed.

Jack surveyed Kennett's apple barn. The door was pad-
locked shut. That was a cinch for Jack to break through.
The lock didn't worry him.

It was the rest of Kennett's elaborate security system

that concerned him. Kennett was an out-of-the-box thinker, as that gun in Jack's oven indicated. What other crazy devices had the Rooster rigged to keep intruders out of his precious apple barn and away from that hidden bomb shelter?

Thoughts of *Home Alone* and a blowtorch that would singe Jack's head when he opened the door raced through his mind. He could disable electronics. He'd already jammed Kennett's monitoring devices and cameras. It was the unexpected homebrew gadgets that worried Jack.

Kennett had apparently gone back to bed. Which didn't give Jack much comfort. Kennett could spring up and awake any moment, recovering from a concussion or not. Jack didn't feel like lingering.

Kennett's system was way too elaborate for protecting a cashbox and a few bins of apples.

Jack shrugged, donned his shielded gloves in case Kennett had electrified the padlock, got out his industrial-strength bolt cutter, and nipped the padlock off.

So far, so good. Jack's hair wasn't standing on end. He moved in and surveyed the barn. It took him a minute to locate the hidden trapdoor. Kennett had concealed it with a covering of hay.

Jack kneeled and brushed the hay away. As he hunkered down in Kennett's barn, staring through his night-vision goggles at the trapdoor that led into Kennett's bomb shelter, he felt the familiar mission thrill. Which was a very good thing, and the payoff for being bored out of his mind as he'd watched Kennett's house and orchard all afternoon, mapping Kennett's pattern of everyday life and watching person after person troop in to pick and buy apples and get another good dose of Kennett's poisonous lies.

Jack took a myriad of devices from his backpack and scanned the door, checking for explosives and electric currents.

*Damn!* Just as he thought. The door was wired. Without knowing how it was rigged, it was too risky to try to break in.

Jack bent down and sniffed the trapdoor. Some people have a nose for fine wine. Jack had a nose for chemicals and explosives.

Oh yeah. He picked up overtones of various apple scents, hay, dirt, and . . .

He grinned. As he suspected, the bastard had a boatload of fertilizer and chemical explosives stored in the bomb shelter. Ingenious and ironic bastard. Who, besides Jack, would look in a bomb shelter for a bomb?

Jack pushed back to a squatting position. Time to call in a favor. He knew a guy with an airplane and a piece of high-tech wonder who could map this bunker out from the air. But first Jack had to sneak back to Aldo's.

Willow lay in bed, thinking about Jack and Con. The way the Sense lit up every time she was around Con, the way her body reacted to him, all the clues . . .

Hang the DNA. Con was Jack. She believed that with every part of her being. Drew was right—no one and no evidence would convince her otherwise.

She just had to prove it. Had to get Con to admit he was Jack. She knew her husband. He'd never break his cover and never abort a mission. She kept going back to that.

Jack was here for a reason. She liked to think it was to see her and make sure she was doing okay. He'd always been protective. But tonight had convinced her there had to be more to it than that. Jack, of all people, would certainly realize the risk to his cover that she presented. He knew about the Sense and her intuitive nature. Emmett Nelson knew it, too. Neither one of them would take it lightly.

So why risk it? What was at stake here, in this tiny,

out-of-the-way town where apples and sunshine reigned supreme? Was evil lurking somewhere she couldn't see? Could she help Jack? How could she help him if she didn't know what his mission was?

Drew hadn't reported back to her yet. She could bug him, but what good would that do?

She had to discover what Jack's mission was. If he was here, something sinister was going on. He was here to stop some serious evil from happening. Jack's whole goal in life was to serve his country and protect its people from horrors they would never even know they faced.

She wasn't a jealous woman. She didn't hold a grudge. She didn't blame people for their actions, especially if their motives were pure. She always believed the best in people. Another kind of woman would have been furious with Jack for cutting her out of his life and choosing his spy career over her.

Willow wasn't that woman. She knew, from the core of her being, that Jack loved her and always would. If he'd chosen to go deep under the cover of death, it was to protect her and the country. Unless that explosion had messed with his head. But judging from the way Con behaved, it hadn't. He seemed to have all his faculties firmly in place.

And, rats, she'd come close to seeing just how firmly.

No, the more she thought about it, the more convinced she was that Jack was here to save her and probably thousands of innocent people, too. Which didn't alter her plan to sleep with him and prove to herself for sure and certain Con was Jack.

Once she had, she'd have Jack right where she wanted him. She'd be able to convince him to take her undercover with him wherever he went, even if she had to fake her death, too.

She lay back, looking up at the ceiling, and thought for a while longer about everything that had happened since she'd first seen Con at the apple growers' dinner. Had that really been less than a week ago?

In those few days since Con turned up, Shane had taken suddenly ill, running completely against type and reputation and getting plastered after only a few drinks. Then someone had spiked the punch and half the town ended up hungover.

Willow suddenly smiled. *Jack! You bad boy.*

Those pranks were exactly the kind of thing Jack would do, especially if he was trying to keep her and Shane apart. She shook her head as her smile widened. Suddenly she saw Jack's hand in everything. Things began to fall into place and make sense—the rooster falling from the second story. The way the Sense had warned her at the exact moment Con had noticed it and tried to protect her. Her sense of imminent danger, the foreboding . . .

Her mouth went dry. She gasped. That crazy, unruly hair on her neck stood straight up again, for the zillionth time. The rooster! She saw the incident in a different light now, as a real attack on Con, not just an accident.

*Jack's here fighting someone and that someone is fighting back.*

Her heartbeat roared in her ears. She took a deep breath and tried to keep her thinking calm and clear. *Think, Willow, think.*

Who could be at the heart of all this?

*Shane.*

The name popped into her head. Everything revolved around him. He was relatively new to town, too. He and Con clearly didn't like each other. And Shane was always pumping her for information about Jack. She shuddered.

Jack would risk the cover of death to come back and protect her from an evil man. She knew he would.

*Oh, Jack.*

She wished she could talk to him, confront him. But she knew it was pointless. He'd never admit to a thing.

She had to know for sure. She had to make certain she wasn't wrong. There was only one thing to do—investigate Shane. Alone. She couldn't share her fears with anyone. They'd think she'd turned into a conspiracy theorist and nutcase.

She'd have to be exceptionally careful. Because if Shane *was* an adversary of Jack's he was an extremely dangerous man.

# CHAPTER TWENTY-TWO

Jack returned to Aldo's. The two cups of spiked tea were still sitting on the coffee table where Willow had left them. He grabbed one and downed it. What the hell? His stomach had finally settled down and he needed a stiff one. For an alcoholic tea drink it wasn't bad cold.

The scent of Willow's perfume lingered in the chair where they'd been groping and on the cold air he'd let in when he'd aired out the bathroom.

He pulled his secure phone from his pocket, plopped into the chair, and inhaled deeply, dreaming just for a minute about Willow and what had almost transpired in the recliner. Damn, he'd have to be more careful from here on out.

He punched in the number of an old buddy of his from the Defense Intelligence Agency, Josiah Zaran, someone Emmett had cleared Jack to talk to, should he ever need Zaran's help.

Zaran answered on the first ring. "Are you the first person in history to break through from the afterlife? Houdini must be mad as hell you beat him to it. I thought you were dead, my man."

Jack laughed. "Stop bullshitting me. You're one of the very few people with clearance to know better."

Zaran was sometimes known as the Mole in intelligence circles because of the years early in his career that he'd spent belowground in Grand Forks, ND., tending intercontinental ballistic missiles in their hardened eighty-foot-deep silos. Now Zaran worked as an intelligence officer in the Underground Facility Analysis Center, a joint effort of various intelligence communities, including the National Security Agency, that was housed not too far from Langley, Virginia. Former CIA director John Deutch had established the center as a think tank where intelligence officers could brainstorm ways to find and destroy the United States' enemies' underground clandestine weapon sites.

Zaran had access to a plane or two equipped with electromagnetic gear that beamed electromagnetic energy down, illuminating underground sites powerfully enough to map a fly on the wall of a bunker beneath the ground.

"I need a plane, Zar."

"What the hell, radio silence for two years and now you need a plane. Where, when, and what the hell for?"

Jack started with the easy questions. "Immediately if not sooner. To map an underground bunker I believe is housing explosives and plans to disrupt the upcoming G Eight auxiliary meeting." He took a deep breath and explained about Orchard Bluff, hoping Zaran didn't laugh in his face.

"Holy shit," Zaran said. "You want me to buzz an apple orchard on U.S. soil?"

"No," Jack said calmly. "I want you to fly over at fifty thousand feet and map out an enemy combatant's lair so I can carry out my mission to stop him from killing innocent people."

Zaran laughed again and let loose a string of casual, conversational curses. "You don't ask for much. You know how much jet fuel I'll use sending out one of my spy planes?"

"Yeah, I have a pretty good idea. Less than you use on most of your test runs." Jack took a breath. "Look, Zar, you know I never ask unless it's important. Take it all the way to the President to get clearance if you have to. Let him decide whether he wants a terrorist attack on his watch or not."

Zaran cursed some more. He used curses as filler words the way some people used *um*. "I don't need the President's approval for a mission like this. Fine, you have your plane. One fly-by should do it."

"When will I have my data? I need to strike quickly and get the hell out of Dodge," Jack said.

"I'll have it to you tomorrow morning. You can wait until oh seven hundred, I assume. It'll take me an hour or two to get the proper clearance to get a pilot and flight plan. And since you've been dead for two years, I imagine you could use your beauty sleep. We should give you a new code name. How about Zombie?"

"I liked Sariel better, but I guess that one's out of commission now."

"Yeah, like you were ever an angel."

Willow opened the caramel shop, thinking of Shane. She needed to get into his house and see what Jack could be interested in.

She'd never paid much attention to Grant's place before, even after she met Shane, other than to decide it was a mess and still reeked of fussy old lady. But Con had gone up into Shane's bedroom and seen something there. Willow was certain of it now that she thought back and remembered how Con had looked when he'd come down from the room Shane was staying in. And it hadn't been a ghost, either. Con had also been particularly curious about the bomb shelter. If Con was Jack, as she believed he was, he had a reason.

Shane. She couldn't believe she was suspecting him of who knows what. She certainly didn't have a clue. He didn't *seem* like an enemy spy. But then, Jack didn't seem like a spy, either. And no one would ever think all-American Drew was a spy. No one in her family even suspected Jack might be one. But the ones you didn't suspect were the best spies, weren't they? The ones who went around destroying cars and buildings like James Bond were a bit too obvious.

Shane's interest in Jack was also suspicious and a little too coincidental. There was something going on there. She just didn't know what.

She hated the thought of being alone with Shane, but she had to know what Jack was up to if she was going to blackmail him into taking her with him when this mission was over. Once she slept with him and confronted him, of course.

She'd have to be careful, very, very careful, if she was going to potentially step into the middle of one of Jack's missions.

She weighed the risk for less than a second. Any peril was worth getting Jack back. Life without him was just too empty.

There was no one in the store. She grabbed her phone and texted Shane: *I need to talk to someone about Jack. Can I see you tonight?*

Jack sat at the kitchen table in the guesthouse and went over the intel Zaran's spy plane had collected. Outside, Aldo cussed and swore as he righted the metal rooster sculpture someone had tipped over in the night.

Rooster tipping. Only in Orchard Bluff.

Jack studied the images with the skill an ultrasound technician uses in detecting cancer or healthy babies. His trained eye picked up on things the casual observer would be oblivious to.

The bunker was a terrorist war room and command

center. Bulletin boards full of airport and hotel floor plans and electronic circuit schematics. An adequate supply of food to last for weeks if Kennett needed to hide out there, waiting for a chance to escape. A decent supply of fertilizer and explosives, enough to blow up the bunker if the need arose. And a freezer filled with Grant Cooper's body. Well, a body, anyway. Who else would it be? Jack wondered why Kennett hadn't disposed of it yet. He liked to keep trophies?

Jack took a sip of coffee he'd made himself. He wasn't chancing the wrath of Ada again at Bluff Country Store. He cursed beneath his breath.

Intel collected by NCS indicated Kennett was masterminding and orchestrating the attack on LA from sleepy little Orchard Bluff. Which was convenient for two reasons—its complete ordinariness and proximity to Willow. The details of that attack were certainly on those bulletin boards and easels. Jack had to get in there to take a look before he blew up Kennett's stash of explosives.

As Jack suspected, Kennett had an elaborate protection system on the bunker. If someone tried to break in, they'd be blown to bits along with any evidence of Kennett's sinister plot.

Archibald Random, head of RIOT, was behind this. Jack didn't know how it fit into Random's overall plot for world domination. And Jack really didn't care. He'd leave that for big-picture minds like that of his boss Emmett Nelson to worry about.

Jack was one little, very important cog in the plot to foil Random. And Jack was damn well going to do his job and have some fun.

Jack was as much an explosives expert as Kennett. And after having been blown up once himself, he had a healthy appreciation for the finesse required. It wouldn't exactly be a piece of cake getting past Kennett's defenses and blowing up his bomb shelter with Kennett in it. But it would make for a hell of a show.

Ada stopped by the shop, arriving with Willow's favorite fall coffee drink—Ada's signature apple harvest pumpkin spice latte.

"What did I do to deserve this treat?" Willow walked around from behind the counter and took the warm paper cup from her.

Ada pulled off her lightweight driving gloves. "I needed a break from the store. I thought I'd save you a trip and pick up my order of caramel sauce myself."

"That's sweet of you. Do you have time to sit and visit for a minute? I'm due for a break, too. I've been up since dawn making caramel." She indicated one of the three small tables reserved for guests. She wished she could confide in Ada. She really needed to talk her plans over with someone. But there was no way she could divulge a word of what she knew to Ada. She couldn't even share her plans with someone in the know about Jack like Staci.

Being a living spy's widow was a lonely, isolated life. What she really wanted to do was talk things over with Jack. He'd get a kick out of her plot. And absolutely stop her from implementing it.

"I've got a minute." Ada pulled out a chair.

The two of them sat. Willow took a sip of latte and sighed. "You've outdone yourself."

Ada smiled back. "I've been working on perfecting the recipe. The secret is a sprinkle of Ceylon cinnamon on top. I get it from a top-secret supplier of mine. I must protect my sources."

Willow laughed at Ada's spy reference, though she was sure Ada had no idea why she found it so funny.

"So, I hear you and Shane have a date tonight. What

happened to your interest in Con?" Ada's lack of enthusiasm for the situation shone on her face.

"Nothing. And it's not a date with Shane. Just friends getting together," Willow lied.

"Well, Shane has a different opinion of your evening together. When he stopped by the store this morning for his coffee, he was simply beaming. And bragging. I think he thinks he's going to get some action, if you know what I mean." She tilted her head and studied Willow. "I can't explain it, Willow, but I don't trust Shane, even though he is Grant's friend. There was something almost sinister about his good mood."

Sometimes close friends were like slipping with the saltshaker while making caramel—a real pain. Ada was scaring Willow.

Willow shook her head. "Sinister happiness? That's a new one." As she took another sip, she was puzzled by Shane's behavior. She'd made it clear they were just friends.

Ada leaned forward. "Just be careful, okay?"

"Sure. And if it makes you feel any better, I'll call you when I get back from Shane's." Jack had taught Willow to always have backup. "And tell you all about it. If you don't hear from me by midnight, call me."

Ada nodded. "And if you're having such a good time you don't answer?"

"Call back. If I still don't answer, I give you permission to charge into Shane's and haul me out of there. Or call the cops."

Ada shook her head and grinned. She obviously thought Willow was just teasing.

"Seriously," Willow said.

"Okay. Deal. But I think you should be cautious around both him *and* Con."

"Oh no! Not you, too? You can't condemn Con based on rumors. Aldo says he's the real deal and so does his *nonna*. And no one doubts his *nonna*." She mimicked Aldo and laughed. "Don't forget my fabulous sleuthing, either. I did a thorough online search on him. I didn't find a bit of evidence of anything criminal, immoral, unethical, or even fattening."

"You can't believe everything you read online," Ada pleaded with her.

Willow gave up. She needed to confide in someone. She wanted someone to understand about Jack. She needed an ally, even if what she was about to do was reckless. Especially given how gossip seemed to funnel through Orchard Bluff Store.

"I can't help liking Con. He reminds me of Jack. Hang on," Willow said. "I want to show you something. Maybe then you'll understand." She set her coffee down, popped up, and went to her locked supply drawer where she kept receipts and other important papers for the shop.

She pulled Jack's picture from beneath a stack of papers and carried it to the table, set it down, and slid it over for Ada to see. "I've never shown this to anyone here. I know people think it's odd I don't have his picture on display." She was just obeying Agency orders. "It's hard to explain why." She shrugged. No one would believe her anyway. "Everyone grieves differently. I'm trying to move forward with life. I can't if I'm reminded of him every day."

It was as good an explanation as any.

She watched Ada study the picture, waiting for an exclamation of recognition.

Finally, Ada smiled and pushed the picture back across the table to her. Her eyes sparkled and she appeared to be touched by Willow's gesture. "Jack was an attractive man. I can see why you miss him. How does Con remind you of him?"

Willow couldn't believe what she was hearing. She sputtered for a minute before coming up with a response.

"What do you mean, how does Con remind me of him? Isn't the similarity obvious?" Drew and Staci had seen it immediately.

Ada grabbed the picture back and studied it again. "They have similar coloring. I can see that. And maybe something about the eyes. But you must be reacting to their personalities. Because, no, really, except for a passing similarity, I don't think they look at all alike."

"B-b-but . . . ," Willow stammered. "They're practically twins. Take a closer look." She pointed at the picture.

Ada obliged her, studying and frowning. "Nope. Nothing." She looked up at Willow. "If anything, Con looks more like Aldo than your Jack. Huh, maybe they are cousins after all."

Willow couldn't get Ada's words out of her head as she mechanically went through her afternoon. How could Ada not see the striking resemblance? It was so blatantly obvious. Willow felt as if she were living in the Twilight Zone. She half-expected Rod Serling to appear at any minute to explain what was going on. Like maybe an alien had body-snatched Ada.

Could Willow have been mistaken? Was she being so stubbornly optimistic and hopeful that she'd deluded herself into believing Con was Jack because she wanted him to be?

As Willow stood in front of her mirror, brushing her hair and getting ready for her visit with Shane, she almost chickened out, almost decided it was a pointless mission. If Con wasn't Jack, Shane wasn't a person of interest to anyone, certainly not her. Not with Con around.

For her evening with Shane, she was going for the opposite look she used when she was trying to seduce Con. She was going barefaced for the fresh, innocent look, with just a hint of mascara and a dash of light-pink lip gloss.

She applied the gloss and frowned at her reflection. Did she look too feral? Like a woman on the hunt?

She hated all these doubts. And she really hated the evil woman she'd become. She'd spent an hour making Shane a special four-piece box of his favorite chocolate-covered lavender caramels—laced with a strong dose of the most powerful over-the-counter antihistamine on the market.

She wasn't taking any chances. She'd learned one thing from Jack and his spy friends Kyle and Drew—when entering a dangerous, clandestine environment, always, always, always stack the deck in your favor. And that's all she'd done, really, just dosed Shane's caramels with a little something to make him drowsy, a little chemical something.

Yes, she was all for all-natural and dead set against chemical additions, but she really couldn't help herself this time.

It was just too bad it had taken her so long to get the recipe just right. Those silly antihistamine pills were bright pink on the outside. But, fortunately, white on the inside. She'd had to crush and strain them to get rid of the bright-pink coating. Then add extra sugar to cover the bitter taste, which messed with her recipe. So she'd had to add extra salt so the caramel wasn't too sweet. Which would seem like an oxymoron to the uninitiated caramel lover.

Adding chemicals to her organic, all-natural caramel seemed like a crime against nature. And to make matters worse, she had a bottle of apple wine to accompany it. Wine was supposed to increase the soporific effects of the antihistamine. Oh, really bad her, she'd looked up how to make it even more potent.

And now she was even beginning to think like a criminal. She had put one untainted caramel in the box in case Shane offered her one. She'd marked it subtly with a little flourish of chocolate on top. And she had an untainted box of caramels in her big purse that she was going to swap for any leftovers of the drugged stuff as soon as Shane was out.

And even more heinous her, while Shane boasted about his tolerance for alcohol and resistance to most drugs, she knew his Achilles' heel. He was particularly sensitive to the drowsy effects of plain old antihistamines. Just two weeks ago, he'd complained to her about his allergies and how he couldn't take the most effective antihistamine because it made him way too sleepy to drive or operate the farm equipment.

So, yes, she was bad to the bone for what she was about to do.

And not as confident as she'd originally been. She was so insecure, she'd nearly broken down and shown Jack's picture to Shiloh when she'd come in for her shift. Just to get her reaction and see whether she couldn't see the resemblance, either. Maybe only people who had known Jack well could see it? Only remembering Emmett's firm warning stopped her. She'd already screwed up once today and look what that had gotten her! More doubt.

# CHAPTER TWENTY-THREE

Willow curled up on Shane's ratty old sofa next to him, shoes off, feet bare, legs tucked beneath her, with a glass of the wine she'd brought in one hand. She was on high alert for any signs Shane was going to make a move on her as she listened to him drone on about his late lost love and pry her for details about Jack.

"Crystal had the cutest little birthmark on her neck. Right here." Shane touched Willow's neck just above the hollow of her throat.

She fought a wave of revulsion. The look he gave her, she couldn't explain it, but if he'd been a vampire searching for her jugular that look and touch wouldn't have creeped her out more. It wasn't the first time during the evening she'd debated the wisdom of coming here. If she hadn't been so desperate to out Jack as himself, she'd have grabbed her purse and run.

"Did Jack have anything like that? Any identifying mark that if you saw it, you'd know it was him right away? Something that took your breath away because it was so uniquely Jack?" He took a drink from his second glass of wine.

*Good. Drink, drink.* The more alcohol he had, the more effective that antihistamine was going to be.

"Yes," she said. "He had the cutest cowlick just here." She reached over and stroked Shane's head, indicating the spot and making a note to remember it. Because, of course, she was lying. Jack didn't have a cowlick. But the Agency had warned her well and good. She never gave out intel about Jack, not to anyone. Least of all to a man she was suspicious about.

A bag of chips and a bowl of dip sat on the coffee table in front of them, untouched.

Shane indicated it. "Have some chips and dip. I made the dip myself. From a mix." He laughed.

The last thing she intended to do was eat anything she hadn't brought herself. For one thing, she'd seen the unsanitary condition of his kitchen. And for another, Jack had always told her that when you're on a spy mission you don't trust the food of the enemy. Wise counsel. It could be poisoned.

"It looks delicious. Maybe later. First, I've brought you something sweet." She popped up to get it, watching him over her shoulder as he finished the glass of wine and she set hers on the table.

Yes, she was an evil woman, sympathizing with him about his grief and plying him with alcohol so the antihistamine would work to maximum effect. She wanted him dozing soundly so she could snoop. She just hoped that if he was indeed an enemy agent, he hadn't planted surveillance cameras all over the place.

A fire crackled in the old fireplace and, although it should have made the room seem homey, did little to mask the sense of gloom in the house.

She went to her purse, which she'd dumped on a nearby chair, and pulled the box of doctored caramels out.

"For you." She held the gold foil box wrapped with a lavender ribbon out to him, poised on her fingers like the apple the witch had offered Snow White. Maybe she shouldn't have been so obvious when offering her poison? "A get well gift. Chocolate and caramel never fail to make a person feel better. I made them specially for you."

Not in a dark dungeon, like Snow White's witch, but concocting poisonous treats is an evil business, even if done in a candy kitchen for the good of Willow's marriage and possibly the world.

Shane didn't seem to notice either her deceptive, too-sweet nature or her nerves as he took the box from her outstretched hand. "Specially for me, huh?"

He pulled off the ribbon and then the lid of the box. "Are these what I think they are?"

NCS chief Emmett Nelson had always told Jack and his buddies that the most convincing way to lie was to tell as much truth as possible. Wedge the lie in the middle, where it would go unseen.

Following that advice, she nodded and smiled as she picked up her wineglass and sat down. "I made them this afternoon. I've been fiddling with the recipe and wanted your opinion on the new blend."

She wanted to know whether the antihistamine flavor was too strong and would kill the market for this new *knock him out* flavor. Not that she had any intention of selling them. Not unless she got her pharmacy license. Though she did have a great name for them—KOs.

Shane waved his hand over them as if wafting their scent toward him and took a long, big sniff, acting as serious as if he were judging the world chocolate contest.

Willow held her breath. Just how sensitive *was* his nose? Was he like Jack, who could sniff out an explosive or foreign chemical from ten feet away?

She felt a sudden chill creep down her spine as she realized her own stupidity. If he was a foe of Jack's, of course he'd be able to sniff out the allergy meds in the candy. Not that they were particularly aromatic, to her nose they didn't smell at all, but she'd seen Jack sniff out things she couldn't smell for the life of her. He had the fine nose sensibilities of a chemical bloodhound.

She fought hard not to cross her fingers in front of Shane. With Jack potentially back in her life, everything had taken on a sinister nature again. But not all spies had Jack's nose for chemicals, right? She couldn't remember Drew having the same knack. At least not to the same degree.

"Ah . . . deep, dark chocolate. Lavender." Shane smiled at her. "Am I missing anything?"

She almost relaxed. "No, I think you got it all. Excellent."

Shane, with his dimples and blond growth of five o'clock shadow, should have been appealing to the point of irresistible. Lettie would have been all over him. But Willow felt a shiver of revulsion. She hid her feelings by taking a sip of wine, hoping it would mellow her fear and make her relax.

She felt a deep sense of foreboding, but she'd felt that since the anniversary of Jack's death, so it was no help to her now. She was on her own.

Shane, however, didn't stop playing his chocolate connoisseur game. He kept wafting and sniffing as she held her breath.

Finally, he smiled. "Liar!"

She jumped, nearly spilling her wine.

"You've added more salt."

The hair on the back of her neck stood up. He was exactly right. How could he tell by simply smelling? He did have Jack's talented nose. She'd been totally reckless. And yet, either Shane was toying with her or she'd gotten away with her deception.

She forced herself to keep smiling. "You really are good!"

Whether he smelled the chemical addition or not, he had a dangerous talent. She had to proceed carefully.

"I'm experimenting with making lavender sea salt

caramels. You picked up the extra salt." She let her surprise show and lowered her voice, hoping to keep him distracted until she drugged him. "You have a talented nose."

He smiled and leaned close to her. "The best."

*Not quite. Or you would have picked up the antihistamine. Jack would have. Or maybe you have and you're toying with me.*

"We'll have to convince you to come back next year and judge the apple pie contest."

"I'd be up for it." He leaned back and spun the box around 180 degrees in his hand with a flourish so that the doped caramels ended up closest to her. He offered the box to her. "Ladies first."

Jack would have cursed at Shane's table-turning chocolate box maneuver. She had made sure to hand the box to him so that the untainted caramel should have been nearest her. Willow tried not to bite her lip and give away that she was nervous.

*Think like a spy.*

It would be impolite and out of character for her to reach across the box and take the caramel farthest from her. An enemy agent would notice her deliberate move and get suspicious. She had to act naturally.

She took the box from his hand, studied it, gave it a gentle half turn as she pretended to make up her mind about which piece of candy to take, and held the box back out to him. "Oh, I couldn't. I made them for you. You have to choose first." Again, nothing but the truth there.

She'd handed him the box in such a way that the drug-free caramel would be near her. She had to protest once more, just to keep up the ruse, but she hoped he still insisted she take the first piece.

"No, seriously. You first. My mama taught me manners. She'd have my head if I didn't treat you like a lady." He spun the box around again.

She smiled and took a drugged caramel. She waited while he selected a candy, fortunately a drugged one, then set the box down.

Her heart hammered in her chest like one of Shane's dogs begging to get out the door. The dogs lay, heads on their paws, at Shane's feet by the sofa, mournfully looking up but refusing to beg for a treat. Shane had them well trained.

"To death by heavenly chocolate and caramel!" Shane raised his caramel almost as a toast and laughed.

At his words, she nearly dropped her caramel, recovering just at the last second to raise it to her lips. She'd put enough allergy medicine in it to put down an elephant. There's no way she wanted to take a bite.

But there was nothing for it. She held her caramel up to her lips to bite and "slipped," dropping it from her fingers.

The candy fell on the floor. Buddy dove for it and licked it up. She and Shane reached for Buddy, each in a fury to stop him from swallowing it.

She watched in horror as Buddy chomped and caramel-tinged saliva rolled down his doggie cheeks.

Shane got to him first. "Drop it!"

Buddy stared at him, looking innocent.

"I said, drop it!"

Buddy barked twice and wagged his tail. His mouth was empty.

"I'm so sorry!" Willow looked on in horror. What had she just done to Shane's dog? "That's dark chocolate he's just eaten. It's almost as bad for a dog as pure cocoa. He'll be sick. We have to take him to the vet."

Shane set his caramel down and shook his head, looking as if the last thing he wanted was to make a run to the vet. "Bud's a big dog, aren't you, boy?" He rubbed the dog's jowls and scratched him beneath his chin. "There wasn't enough chocolate to make a dog his size sick enough to worry about. He'll be fine."

Shane gave Buddy the evil eye. "I just hope he doesn't get a taste for chocolate. If he does, he's no good to me."

Something about his tone sent a shiver down her back. He meant it. And a dog who was no good to him—what did he do with such an animal?

"But, really, Shane, I think we should—"

Shane cut her off with a look.

She felt awful, absolutely horrible. She didn't believe Shane. She'd put an extra-thick coating of chocolate on those caramels to disguise the taste of antihistamine. And she'd used 70 percent cacao chocolate. The higher the cacao content, the more dangerous it was for dogs. What if poor Buddy got sick?

She'd never be able to drug Shane then. And she wouldn't forgive herself for accidentally hurting Buddy.

Shane grabbed Buddy's collar, called to Duke to follow him, and led them out of the room, returning shaking his head.

He sat down right next to her on the sofa. "Now, where were we? Oh yes, deep, dark-chocolate–covered caramels." He picked up his caramel, grinned at Willow, and put it into his mouth whole.

That was easy.

He rolled his eyes back in pleasure as he sucked on the caramel. "Heavenly."

*Play the game. Never give yourself away or you're dead.*

She heard Jack's warning in her mind almost as clearly as if it were audible.

She held the candy box out to Shane again. "Have another."

Jack stood at the edge of the Rooster's apple orchards at the top of the path of flowers just outside the apple barn.

He wore black camo, his typical *sneaking out and spying at night* garb. He was nothing more than a shadow. Death coming in little army combat–booted feet. Kennett's dogs hadn't even picked him up.

He stared at Willow's car in the driveway, frowning. *What the hell is Willow's doing here?*

Yes, he'd been tracking her. When her car headed for Kennett's, he had to follow. Happily, her visit coincided with his mission to infiltrate Kennett's, so he could kill two birds with one stone, so to speak. Although he intended to kill only one bird, a great big cocky one.

His heart stopped for just a minute before kicking back into gear with an unreasonable stab of jealousy. And a pang of denial—maybe she was just hanging with the dogs. Yeah, everyone in there was a dog, including Kennett. But Jack was thinking of Buddy and Duke, who were a higher class of animal altogether than the Rooster.

Jack bit back a long string of curses in Portuguese that Kyle had taught him years ago. There was nothing quite as impressive as Portuguese cursing. Jack had an irrational urge to ram Kennett's door in.

Which, of course, was not covert at all. That didn't stop Jack from wanting to charge in, take back his wife, and carry her caveman-style the hell out of there. Kennett anywhere around Willow gave Jack barbarian urges.

Was she taking pity on a poor invalid? Just being friendly? Or something more dangerous? Had she finally made the connection between Kennett and Con? He hoped not.

Jack's pulse pounded out of control at a time when he needed calm and clear thinking.

The woman was stubborn. She wouldn't rest until she found out for sure whether he was himself or not. None of which explained exactly what she was doing here. Or why he was so damn jealous and distracted. He forced his attention back on his mission.

The apple barn beckoned before him, locked tightly with an alarmed padlock. Breaking through it was not a problem for Jack.

The curtained, warmly lit living room window before him, however, was a huge temptation. There was just the tiniest of cracks between the bottom of the curtain and the window ledge. *Enough for a spy camera to peep through.*

Jack just hoped the Rooster hadn't armed any devices to jam Jack's night-vision goggles or spy cams. Jack slunk to the side of the house with his bag of spy gear slung over his shoulder, tiptoed through the fall asters and mums, insinuated himself between Kennett's siding and his bushes, and inconspicuously put his high-def, night-vision spy cam key chain on the outside window ledge so it could focus through the tiny slit beneath the curtain. After activating it, of course. This wasn't the cheap kind with a flashing red light to give it away. This was the real-deal CIA-grade device.

Jack wore night-vision goggles with spy cam receptor video. He hunkered down in the bushes and turned on the video receiver. Almost instantaneously he was watching Kennett cuddle up next to Willow.

Nope, Kennett hadn't set up a jammer.

There's jealousy and then there's soul-baring, blinding, raging, protective jealousy, the kind that makes a guy want to kill. Jack experienced a high-voltage jolt of the second kind. He did not want that killer touching Willow, not even to shake her hand. Before Jack could master his emotions, he rammed his shoulder against the outer wall of Kennett's house.

It was a foolish thing to do.

*Calm down, idiot in love, before you blow things.*

Jack hunkered down, squatting and resting on the balls of his feet. He slammed one fist into his other palm, imagining it was Kennett's face he was hitting. Bad idea. His hand hurt like hell and he needed it for his mission. Love made a guy do stupid things and Jack was behaving like the world's dumbest spy. He could take that bastard out with one well-placed sniper shot. And throw his entire career away with that one bullet.

*I'm going to kill that SOB.* And he meant it.

Jack took a deep breath and counted to three the way the Agency psychiatrist had taught him to do when he felt his anger raging out of control. He separated himself into two separate beings—Jack the professional spy who never got riled and Jack the jealous husband. He let Jack the spy push Jack the husband into the background and take over. He'd been using this kind of compartmentalization to survive his entire life. It kept him sane doing what he did for a living and had saved his sanity more than once when he was a bullied kid.

Somewhat under control, he glanced at the apple-shed door. He had to get into that bunker. Watching Willow schmoozing with the enemy wasn't going to help him accomplish his mission. But he couldn't leave her unprotected.

Jack left the key-chain cam where it was and headed to the shed. If she needed him, and he planned on keeping an eye on her, he was only seconds away.

Shane turned toward the window. "Did you hear that?"

"What?" Willow hadn't heard a thing.

"I heard a noise outside. By the window."

Willow shook her head. "You must have supersonic hearing. I didn't hear a thing."

Shane cocked an ear, acting more nervous than she'd ever seen him. Yes, he was always cautious, and maybe the tiniest bit paranoid about his privacy, but this went beyond normal. Which made the case that he was Jack's target. An enemy spy would be extremely conscious of his surroundings and always on guard. Jack always was.

"I heard something." Shane stared at the curtained window, frowning. His chest rose and fell in a pattern that indicated he was getting worked up and was afraid of something or someone. "I'd better check it out."

"Now?" Willow couldn't let him go outside. Any minute now that allergy med would blend with the wine and kick in and Shane would go down like a bull moose. Even hitching him to Buddy and Duke she'd never be able to drag him back inside. At least, not without a lot of bruising and unexplainable bondage burns. She did not need the rumors those would cause.

She was trying to keep this visit clandestine and below the radar, particularly Jack's.

How could she ever explain to the neighbors why Shane was outside and passed out cold, under the influence of antihistamines?

"I'll be right back." He rubbed his eyes and yawned.

*It's kicking in already.*

She grabbed his hand to stop him. "It's probably nothing," she said. "Just a mouse or rabbit. Maybe one of those pesky raccoons. Didn't you tell me you've seen several in your maple tree?" She gave him a warm smile. "Can't we just ignore it? We were having such a nice . . . time."

Shane squeezed her hand, gave it a pat, and pulled his hand free from hers. "I won't be gone long."

Darn, she wasn't quite convincing enough.

Shane stood up and immediately swayed on his feet. "Whoa. Stood up too fast."

She was in big trouble now. The drugs were kicking in.

She sprang to her feet and threw her arm around him,

bracing him against her to steady him. "Don't worry, I've got you. You don't look well. What's wrong?"

"I feel dizzy." He blinked. "And suddenly very tired."

"The concussion," she said. "You're still suffering from the concussion."

In Jack's line of work, he'd suffered many concussions. He usually bounced back quickly, but a couple of times he'd suffered Post-Concussion Syndrome, PCS. She knew enough of the symptoms to try to pawn these off on the effects of the antihistamines she'd dosed Shane with kicking in.

"But it's been days. I've never—" He stopped short.

Never what? Had one before? There were a million ways to bang his head working on a farm in an orchard. Something like falling off a ladder, for example.

He rested his weight more heavily against her. She shifted him around until he was facing her. "Hang on to me." She put his arms around her waist. "We need to get you to bed. Now. Then I'll call the doctor—"

"No doctor. I'll be fine." He swayed in her arms. "I've had concussions before."

She shot him an uncertain look. "Shane—"

"I'll be okay. No doctor. I don't like strangers in my place."

"I'll drive you to Emergency."

"Just get me to bed." He swayed.

She swayed with him, nearly buckling as he shifted more of his weight to her. "Can you make it up the stairs?"

He nodded. "I think so. With your help."

She tried to get him sideways to her with her arm around his waist and his around her shoulder. But he was so large and unsteady, she couldn't maneuver him. And she couldn't carry him on her back.

The only way that seemed to work was for him to hang

on to her as if they were slow dancing and gently glide him toward the stairs in an awkward waltz.

"I feel like there should be dance music," she said. "Here. Glide with me."

He was fading quickly. She had to get him upstairs. Now.

"This is fun." Even his voice was fading away. He nuzzled her neck. "I should take you dancing sometime."

"I'd love that," she said, feeling fully awake and anxious. She had to get Shane to bed, search his room, and get home. "Right now, dance with me up the stairs to bed."

# CHAPTER TWENTY-FOUR

Jack disabled the lock and security system for the barn. It wasn't elaborate. It didn't need to be. The bomb shelter defense system was another matter.

Jack set a motion-detecting warning sensor by the barn door and a guard cam. If anyone came in, it would buzz and alert Jack to an intruder. He positioned a portable spy cam toward Kennett's house, too, aiming it so he got a view of both the living room and master bedroom windows. Every smart spy and assassin covered his back.

Before attacking the bomb shelter, Jack took a final look at Kennett's window. Two figures were silhouetted against it, clenched together way too closely for Jack's comfort, swaying almost as if in time to music.

Jack the husband broke through his compartment into mission territory. Jack the spy stopped him just in time, before he did something stupid. He watched Kennett and Willow sway as they moved away and out of his range of vision.

Something was off with their movements. Kennett moved as if he was drunk or drugged. Jack knew drunk and drugged well enough to recognize it even in shadow. Either that or the Rooster had no rhythm and couldn't dance. But the dance-off had proved otherwise.

Jack knew the layout of Kennett's house. He and Willow were heading toward the stairs. Jack stared at the window, scowling and vowing to set an extra charge just to teach Kennett a lesson for leaning on her. Willow was obviously in control and trying to help Kennett.

Jack should have kept moving and gotten on with his mission, but he was mesmerized by the window. Watching. Waiting for a light to go on upstairs. It took much longer than it should have for a light to come on on the second story. Long enough for Jack to imagine all kinds of horrible scenarios.

Just as he was about to charge to the house and rescue her, a light came on in Kennett's bedroom and two silhouettes emerged. It now appeared as if Willow were putting a drunk Kennett to bed.

What was Willow up to? Jack didn't have much time to consider. As long as Kennett was out, Willow was safe. And he wouldn't be surprising Jack as he worked. Jack turned away. Time to get back to spying for the mission at hand.

By the time Willow got Shane to the upstairs hallway he was almost dead on his feet. She hoped not literally. What had she done? She'd never seen anyone react so quickly and so severely to allergy meds. But Shane was fighting to stay awake.

"Hang on, Shane," she whispered softly in his ear. "I've got you. We're almost there."

She maneuvered Shane through the doorway, accidentally smacking his shoulder on the frame in the process. "Sorry! Sorry." She winced, hating the thought that she might have hurt him.

He murmured something back to her. She hoped it was something forgiving like, D*on't worry.* Or, *No problem.* Or, *It only hurts when I move.* Which was what Jack would have said.

She limped toward the bed with Shane's arm looped around her, nearly dragging him. This was turning out to be a bad idea. Very bad. Spying wasn't as easy as Jack and Drew made it look.

"Come on, Shane," she crooned in Shane's ear. "Just a few more steps."

Shane moved like a zombie, but at least he moved.

"Hang on," she said. "Let me just pull back the covers." She balanced him against her, spinning and sticking out her butt with him flopping over her back from behind so she could reach the covers and open the bed for him.

As she pulled back the comforter and glanced at the disaster area he called a bedroom he copped a feel of her breast and she felt him go hard against her backside.

*Men!* Nearly dead to the world and still getting aroused.

If she ever had any doubts as to whether Shane was the one for her or not, they were now totally disabused. With his member pressed against her butt and his hand on her breast she felt mostly revulsion and nothing more.

She did a magician's flip of the comforter, accidentally wiggling her butt against Shane as she did.

"Oh, baby," Shane whispered. "I was hoping the night would end like this—with the two of us taking a tumble."

He was definitely out of it if he thought he was getting lucky. In a few minutes, maybe seconds, he'd be out cold. Since arriving, she'd been puzzling over why he hadn't made a move on her. What had all that bragging been about at the store? He must have been waiting for the right moment. Fortunately, he'd waited too long.

With the bed open, Willow wondered whether she could just step aside and let Shane tumble onto the bed sideways. Then maybe she could swing his legs up. It was worth a try.

"To bed with you now." She removed Shane's hand from her breast and tried to sidestep out of his way.

Shane grabbed her and spun her around to face him.

"Willow," he said as he stared into her eyes with an

unfocused gaze and swayed like the apple trees in his orchard under the influence of a stiff breeze.

"Shane?"

He fell forward onto her, pushing her back on the bed. She landed beneath him with an *oomph*, her legs straddling him.

"Shane!" she yelled.

But he was out for the count.

His chest rose and fell—right in her face. She could barely breathe, smothered beneath his chest and weight. He smelled hot, in the sweaty sense. Was that a side effect, too? It was definitely not a turn-on.

What was she going to do now?

She stuck both legs in the air, hoping to get some momentum and get her legs beneath her onto the bed. Maybe she could brace them and somehow inch herself and Shane fully on the bed. Then she'd wriggle out from beneath him. Maybe. She hoped. If she could just keep breathing long enough.

Jack plowed through the hay behind the apple-weighing counter in Kennett's apple shed until he found the trapdoor into the bomb shelter.

It was equipped with another electronic lock. He grinned. He knew this kind of lock. No problem. He leaned down and got to work. Within minutes, the lock released.

Jack took a deep breath, bracing himself to open the shelter door. For just being in his early thirties Kennett was surprisingly old-school and creative with his methods of defense and killing, as evidenced by the gun in Jack's oven.

The magnetic imaging scan Zaran had sent Jack was as detailed as modern technology allowed. From what Jack could read on the scan, the Rooster hadn't booby-trapped the door. Jack threw it open and jumped back. His heart pounded as he hunkered against the barn wall, ready to flee. All was quiet on the barn front. He'd gambled correctly.

He went to the entrance and peered in. Just as he suspected, Kennett had armed it with a laser maze. In the movies, spies have to jump and tumble their way through such a maze, hoping they don't break a beam and end up dead.

Real spies, like Jack, carried laser-jamming devices. He pulled his from his tool belt and went to work. In just a few minutes, he'd cleared the maze.

He slid through the bunker trapdoor and climbed down the ladder into the Rooster's lair. The place was surprisingly low-tech. Just a single laptop, a bed, a TV, a whiteboard, a large easel and pad of paper, a supply of food, a microwave, a freezer—Jack knew what was in there and wasn't going to look—and fertilizer and bomb-making equipment.

From the base of the ladder Jack studied the whiteboard, which held drawings that made no sense to the common eye. Jack, however, recognized RIOT code when he saw it. These were the plans for Kennett's next mission—causing chaos and destruction at the G8 meeting.

Jack could zoom in on the first page from here, but he needed to be closer to flip the pages and get the rest of the plan. He studied the surrounding floor and walls for booby traps. If Kennett was smart and savvy, which Jack was sure he was, he'd have a way of spotting his own traps.

Jack pulled a small black light from his pocket and shone it around the room. A maze of fluorescent trip wires just inches off the floor lit up, along with a disgusting number of stains that explained some of the foul odor in the bomb shelter. Kennett had evidently been using a drain in the floor as a urinal.

Certain markings on the whiteboard also became visible under the beam of Jack's flashlight. Ah yes, Kennett must have played with one too many spy kits as a kid.

Jack cautiously stepped through the maze of trip wires

as he made his way toward the whiteboard. What the hell would happen if he slipped up and struck a wire? They were obviously plastic, like fishing line, only made or coated with phosphorous. No fear of being electrocuted here. So what did all these wires do?

Near the whiteboard and laptop, he fell to a squat. At that level, he had a view of the maze of wires. They were connected to a string of dart guns and blowguns.

*Poison-tipped darts,* Jack thought. *Probably tipped with something undetectable and fast acting.*

Off the top of his head, Jack could think of half a dozen poisons that would do the trick. He even had a few favorites. He didn't, however, have any intention of finding out firsthand which one was Kennett's poison of choice.

Jack stood and went to work on the laptop, installing a flash drive to back up the contents. While the backup was in progress, he got out his smartphone with its dozens of CIA apps. While shining the black light on the easel, he snapped picture after picture as he flipped through the pages. Using sophisticated encryption and shielding techniques, he sent them off to NCS headquarters.

He didn't have much fear they would be intercepted. The bomb shelter was shielded by Kennett, too.

Jack was just finishing up with his photo shoot and getting ready to set the ignition devices he was going to use to blow up Kennett and his stash of fertilizer-inducing death when a motion in his receptor goggles from the spy cam he'd set by the barn entrance caught his attention in the corner of his glasses. Willow was searching Kennett's room. *Shit.*

Willow wiggled and wriggled and poked Shane until he rolled off her slightly and she managed to get out from beneath him. On the positive side, at least she had up-close knowledge that he was fine. His breathing was regular and he was making happy noises as if dreamland was treating him well. No need to call the doctor as far as she could tell.

But as deadweight the man was substantial. Her pulse raced as she grabbed his legs, which were heavy and hard to move, too. With enough effort to cause her to break a sweat, she hefted Shane's legs around onto the bed. She pulled off his boots, stared at the zipper of his jeans for a quick second, shook her head, and decided not to go there. Shane could sleep in his clothes. She'd rather not touch him.

She grabbed the comforter and pulled it over him before surveying the room, which was a pit. And that was putting it mildly. Shane needed a maid. In the worst way.

Willow frowned. What had Jack seen in here that caused the alarm she'd seen on his face? How was she going to find it? How was she going to find *anything* in here?

The only housekeeping Shane had done in the room was to make the bed. Small consolation—that had caused her a problem, too.

Willow got on her hands and knees and looked under the bed, hoping to find Shane's store of treasures. That's where she kept hers; why wouldn't he?

But the only things beneath the bed were dust bunnies. She got up and tried the closet. Nothing out of the ordinary. Just a musty odor. He needed some cedar hangers and lavender sachets to put in there.

She paused and tried to think like Jack. What would he be looking for? Unfortunately, she wouldn't recognize an electronic bug if it zapped her onto her butt. Or a hidden spy cam, encoded secret message, or dead drop.

Dead drop! Maybe Shane kept a hollowed-out rock? One with secret messages inside. Low-tech, yes. But Jack had told her a dead drop was still the most effective method of getting a message out without it being intercepted.

She scanned the room. No rocks. Just a lot of dirty, smelly socks on the floor. She went to the dresser Shane was using and gently opened the top drawer—underwear and more socks, ostensibly clean ones.

Shane snored and flipped over.

The movement startled Willow. She jumped and put her hand over her heart.

*This is a dumb idea. Really stupid.*

Which didn't stop her from opening drawer after drawer. And finding nothing.

Finally, she tiptoed out of the room, gently shutting the door behind her. She felt disappointed beyond belief. There was nothing in Shane's room that she could see that would have set Jack off.

Con, with his immaculate personal habits, would have been appalled at the state of the room. That could have set him off.

She gently crept down the stairs, careful to not wake Shane. As she was heading toward the chair to get her coat and purse, she passed Grant's study. The door was open.

She hesitated.

Well, why not? She'd snooped everywhere else. Maybe Shane was using Grant's study while he house-sat and ran the orchard for him. She still held out hope that Con was Jack and Shane was a dangerous terrorist or foreign spy. If there was anything in that study that would make her case . . .

She gently pushed the door open, letting light from the living room flood the study. She didn't dare risk turning on a light.

Grant's study was not what Willow would call perfect and ordered, but it was less messy and seemingly more cared for than the bedroom.

She tiptoed to the desk. A computer was on. She took a peek at the screen, but it was password protected. She tried a stab at a few passwords, typing in Duke's and Buddy's names and even Shane's birth date, but none of them worked.

She didn't have time for twenty questions, or the million or so it might take for her to guess correctly. An invoice receipt on the desk caught her attention.

She picked it up and read it.

What? She couldn't believe her eyes. This was a receipt for pesticides and fertilizer.

Her mouth fell open. Nothing sinister in that. Just . . .

*Shane, you big cheat! You're helping Grant perpetrate fraud.*

Everyone marveled at the quality of Grant's organic fruit and the high yields he got without using pesticide. Because his apples were "organic" he commanded a higher price.

Well, this explained a lot, including the yield. Shane was helping Grant deceive—claiming to be an organic farmer while using tons of chemicals.

If she hadn't already dosed Shane with chemicals, she'd be tempted to slap him. Not that she believed in violence. But the man was swindling people. Or helping Grant to, anyway.

She gently set the receipt back in its place on the desk, being careful to make sure it was exactly where she'd found it.

What was she going to do about Shane and Grant's deception? Where in the world was Shane storing all those pesticides and chemicals? And how was he able to use them without anyone ever seeing him do it?

# CHAPTER TWENTY-FIVE

Willow checked on Shane once more before she left. He was sleeping with a smile on his face. She shook her head, wondering what he'd remember in the morning. Willow hoped he wouldn't be at all suspicious that she'd drugged him. And why should he be? If he were an innocent man and not an enemy agent. And besides, she had Buddy as backup. He was okay after eating a caramel. Surely Shane would see that.

Thinking like a true spy, Willow remembered to switch out the doped caramel for the good on her way out. She stopped by to pet Buddy and Duke where Shane had penned them in the kitchen. Buddy looked fine, totally healthy, as he let her pet him and licked her hand. *Whew!*

"Nice dog. Good Buddy." She rubbed his face and avoided his wet dog kiss, laughing. "What is it with the males in the house, huh? They all want to slobber all over me."

Well, Shane had been right about Buddy. That, at least, was a relief.

Willow slipped on her coat, pulled on her gloves, and let herself out of Shane's house, latching the door behind her.

She slid into her car and banged the steering wheel in frustration. She hadn't learned a thing. She'd completely failed in her mission. She still had no idea whether Shane was an enemy agent or not. And she'd gotten nothing to blackmail Jack with to make him take her with him when he left.

All that fear and being pawed over for nothing.

Jack had just let himself out of the bomb shelter when he heard the door to Shane's house swing open and slam shut. Willow leaving, he hoped. He could have watched the action from his receptor goggles, but he slid through the shadows to the apple-barn door and peeked through a crack.

Willow was walking to her car. He took a deep breath, relieved to see her leaving Kennett's unharmed, and filled with too many emotions to separate and name.

What was up with him? He'd only wanted to protect Willow and get the hell out with his feelings intact and the protective scar he'd formed over his heart in place. But over the last week something had happened. Something had changed. The scar had ruptured and now he was bleeding love and emotions all over the place. Not good for a man in his position.

In the end, he'd still have to leave her. And stay the hell away from her forever. No more peeking. No more coming back for just a look. Or to save her from an enemy combatant. Damn, what if someone came after her again looking for him?

He shook his head. Once he left, that was the end. No turning back. He'd be dead to her. Forever. It was just too damned dangerous—for her and him. She was too intuitive. Too close to the truth.

He didn't like the thought of stepping into an eternity without her. It wrenched his heart out.

What about Con? Could *he* win Willow's heart and make her forget Jack? Could she live with him—a straight-laced, normal guy with a slightly exotic accent and no assassin tendencies? At least none that were in the cover brief. He was perfect for Willow—Jack without the faults. Guilt-free. And family to her neighbor.

The bigger question was—could Jack fool her forever? Would the Agency let him? And did he want to? Would he be happy in Con's shadow? And then there was that damned chuff—how would Con ever explain that?

The house was suspiciously quiet when Willow walked in her front door. No tapping of tiny paws on her wood floors. No cute, yelpy little squeaks that passed for barks. No pleasant aroma of caramel and scented wallflower plug-ins.

She wrinkled her nose and took a deep sniff. The house smelled faintly of vomit and urine. And her floors—covered with excrement and accidents.

Willow's heart thumped wildly in her chest. She slapped her thighs and whistled. "Spookie! Here, girl." Willow's voice shook. She was supposed to sound reassuring.

She raced through the entryway past the dining room and scanned the living room. When she turned back over her shoulder into the kitchen, her heart stopped. An overturned can of dark Dutch cocoa lay at the edge of the kitchen counter, its contents spilled into a pile on the floor. A pile with paw prints in it. A pile that had been tracked around the kitchen floor.

"Spookie! Spookie, where are you?" Willow was screaming now, not even trying to hide her worry.

Being a Halloween pup, Spookie had gotten into the Halloween candy the very first week Willow had her. How the tiny pup had managed to bump the table, knock over a bowl of mini chocolate bars, chew through the wrappers, and consume two of them Willow never knew. But ever since, no matter how sick it made Spookie, she sought out chocolate wherever Willow hid it, however cleverly concealed and seemingly out of reach it was. For that reason, Spookie was never allowed in the shop—too much temptation and opportunity for chocolate tragedy.

Willow rarely kept chocolate in the house. But she'd gotten out the cocoa from the high shelf where she kept it to dust the caramels with at the last minute, hoping to hide any lingering bitterness of the allergy meds. She'd been so distracted and caught up in her own plans, she must have gotten careless.

She didn't even remember setting it on the counter. She would have sworn she'd put it away. She'd certainly put the lid on tightly, hadn't she? No, she must not have sealed it. And now her little dog—

Willow raced toward the bedroom following an awful trail of doggie vomit. "Spookie!"

Just then, Spookie staggered out of the corner of the living room from behind the chair, her little white face covered with cocoa that looked comically like a fake beard. Her muscles were twitching so that she walked jerkily and tottered as if she were drunk. She had absolutely no coordination.

Willow ran to her and scooped her up, cradling her and crying at the same time. "What have you done, baby? How long ago did you eat that nasty cocoa powder?" Willow rubbed her cheek against her poor dog's face, fearing the worst and almost glad Spookie couldn't answer.

The lack of coordination and muscle control was a bad sign. A very bad sign. The nearest twenty-four-hour emergency veterinary clinic was almost half an hour away. The bad way Spookie looked, Willow feared they didn't have half an hour. Any minute now the seizures could start.

The last time this had happened, that time when Spookie was a pup, Jack had administered something to make Spookie throw up and had rushed her to the vet just in time. The man took extreme driving to a new level. He could drive like James Bond on the best of Bond's days.

Willow scratched Spookie's poor, aching tummy.

It took practically no chocolate at all to kill a small dog Spookie's size. And pure cocoa powder was the most lethal form of it. Half an ounce could be fatal.

Willow grabbed her cell phone and dialed Con's number.

Jack let himself into Aldo's guesthouse, hyped up and angry at the situation he was in. He hadn't felt this potent combo of emotions since his junior high years, the years he was bullied before he got the courage to fight back. It was the kind of emotion that made some teenage boys into killers who shot up their high schools, and others into heroes. It was the kind of emotion Jack had vowed never to feel again.

He disabled his alarm systems and took the stairs two at a time. In the main apartment, he began to pace, which was what he did when he needed to think and work things out.

Tomorrow morning, Kennett would go into his apple barn as usual, well before he opened for business and there was any chance of a customer stopping by. He'd open his cash register, which would set off a charge that would blow him to bits.

It wasn't the cleanest kill, but it would have to do. Jack would be positioned nearby to hit the disable button, just in case anyone else happened by. Jack had a zero collateral damage record and he sure as hell wasn't going to blow it now.

But after the explosion, what did he do? Leave town without a word? Without saying good-bye to Willow? Never to see her again?

Wouldn't that make Con look guilty of something? Emmett would give Jack time to close out business. But did he want it?

Just then his smartphone buzzed in his pocket. He pulled it out and looked at the screen, picking up the call as soon as he saw who was phoning. "Willow?"

"Con, come quickly! It's Spookie. I was out and she got into the cocoa powder. Now she's . . . she's losing muscle control and starting to twitch. I need help. I can't lose her. She's the last living thing I have from Jack. I don't know what to do." Willow sounded on the edge of tears.

Jack's heart simply stopped for a beat as a memory of Spookie as a pup and the first time he and Willow had nearly lost her flashed through his mind. Then his heartbeat kicked in with a fury and he sprang into action, rushing to the bedroom for his kit of chemicals and meds. "Hang on, Wills. I'll be there in a minute. Just make Spookie comfortable."

He clicked his phone shut, remembering too late he shouldn't have called her Wills. He'd broken his cover for an instant.

It took Jack less than a minute to get to Willow's house. Willow was waiting for him by the door with Spookie trembling in her arms. When she saw him, she ran to the car.

He reached across and opened the door for her. "How's she doing?"

Willow shook her head as she slid into the passenger seat with Spookie.

Jack looked at his dog. The dog looked back at him with pleading eyes, begging for help. Damn it all, he felt helpless. "Has she vomited?"

"Yes."

"Good." He wouldn't need the hydrogen peroxide to induce vomiting. Instead, he pulled out a bottle of activated charcoal and held it out for Willow to see, dropping all pretense of uninterested stranger. "Give her this." He told Willow the dose. "It will prevent her body from absorbing more of the poison."

He rubbed the dog's head. "It'll be all right, girl." He wanted to say, *Daddy will take care of you,* but he bit it back just in time.

"What kind of chocolate did she eat and how much?"

Willow was already coaxing Spookie to eat the charcoal. And Spookie was balking. Why was it that dogs would eat shit and resist what would save them?

Willow somehow managed to get a pill down Spookie's throat as the dog whined and cried. "Dutch cocoa. Too much."

Jack nodded. "Where's the nearest emergency vet clinic?"

"Half an hour away." Willow looked into his eyes, pleading more poignantly than even his dog's eyes for help.

*Ah, the hell with it.* He was going to have to drive like Jack to save Spookie. "Give me directions. I'll get us there in ten."

"Alive?" she asked.

He grinned, shifted into reverse, swung the car around, and peeled down the driveway with gravel flying behind him.

Con's cover car was not the vehicle he would have picked for a drive to survive, but it would have to do. He preferred the precision and control of a stick shift. Sometimes an automatic such as this was just too sluggish.

Using his peripheral vision, he pulled onto the road without stopping. There was nothing coming.

"Take a left here," Willow said at the first intersection.

Jack didn't stop at that stop sign, either. He fired up the car to over 60 on the 35 mph speed limit road.

The moon shone, nearly full, lighting their way as he took the corners of the curving road at full speed. Despite the worry and concern, he couldn't help grinning. He hadn't had an opportunity to drive like this, with Willow by his side, in two terrible years.

He cruised up to 80, in his element. He'd taken every need-for-speed driving course the Agency would send him to and he'd been the star pupil in every one. He was born to drive. He didn't have a single worry that he wouldn't get them to the clinic alive. Well, maybe one.

"Pray that a deer doesn't decide to cross our path." He glanced over at Willow to see how she was reacting to his driving.

Most women would have told him to slow down. Not Willow, she had a small smile on her face, as if enjoying herself and remembering something pleasant. If she weren't so worried about Spookie, Jack was sure she'd have been smiling full out and laughing.

They sped through town and out onto the open highway, where he accelerated to over 100. The roads were nearly deserted at that hour and any car he came upon he passed easily. Someone gave him the finger. He caught only a glimpse of it as he flew by them. Probably everyone he passed was calling him a maniac. He hoped none of them called the cops.

"Take the next exit." Willow pointed.

*Good girl.* She knew what she was doing. Giving him as much time as possible to prepare for the turn.

He took the exit, barely slowing down.

"Right at the light." She sounded calm and almost content as he took the corner on two wheels. "Left at the next. Then straight-ahead two miles. Second driveway on the right." She glanced at her watch and back at him with a look of awe and knowing. As if she'd pinned him as being Jack. As if it were old times again, before his untimely death, and they were out practicing his spy driving, in other words joyriding.

She was one woman in a million, the kind who never told her husband to slow down or not follow so closely. He loved that woman. Her look of approval made his heart sing.

Spookie whimpered, bringing back the gravity of the situation.

"There." Willow pointed to a neon sign advertising twenty-four-hour veterinary care.

Jack slowed just slightly and then, for no reason, decided to show off. Just shy of the driveway, he pulled the hand brake, swung the wheel, and performed a perfect bootlegger turn, sliding backward into a parking spot perfectly within the lines.

Willow glanced at her watch. "Nine minutes and thirty-five seconds. A man who keeps his promise. Not bad." She beamed at him and jumped out of the car almost before it came to a complete stop. "I called ahead. They're expecting us."

*Us.* The word sounded good, even to a loner like him. Willow was the only "us" he'd really ever wanted to be a part of. Her and the Agency.

Jack jumped out, beeped the car locked, and held open the clinic door for Willow and Spookie. He stared at the dog, trying to determine how she looked. *Better,* he thought. *At least, not worse.*

He was no veterinarian, but he knew about animals, biology, and chemistry. Spookie would make it. Or maybe that was only wishful thinking.

The vet's assistant was waiting for them. "They're here!" she called back to the doctor before nodding to Willow. "Follow me."

Jack followed without thinking.

The assistant stopped him short. "Just one person goes back with the patient, please." Her gaze bounced between them. "Which will it be? The mama or the daddy?"

Jack cleared his throat and stepped back, feeling out of
sorts and out of synch with the way life had become. He'd
almost blown his cover again. As if the driving hadn't
given him away. Willow had always told him that no one
drove like he did. His driving was practically so unique, it
could have identified him as easily as his fingerprint.

"I'm just the neighbor who gave them a ride." He
looked at Willow. "I'll wait here."

She didn't see him. She'd already turned and was following the assistant back to the surgery. It was probably
all for the best. Jack was looking at Willow in a way he
shouldn't be.

By the time the vet finished his examination and ministra-
tions, Spookie was already looking perkier.

"You gave her activated charcoal?" Dr. Broderick
looked at Willow.

"Yes, Jack, I mean, my neighbor, Con, told me to."

The doctor nodded approvingly. "Probably saved this
little dog's life. Make sure you thank him properly."

Oh, she intended to. Jack was her hero. Always had been.
And yes, by his driving she was sure Con was Jack. Who
else could take a city corner so smoothly at 70 miles per
hour and not even break a sweat? Oh, maybe Drew, but she
doubted it. Jack had always been the best driver among his
group of spies.

"I will," she said.

"You can take her home. Watch her, but I'm sure she'll
be fine." He rubbed Spookie's tummy and Spookie gave a
weak but happy bark. He handed her to Willow. "My assistant will give you instructions." He showed Willow the
way out.

Jack was waiting for them in the lobby. He sat, legs
splayed wide, feet planted firmly, resting his elbows on his
knees and his head in his hands. In profile, his nose was

different, but everything from his posture to his being was Jack. He looked military and handsome, the way Willow had been remembering him.

And he'd dropped out of his cover character for her. Because of her and Spookie. Because he still cared. Or so Willow told herself. She just had to get him to admit it. Which meant, she had to get him to make love to her. Yes, it still boiled down to that.

She no longer wanted to sleep with him to prove he was Jack, though it would be the final proof. She wanted to sleep with him because he *was* Jack. It was as simple as that.

He looked up at her. As their eyes locked, a look of relief washed over him.

"She's fine," Willow said. "Take us home. Can you get us there in less than ten?"

She was implying she couldn't wait. She hoped he caught her message. She wasn't letting him go this time.

# CHAPTER TWENTY-SIX

Willow insisted on carrying Spookie, who had fallen asleep on the ride. Jack walked them to her door.

Willow handed him her keys. "Will you help me get her settled in?"

Willow looked at him with those hero-worship, bedroom eyes. It was all he could do to swallow, let alone talk.

He nodded. "Sure." He unlocked the door and let them in.

"She sleeps in the bedroom with me." Willow nodded toward the hallway.

Was that innuendo he heard in Willow's voice? As in, he'd be welcome to sleep there, too? Jack swallowed hard. This was a notoriously bad idea. But what was a guy to do? Appear hard-hearted? He followed her down the hall.

Willow turned into her bedroom, which smelled sweet, like her perfume. Obviously Spookie hadn't made it to this room during her bout with the cocoa.

Willow stood above Spookie's dog bed. "Here. Take her while I get her bed ready."

The bed looked fine to him, but he took his dog gratefully. When Willow smiled at him, he realized that's what she intended. She was giving him the gift of a cuddle with his pup.

He watched while she arranged a soft blanket for Spookie. When Willow indicated she was ready, he kneeled and gently put Spookie to bed.

They stood over her, side by side, watching their dog sleep like two anxious parents over a crib. There should have been a crib. They should have had kids before he died. There was a lot of stuff they should have done before he'd passed into the ether of the cover of death.

Willow looked up at him. The light was off in the room, but a shaft of light shone in from the hall. Backlit, she looked like an angel. His angel. Her green eyes caught the light and sparkled. He could stare at her forever.

"You saved her life." Willow touched his arm gently to show her gratitude.

He shrugged.

She pulled him around to face her. "You're my hero." She cupped his face and gently went up on her toes until her lips met his.

*All right, asshole, step away from the girl,* he told himself. But he couldn't make himself move. He was afraid if he did, he'd lose all control and simply throw her on the bed and take her.

She kissed him softly, provocatively, in the way that he liked, the way that always made him groan.

He should move away, just step away from the temptation and danger Willow posed. He knew where this was going. Particularly if he didn't get his ass out of here this instant. He made a fist and squeezed it tight, trying to control his baser urges.

There was a point in every mission when Jack rationalized the risks he was about to take. This was this mission's moment and the rationalization was a doozy he wouldn't have considered if he hadn't been in a *needing his wife with a passion that kills* lust-induced emotional frenzy. He'd gone way beyond the point of no return or taking a suicide pill.

He'd have to try to compartmentalize. Make love to her

as Con and hope Con didn't have an involuntary chuff. Or could somehow cover it.

Willow slid her arms around his neck and cuddled up against him. The simple fact of being so near her, in her loving embrace, made his toes tingle and the rest of him burn.

Oh no, no, no, no, no, he was losing control.

Sappy love songs talk about aching for a woman's touch. He was aching now. All over, but one long, hard part of him particularly.

He knew how Willow liked to be kissed—softly at first, building to lip-bruising passion. Jack didn't trust Con to show any restraint once he started kissing, so he remained fixed in a place, a statue afraid to move.

"Don't be afraid," she whispered into his ear. "Let yourself go." She rubbed up against him and ran her fingers through his hair.

Willow knew how to torment him. The feel of her fingers in his hair had always soothed him and calmed the storm of emotions he felt after a mission. Her touch now was anything but calming. Goose bumps rose on his arms. Every part of him ached to take her.

She tilted her head and studied him, her eyes dancing with mirth and passion. "You Italian lovers are more reserved than I've been led to believe. I thought you liked to talk with your hands. Talk to me now, Con."

"Right now, I'm happy just listening." His voice came out hoarse.

"Listen well." She pulled his shirt loose from his jeans and ran her hands up his bare back. Before he could move, she dragged her nails down his back, roughly, until he shuddered.

"Like what you're hearing?" she said.

Damn her, she knew what he liked and she was playing

dirty, trying to get him to break his cover. He was on the edge as it was, hanging on by the thinnest thread of self-control, trying to remember his training on resisting torture. Sadly, NCS had never trained him to resist mind-numbing, mind-bending pleasure.

She unbuttoned his shirt. He stood as still as the *David*, and definitely more erect, itching, aching to touch her as he tried to remember everything he'd been taught about how not to crack under interrogation. He had to imagine he was someplace else. Not here, alone with the wife he loved and longed for. He couldn't act, not even as Con, until he was certain he wouldn't crack.

She could torture him with pleasure, but he would not move.

"It must be excruciating standing still. Dance with me." She danced him around until he faced her closed closet doors—her mirrored closet doors.

When she had him in perfect mirror-viewing position, she kicked off her shoes and shimmied out of her jeans as he stood mesmerized by the movement of her hips. And then by the sight of a thong panty that disappeared between the shapely cheeks of her butt.

She pulled her blouse over her head, drawing his gaze from the mirror to her body. She held the blouse out at arm's length by a finger. And then with a seductive, teasing smile dropped it onto the floor and winked.

She wore a see-through lace bra that matched the tiny triangle of her thong panty. He couldn't breathe. If she made one more move toward him, he was done for.

Time for some mental evasive action. He forced his thoughts to places they shouldn't roam. Back to how bad he was for Willow.

The thoughts came a second too late and were too obvious in his expression. Willow knew his coping tactics.

A frown passed quickly over her face and then her eyes lit with determination.

She slid her hands over his chest and pulled his shirt off his shoulders and arms, dropping it to the floor as she bent to suck his nipples.

He had a perfect view in the mirror of her hair falling over her back, her narrow waist, and her bare bottom as her tongue teased his nipples.

He groaned and his breath caught. "What about the dog? Won't she see?"

"You Europeans really aren't living up to your rep. I thought you had no body or embarrassment issues. Don't tell me you're shy about a little dog watching us?" Willow gave his nipple another quick lick.

He threw his head back. His mouth was dry. "I don't want to disturb her."

"Don't worry." Willow unzipped his jeans and thrust her hand down them, grabbing and stroking his bulging member. "We won't. The vet gave her something to make her sleep so she could rest and recover."

Jack had always told her it turned him on when she took charge and she'd taken his admission to heart.

*Shit.*

"Besides, I think it's time she learned something about the birds and the bees."

Willow was definitely playing dirty and going for broke, not caring whether he thought she was a bad girl or not. She'd once told him women were intimidated during sex because they wanted their men to see them as good-girl girlfriend/wife material. He was intrigued to see how far she'd take this act, knowing it would mean his downfall.

It would be hell to stop her now. He liked this game of heavenly torture, wanting to see just how far she'd go to make a point. His flesh was willing and his spirit weak with desire. He wanted her.

She stood up straight, reached behind her, unlatched her bra, pulled it off, let it fall to the floor, and smiled. "Don't move."

As if he could.

She went to the nightstand and removed a tube of sexual lubricant. A new tube, Jack couldn't help noticing. A brand-new tube.

She used the lid to pierce it. Piercing gave him a mental image he tried to resist.

In the dim light he couldn't read the label, but he got the feeling, from the way she was grinning, it was something that would do him in.

She walked over, boldly, like a femme fatale spy on a mission, and pulled his member out, sliding her lubricated hand along it with one hard, smooth stroke after another while he watched her do it in the mirror and gasped with pleasure. Then she put her other hand on and stroked with both. And then . . .

Every couple has a signature sex move. This was theirs. Willow watched Jack's eyes as she put her second hand on him. Sure enough, recognition lit them. He knew what was coming. His eyes dilated. And not just from the dark.

*Resist this, Jack.*

She'd used the heated, for men's pleasure, lubricant. She'd bought it hoping she'd get a chance to use it on Jack, to prove he was Jack.

He was showing unusual restraint. This had to be killing him. At least, she hoped it was. She wanted to break him. She had to get him to toss his cover aside again and she was going to use every dirty trick in the book.

She began to twist her hands in different directions as

she corkscrewed them up his shaft. Jack gasped and froze. But she refused to stop. Twisting. Stroking.

"Damn it," he muttered, and pulled her hands free from him.

He slid out of his jeans and underwear, scooped her into his arms, and carried her to the bed.

*My hero,* she thought, wanting him to ravish her completely, utterly, totally. *Give me everything you've got, Jack. Show me that you're the man I know you are.*

He tossed her onto her back on the bed with her head to the foot of it so that he had a perfect view of them in the mirror.

"A man can only take so much." His voice was ragged.

He stared down at her, smoothed her hair as it fanned out on the bed, stooped, and gently kissed her mouth, her neck, trailing down to her breasts, kissing them in the way Jack knew how to do.

She cupped his head and arched against him. "Now, take me now." She was ready, so ready.

He didn't need any more encouragement. He lifted his head and watched them shadowed in the mirror. Grinned. And plunged in.

It had been two years. She felt like the first time, only with none of the pain.

And then it was just the two of them lost in pleasure—her and Jack on top of her, thrusting in the way he knew gave her the most pleasure. Quick. Hard and dirty. Fast.

Suddenly slowing, lingering, gentle. Thrusting and pausing. Cupping her bottom so that he could slide in deeply to the spot that always made her gasp with ecstasy.

She didn't have much experience with other lovers. But no one but Jack could move like this, move her like this.

She clamped her legs around him, pressing him deeply into her. Her legs fit around his long waist just as perfectly as they had around Jack's.

She knew the feel of her husband. And this was him. Even though his body was scarred and his chest hair was gone, he was unequivocally Jack.

She sighed and moaned.

Jack stiffened. She could feel him getting ready to crash over the edge of delight. He completely covered her, thrusting fast, and hard.

She bit his shoulder and grabbed his butt, holding on hard as the pleasure built and built. She gasped. "Jack, Jack, Jack!"

He grunted as he climaxed and collapsed on top of her. But he made absolutely no chuffing sound. *None.*

Willow's heart sank. "Jack?"

# CHAPTER TWENTY-SEVEN

Willow felt as tight as a virgin, Jack realized with happy satisfaction. She probably hadn't had sex in two years.

The thought, and his name on her lips, made him unaccountably happy. And then he heard the doubt, saw it written on her face, and realized . . .

He hadn't chuffed. What the hell had happened? It surprised him as much as it did her. The explosion in Ciudad, which had given him a foreign accent and a gravelly voice, had stolen his chuff. He was no longer her tiger.

Willow had gotten what she wanted—her chance to prove that he was Jack—and fate had ripped her off and tripped her up. No chuff, no Jack. He could keep his cover, refuse to reveal himself. Just walk away as he'd planned. Let Willow think he was Con, a man so similar to Jack it was eerie.

He wasn't even tempted. He wanted her to know he was her husband. He reacted, gently put his fingers on her mouth, and shook his head. "Shhhh, Wills. It's me. I can't be Jack anymore. Jack's dead; you know that. And apparently, so is my chuff."

Her eyes went wide and welled with tears. Of joy, he hoped.

She smiled up at him with relief. "It's really you?"

He nodded.

"I knew all along. You could never fool me, tiger. Never."

"You doubted for a second there, when you didn't hear the chuff. Admit it."

"Never." She brought his face to hers and kissed him. "I love you. Don't leave me, Jack. Take me with you wherever you're going next. We'll be whoever we have to be."

He kissed her lightly. How could he leave her?

"I love you, too, Wills." His voice broke as he ran his fingers through her hair. "I always will."

"Stay the night, at least," she said as she caressed his cheek.

Willow wrapped herself around Jack. There was no chance of escaping, or refusing her request. Not that he had any will to leave her.

Jack lay back on the bed, thinking hard. He'd carefully staged the explosion that would take place in the morning to look like an accident. Willow had never known he was an assassin, just that he was a spy. There was no reason for her to connect the explosion and Kennett's death with him. He stared at her, drinking in the sight of her and her blissful expression. He had an audacious plan. But would she go for it?

"No recriminations?" he asked, marveling at her ability to forgive. If she'd left him for two years, he'd damn well expect an explanation, at the very least. "You're not mad?"

"No. You're back. That's all that matters." She ran her fingers along his chest. "I may not like the business you're in, but I understand the need for secrecy. I understand, too, that sometimes you have to do things that hurt other people, for the good of all. Sometimes you even have to hurt me." She kissed his shoulder.

He cupped her face and looked deep into her eyes, wanting her to know he hadn't planned this. He would never have agreed to intentionally hurt her the way he'd ended up doing. "It wasn't like that, Wills. I wouldn't have done this to you on purpose. After I was blown up, things evolved. Some locals took me in. They knew enough to hide me from the drug lords we'd been after. They smuggled me out to the country.

"No one thought I'd live. I was unconscious and delirious for weeks. I was in a coma for several more. Even the Agency and Emmett didn't know I was alive or where I was."

"But they told me you were dead. Did they believe that?"

Jack sighed. "They did that to protect both of us. The operation had gone bad. They had no idea how much the drug lords knew or who was feeding them intel.

"If I was still alive somewhere, the fewer people who suspected it the better. Emmett told me later no one in NCS believed I could have survived that blast, especially given Drew's eyewitness account.

"Even my best friend thought I was gone."

"Oh, baby. What you've been through." She rested her head on his shoulder and stroked his chest with soothing, featherlight stokes, massaging the scars the plastic surgeon had been unable to fix.

Her sympathy almost broke him completely. "By the time I recovered enough to know I was going to live, I was a wreck. And you'd already buried me and moved on—"

"I never moved on." Her hand stilled on his chest.

He covered it with his and squeezed it. "I know. NCS and I couldn't resist the cover of death. I thought you'd have a better life without me in it. I know you never agreed with all the things I did as a spy."

"Jack, how could you think that?" She lightly kissed his shoulder. "My life is empty without you."

He smiled at her. If she knew the whole truth . . .

"The past really doesn't matter to me. You're back now

with a new nose and a sexy accent that you never break out of. But I do miss the chuff." She gave him a playful smile.

"Let's hope the next time I'm blown up it comes back." He stroked her cheek.

"Let's hope there isn't a next time. I can live without it as long as I have you." She studied him. "How do you keep your accent? You can talk to me in your regular way now; no one will hear and I'm not going to tell."

He shook his head. "I can't. I have Foreign Accent Syndrome. It's a side effect of the injury."

She frowned. "Drew was right, then," she whispered, half to herself. "You'll never sound like my Jack again?"

"No. Think you can live with that?"

She grinned. "If I have to." She paused. "Jack, why did you come back? What's your mission here?"

"To see you and make sure you're safe," he said without hesitating. Well, it was the truth. The partial truth.

Her eyes misted. "But you can't stay."

"Not as myself." He sighed. "And I can't take you away from this life. I've seen how happy you are here." He stroked her hair. "I have a crazy idea, though. How would you like to be part of Aldo's extended family?"

She grinned. "What are you saying?"

He propped up on one elbow and stared down at her. She was beautiful in more ways than he deserved. "I was thinking you and Con could have a thing. A serious thing that could eventually end in marriage."

"That is the lamest marriage proposal I've ever had." Then she laughed. "What would Emmett and NCS think of that?"

"I don't give a damn. They'd just have to live with it." She laughed.

"Well?" he asked, knowing he could hurt her again if she ever found out the truth about him but unable to stop himself. "Will you marry Con someday?"

"Yes, I'll marry Con. Will that make me a bigamist?"

"Not in the eyes of the law. I'm officially dead." He leaned down and kissed her before sitting up and swinging his legs off the side of the bed. Where were his pants?

"Wait. Where are you going?"

"I have a few things to take care of."

"Now?"

"Yeah. The sooner, the better. Trust me."

"You mean you have to get Emmett's blessing?" She eyed him cautiously.

"Something like that. It's already six in the morning in Virginia. Emmett will be up and about."

"You can't do it from here?"

"No, baby." He brushed her lips with a light kiss. "And we don't want to scandalize Orchard Bluff by broadcasting our affair, either. I need some time to clear Con's good name." And blow the Rooster to bits without making Willow the least bit suspicious.

She shook her head. "This is a ridiculous situation." She sounded totally happy.

"Yeah, it is. Isn't it great?"

She laughed. "You are coming back? Promise not to leave without telling me?"

"No way. You'll just have to trust me on this."

By seven, Willow was up, showered, breakfasted, dressed, and ready to head downstairs to start making caramel. Spookie was back to her lively self. Jack was back.

*Jack is back!*

Even with the added complications of this new cover, Willow would have to assume as Con's future wife, her world was perfect and sweet.

She hummed to herself as she grabbed a clean apron from the dryer and tied it around her waist. *When will we be able to share the details?*

She wanted to tell Drew and Staci. Was convinced that they had to. Staci deserved to be free of her guilt and Drew would be ecstatic.

*In time,* Willow told herself. *Give Jack a little time to work out the details.* She thought about Emmett Nelson and frowned. That liar.

Her cell phone vibrated. As she grabbed it from the counter her heart danced with hope that Jack was calling. She wanted to trust him, but part of her feared he'd run out on her. There was something he was hiding from her. Something that made him uneasy.

It was a text from her mother. *Be extra careful today. I still have the bad feeling. And it's getting worse.*

Willow had been so happy, she hadn't felt any foreboding. Had glossed over it. But now that her mom had prompted her . . .

No. It couldn't be. Her mom was probably reacting to Jack. Both Willow and her mom had to be. Still, she'd have to warn him and keep an eye on him, just to be on the safe side.

She texted her mom back, saying she'd be on her guard. The phone rang in her hand before she could put it down. She glanced at the screen. Still not Jack. Shane.

Her heart fell. She didn't want to talk to Shane, of all people. But she probably owed it to him to pick up and see if he sounded okay.

"Willow," he said when she answered. "I'm calling to apologize. I can't believe I crapped out on you again last night. For the second date in a row. I'm usually not such a lightweight. The accident's affecting me worse than I thought." He sounded very much alive and okay.

Which was a big relief. If she'd killed him or hurt him in some permanent way she'd never forgive herself. She was feeling guilty enough as it was about drugging him. At least his allergies shouldn't be bothering him.

Small mercies. And a lot of justifying going on by her.

"There's no need to apologize." There really wasn't, especially given that she was the guilty party.

"To be honest, I'm not just calling to beg your forgiveness. I have a situation here and hoped you could help me out. You're the first person I thought of.

"Someone dumped off a litter of kittens last night. I found them in a sack at the end of my driveway this morning."

"What!" Now she was indignant. "Kittens?"

"Yeah, I know. Terrible. People do horrible, cruel things. They're not even weaned and it was a cold night last night, too. They could've frozen to death."

"Oh no. How are they?" Now she was mad and indignant, and worried, too. Who would harm kittens? Why didn't people think to find them good homes? People who couldn't be bothered made her sick.

He paused. "They're okay." Hesitation echoed in his voice. "I've done my best for them. I made them a bed and put them in the apple shed where they'll be warm. But I have a mean old tom around. I can't keep them.

"If I don't watch them every minute, he's bound to get them. And with my head the way it's been the last few days, I'm not the best guy to guard them, nurse them into full health, and find them homes right now.

"I was hoping you could take them. Just until the weekend when the crowds show up. I'm sure I could find them good homes then."

She was already reaching for her coat. "I'll be right over."

# CHAPTER TWENTY-EIGHT

Jack watched Kennett's apple barn and house from a hidden location in the orchard across the street a safe distance away. If the Rooster followed his morning routine, any minute now he'd come out of the house and head to the barn. He'd open the old-fashioned till Grant had kept for atmosphere as much as to store business proceeds.

That one small action would set off an explosive that would make it appear as if the space heater in the apple barn had ignited some gas Kennett kept there and *kaboom*! Horrible SMASH assassin dead.

When the fire marshal did his official inspection, he'd discover Kennett's secret pesticides had exploded. Grant Cooper's good name would be ruined forever. But at least his body would be found.

And then Con and Willow could live happily ever after. After that scandal over Kennett, Con would look damn good by comparison.

Jack rocked back on his heels. He didn't take ending a life lightly. Right now he didn't look at it as ending Kennett's. He preferred to think of the lives he was ultimately saving.

Everything was going to plan. Until Willow's car came into view and he heard the crunch of gravel as she turned up Kennett's driveway.

Jack's heart stopped. This didn't feel right. What was

Willow doing at Kennett's so early in the morning? Especially after last night.

Willow jumped out of her car just as Kennett stepped out from his house. He grabbed Willow and gave her a hug as Jack's worry grew and his rage kicked in. Kennett said something to Willow. Jack had a CIA-grade pair of listening ears, earpieces that magnified sound from yards away, but he still couldn't pick up what Willow and Kennett were saying to each other. Instead, he picked up an earsplitting buzz.

Kennett, that suspicious bastard, was no doubt jamming them. Kennett slid his arm around Willow's shoulder and guided her toward the apple shed.

*Shit.*

Jack hit the kill switch on his explosive device. He'd never take a chance with Willow's life. He wouldn't be the guy who blew her up. Exploded her world with his lovemaking, sure, but not the other.

Jack's spy senses were on high alert. Something felt terribly wrong. He jumped out of the squat he was in and took off at a run toward the barn.

Inside, the barn was dimly lit and the Sense was going crazy inside Willow in a way it never had before. And yet everything seemed calm and safe.

*Jack.*

She couldn't help worrying about him, and yet this felt different. It felt personal. That was ridiculous. Unless, of course, Shane really was a dangerous enemy spy. Jack had assured her that his only mission here was to see her and make sure she was safe. But from what? Or who? She had to get the kittens and get out of here.

"Where are they?" she asked as her eyes adjusted to the dim lighting. She didn't see any kittens or hear any mewing.

Shane took her arm. "This way. Behind the till, where I could watch them."

Jack peeked into the apple barn through a crack in the door as Kennett led Willow toward the trapdoor of the bomb shelter.

*Damn.* Jack couldn't let Kennett get Willow down there. That would be certain death. If Kennett was taking Willow to his operation headquarters, it only meant one thing—he was going to kill her. Maybe torture her first for intel. Or use her to draw Jack out. Then stash her in the freezer with Grant Cooper.

Jack pushed the apple-shed door open just enough to get the barrel of his gun through. He drew a bead on Kennett. This was close range for Jack and he was a damn good shot. Totally precise. At this distance there was no need for calculations or worrying about wind speed, curvature of the Earth, any of those complications of a long-range shot.

It should have been an easy kill. Except for Willow standing too near Kennett for Jack's comfort. If she'd been a stranger, he could have hit his shot without a worry. But this was a bit like a surgeon operating on his own wife or child.

And then there was the matter of escaping without Willow seeing him.

As Jack weighed his options he heard barking and the heavy pounding of large dogs racing toward him. He looked over his shoulder just in time. Buddy and Duke were barreling toward him, teeth bared and looking decidedly unfriendly and out for blood. Jack knew well-trained dogs when he saw them. Without Willow with him or unless Kennett called them off, they were going to eat Jack alive. And alert Kennett to his presence.

He had no choice. Cursing to himself, he slid into the barn and slammed the door behind him just as Buddy and

Duke pounded against it, barking and sounding as if they'd like to take a bite out of it and wouldn't stop their battering until they broke in and finished Jack off. So this was how they showed their gratitude for the sexual frustration he'd given them?

*Come on, boys. I gave you a merry chase. Be good sports.*

Kennett looked up at Jack, pushed Willow behind him, and drew a pistol. Jack pointed his Beretta M9 back. *Showdown at the apple barn.* It didn't quite have the ring of *the OK Corral.*

In that instant, Jack knew he should shoot Kennett. He would have if Willow hadn't been behind Kennett. In this case, putting her directly behind him was as effective as using her as a shield. Jack couldn't shoot Kennett without risking an unintentional Quigley, killing two with one bullet.

Kennett held his gun in one hand and the other arm out to keep Willow behind him, ostensibly out of danger. "Stay behind me, Willow. I'll protect you." Kennett's voice was as smooth as the polished surface of a perfect Red Delicious apple. "Finally come to finish the job? Didn't count on my dogs? That's poor planning for such a reputed assassin. I expected better from you. RIOT only hires the best."

"What?" Willow peered around Kennett's shoulder, eyes wide. "Assassin," she whispered. "RIOT?"

Jack cursed beneath his breath.

Kennett barked a command to his dogs. The assault on the shed door stopped and silence echoed in the room. Still in a protective stance, he stepped back into Willow. "That man is a dangerous assassin sent to kill me. Isn't that right, Con?"

Willow shook her head. "No! Why?"

"I work for the CIA," Kennett said. "I've been deep

undercover infiltrating a dangerous terrorist cell that's planning to bomb an important summit meeting."

"A terrorist cell here? In Orchard Bluff?" Willow sounded as completely surprised as she should have.

She was definitely playing along, playing the innocent. But she was looking at Jack and that gun of his with terror in her eyes.

"What better place? They've been passing explosives through here from Canada." Like the pro he was, he kept his gun precisely aimed at Jack. If Kennett fired, Jack was dead on contact.

Jack was busily planning his own shot and method of attack and escape.

Willow looked stunned. Jack couldn't tell how much she believed Kennett.

"That man"—Kennett pointed at Jack—"works for the enemy and has been assigned to kill me." He laughed confidently and grinned.

Kennett wasn't at all scared. He was high on the adrenaline of the situation. So was Jack, but he had Willow to worry about and that complicated things.

"But he's Aldo's cousin," Willow protested.

Jack couldn't tell whether she was protecting him or not or what she was up to. But he didn't like the look of betrayal in her eyes.

Kennett laughed. "No, he's a killer who's been altered by plastic surgery to look like Sariel, a CIA assassin who was killed in an explosion in Ciudad del Este. RIOT has been using him to confuse us and get close enough to kill our agents."

*What the hell?*

Jack couldn't believe what he was hearing. Kennett was accusing him of being the bad guy? Why would Kennett pretend to be the good guy? Unless it was to build Willow's trust until he could kill her quietly. After he took care of Jack. The old divide and conquer strategy.

"Willow, don't listen to him." Jack stared into her eyes.

She was staring back at him as if she didn't know him anymore.

*Damn it all to hell! This is exactly what I've been afraid of.*

"Wills, you know who I am," he said.

She was staring at him as if taking inventory and cataloging all the ways he was different from her Jack. As if she believed Kennett and his lies. She didn't reply, just stared at Jack mutely.

"Kennett is the assassin," Jack said. "He's known in intelligence circles as the Rooster and works for the Revolutionary International Organization of Terrorists. He's the one planning to kill thousands of innocent civilians. I'm here to stop him."

"Don't believe him," Kennett said to Willow, without taking his eyes off Jack. "He's been here for less than a week, showing up out of the blue and pretending to be Aldo's cousin.

"You *know* me. I'm steady and committed."

Willow opened her mouth to speak, shook her head, and closed her mouth without saying anything.

In the meantime, Jack was praying for a lucky break. He hated relying on luck, but it had gotten him out of a tricky situation or two in the past. Though, as his bastard of an old man used to say, *you make your own luck.*

"Let the lady go, Con," Kennett said. "She's innocent."

Jack was all for getting Willow out of here, but he didn't trust Kennett. There was no way Kennett was letting her leave alive.

"Fine with me." Jack nodded to Kennett and then toward the door. "Let her walk out of here."

Kennett shook his head. "Nice try, Con. I let her walk past and you kill me while I can't fire back for fear of hitting her? Then you shoot me and her. Men like you have no compassion or honor.

"There's a trapdoor to an old bomb shelter behind me, hidden beneath the hay. It's safe. Let her go down there and then we'll settle this between us. The winner can rescue her."

Jack kept his poker face on. He knew why Kennett wanted Willow in the bomb shelter, and it sure as hell wasn't to protect her.

"No deal. That's a trap. You have enough explosives stored down there to blow this place so high it will never be found."

Kennett lifted the barrel of his gun slightly, aiming for Jack's head. "It's that or shoot it out now."

Jack was thinking hard and fast, but nothing was coming to him. All he knew for sure was that he wouldn't risk shooting Willow.

"Fine," he said, at last. "But first, you move away from the door. The last thing I need is you disappearing like a rabbit down a hole."

Jack was trying to telegraph a message to Willow. He wanted Willow to duck so he could take out Kennett.

Kennett shrugged and did as Jack told him, moving closer to the window. "Satisfied?"

Jack shrugged. "Good enough."

"Kick the hay out of the way," Kennett told Willow.

She did as she was told.

"Do you see the door?"

She nodded. "Yes."

"Give it a gentle tug. It sticks a bit, but it will come up with a little pressure. A light will come on and you'll see a ladder." He stared at Jack and smiled. "Once she's down the hatch, I'm taking you out for good."

Willow opened the door, tugging as Kennett had told her to do.

*Where's the lock?* Jack thought. He'd been right—Kennett had been planning to take her down there all along.

"Willow, no!" Jack yelled just as Willow looked as if she was going to start down the ladder into hell.

Kennett grinned and everything happened in slow motion as Jack's senses went on high alert.

Kennett aimed at him and pulled the trigger.

Jack ducked behind a stack of apple crates.

"No!" Willow screamed. She lunged forward and pulled Kennett's arm down.

The shot went into the floor. Grabbing him from behind, she swung him toward the bomb shelter trapdoor. Kennett tumbled backward off balance right into the opening.

Jack heard the sickening thuds as Kennett fell down the ladder.

*Damn,* Jack thought. *The bomb shelter's booby-trapped.* Kennett fell too fast to disable his safeguards.

Willow froze, looking horrified at what she'd just done.

"Run!" Jack yelled to her as he raced toward her. "This place is going to blow!"

He grabbed her hand and pulled her toward the door. She squeezed his hand back and ran with him.

They burst through the door, stumbling over the dogs as Willow called to them to follow her.

They were less than twenty feet away when the apple shed exploded, a ball of fire and heat behind them.

The dogs whined and cowered.

Willow tumbled into Jack's arms, coughing and crying. "I knew it was you. I never doubted."

Jack pulled her into his chest and led her away, sheltering her with his body as debris rained down around them.

They stopped in the safety of the orchard across the street.

"You believed me? You scared me there for a minute."

Willow turned to stare at the fully engulfed apple shed and shuddered in his arms. "Of course I did. The Sense was screaming at me and there were no kittens."

He frowned at her.

"Shane called me over here this morning saying he needed some help saving some abandoned kittens. There weren't any."

Her lips trembled. "I killed him," she whispered. "I only meant to lock him in the shelter."

Jack pulled her close. "I know, babe."

"Oh, my gosh, I killed him."

"That man was an enemy terrorist assassin responsible for the deaths of thousands of innocent civilians and half a dozen NCS agents." Jack used the most calming voice he could. "You saved countless lives."

She shook in his arms.

He tipped her face up to meet his gaze. "Wills, he's the man who blew me up in Ciudad."

"You were going to kill him?" She looked horrified and stunned.

"Yes."

"Revenge?"

"No. Mission."

She stared at him in a way that broke his heart. "Are you really an assassin for the Agency?"

He nodded. "I am. I always have been."

She took a deep breath and blinked as she looked at him.

He took a deep breath, too. Just as he feared, it was over between them. He had to explain. "That's why I stayed away after I died. I knew you'd be better off without me. You still will be. The Agency will keep paying you my pension. I'll maintain the cover of death. Things will go back to the way they were a few weeks ago, before I came to Orchard Bluff.

"You'll be fine, Willow. I just want you to know . . ." The words stuck in his mouth. He felt like a world-class jerk, but he had to say them. "I love you, Wills. I always will."

She stared at him. "You fool. Don't you dare leave me again."

He was so surprised, he nearly took a step back.

"Better for me? Better for me without you?" She pulled his face down to hers. "Look at me, Jack. I don't believe in killing, but I believe in you. I know you. You're only doing what you believe is right to save others."

She glanced at the flaming barn. "Given what I just did, I'd be the world's biggest hypocrite if I didn't understand your motivation and threw you out.

"I love you, too. And always will. You promised Con would marry me and you'd darn well better stick to your promise. And marry me soon." She stroked his cheek. "Now, call nine-one-one. But kiss me first."

When a wife commanded, a husband obeyed. Jack leaned down and kissed her as if he'd never let her go.

# STINGER

## TWO MONTHS LATER, DECEMBER 18

Emmett Nelson smiled to himself as he waited his turn in the reception line at the Orchard Bluff Grange Hall to congratulate the new couple. Jack beamed ear-to-ear and Willow looked radiant and as happy as Emmett had ever seen her. Neither one looked upset by the new arrangements—Jack would be Con in his personal life and continue on as Emmett's top assassin in his profession.

The hall was decorated in country finery—boughs and wreaths made of fragrant fresh greens, apples, dried apples, candied apples, every kind of apple imaginable on wreaths and in table centerpieces. Poinsettias in red, pink, and white from a local greenhouse sat on each table and by the roaring fire in the oversize fireplace at the grange. A ten-foot-tall Christmas tree grown by a local farm was decorated in white lights and homespun garlands. The wedding gifts sat beneath it.

There was a huge Italian spread on buffet tables lining the far wall—lasagna, spaghetti, pesto, salad, bread, meatballs, and apple wine. Con's cousin Aldo catered the event, of course, looking on proudly from his perch behind the buffet table where he urged people to eat, acting like an Italian mama. "You're too skinny. Eat! Eat! The meatballs melt in your mouth."

Willow wore a simple knee-length white dress and

shoulder-length veil held in her hair by a crystal comb. Jack wore a fancy Italian suit that the Agency's cover artist Malene had picked out for him and the Agency had paid for. If Emmett pegged Jack right, and of course he did, Jack was as uncomfortable as hell in that suit. Ah, the price of love. Jack was going to have to dress out of his comfort zone for quite a while.

In time, he might be able to claim he'd gone country and dress in the casual way he preferred.

Drew Fields stood beside Jack in the line as his best man. Drew hadn't exactly been thrilled with Emmett for keeping the secret of Jack's being alive from him. But as a first-class spy he understood the necessity. He'd mostly been furious that his wife, Staci, had suffered so much guilt over Jack's death.

Well, Emmett had set it right now. This wedding was costing Emmett a chunk of his budget. Good thing it was the *use it or lose it* time of year.

*Enjoy your Christmas bonus, Jack. This is all you're getting this year.*

Conversation buzzed all around Emmett, and Emmett, being head of NCS and a world-class eavesdropper, took in every syllable.

"They look so sweet together," one woman behind Emmett whispered to another. "But can you believe their whirlwind courtship? Two months. And her a widow only two years. They met on the anniversary of her husband's death. Looks like she's forgotten all about her first husband."

"Oh, I think it's romantic," the second woman said. "I'm glad she found someone who makes her so happy. Look at her!" The woman sighed with great joy in her voice. "She's glowing."

"Yes, but I thought for sure she'd end up with Shane." She sounded just the tiniest bit regretful.

"Oh, now there's a scandal for you! Claiming to be an organic farmer while stockpiling fertilizer and pesticide to help Grant Cooper. They were both frauds." She sounded as if this was the worst possible thing she could imagine.

"Yes, I know. It's all anyone can talk about. And the way they died . . ."

Emmett had to fight to keep a straight face. If only the women knew the worst of it.

Chalk up another mission and matchmaking win for the chief. He had an impeccable record.

The line moved forward. Emmett shook Drew's hand and moved forward to clap Jack on the back. "Congrats, buddy. It's about time you got the girl."

He winked at Jack and grabbed Willow, hugging her and kissing her on the cheek.

She whispered in his ear, "I should be mad at you for keeping him from me for two years, but somehow I can't hold it against you, you old charmer. Call it the Sense working overtime, but I can't help thinking you orchestrated this somehow.

"After all, you could have refused to ever send him here in the first place."

Emmett laughed and whispered back, "I should hire you. With that Sense of yours, you're a dangerous woman."

"I think I'll pass. I prefer making candy." Willow smiled and introduced him to her mother, who stood next to her, as an old friend of hers and Jack's. "Meet another dangerous woman. Mom, Emmett was just saying how dangerous the Sense is."

"Oh, I don't know about that," Diana said. "But it does come in handy." She beamed at her daughter and then smiled at Emmett. "It was so nice of you to come. I'm just so happy for Willow and Con." She looked Emmett straight in the eye. "He reminds me an awful lot of Jack. I suppose I'll get used to it." She winked at Emmett and passed him on to Willow's matron of honor, Staci, as he wondered what Diana knew.

"Good to see you, you old liar. I think," Staci said.

"What do you mean, you think? Don't forget, you owe me your marriage, too. My methods may be unconventional, but I get results."

Staci glanced at Willow and Jack and smiled. "Yeah, I'll give you that."

Next Emmett hugged Willow's bridesmaid Mandy, the widow of one of his best spies, Kyle.

"I don't suppose you have a resurrection up your sleeve for me?" she whispered in Emmett's ear.

"I'm sorry, darling. I wish I did." He squeezed her back. "But I could probably see about getting you some work in Canada." He winked at her. She'd been secretly seeing a Canadian secret agent. "I have some pull with the Canadians."

"I bet you do." Mandy handed him off to Ada, introduced as one of Willow's Orchard Bluff friends. "This is Emmett. He's part of the family."

Ada's eyes lit up. "Oh, how nice. Are you related to Aldo, too, then?"

"No, sadly not." Emmett took her hand and gave it a gentle squeeze.

"He's from the . . ."—Mandy's lips twitched—"other family, the other side of the family. We all love Emmett. What would we ever do without him? He always seems to work magic in our lives."

Yes, Magic. He had a little prestidigitation he needed to work for her next. There was a mad magician on the loose in Vegas and NCS was in need of an illusionist. Vegas—it would be good to get back there.

8470

Coming soon…

# LICENSE TO LOVE

Available in September 2013 from St. Martin's Paperbacks

And don't miss Gina Robinson's other
Agent Ex novels

## THE SPY WHO LEFT ME

## DIAMONDS ARE TRULY FOREVER

From St. Martin's Paperbacks